# BLUE DARKNESS

For Yvonne
10-23-2010 Grand Forks, ND

By Ernest Francis Schanilec

BLUE DARKNESS


Second Printing February 2003
Third Printing November 2009



Author - Ernest Francis Schanilec
Publisher - J&M Printing, PO Box 248, Gwinner, ND 58040 - 1-800-437-1033

Library of Congress Number: 2002091670
International Standard Book Number: 978-931916-21-9

Printed in the United States of America

# *Dedication*

*To Joyce, grandmother of*
*Robby*
*Alicia*
*Grace*
*William*
*Cosette*
*Anicka*
*Josie*
*Henry*
*Alison*
*Ellie*
*Emily*
*Thomas*

# ACKNOWLEDGEMENTS

I AM GRATEFUL to the following for their contributions during the process of writing my first novel: Pat Schumacher and Ardith Hoehn, who both guided and encouraged me along the way; Three of my sons, Clayton, Gaylord and Rob, for editing, page formatting and cover design assistance; and my brother Vern and his wife Faye, who assisted as critics.

# 1

FLASHING LIGHTS AT MAYNARD'S HOUSE could mean trouble. Maynard Cushing was a neighbor and friend—a darn good guy. He lived alone and Tom Hastings was thinking the worst, a heart attack. His friend was also a client.

Dinner had been good at Mary Ann's, the local restaurant located on the east shore of the lake. Pending darkness augmented by heavy cloud cover enhanced the effect of the flashers. Just before Maynard's driveway, a turn in the township road led to a small hill leading to Tom's roadway and home. The flashing lights were no longer visible after reaching the top but his concern for Maynard's welfare deepened.

Maynard Cushing began writing his memoirs two years ago. He hired Hastings, needing assistance in purchasing and learning a computer. After retiring from a career in medical science that spanned twenty-five years, Tom Hastings was available. He ran a part time computer consulting business. The majority of his clients were small businesses and individuals like Maynard. Computers became a passion of his when they became commonplace in the eighties.

Maynard Cushing was retired after a long, successful career with the CIA. His wife died of cancer four years ago. Hastings was also widowed. An airplane crash took the life of his spouse almost five years ago. The details surrounding his tragedy were difficult for Hastings to forget. His wife was one of the victims of a hijacking.

Oh, to banish those dreadful thoughts. What happened in the past is over. Tom feared that something serious happened to his friend, Maynard Cushing. Approaching the gravel roadway that led to his house, Tom slowed the truck. He was a little over half-mile away from the flashing lights. The roadway rises and dips through a wooded area before it fuses into a large asphalt driveway. The house that Tom

Hastings called home was nestled into a hillside at the south edge of the driveway. Thoughts of flashing lights and what they might mean to his friend Maynard became overwhelming. After stopping the pickup truck, he remained seated for a couple of minutes. Tom was not the type of guy to gawk or snoop into other peoples business but this was a matter of needing to know. He drove back up his roadway, onto the township road, down the small hill, and turned right toward the Maynard Cushing house.

He left his truck on the shoulder of the road and walked up the driveway. His hopes sank when seeing the ambulance. Two county sheriff cars were also parked in the driveway. Tom's hands were in his pockets—his muscles tightened—he was afraid to learn what had happened.

Two uniformed officers, standing near the ambulance, were watching Tom approach.

"Good evening sir, can we help you with something?" one of the officers asked.

"Ah, I'm a neighbor. What's going on?"

"We're sorry to inform you that your neighbor is dead."

Tom was shocked. He worked hard to contain emotions. "What happened? How did he die? Was it a heart attack?"

"I don't know, sir. We'll know more later," replied one of the officers.

Tom said, "Thanks," turned, and slowly walked back to his truck.

Shocked and stunned, he returned home, walked out onto the wooden deck and gazed out over the water. The long, narrow bay extended westward for a mile terminating in a wide, shallow, grassy area. Eastward, the mouth of the bay was just out of view, where it widened into the main part of the lake. Wedged between his bay and the main body of the lake was a large peninsula, narrowing into an area known as Rocky Point.

He stood on the deck with both hands on the rail, attempting to absorb the beauty of the waters surface, active with never ending, blue gray ripples.

Tom looked at the hot tub snuggled into a corner of the deck. The thought of hot bubbling water was appealing. He needed a tool to divert attention from distasteful thoughts about Maynard's death. In a matter of minutes he was enjoying the soothing, hot, turbulent water and the unobstructed view. He noticed his neighbor Sylvan, who lives in a lake home a short distance along the shoreline towards the mouth of the bay, returning with his new sailboat.

The lengthy mast came into view as the boat made a turn and approached the dock. There weren't any sails, the running lights were on and the motor attached to the stern was gently nudging the boat to the side of the dock. Sylvan purchased the boat earlier that spring and hadn't gotten around to rigging the mast. Sleeping was difficult for Tom that night. He tossed and turned with ever-returning visions of Maynard's pleasant face.

Early the next morning the doorbell rang. Tom was startled out of a deep sleep. He wasn't expecting anyone and felt fearful pangs of apprehension while pushing the blankets aside. He put on his robe and headed down the short stairway. A peek outside caught a glimpse of a car in the driveway.

It was a county sheriff's car. Tom felt his stomach tighten.

"I'm Deputy Paul Johnson," the man said. "Are you Tom Hastings?"

"Yes, that's me. What can I do for you?"

"I'd like to ask you a few questions. One of your neighbors was found dead last night."

Tom looked at the treetops beyond the deputy. The upper branches were swaying with the wind. Feelings of loneliness radiated through his body. He had lost his wife and now a close friend. Maynard was gone.

The deputy shifted his feet awaiting an answer.

Without clearing his throat, Tom said, "Yes, I know. I stopped by his house late yesterday evening. The police cars and ambulance were there."

"How long have you lived here, Mr. Hastings?"

"Full time for about seven years—part time for twenty years."

"How well did you know Mr. Cushing?"

"Actually, quite well. He was a client of mine. Two years ago he contacted me to help in selecting a computer. He needed one to write memoirs of his career with the CIA."

"Do you remember when you saw him last?"

"I was over at his house this past week. Pretty sure it was Wednesday. Yeah, we worked on keyboard stuff, usage of the special keys, delete and backspace."

"Did you notice any vehicles on the township road that were different or unusual?"

"I'm not sure. I'll have to think about that question for a bit. How did he die?"

The deputy looked Tom right in the eye and said, "He was murdered...head bashed in with a club."

Tom was stunned. He was absorbed with the memory of Maynard's kindness and the thought of someone hitting his friend with a club—on the head. After recovering from the deputy's shocking statement, he tried thinking about vehicles seen on the township road recently. Most of them were locals from Rocky Point and those belonging to other residents in the peninsula. Tom had a habit of making mental notes of any strange vehicles because of living alone down an isolated road.

"Deputy, I remember seeing a black car on the township road earlier in the day, yesterday. That would be the day Maynard was, ah died. As far as I know, no one at the Point or any of my neighbors own a black car."

After discussing the car sighting with Tom, the deputy wanted more details regarding the relationship with Maynard and his computer needs.

The treetops were still swaying as Tom's eyes looked beyond the deputy. He was accustomed in taking refuge from harsh realities by taking long walks in the woods. They refreshed and calmed his mind. Tom wished he were out there, amongst the trees.

He looked the deputy in the eye and replied, "After retiring six years ago, I started a part-time computer consulting business. Objective was to earn spending money and to pass on some of my knowledge. Maynard called me a couple of years ago and said he needed help in learning how to use a computer, for writing his memoirs."

"Did he talk much about his experiences with the CIA?"

"Maynard told me some interesting stories. A lot of them were about things that happened when he was an agent. Though I read all of his writings, I didn't pay much attention to what most of the stories were about. My main objective was to help with learning the word processor."

"We have the understanding that Maynard's career with the CIA was long, many years. Did he ever talk about any threats or people he was afraid of?"

"No, not at all. He was an honest, likable person. I can't imagine anyone harming him. Was it something from his past that killed him?"

"Ah, don't know yet. Thanks very much, Mr. Hastings. I'm all finished with the questions for now. Here's my card. Please call if you remember anything...anybody that may have been threatening to your neighbor."

Tom reached out and grabbed the card. "Be glad to, but he didn't have any enemies that I know of. Thanks for coming by, sir."

The deputy turned his car around. Tom watched as the white sheriff's patrol car drove up the driveway and disappeared beyond a bank of trees. He lowered his head and examined the card. The deputy was an impressive person with a pleasant mannerism. He had a kind-looking face, in spite of two large front teeth hanging down below the upper lip. Six-four tall, Tom estimated. His questions had been clear—difficult for Tom to answer.

# 2

**A**FTER GETTING DRESSED, checking the markets and e-mail on the Internet, Tom backed his pickup truck out of the garage and headed for New Dresden. Anyone living in the country had a hometown. His was located three miles south of where the township road intersected a county highway. The approximate distance from his home to New

Dresden was four miles.

A farmhouse overlooked the township road-county highway intersection. Tom Hastings's friends, Byron and Eva, lived there. Tom wondered if they had seen the black car the deputy asked about. Located one mile down the road, towards town, was a dairy farm. It occupied a large expanse of land on the same side of the highway as the Byron and Eva farmhouse.

The five flags at the peak of a hill next to the dairy farm marked the location of a cemetery. One of the gravestones was carved with the inscription, *Becky Hastings*.

The county highway curved after it merged with a state highway. It led directly to Main Street in New Dresden. After passing by several homes, Tom looked to his right and observed the blue water of Borders Lake.

Settlers of Germanic descent founded the small town back in the 19th century. Considering the low population of New Dresden, about six hundred strong, it was a haven for small businesses.

New Dresden had two restaurants, a sports bar, super market grocery store, bank, lumber yard, body shop, several gift and antique shops, used car dealership, funeral parlor, vacuum cleaner shop, plumbing firm, electrical firm, barber shop and most importantly, a full-line hardware store.

Tom parked on Main Street and headed for the post office. Because the town didn't have enough population to qualify for home delivery, every household and business got their mail from a post office box. Just about everyone in town passed through its doors each day, Monday through Friday.

The Main Street door of the post office opened into a small vestibule. Tom entered and passed through the door to his right. He used a key from the pickup truck key chain to open the postal box. Fishing out the mail with both hands, he laid the bundle on a counter across the room. A man came through the door, grunted a greeting, and opened his box.

"Good morning," Tom said.

The man didn't respond and quickly left the room.

After sorting through his mail, he remembered needing stamps.

Walking back through the vestibule, he opened the door to the business section of the post office.

"Hi, Tom, what can I do for you today?" asked Jerry, the postmaster.

"I need a roll of stamps."

"That'll be thirty-four dollars," Jerry said, tossing the roll of stamps onto the counter. Tom caught them on the second bounce.

Jerry had a confidant, warm personality. He was an accommodating postal employee who enjoyed visiting with citizenry. The local weather was always discussed thoroughly during the course of a normal day. This morning Jerry felt subdued because of the news about Maynard Cushing. Neither Tom nor Jerry brought up the subject during the visit. Tom wrote out a check for the stamps and left the building.

Tom's next stop was the grocery store. He picked up a grocery basket and lifted a copy of the *Star Tribune* from a rack. Before heading for the aisle to pick up orange juice, he flipped through the paper looking for a story about New Dresden and a murder.

The story about Maynard's murder was on the page five. According to the writer, state officials had been assigned to the case because a quantity of methamphetamine was found in the victim's house.

Tom was shocked and irritated by the mention of drugs because he had worked for Maynard the last two years. The idea that his friend Maynard was involved in drugs was preposterous.

The murder was on the mind and lips of most everyone milling in and around the grocery store that morning. Words including *Mafia* and *drug lords* were overheard by Tom when selecting a bunch of bananas. The mention of drugs in the *Star Tribune* story aroused a few of the locals. They were proud of their community and the possibility of drugs being involved was not a popular concept.

While passing the meat counter, Tom overheard an employee say, "He must have been on the stuff for a long time."

Standing in line at the checkout, he overheard a lady tell the person ahead, "I knew he was on drugs all the time, otherwise why would he keep to himself so much?"

Tom was disgusted with the talk at the grocery. What do they know about Maynard?

Most small towns have a Main Street café. New Dresden is no exception. The Borders Café was located across the street from the post office. It was a typical small town restaurant where people gathered to have coffee and talk over the news. Contributing to the restaurant's popularity were the breakfast and lunch specials. The food was good and the price reasonable.

After Tom left the grocery, he crossed the street and headed for the café. When approaching the restaurant door, a elderly lady with beautiful gray hair was having a difficult time opening the door. She insisted on a pull but this door needed a push.

Tom reached over her shoulder and pushed the door inward, it opened. "Oh, thank you," she responded.

When Tom entered, he looked about for a place to sit. Ah, there was Henry, a friend of his, sitting at a table by himself. Henry owned and operated a plumbing business on the south side of town. His home was on the north shore of the same lake that Hastings lived on.

"Have a seat, Tom," Henry said as he gestured toward an empty chair across the table. Tom accepted, laid the newspaper on the table, and sat down.

"Hello, Henry, what looks good today?"

"I ordered the special-fish sandwich."

Their conversation, as most others in the restaurant, was about what happened at the Cushing house yesterday. Rather than a buzzing of loud voices and multi-table conversations, the restaurant was subdued. It was apparent Maynard's death affected the mood of the locals hanging out at the restaurant—whispers instead of loud voices.

Henry was a good-natured, interesting person. He thrived in telling stories about the historical past of the New Dresden community, but like most everyone else, his mind was on the murder.

"A couple of my service people drove over for a service call at the Cushing house just last week, a plugged drain," Henry said as his eyes narrowed and looked up at the ceiling.

"Henry, I'm going to miss Maynard. I don't know how well you knew him, but my experiences with him were all good. He was likable and had an interesting personality. Maynard was no dummy either, catching on to the computer like he did."

"Yeah, he was nice doing business with...always paid his bill," said Henry as his frown converted to a smile.

Tom chuckled and added, "He got caught dozing ever so often—right in front of the computer, his fingers on the keyboard."

"Oh, he did, did he?" said Henry. "This is one of the worst things that has happened here since old man Brusky killed his wife back in the '30s. I still have the newspaper clipping, picture and all, from back then. Brusky ran a logging mill and he came home one day and found his wife in bed with another man. The jury didn't have much sympathy and they sent him to prison for the rest of his life. He died in prison six years later, poor fellow."

Henry stood up and said, "Got to get back to work."

Reaching in his pocket, he drew out some coins, laid them on the table and proceeded to checkout.

A few minutes later, Tom left the restaurant, got in his truck and drove northward across the railroad tracks and out of town.

— —

THE HOME WHERE PETE AND LISA SMILIE LIVED was located in a fifteen-acre patch of woods adjoining the Hastings's roadway. When they bought the property two years ago, the house and outbuildings needed extensive repairs. Working together, they got rid of a ton of junk and remodeled the house. Except for the living room carpet, the project was finished. Their house was an example of comfort and coziness.

The couple was sitting in the kitchen, on their day off from work, sipping coffee when Lisa gestured toward the window and said, "Someone's here, Pete. Looks like a pickup truck."

"Oh, yeah. Hey, that's probably Tom Hastings."

Lisa was born and raised in Italy. She and Pete met in Naples when he was in the army. They fell in love and Pete talked her into moving to America. She struggled with adjusting to country living during the first few months. Pete's love and support helped her overcome lonesomeness for her family. Her new life was a rich and happy experience. She worked in a factory in Big Lakes, the county seat fifteen miles northwest of New Dresden.

Pete shopped real estate for almost a year before finding the perfect place for his new bride. He worked for Lakes Electronics, a high-tech business a few miles north of Big Lakes. His big passion was wildlife. He always kept a sack of corn in the garage to feed a small flock of wild turkeys. One of the workers at the grain elevator in New Dresden would automatically retrieve a sack of corn from storage when Pete pulled up in his pickup truck.

Last year Pete built an elaborate deer stand at the south edge of his woods. It overlooked an open field that was planted to corn this year. Frequently, he and Lisa would spend evenings perched in the deer stand. They'd sip beers and enjoy deer and other wildlife that came to feed.

Lisa's face was pale this morning. She didn't sleep well. Word had gotten to them that Maynard Cushing was dead. In addition to her job in Big Lakes, she performed household chores for Maynard on weekends.

"I wonder if Tom's heard the news." She said to Pete.

"It would be pretty hard to avoid it if he went into New Dresden for the mail this morning."

Tom Hastings was thinking about the same thing as he brought his pickup truck to a halt next to Pete's. He got out and gazed at the landscaping. No longer an eyesore, it was a model of beautiful scenery.

Hastings enjoyed the outdoors as much as his neighbor. The main reason both selected this area for their homes was because of the abundance of deer and other wildlife.

He knocked on their door.

Pete emerged, sporting a big smile. Tom, close to six feet tall, was towered over by the big guy in the doorway. Pete was about six-three and two hundred pounds of muscle.

"Hello, Tom, how goes it today? Let's talk out on the deck," Pete said. "Lisa is getting dressed. We're really shocked about what happened to Maynard. Who could have done such a thing?"

"So you know about it. Yeah, Pete, it's a bad deal."

"We were coming home from my dad's place yesterday evening

when we noticed the lights over there...at Maynard's place. We heard about it this morning. Hey, how about some coffee?"

"Sure, I always have room for another cup."

Pete got up and was on his way back into the house when Lisa met him in the doorway.

"Oh, you must have read my mind, Lisa."

She was carrying a tray, three cups of coffee nestled in the middle.

"Hi there, Tom. I'm so sorry about Maynard. He was your friend, wasn't he?"

Tom stood up and accepted Lisa's gentle hug. "Thanks, Lisa. Yes, he was my friend. I understand you were working for him too."

"Yes and I feel just awful about what happened."

"Pete, did you happen to notice a black car anywhere in the vicinity of the township road yesterday?"

"Yeah I did, why?"

"Well, a deputy sheriff stopped at my house early this morning and asked about it."

"Was the deputy a real tall guy?"

"Yes, his name is Johnson. Did he stop here too?"

"He sure did," added Lisa. "It scared the heck out of me."

Pete said, "About the black car...I was heading into town with the pickup yesterday and saw one going east on the north branch, just beyond Maynard's place."

"What time of the day was that?"

"Ah, lets see, that must have been late afternoon. I was going into town for tractor gas about then...ran out earlier. When I slowed at the top of the hill, that's when I saw it."

"It wasn't coming from Maynard's driveway, was it?"

"Dunno'....I don't think so...but wait, it could have. The deputy didn't ask anything about a black car."

"Geez, Pete, I'm not aware that anyone living on the peninsula drives a black car. Have you seen any around the past year?"

"No, just the one yesterday. Most vehicles that use the public access are pickup trucks and SUV. But then, during the summer months, South Ridge Resort has a lot of people coming and going. Could have been one of them."

South Ridge Resort was located on a parcel of land wedged between the county highway and the public access road. It had a long stretch of shoreline beach along the main body of the lake. The resort had fourteen rental cottages and about twenty-five trailer rentals. The owner's house was located on a ridge in the center of the property and was visible almost a mile away from the entry to the Hastings and Smilie roadway.

"Thanks for the coffee, Lisa. I've got to get going. Let's stay in touch."

"You're welcome, Tom, anytime."

# 3

**D**EPUTY JOHNSON VISITED THE HASTINGS'S HOME again the next day. Tom was working in the shop when he had heard the sound of a vehicle come to a stop in the driveway. He looked out the window and was surprised to see a county sheriff's car, again.

The tall deputy got out and said, "Good morning, Mr. Hastings. How are you today?"

"Just fine, deputy. What's up?"

"Ah, a couple of things. First, the investigation of the Cushing murder is being taken over by the State Criminal Department. This means someone from there will be visiting you."

"Secondly, if you don't mind, I have some more questions."

"No, by all means I don't. I'd like to help all I can."

"It's about the black car. You originally said seeing it early afternoon on the day of the murder. Is that correct?"

"Yes, I believe it was on my way back from lunch at New Dresden."

"Could you tell if it was a four-door or a coupe?"

"My closest guess was that it was a four-door sedan, likely a General Motors make, probably a Buick Regal, or perhaps an Olds."

"Also, did you notice if it had a sky roof?"

"I don't think so, but it could have. I just don't know."

"Where exactly did you see the car?"

"I met it on the township road about half way between the public access road and my roadway."

"Thanks a lot, Mr. Hastings. Ah, there's one more thing. Someone from the State Criminal Department is going to ask you about your business card. One of them mentioned finding it in the Cushing house."

"Yeah, I left two cards on Maynard's computer desk."

Maynard's computer was located in a spare bedroom that was converted into an office. Along with a printer, it perched on a desk under the east window offering a view of a farm field. A section of the township road was also visible from the window. There was a second window in the room that overlooked the hillside to the south. Tom appreciated the room, it was a comfortable place to work.

After Deputy Johnson left, Tom backed his pickup truck out of the garage, drove up the roadway, and onto the township road. While going down the small hill, he glanced toward the Cushing home and noticed there were a couple of vehicles in the driveway, neither was a sheriff's car.

Tom waited for a milk truck to pass before turning onto the county highway. Uneven silos, three in number, reached for the clouds at the Byron Schultz dairy farm. The farmhouse was perched like a beacon, overlooking the township road. Byron retired after selling his herd to his neighbor three years ago. His wife, Eva, was also retired following a long career as a public school administrator.

Byron was a lean, tall man with a full head of dark hair. He was born and raised on that farm. Dairy cattle were his entire life. Skills that he developed during his farming days came in handy when applying for a part-time job. He was currently employed part time at a welding plant in Big Lakes.

Eva was also working part-time. She was called on to substitute teach at one of the schools in Cornwall, a town ten miles to the east.

In recent years, Byron farmed bits and pieces of land surrounding the Hastings and Smilie properties. Tractor-pickup talk sessions including Tom and Byron were common along the township road during stops for machinery repairs and adjustments.

A cluster of mallard ducks relaxed in a small muddy pond next to the road just beyond the Schultz farm. Some of the ducks were dipping for food in the shallow water while others were sunning on the muddy field next to the water. The head of green head mallard gleamed, reflecting the rays of the bright sun.

— —

MAIN STREET OF NEW DRESDEN was only one block long. Buildings occupied most of the lots on both sides of the street. Tom drove around the block and found a parking spot directly in front of the post office. He entered and plucked a yellow slip from his postal box. Opening the door into the business room set off a jingle to alert the postmaster. Tom laid the slip on the counter when Jerry returned from sorting mail in the back room.

"Good morning, Tom. Nice day out there today?" he asked.

"Sure is, Jerry. Are people talking about Maynard Cushing's death a lot?"

"Are they talking...you've got that right. That's all they're talking about. Your name even gets brought up now and then."

"Am I a suspect or what?"

Jerry laughed and told Tom, "No, but maybe you should be. Oh, I'm just kidding."

Tom picked up his package and strolled down Main Street toward the grocery store. Ellie, the grocery store clerk, wasn't displaying her usual smile.

She frowned and said, "Maynard stopped by for some groceries the day before he died. I saw him go into the bank. He was in there for about an hour before coming over here. We're going to miss him."

The large windows on the main street side of the grocery store rendered an excellent view of the street. Ellie and Tom watched a limping Sylvan Tullaby approach the bank.

Tom asked Ellie, "Do you know my neighbor, Sylvan?"

"Yes, know who he is, but not personally. I heard he was wounded in the military. That's probably why he limps. He always wears those ugly striped coveralls," Ellie added as she abandoned the conversation with Tom to assist a customer.

Sylvan and his wife, Missy, lived in a house overlooking the same bay as Tom Hastings. Their home was eastward, approximately a quarter-mile from the Hastings's house. They had access to their lake home via a gravel road that ran parallel to Tom Hastings's roadway. Both intersected with the south branch of the township gravel road.

On Tom's drive home, instead of turning up the small hill, he continued down the north branch of the township road and passed by Maynard's driveway. Three vehicles occupied the driveway—a county sheriff's car, a van, and a regular car. The van was white with black lettering on the doors; Flasher on the roof suggested it belonged to the sheriff's department. Civilian car was a two-tone dark blue and gray.

He continued down the road, following a long gradual curve, until it intersected with the south branch. After stopping at the stop sign, he turned left and drove up the Rocky Point roadway.

During one of many discussions that Tom and Henry engaged in at the Borders Café, Charley Smith's name was brought up. Henry talked about the pioneer who originally purchased the Rocky Point property and built a house at the tip of the peninsula, perhaps sixty years ago. As years went by other family members built houses, all of them along the shoreline.

The Rocky Point roadway was gravel, paralleling the curved shoreline. It provided access to driveways of all the houses. Tom drove slowly, looking for a black car parked in a driveway or an exposed garage. After passing by the seventh home, he pulled into the driveway of Nick Smith.

Nick was a retired corporate executive, one of the residents that Tom had previously met. He was mowing the lawn when the pickup truck drove into his driveway.

Nick was trim and looked great because he remained physically active during his retirement years. His hair was thinning and partially gray but he had more than enough strength to push the lawn mower over a large area of grass. Nick was an avid golfer and took pride in walking the course instead of using a golf cart. Noticeable was a generous amount of perspiration on his forehead when he stopped the mower to greet his visitor.

"Good afternoon, Nick. I see you're getting your daily workout."

"Hi, Tom, I gotta keep doing this as long as I can. Have you heard what happened to Maynard Cushing?"

"Yes, I sure have. Have the sheriff people been over here?" asked Tom.

"No, they haven't been over to see anyone at this end of the point. They could have visited some of the homes around the curve. Did the sheriff visit you?"

"Yup, he sure did."

"Well I sure hope whoever killed Maynard doesn't live around here."

Tom asked, "Do any residents of Rocky Point own or drive a black car?"

"Ah, not that I know of. Why is that important?"

"The sheriff has been asking. I saw one and so did Pete Smilie...same day as the murder."

"Oh wait a minute, I do remember seeing a black car coming up the north branch when I was heading out to golf about four or five days ago. I didn't pay much attention because, as you know, there is a fair amount of traffic on the township road this time of the year."

"Nick, can you remember exactly what day that was?"

"No, I'm not real sure, but it may have been on Saturday."

"Well, that's about four days before the murder. Probably a different one."

"Was a black car involved in the murder?"

"Nick, I really don't know, but the sheriff is sure interested."

"The drug talk is what I don't like. Being this far away from the city, we shouldn't have to put up with that kind of stuff. This is too close."

"Ah, Geez, Nick, there's no way Maynard was involved in drugs. Maynard had a lot of class. I knew him well...was with him a lot. No way."

"Well, I hope you're right, Tom. But what kind of a nut are we dealing with...goes around killing people!"

Tom and Nick talked for another ten minutes. After leaving Rocky Point, Tom drove back to the township road. He counted ten homes and no black cars.

# 4

**SYLVAN TULLABY WAS TROUBLED** after returning home from New Dresden. He was tired of hearing about the murder of Maynard Cushing.

He said out loud, "They talked as if no one ever died around here. Lots of people die and for lots of different reasons. What's the big deal about this one?"

He suspected that the people in the grocery store were talking about him when he was walking to the bank. Tom Hastings and that checkout lady were watching him. He could feel their eyes.

His dog, Casper, ran out to meet him while parking the van in the garage. When Sylvan opened the door, the dog was all over him. He petted the dog for a minute and headed for the house. Working on the remodeling job, after buying this place, helped him cope. His former wife was killed in an auto accident a little over six years ago. By moving here, and marrying Missy, he was able to salvage something from the years left in his life.

He shuddered when thinking what the doctor told him during his last checkup. On to more pleasant thoughts—Missy was expected in about an hour. She was making pork tenderloin for dinner—his favorite. What would he do without Missy? Probably go insane, he thought. The doctor said he had a rare disease. His life expectancy was anywhere from one to ten years.

That's why he bought the expensive sailboat. *Why not spend the money*? He experienced feelings of guilt. He thought of Missy. He couldn't ignore the fact that she was his wife and had something coming.

Arthritis in his right knee was hurting a ton since getting up this morning. The prescription pills weren't doing any good. He didn't like limping but it hurt too much to walk straight. The knee caused him to call in sick this morning. His boss, Val Peterson, wasn't happy when Sylvan's secretary broke the news. Sylvan worked his way up the ladder into the executive offices of Lorry Manufacturing. It wasn't easy. He had to crunch a few toes while moving up the ladder.

*Where is that Missy? She's late. I'm starved.* Sylvan grabbed a pack of cigarettes and climbed the steps to the deck. The doctor gave strict orders that he wasn't to smoke. Oh, what the heck, he thought. You gotta die from something.

— —

THE NEXT DAY, MID-MORNING, Tom Hastings's doorbell rang. He opened the door, two men dressed in suits, city guys.

The younger of the two spoke first. "Hello. Sorry to bother you. I'm Agent Ben and this is Agent Perry. We're from the Bureau of Criminal Apprehension of Minnesota. Are you Tom Hastings?"

Agent Ben was the spokesman in spite of his youthful appearance. He was a slim and small man, about five-seven. His partner Perry was taller and heavier—a round pouch instead of a waist. Perry had a perpetual smile. His partner Ben wasn't smiling.

"Yes, I am Tom Hastings. What can I do for you?"

They both flashed their ID and Ben began to ask questions. "Are you the person represented by the business card discovered in Maynard Cushing's office?"

"Yes, I am."

Tom went on to explain the computer work he had done for Maynard the last two years. Ben was fishing for answers that hinted at erratic personal behavior on Maynard's part. He became irritated when Tom refused to go along with the idea Maynard was a weird person.

Because Hastings was familiar with Maynard's computer, they asked him to accompany them to the house to help them retrieve information from the hard drive. Tom agreed and was escorted into the back seat of their vehicle. Ben got into the passengers' seat and Perry got behind the wheel.

Agent Perry pulled up next to a county sheriff's vehicle in Maynard Cushing's driveway. After crossing the yellow tape, the three men, led by Ben, climbed three steps to a small deck. The front door opened and Deputy Johnson stepped out.

"Hello again. I see you have the computer guy with you." he said to Agent Ben.

Ben nodded, the deputy stepped aside, and led them into a small middle hallway. Hastings experienced feelings of apprehension when seeing the chalked outline on the floor. He glanced to the left into an empty kitchen. The last time he was in this house, Maynard was in there making coffee.

His feelings changed to nostalgia when looking in the empty living room to his right. He remembered sitting on the couch waiting for Maynard to dress for dinner. He was especially fond of the panoramic view afforded by the large picture window. When the leaves were off the trees, the lake was visible from that room.

Agent Ben tiptoed around the chalk created outline, looked back and said, "Please be careful not to step on the chalk."

Tom followed Ben and Perry into Maynard's office. He pressed the on-off button after getting the go-ahead from the agents. The computer booted normally. After desktop icons appeared, he sat down in the black office chair and looked for a *My Documents* folder icon—it was missing. Tom was aware that all of Maynard's memoir files were stored in that folder.

He double-clicked the *My Computer* icon to access the hard drive. He became frustrated in failing to locate the *My Documents* folder. He searched the *Recycle Bin* where deleted folders and files were routed before final removal. It was empty. In desperation, he did a complete *Find/Search* of the entire hard drive for the missing folder. He experienced a sinking feeling in the pit of the stomach when the result read, *Zero folders/files found.*

"How are we doing so far?" asked Ben.

"Not good at all," Tom answered. "The memoir files are all missing. Someone must have deleted them."

"Did Mr. Cushing have any backups?"

"Yeah, there should be four back-up diskettes up there in the plastic box."

Agent Ben needed to stand on his toes to reach the diskette container. He set it down on the desk.

"Would you take a look?" he asked Tom.

Hastings remembered helping Maynard create back-up copies of the memoir files onto four floppy disks. They were organized into four separate files, each on a separate disk.

"Look at this tray. Someone other than Maynard or I has been messing with these disks." Tom flipped through the diskettes three times.

"I'm sorry, gentlemen, but Maynard's back-up diskettes, the memoirs, are missing."

"Could he have stored the diskettes somewhere else?" asked Agent Perry.

"It's possible, but as far as I know this was the only place where he kept them. I doubt he would have stored them somewhere else, on his own."

"How about hard copy?" asked Agent Ben.

"The files weren't ready for printing. There again, it's possible he printed them on his own."

Perry left the room and momentarily returned to inform Ben that the keyboard and computer accessories had not been checked for prints.

Ben became angry. He raised his voice and said, "These small town sheriff people have corn flakes for brains."

Deputy Johnson's ears, in the next room, were burning.

"Thanks a lot for your help, Mr. Hastings, Perry will drive you home now," said Agent Ben.

Tom followed Perry out the front door and into the car. As they were climbing the small hill, he looked at Maynard's house and said, "I sure miss that old guy. We had a lot of good times."

"Sure a nice place you have here," Agent Perry said when dropping Hastings off. "Here's our card. If you figure out what happened to those files, please give us a call."

As his car disappeared beyond the driveway, Tom remembered that he had dropped off *two business cards* on Maynard's computer desk. The state agents mentioned only one. *What happened to the second card?*

# 5

TOM NEEDED A BREAK after the frustrating visit to Maynard's house. He turned to his number-one passion—tennis. Retiring and moving into the country provided the space needed to build a court. It was completed three years ago. Tom used it often during non-snow summer season. Purchasing a ball machine allowed him to use the court alone.

After an invigorating tennis workout, he showered, poured a glassful of vintage French Chardonnay, and glided into the hot tub. The initial feeling derived from the hot, turbulent water removed all his unpleasant thoughts.

The hot tub location afforded an excellent view of the bay. He noticed two fishing boats parked next to weed beds directly across the bay. There must be something special about that weed bed. It attracted more fishing boats than any other part of the bay. He could see Sylvan's dock from the hot tub section of the deck. The white sailboat was missing. Sylvan had the nicest boat in the bay—shiny new.

Tom thought about Sylvan and his wife moving into the neighborhood six years ago. They went through a difficult ordeal getting a building permit for the addition. One day Sylvan showed up at his doorstep with a petition. He needed a special variance from the county in order to get the building permit. Tom signed the petition but not before asking some questions. Sylvan wasn't pleased.

For most of one summer the annoying sound of saws and hammers drifted over to the Hastings's house. By the time leaves began to color in the fall, the house was finished except for the deck. It didn't get completed until the last leaf spiraled to the ground.

A generous stand of trees dominated Sylvan's sloping landscape.

The landscape of the Hastings home, between deck and water, was free of trees. Boaters had a clear view of Tom's place, only limited at Sylvan's house.

Tom remained in the hot tub for forty-five minutes. As he was getting out, the sailboat entered the bay. Running lights were on, it was cruising at low speed. Since there was a nice breeze, he wondered why Sylvan didn't have the sails mounted. The sailboat didn't turn into Sylvan's dock but rather cruised on beyond the Hastings home toward the closed end of the bay.

As the boat passed, Tom became aware that one of the two people aboard was watching him with binoculars. The sailboat made a long turn and cruised along the opposite shoreline before docking at Sylvan's shore.

As the sun was lowering in the west, its glistening rays lit up the tree line across the bay. Nearly perfect reflections of the trees in the water were truly a sight to behold. As the sun continued to lower it eventually moved behind a wall of trees and disappeared from view. The disadvantage of not being able to observe the sunsets during the summer months was offset in other ways. The trees protected the building from summer storms and winter winds.

After the dazzling affect of the sun was gone, Tom moved indoors and spent the rest of the evening watching Atlanta Braves baseball on television.

His thoughts drifted to Maynard and his last computer session. *What about the second business card*? He remembered laying two cards on the desk—no mistake about that. The state guys had one of them. The memoir files were missing. Four diskettes were missing. Feelings of fear crept into Tom's mind.

He left the couch and began shuffling through the cards in his billfold. The card that Agent Perry gave him wasn't amongst them. He eventually found the card lying on the computer desk.

He dialed the number. Perry answered and listened as Tom explained the second card. Perry thanked him for the call and said he would discuss it with Agent Ben.

# 6

**T**HE SOUND OF SPLATTERING RAIN ON THE ROOF, next morning, awakened Tom Hastings. Peeking out the bedroom window, he knew outdoor work was going to take a holiday. After checking e-mail and markets, he headed for New Dresden in the pickup truck.

Water puddles had formed in several low areas of his roadway. The township road was dryer until he got to the small hill where the gravel had partly washed away. Reducing speed, he glanced toward Maynard's house. The yellow tape was gone. The driveway was void of vehicles. Tom Hastings's feelings of sorrow were still present.

Tom was alone in the post office mailbox room when he opened his box and plucked out the mail. After sorting on a side counter, he discarded the junk and placed two bills in his pocket. Nick Smith from Rocky Point was checking out groceries when Tom entered to buy a newspaper.

"No golf today," he said. "Guess I'll go home and work out on my bicycle."

Tom paid for the newspaper and followed Nick outside. They paused underneath the canopy projecting from above the building.

"Anything new on the Maynard Cushing murder?" Nick asked.

"There doesn't seem to be anything in the *Star Tribune*. Haven't heard anything new, except the police tape was gone this morning. Did you notice?"

"No, I didn't. Had my mind on golf and the rain, I guess."

"Have you talked to Rollie? He spent a lot of time at Maynard's house," said Tom.

"No, but I talked to his wife, Sarah, yesterday. She said he was upset. They played a ton of checkers, you know."

"That's true. Rollie visited Maynard on some days when I was there, working with the computer. They either played before or after."

"Well, I better get these groceries in the car. See you later. Stop by if you hear any big news."

The two men parted. Nick hurried across the street to stay dry. Tom got into his pickup.

— —

MARY JONES WAS CLEANING A COTTAGE. She glanced out the window and said out loud, "Our guests will be grounded today."

Mary and her husband, Bill, owned and operated South Shores Resort. They bought the property twelve years ago.

Mary was a career, business lady. Her hair was graying but she had a youthful figure. She wasn't as carefree and easygoing as her husband Bill, but did manage a wide smile on occasion. Bill was tall and slim. He didn't seem to worry about anything.

When finishing the cottage, she opened the door and made haste in getting to the office. She put the cleaning materials in a closet and entered the kitchen. Bill was sitting at the table reading a newspaper.

"Did you get the tractor fixed?" asked Mary.

"Naw, that darn thing just won't shift. I may have to take it in."

"What next? I just noticed the drain in number five wasn't doing very well."

Bill looked up at her and frowned, "Damn that thing. Who knows what some of these people put down the drain. That's the third time this year."

"I hope there's nothing in the paper about the murder. We've had two cancellations already."

Bill lifted a cup to his lips. After a couple of sips, he said, "Naw, nothing in the paper. That's a break. You know, Mary, we should sell this place. It's just too damn much work. I talked to the realtor the other day and he said property values are skyrocketing."

"Which realtor did you talk to?"

"Ah, it was the guy in New Dresden. Kyle is his name, I think."

"There's another realty office there too, you know. Adams Realty."

"Yeah, I know. They're both pretty new. I happened to run into the Kyle guy in the hardware store."

Mary heard the door open into the office. She stepped in and saw Tom Hastings.

"Well, hello stranger. Come on in and have some coffee," she said.

"Hi, Mary. Yes, I sure will."

Bill stood up when Tom entered and extended his callused right hand. "What's up?" he asked.

Tom's handshake was firm. His palm wasn't as hard as Bills, but it wasn't soft either.

"I'm trying to get over losing my friend, Maynard. Did you two know him well?"

"No, we didn't. I've talked to him on occasion. I don't think Mary ever met him," said Bill looking up at his wife.

"Oh, but I did meet him. Remember when Lisa Smilie called. She was sick," responded Mary. "It's sure too bad what happened. Why do you suppose he was killed?"

"According to the state people, it was because of drugs. The sheriff doesn't agree. They think it was the CIA connection," answered Tom.

Mary looked at Tom in disdain and said, "Either way, it's bad for us. We've put a ton of money in here, not to mention the time, then some whacko murders someone to scare people away."

Bill chipped in, "A couple of deputies came around the day after the murder. They spent a couple of hours talking to whoever was around. They were especially interested in those that had cabins or trailers over near the public water access."

Mary pointed east and said, "Yeah, there's this guy who lives in a trailer, year around, next to the public water-access-road. He stopped by for a chat and coffee a couple of days ago. He and his wife were walking their dog around the campsite after supper when they saw a man walking up the road...it was the day of the murder."

"Do you suppose they told the sheriff deputies?" Tom asked.

"Gee, I really don't know," said Bill.

"Eric never mentioned talking to the sheriff's people," said Mary.

"Do you have any customers driving a black car?" Tom asked.

"Yes, about a week before the murder, two people from Illinois arrived in a black car. It may have been a Buick Regal. I don't know cars that well," answered Mary.

"Were they ever guests before?" Tom asked.

"I don't think so. They seemed like a nice couple, but they kept to themselves. Bill, did you see much of them?"

"No, I don't think they spent any time on the beach or around the dock. Their car wasn't around all that much either."

"When they checked out, they paid with cash," added Mary.

Bill said, "I was surprised the state agents didn't interview either of us, and as far as I know, they didn't interview any of our guests either."

"Nice talking to you guys. Thanks for the coffee. Time to move on."

"Take it easy," said Bill.

Tom pondered calling Deputy Johnson about the black car at South Shores. After working on the computer catching up on bookwork for an hour, he picked up the card on the desk and dialed.

"Deputy Johnson, here. What can I do for you?"

"Hello, this is Tom Hastings. You visited my house the other day, remember?"

"Yes, I remember.  What's on your mind?"

Tom told him about the black Buick at the resort.

"Thanks for the call, Mr. Hastings. Is there anything else?"

"Yes, there is. Deputy, I'm concerned because one of my business cards, left for Maynard in his computer room, is missing. I mentioned it to one of the state guys on the phone last night."

"I thought Agents Ben and Perry found you because of your card."

"They did find me because of my card, but I'm positive of leaving two cards on Maynard's desk, the very last visit. Not only is the second card missing, but also the backup diskettes."

"Tom, I'm really glad you mentioned the missing card. We have reason to believe that whoever killed Maynard may kill again. In all honesty, it is possible you could become a target. Because you have the right to protect yourself, I think you should know what's going on.  I'll come over for some talk."

In about an hour, the deputy's car arrived and parked in Tom

Hastings's driveway.

Deputy Johnson got right to the point. "The state guys brought in a BCA technicians team, who spent the best part of yesterday messing in Maynard's house lifting prints and taking photographs. When the technicians finished, one of the BCA agents told me they were all through with the house and turned it over to us. They were a little vague about who is in charge of the case and they returned to St. Paul yesterday.

"In spite of what the state officers said, I decided not to release the house to Maynard's son just yet. I want to go over it one more time. Perhaps your card will show up. Either way I'll let you know. This is a confusing case, Mr. Hastings. We may need each other's help."

# 7

**F**LASHING LIGHTS, DIFFERENT LOCATION, on the country highway. Tom was returning from New Dresden. His stomach tightened—thoughts about Maynard. Deputy Johnson's words, *you could become a target*. A couple of weeks had gone by since the visit. Tom was locking his doors at night, turning the knobs, making sure.

There was no ambulance, state trooper's car parked on the shoulder of the road. Uniformed trooper, standing behind his car, writing on a clipboard. Three persons were milling about, a few steps away. Tom approached with the pickup truck, rear view mirror filled with a semi-truck, not far behind. Slowing was okay, stopping was not safe, he thought.

Black sedan in the ditch. The other vehicle, a pickup truck, was parked on the shoulder in front of the trooper car. Tom noticed the driver side headlight area was crunched. Tom was the type a guy who minded his own business. That plus the semi-truck was why he didn't stop and join the onlookers. A mile later, when he was about to make a right turn off the county highway, he saw the tow truck approaching from the north.

"It's coming for the black sedan," he said out loud.

There are a lot of black sedans, Tom was thinking while parking the pickup truck in the garage. Nevertheless, this could be the one. Backing the truck out, he headed back to the accident site. When arriving, the patrolman was gone and so was the dented pickup truck. The wrecker operator was hooking onto the black sedan. Perfect, Tom thought.

He parked in an abandoned driveway and approached the scene on foot.

"Anyone get hurt?" he asked the operator.

"I don't think so, except for a pickup truck and that black car down in the ditch. A busted radiator."

Tom watched as the cable tightened and slow but sure dragged the car from the ditch.

"Is that a Buick Regal?" he asked the operator.

"Yup, a 98."

Tom observed the wrecker truck had a Big Lakes emblem on the door. He busied memorizing the license number of the Regal, *BPX542*.

The operator peeked under the front end of the Buick. He looked up at Tom and said, "Well, that'll do'er, I guess."

Tom walked back to his truck, watching as the joined vehicles rolled up the highway.

— —

KYLE FREDRICKSON WAS NERVOUS about the Cushing house listing. He moved to New Dresden six years ago, splurged and bought the only realty business in town. Property sales were good. They remained satisfactory until Adam's Realty started up down the street. Kyle was not pleased with the unexpected competition. In just two years, his listings went down sixty percent.

He overheard two people talking at the post office yesterday. One of them said the yellow tape at the Cushing home was removed. Kyle called Mr. Cushing's son, hoping to get in a good word and work toward a listing. The initial conversation with Norm was constructive. Kyle asked for the listing and got a favorable response. He should be confident and happy. This morning, Norm and Linda Barr were visiting on the sidewalk. Linda was the manager and top sales-person at Adam's Realty—happiness turned to worry.

Kyle blamed his recent downturn in business on Linda Barr. He thought of her as a deceiving, conniving broad who needed to be taken down a notch. She had stolen two recent listings that Kyle was sure he had secured. At all costs, he could not let her get the Cushing job. Out of curiosity and anxiety, he decided to drive out to the Cushing place.

He touched his brakes when he saw a flashing light about a quarter mile ahead. Looking at the speedometer, sixty-nine miles per hour, he feared the worst—a speeding ticket. Kyle was relieved the flashers were perched on a wrecker, not a patrol car. As Kyle passed, he noticed Tom Hastings's pickup truck parked in a grassy approach of a farm field. *What was he doing there*? Kyle was curious.

Mental note: visit the Hastings house soon. Tom Hastings was a friend of Maynard Cushing and a good word might do some good.

Keeping his head above water financially wasn't easy after that meddling Linda Barr moved to town. Debts from the past never seemed to go away. He had thought about approaching the Barr lady and making a deal. He could start over somewhere else.

# 8

TOM HASTINGS SHIVERED WHILE STEPPING DOWN THE STEPS. The morning was damp and cool following yesterdays rain. A split section of firewood, three pieces of dry kindling, and a chunk of cardboard paper along with crumpled pages of newspaper. The wood burner on an inside wall in the dining room was ready. After lighting the paper, he loaded the coffee percolator, flicked the switch, and headed for his computer corner. The room was too chilly to check e-mail and the Internet so he snuggled up next to the fire patiently waiting for the coffee to brew.

The scare he received listening to the words of Deputy Johnson had gradually diminished during the recent two weeks. His life was settling back to normal, hardly even glanced at Maynard's house any more.

After the room warmed, he returned to the computer desk and opened the file drawer. While sifting through the tabs looking for the folder of a client, he saw the title, *Maynard*. Waves of excitement passed through his body—the regenerated memory of making a second set of backup diskettes of the memoirs. Pulling the folder out, he was expecting to feel the bulk of four diskettes. To his disappointment, they weren't there.

"Now where the heck did I put those diskettes?" he said out loud. He shuffled through stacks stored in three plastic boxes on a shelf above the computer. Frustration soared by failing to find the Maynard backups. The possibility of leaving them at Maynard's house was unlikely—they had to be here somewhere.

"Take a break," he whispered. "Have some coffee and try to remember. Did I make backups? If so, where did he put them?"

Tom took a cup of coffee upstairs to his bedroom and got dressed. After returning, he put on a jacket and walked out on the deck, steaming cup in his hand. As he looked out over the water, a series of surface ripples were moving through the bay. The wind behind the ripples was cool. Shivering, he returned into the house.

On a bench next to the desk lay his briefcase, partially opened. His memory of the backup diskettes returned. In a sleeve of the briefcase, he found the Maynard memoirs diskette copies. Feeling waves of excitement, he created a Maynard folder on the hard drive and copied the contents of each diskette into the folder. One step further he went, duplicate copies of the diskettes.

Deputy Johnson's card was lying on the desk.

Confidently, he dialed the number. "This is Tom Hastings. I'd like to speak to Deputy Johnson."

"Just a second, I'll check to see if he's in," replied the dispatcher, a ladies voice.

He heard a shuffle of feet and a click. "Hello there, Tom Hastings. This is Deputy Johnson. What's up?"

"Deputy, I found a copy of Maynard's memoirs. They were in my briefcase."

"Nice going, Tom. I'll stop by right after lunch and pick them up. Will you be home?"

"I sure will. See you then."

He had done his duty—reported the discovery to the officials. While waiting for the deputy to arrive, he loaded the memoir file. Right there in front of him was the content of file number-one. Scrolling down, he scanned Maynard's family history. Nothing in it made a case for murder.

In file number-two, Maynard wrote about his experiences in grade school and high school. Noteworthy, but not significant, was a story about getting into trouble in high school. Nasty Maynard and a couple of other boys placed a snake in a desk—the girl screamed. They got caught—off to the principal's office. That night at dinner, Mr. Cushing had a fit. Privileges of young Maynard were lost for two weeks.

The contents of diskettes three and four included Maynard's experiences as a CIA agent. Just the ticket, Tom thought. He looked out the window. The deputy hadn't arrived. He was confident and eager that something in those writings was going to provide a clue as to why Maynard was murdered.

Reading them was tedious, Maynard wrote about hundreds of incidents. Tom reviewed each one and placed triple asterisks by those that appeared suspect. Still no Deputy Johnson—he must have been delayed.

An hour passed. Cataloging the incidents was complete. Ten were marked with asterisks. After reviewing, Tom thought any one of them could have a bearing on the murder. Two were especially interesting.

First, there was a tale about a foreign agent. Fifteen years before Maynard retired, the agent verbally threatened to kill him. The FBI investigated and the agent in question was eventually expelled from service. Just two years ago, Maynard received a threatening phone call. The call was traced to an apartment in DC that had recently been vacated. From FBI description of the recent occupant, Maynard suspected the call came from the expelled agent.

The second was in the last and fourth file. Maynard wrote about an incident that happened when he was stationed in Virginia. He had uncovered evidence that one of the CIA agents working in the same office was selling secrets to a foreign government. Maynard told his boss. The FBI became involved and the agent was arrested.

While free on bond and awaiting a hearing, the agent, whose name was Robert Ranforth, disappeared. He was never heard from again. During the past ten years, Maynard contacted his friends, current agents with the CIA, and inquired as to the status of Agent Ranforth. As of this writing, Ranforth's whereabouts remained unknown.

Tom was still on the computer when Deputy Johnson's car appeared in the driveway. He opened the door as the deputy came down the sidewalk.

"Hello, Tom. You've got something for me?"

"Sure do. Come on in. Have a seat, I'll get you a cup."

"Thanks, I could use one. Missed lunch today."

The deputy sat on a chair at the dining room table and waited.

"There you are," Tom said, as the coffee splashed over the edge and onto the table.

"Whoops, I'll get a rag."

After drying the table, Tom brought over the diskettes, packaged and bound together with a rubber band.

"There are four diskettes, each one contains a separate memoir file. The stories are complete but the contents have not been edited, professionally."

"Thank you. These could be very important. I'll have someone put these in our computer at the office."

"Tom, I had a talk with my boss yesterday. We decided you are in serious danger because of your previous involvement with Maynard Cushing. He is willing to take you into our confidence. Your strategic location will help in the investigation. You have to promise me that all the information shared with you will remain right here."

"Deputy, I appreciate what you are doing and I will cooperate in any way I can."

"Okay, Tom, you can call me Paul. Here's the latest. The Minnesota

State Bureau of Criminal Apprehension agency has concluded that Maynard Cushing's murder was drug related. The reasoning is Cushing owed the big boys money, behind on his drug payments. He was murdered to send a message to others who weren't paying."

"I don't buy the drug theory. No way was Maynard involved with drugs," Tom responded. "Do you think it's possible Maynard was murdered because of something that happened during his CIA career?"

"It's possible, but doubtful, since Maynard had been retired from the CIA for about ten years. Nice job on recovering the disks, Tom. We may change our minds after reading the memoirs."

Tom didn't mention making copies for himself.

Deputy Johnson rose from his chair, announcing, "The Maynard Cushing property has been released to his son. He's real anxious to sell, almost too anxious. Oh, by the way, we didn't find your other business card."

Tom imagined a dark room, a bright light shining down on his card, a set of evil eyes studying his name.

"Would it be okay if I walked out on the deck and checked out the view?" asked the deputy.

"Sure, help yourself,"

The deputy observed the hot tub and said, "That must be a nice way to end a long, hard day."

He looked east, down the shoreline, and spotted Sylvan's mast. "Who belongs to the sailboat?"

"A guy by the name of Sylvan. I can't remember his last name."

"Do you see him much?"

"Now and then in New Dresden."

"Since you've forgotten his last name, may I assume you don't know him very well?"

'That's right. Our connections are limited."

"How long has he lived there?"

"He bought the property and moved in about six years ago."

"Is he married?"

"Yup, sure is...wife's name is Missy."

"What does he do for a living?"

"I heard he's an executive, works for a Big Lakes manufacturing firm."

Paul said, "This sure is a nice lake. I might be interested in one of the lots across the township road from the Cushing property. Who owns all those lots?"

"I'm not sure, but Kyle Fredrickson in New Dresden would certainly know."

"I've never met Kyle...perhaps the time has come to give him a call."

As Deputy Johnson was leaving, he said, "I'll stay in touch. Be careful."

# 9

**D**ISKETTES AND MAYNARD'S MURDER were on Tom's mind all afternoon. His garden tractor labored as the attached mower deck spit out wads of damp clippings. Grass grew thicker in the low damp areas of the greenway.

By this time, only Deputy Johnson knew he'd had copies of the memoirs. Who else was going to find out, he thought—probably be all over town by next morning. Not a funny matter. He could be in even greater danger than the deputy mentioned. Maynard's killer has his business card, a link to the diskettes.

Tom enjoyed mowing grass with the twenty-two-horse riding mower. He pulled back on the throttle and eased the machine into the garage, his biggest one. Tom was a garage person—a man who felt the most important part of a home was the garage. He had two of them. The larger one housed his car, pickup truck and all those other things that people refer to as toys.

The driveway was huge—it resembled a mall. The house lined the south edge, large garage did the same on the north. A smaller and older garage bordered the west. The smaller garage stored his farm tractor and his dad's old black-and-white Chevy pickup truck, an antique. Also a treasure of Tom Hastings's, bringing back nostalgic memories of life on a farm in the Red River Valley of the north.

Slinging a camera bag over his shoulder, Tom began the daily walk. His mind was heavy, thoughts of losing Maynard. He walked up the asphalt pathway, extending from the driveway to the tennis court—evolution from a cornfield of a few years ago. The court was surrounded by a greenway approximately the size of two and a half football fields.

*Serious danger.* Those were the words spoken by Deputy Johnson, Tom remembered as he walked along the substantial stand of hardwood and aspen trees that lined the greenway on the lakeside. He paused to peer into the woods, denseness of the trees and leaves prevented a view of the lake. Glancing northward, he admired the rows of young spruce and pine trees, cultivated and free of weeds. Looking eastward, he saw the roadway.

*Head bashed in with a club.* Another statement made by the deputy. Tom imagined someone, the killer of Maynard, coming after him with a club as he reached the four-acre patch of sunflowers bordering the greenway on the west.

Concerns and fears were put aside as Tom's mind became absorbed with the progress of the sunflower plants. Three feet high, he estimated. Small heads were forming at the top of the stalks.

He walked along the trail between the sunflower field and the wall of trees next to the lake. It led to another substantial stand of young spruce and pine trees, rows running north and south. He was proud of those trees. Each year he planted close to 200 seedlings. Watering and nurturing was rewarding. The objective: to find a new home for every alternate tree after attaining a height of seven feet. Camera plucked from the shoulder bag, he took a picture of the landscape. One of his passions, other than tennis, was wildlife and nature photography.

Deer tracks showed up clearly in the cultivated area amongst the small trees. Fifty deer must pass through this field every day, he thought. Tom paused, there amongst all the others was the big one—Prancer had been there. He considered Prancer a partner. Tom was boss of the tennis court. Prancer was boss in the woods.

Like most deer, Prancer didn't hang around long when man was near. Tom remembered the last time seeing him. He went face to face with the big deer late one evening, next to the sunflower field. Neither moved for a few moments. The deer raised his right leg—just a little, the hoof barely cleared the ground. Prancer began tapping a pointed hoof into the dirt, up and down about four times in rapid succession—the warning. If Tom moved, the deer was gone in a flash.

Tom smiled and waved while watching the white tail disappear into the woods. He had pictures to prove that Prancer was a magnificent animal. Tom lit a cigar and followed behind, knowing Prancer would become invisible. He revisited wildlife memories while moving up the trail.

Over there, next to the tall grass, once he saw a fox make calculated leaps attempting to claw prey from its hiding place. To his left, high in that tree branch, he identified a ruffed leg hawk earlier that spring.

Middle of the trail, in a clump of dirt, manufactured by a gopher, he saw a fox track.

*Or was it a coyote track*? How could he ever forget the winter? Wolves were hunting the trails daily. To play it safe, he carried a rifle while cross-country skiing. To top it all, a pair of moose visited earlier this summer.

Tom's mind drifted back in time, his wife would be at his side enjoying the nature. Her death was a severe blow, especially since they were both approaching retirement and had so many plans. He thought about their cozy apartment in Brownstown. Their plans, gracefully leave the city, move to the country. Tom's love of nature eased some of the pain, but out on these trails he would remember—he missed Becky.

A few months ago, the thought of living alone the rest of his life was depressing. The Internet, why didn't he think of it earlier? The perfect searching tool for seeking a new partner—someone to share his life.

Tom was successful in finding a delightful lady from the Twin Cities who had similar interests. She was a good tennis player and enjoyed the outdoors at least as much. He looked up beyond the treetops, to the white rolling clouds and blue sky—somewhere up there, someone sent Julie to him.

Tom would never forget her first visit. She came equipped with a tennis racquet and a backpack, binoculars, bird books, a camera. Nervous feelings, sweaty palms, and a congested voice box during the initial visit. They walked the trails, played tennis, and dipped in the hot tub. In spite of a great beginning to their relationship, Tom endured periods of feeling uncertain about the future. He was hoping Julie would visit this weekend.

The trail ended at two mature rows of evergreens and a fence line marking the western border of his property. As he headed northward between the fence and large evergreens, numerous birds skittered ahead.

The greenway, fields of trees and sunflowers were only a part of his property. A large wooded area seventy acres in size lay to the north. The woods were dotted with grassy ponds, some were viewable from a network of meandering hiking trails. Diskettes and one business card were on his mind as he continued the late evening walk westward.

Beyond the two rows of large evergreens, a wooden bench adorned the top of a hill overlooking the fields. Fluffs of smoke came from the bench—Tom sat quietly, watching for deer, puffing on a cigar.

He entered the woods on the main trail that diagonals toward the beginning of his roadway. The dampness of the ground allowed him to walk quietly. When rounding a bend, he caught sight of a deer's tail as the animal bounded out of sight. A covey of crows were having tantrums. Tom looked up and saw them harassing a red shouldered hawk.

He stopped atop a small wooden bridge that spanned a nearly dry creek bed. A short distance upstream, he could see the beaver dam. Their house was built in a pond, deeper water. The beaver was a smart animal.

When Tom arrived at the largest pond on his property, he marveled at the beavers long, narrow waterways dug in a shallow, grassy extension. He imagined the waterways to be super highways—a means for floating tree branches. Back on the main trail, he surprised a large gray owl that hooted and moved on to safety. A few steps later, a second owl, the mate, clumsily escaped through the crowded trees.

The main trail ended at the roadway. He stepped onto the gravel and began walking back to his house, a distance slightly over half-mile. The gravel roadway was damp, morning rain, deer tracks appeared fresh. He was about half the distance home when three large deer loped across the roadway. He wondered if Prancer was one of them.

— —

WHEN TOM'S DRIVEWAY CAME INTO VIEW, his thoughts returned to Maynard, loss of my friend. He missed his wife and he missed Maynard. An evening at Mary Ann's restaurant wasn't the same. His loved one was gone. His friend was gone.

He thought of Maynard's mind resembling a library, a source of stories, some from his life with the CIA. He shared them with enthusiasm. One in particular that Tom remembered took place in Europe. *Maynard had too much to drink in a German pub and woke up the next morning in a strange bed. He had no idea where he was or how he got there.*

*The good news, his clothes were on a chair by the bed. The bad news, his head was throbbing. After dressing, he cautiously started down a long stairway. A nasty, mean looking German Shepherd dog was stationed at the bottom. One step at a time, a noisier, more threatening growl each time.*

Maynard broke out in a laugh when telling the next part of the story. *The mutt looked about as mean as any I've ever seen. I tried to nice-dog the problem—it didn't work. The dog's mind was made up. I was not coming down those steps. The dog and I were at a stalemate. My headache made matters worse.*

*When hearing the front door open, I stepped back and peaked over the rail. A lady and a police officer had just entered the front hallway. Panic, My wallet was missing, no identity. Returning to the bedroom, I opened a window that overlooked an alley, two stories below.*

*Quickly, I threw the covers off the bed and tied two sheets together. Tying one end to a radiator, the other went out the window. Holding my breath, sliding down the sheets, about five feet from the alley surface the sheet tore and I fell into a heap...into the arms of a waiting police officer.*

Tom couldn't remember how the story ended.

# 10

SYLVAN WAS WORRIED BECAUSE OF A VISIT THE PREVIOUS DAY—a deputy sheriff. The guy asked a ton of questions. Sylvan could not afford to have his past bubble to the surface. Missy didn't know anything about what he was doing ten years ago. Nobody around here did—at least until now. That meddling deputy might uncover his secret.

He had seen the white vehicle with the bank of lights on the roof driving down Tom Hastings's roadway. Sylvan wondered if Tom Hastings was also getting the questions. It was another day off from work. He was having a lot of those lately. So what if I get fired, he thought. There were numerous projects waiting for his attention. Missy was on his case just last week—electrical outlets in the lower level still had live wires sticking out.

"They're dangerous, leaving them exposed like that," she said.

Casper sensed his master was leaving. He followed him to the garage.

"Not today, Casper, you're staying home. I'm headed for the hardware store."

He drove slowly while thinking about the parts needed and the visit by the deputy. Sylvan made the turn onto the county highway and drew a horn from a red pickup truck. The squealing sound of brakes prevented the truck from hitting the blue van.

Sylvan shuddered and whispered, "I need to focus."

Plenty of available parking places on Main Street of New Dresden. After working the van into a curbside space, he entered the hardware store.

— —

TOM WAS WORKING ON HIS COMPUTER, sipping coffee, when the halogen lamp that serves the keyboard burned out. He was working with accounting software, tilting his head upward to catch the numbers in the bifocal section of the glasses. His eyes strained attempting to match the amounts from his bank statement with the rows of transaction items in the reconcile window. Over half an hour passed while searching for a two-penny error in the checking register.

After sealing the final bill envelope, he placed them in his jacket pocket and headed for the garage. One push of the button—the door went up and he got into the pickup truck. He didn't think it possible to survive living in the country without a pickup truck. The four-by-eight box had hauled its share of plywood and two-by-fours. Pulling into a parking place directly across the street from the hardware store, he stepped out of the truck. The lady visible in the window of the antique store was smiling at him. Not sure why, he thought, returning the smile.

The hardware store in New Dresden was a real classic. It was saturated with merchandise, stacked and piled up everywhere. The old floorboards creaked as Tom walked up the main aisle. He stopped to look at chain saws and accessories that were piled in a corner next to a display case. Tom cut and stacked piles of firewood each fall. Both saws in the small garage were working fine, but looking for new products and favorable prices was a habit. The wood shop tools aisle was his favorite. Last week, he plucked the neat mini-planer from the hanging bracket of the massive pegboard. If his wife were around, he would have bought it. Alone, he needed convincing the tool was needed. It wasn't.

Remembering the purpose of his visit, he headed for the electrical aisle. He became aware of another person in the aisle when he placed his hand on a halogen lamp packet. Turning his head, he came face to face with his neighbor, Sylvan.

"Oh, hello, Hastings. Are you working on a project too?"

"No, not really, just need some bulbs. How's your remodeling coming?"

"It's about finished, except for lots of loose ends. Did the sheriff's office pay you a visit?"

"Yes, they sure did. How about you?"

"Yeah, this big deputy came by yesterday. He worked me over pretty good."

"Did you know Maynard Cushing very well?"

Sylvan became irritated and answered abruptly, "Not at all, why do you want to know?"

Tom realized he had asked the wrong question, "Ah, no reason, just routine curiosity. How's the sailboat?"

Sylvan appeared to appreciate the change in subject. "It's quite the challenge. As soon as my rigging arrives you'll see some sails on the bay. I ordered the rigging on the Internet and it's been back-ordered for a month. Should be here any day."

Tom left the aisle and headed for checkout. He partially tripped over a bag of birdseed when approaching the sales counter. The staff behind the counter ignored Tom's successful attempt to recover his balance. To offset the embarrassment, Tom began cracking open peanut shells from a large wooden barrel next to the closed end of the checkout counter.

When a brown-shirted UPS agent came in the back door and distracted the clerks, Tom placed his purchase on the counter. He filled a Styrofoam cup with coffee and focused on the television mounted on a pillar near the counter, while waiting for service.

The television was showing the business news. He continued watching, sipping coffee, waiting for a clerk. One approached from around the corner of the back room. She successfully avoided brushing a wood stove that partially jutted into the room. Even though it was dormant today, it warmed this entire room on cold winter days.

"Did you find everything you needed?" the clerk asked.

"Yup, this is it."

Matt Nelson came down from his office perch that overlooked the checkout counter. He was the owner, inheriting the store from his grandfather, who created the business back in the thirties.

After the lady clerk scanned Tom's purchase, she said, "That'll be eleven-twenty."

Matt's friendly mannerism plus unmatchable knowledge of the hardware business made for an outstanding service for the small community of New Dresden.

While Tom was writing a check, Matt looked up at him and said, "I see you lost a neighbor."

"Yeah, Matt, pretty darn close to home."

The discussion about Tom's neighbor ended. Other customers had entered and were milling about the checkout counter.

"How about a tube of popcorn?" Tom asked.

"Sure thing," Matt replied.

Tom finished writing the check and handed it to the lady clerk.

"Thank you," she said.

Tom left the hardware store and noticed Sylvan getting into a blue van. The sound of a barking dog was coming from the partially opened window of a car parked next to the post office. The barking ceased when Tom entered to pick up his mail. The shaggy little canine started up again when he headed toward the grocery store. What did I ever do to that little mutt, Tom thought.

— —

FRED HOOD, OWNER OF THE VACUUM CLEANER SHOP in New Dresden, pushed the outer bank door open and began walking across the street toward the grocery store. His stiff-like strides and posture suggested a previous military career. He was wearing a flat top gray cap, not the usual kind of attire seen up and down Main Street.

A rusty pickup truck, towing a horse trailer, was noisily approaching from the north. The driver hit the brakes to avoid hitting the jaywalker. Fred's meeting at the bank didn't go well. The loan officer needed more documents before processing his loan.

"My God, what do those guys want, anyhow?" Fred muttered to himself as he hopped the curb in front of the grocery. He cringed from the jolt his spine felt.

Fred would have sued the doctors but he didn't dare. All he wanted was a facelift. An infection ensued and it spread into his neck. The spinal column never completely recovered from the infection.

Business was going well, bills were getting paid. Fred was frustrated with the building that housed his vacuum cleaner shop. Winters were grossly uncomfortable because of chilly drafts—the building leaked. The loan officer at the bank wanted federal tax returns for the previous three years. Fred could only come up with two.

He had many second thoughts about moving here five years ago. The city was too crowded—traffic was impossible, he needed space. New Dresden was perfect. He felt safe—the past was dead and gone—covered with simple scoops of a shovel.

He glanced up the sidewalk toward the post office and saw Tom Hastings approaching. Fred put his head down and continued past the corner of the grocery store. He crossed the side street and headed toward his place of business, Fred's Vacuum Cleaner Shop. The lady standing by his shop door stimulated his pace. She was carrying a vacuum cleaner.

— —

TOM SAW FRED HOOD CROSSING THE STREET. He was startled and held his breath when Fred ignored the horse trailer. Relieved that Fred wasn't hit, Tom stopped and observed Fred, curious about the stiff walk. As Tom was entering the grocery, he glanced at Fred reaching his destination, the lady carrying a vacuum cleaner.

Tom's grocery selections were miniscule, a couple of newspapers and a carton of orange juice.

"Did you see Fred almost get hit out in the street?" he asked Ellie.

"No, but I heard the brakes. That Fred seems to be in a daze most of the time."

Tom left the grocery and crossed at the place where Fred had the close call. Turning northward at the bank, he walked toward his pickup truck. He passed by the Borders Café and Kyle's Realty. A vacant lot separated Kyle's Realty from two gift shops, a barbershop and the Adam's Realty office. The building on the corner, next to where his truck was parked, housed a large antique store.

Tom didn't have any pity for a jeep that was parked behind his truck, only a few inches between bumpers. The third rap pushed the jeep backward a little, enough to wiggle out the truck.

He drove down Main Street toward the two-story brick building that housed Hector's Bar, Main Street's dead end. Turning left, he passed by Fred's Vacuum Cleaner Shop. After circling the block, he braked at the stop sign, turned right and crossed the railroad tracks.

The still waters of Borders Lake, a distance beyond the tracks, were appealing. A city park was squeezed into a narrow area of land between the lake and county highway. Looking to the right, he felt excited when noticing a group of young men hitting baseballs on a beautiful ball diamond.

Baseball was his main sport during his high school, youthful years—the tournaments, the championships and the fantastic memories. After all those years, Tom still visualized the ball sailing over the center fielder's head, while running toward first. Fans were yelling and on their feet as the winning run crossed home plate. Beyond the lake and the ball diamond, Tom flicked the left turn signal and made the turn up the county highway where it forked with state highway 200.

A mile up the road, he slowed and stared at the cemetery to his left. His wife was buried there under the branches of a splendid oak. The far side of the hill that housed the cemetery sloped down to a duck pond and green farm fields. He admired the quality and neatness of the corn and soybeans. The dairy farmers showed remarkable skill in maintaining their land and crops.

After passing the dairy farm, he was passed by a blue van. It turned right onto the township road. Tom wondered if either Byron or Eva saw Sylvan make the turn on two wheels. Their house stood like a sentry overlooking the intersection, they didn't miss much.

Tom noticed a for-sale sign projecting from the lawn next to Maynard's driveway. Kyle Fredrickson was victorious—defeat to Linda Barr and Adam's Realty. She wasn't going to be happy with Norm. Her piercing, loud voice would express her adverse feelings at the Borders Café. The locals would be listening but not hearing.

# 11

**H**ASTINGS'S ROADWAY WAS LONG AND NARROW. Tom hit the brakes to avoid hitting a deer that darted out of the woods and leaped across the road. Close call, but he was more concerned for the safety of the deer than potential damage to his truck. He knew it wasn't Prancer—the deer was smarter than that.

After arriving at his home, he entered the house and took the newspaper out onto the deck. The bay was quiet that morning, not a boat or person to be seen. A blue heron was standing on the last section of the dock. The heron's head was bent sideways and tucked downward against the side of its breast—asleep, supported by the long slender legs.

After finishing with the newspaper, Tom started the riding mower and spent some of the afternoon mowing grass. Mowing finished, he filled a jug with anti-weed spray and sprayed the edges of flowerbeds and the driveway. The spray he was using worked quite well on most broad leaf plants but didn't even bend the creeping charley weeds that were invading the grass on the west side of the house. Creeping Charlie was as resistant to the chemical as a corporate, customer-relations representative to a regular phone customer.

The spraying chore ended when the jug nozzle fizzled. Instead of refilling, he put away the spray equipment and headed out to the tennis court. The ball machine was his opponent that afternoon. Tom was a darn good tennis player. During his youthful days, he played tournaments. His recreation room bore the evidence—several trophies.

The machine was set to oscillation, 'pop-pop' like sounds permeated the area. An hour of dashing back and forth, corner to corner. Tom was ready for a shower. The soothing water in the hot tub relieved muscle and joint strains. The quietness in the bay was interrupted by the sound of a boat motor. Tom raised his wet head above the rim of the tub and watched Sylvan's sailboat backing away from the dock. Sylvan wasn't alone. His wife, Missy, was sitting on the cabin roof near the base of the mast. The boat cruised slowly eastward. Tom heard the phone ringing after leaving the spa.

— —

JULIE HOFFMAN LIVED IN AN APARTMENT COMPLEX in St. Paul. She had long recovered from a heart-breaking divorce that happened over ten years ago. Her two children lived in Denver, Colorado. Too far away, she thought. She liked her job at Glacial Computers located in downtown Minneapolis. As a marketing coordinator, she met many interesting people. But when the working day ended, returning alone to a quiet apartment was depressing.

Julie was an attractive blonde, had sparkling blue eyes. She was medium tall and maintained a respectable waist. In spite of the years, she still attracted the wandering male eyes. She was born and raised in northern Minnesota, the land of moose, bear, and wolves.

Loneliness motivated her to place a profile with an Internet dating service. Early experiences in meeting new gentlemen were failures until she met a man that lived in the lake country, north of the Twin Cities. His name was Tom Hastings. They hit it off on the first date. Julie loved his country place, especially the birds and wildlife. She was sitting on her sofa enjoying a glass of wine while dialing his number.

"Hi, this is Julie. How are you?"

"I'm just fine, and what's new with you?"

"This computer business is driving me whacky and I could sure use some peace and relaxation. How about this coming weekend?"

"It's a deal. Can you make it for dinner on Friday?"

"A team of oxen couldn't keep me away."

They chatted about the recent news and activities for about half an hour.

"I'm so looking forward to seeing you. It's been a long week."

"See you on Friday, Julie, bring your tennis racquet."

"Oh, I certainly will. Goodbye, Tom."

Tom hung up the phone and smiled, the weekend was right around the corner. He thought about the restaurant where he met Julie five months ago. Quaint and private Lucy's, overlooking the Minnesota River in St. Paul.

Because Julie liked birds, Tom knew she would have enjoyed the osprey that swooped down near the dock. Talons splashed in the water. A fish was having its only and last ride. The shoreline of the bay was a natural feeding area for the osprey as well as blue herons and eagles.

During Julie's last visit, she saw a heron feeding in a shallow area along the shoreline between here and Sylvan's dock. The heron was motionless—long legs and narrow body camouflaged amongst the rushes. Tom tried but failed to spot the heron.

"Over there," she said.

"Oh yeah, I see it now," he said when the heron's blue and gray head plunged into the water.

The head of the bird reappeared with tail of a fish protruding from its beak.

"Look at that snaky neck," said Tom.

The long neck undulated—the fish was down.

— —

SOUNDS OF A VACUUM CLEANER permeated the rooms of the Hastings's house on Friday. Beads of perspiration formed on Tom's forehead as he prepared for Julie's visit. He had learned a few tricks from the house cleaner he employed for a few months after his wife died.

A quick dusting of furniture, a run over the carpets with the vacuum and he was off to New Dresden in the pickup truck, armed with a grocery list. Tom maneuvered the truck into a parking place on Main Street just across from Adam's Realty. The vehicle parked ahead of his truck was a black Chevy Celebrity. He studied the license number but it didn't match the one seen at the accident site near the cemetery.

Tom opened the truck door and headed across the street. Next to the curb, directly in front of the post office another black car was parked. Tom slowed his walk. He stopped and saw no one in the recent model Buick Regal. A dead ringer for the one he saw in the ditch.

Before entering the post office, he studied the license number—the same, he was sure.

After getting the mail from his postal box, he watched from the window in the post office. A few minutes passed and the car remained unoccupied. Losing patience, Tom crossed the street and entered Borders Café.

Pausing by the door, he looked across the room seeking his friend, Henry. The usual table was unoccupied. By sitting down on the far chair that faced the window, he had a good view of the black Regal across the street.

The sports page in the *Star Tribune* dominated Tom's attention and his glances at the Regal became less frequent. The car remained unoccupied after reviewing the Twins box score. Two couples seated at the next table began conversing about Maynard's murder. He glanced at the Regal, back at the sports page.

One of the men at the next table said, "I heard drugs were involved, it's hard to believe."

The other guy said, "Nowadays, one never knows. Nothing would shock me. Just read the paper."

Conversation noises, created by many people talking at once, were making it difficult to hear much from the two couples. He did overhear the mention of names, *Byron*, and *Eva*—words, *county highway*. He assumed they were referring to his neighbors that lived in the farmhouse overlooking the township road.

"Need some more coffee?" asked the waitress.

He couldn't resist one more coffee fill before reading the last section of the *Star Tribune*.

"There you are," said the waitress as she dropped the slip on the table.

Tom jerked his head up when realizing his surveillance of the black Regal across the street had been neglected. A quick glance outside, to his disappointment, the black Regal was gone.

He paid at the counter, dropped a cluster of coins on the table, and quickly exited. Out in the street he scanned all directions. While looking northward, he saw the rear end of the black Regal crossing the railroad tracks. His attempt to identify the occupants of the Regal had failed.

The black Chevy Celebrity parked in front of his pickup truck hadn't moved, A convertible had parked in close behind Tom's pickup. Tom was careful not to engage the bumpers while edging out of the parking place. A jeep is one thing—a nice convertible, he had to be careful. Realizing his chances of catching up with the Regal were slim, he hurried, bouncing the truck when crossing the tracks. Tom reached the top of the hill by the cemetery hoping he would see the black car, he didn't.

The black car affair shouldn't be my concern, Tom thought. Damn, the black Regal anyhow. That's the sheriff's job. Why am I so obsessed? Aggressively, he jerked the steering wheel to the left and drove into the Byron Schultz farmstead. Byron answered the door a few seconds after he pressed the doorbell.

"How ya doin', Tom? You came at a good time. Eva is gone for the day. The school called this morning and needed some help. She left me in charge. Somewhat risky, huh?"

"Hi, Byron. I think you can handle this place. As you probably have heard, one of our neighbors has been killed."

Byron didn't answer and gestured Tom to sit in a chair next to the kitchen table. He had been reading the newspaper while sipping on a creamy cup of coffee.

It was typical for a dairy farmer to use milk in their coffee. Tom was just the opposite—totally black with no sugar. Byron was happy to have company and conversation. When he operated the dairy farm, he was much too busy to dally around the house.

Tom admired the perfect view of the township road from the kitchen window while Byron was busy in the kitchen brewing another pot. Returning from the kitchen, Byron set the pot on the table and sat down. He topped his cup and filled one for Tom.

"So, Tom, what do you think is going on? The murder in our neighborhood is scaring Eva to death."

"It's pretty awful, Byron. I miss the guy, he was a close friend. Hopefully, Eva will get over it."

Byron said, "I heard Maynard's son found him lying on the floor. It took about half an hour for help to arrive, but it didn't matter, Maynard was already dead."

"Byron, did you see a black car go by a few minutes ago?"

"Yup, I sure did. It was moving right along and made a quick turn into South Shores Resort."

"Have you ever seen it before?"

"No, I don't think so. But Eva mentioned seeing a black car driving east, beyond the turn to your place, toward Maynard's house."

"Do you remember what day that was?"

"Sort of, it was last week sometime. You'll have to ask her."

"Did the sheriff's office ask you and Eva any questions?"

"No, they didn't."

"They were real interested in a black car that some of us saw on the township road the day of the murder. If Eva saw the car that day, perhaps it may have come from Maynard's driveway...it could be real important."

"She never mentioned seeing the car in the driveway. Eva has been commenting about the unusual amount of traffic on the township road this summer. I think the heavier traffic load is due to the lots, the ones for sale." Byron said, pointing a finger toward the window.

"Yeah, there has been a lot of traffic, especially along the north branch where the new lots are. I walked some of the lots a few years ago. They're nice and big with interesting landscape, a ton of trees. Each lakefront must be at least three-hundred feet."

"Lots of times, we see people park their cars on the side of the road and just walk around."

As Tom was looking out the window, sipping coffee, a red pickup truck appeared, coming from the north. It turned and headed down the township road. After creating a large dust cloud, it turned left at the public access road. When the pickup truck disappeared from sight and the dust settled, two joggers appeared. They were headed toward the county highway.

"Eva and I see our share of bikers, walkers, and joggers. Most of them come from South Shores.

"Oh, I almost forgot, Eva was doing dishes and looking out the kitchen window when she saw a man walking diagonally across that first lot. That's the one located across from Maynard's driveway and next to the public water access road. He was walking away from Maynard's house and in the direction of the public access. She was quite sure it was the day of the murder."

The cups were almost empty when Byron reached over, grabbed the pot and re-filled both cups. A light brown car coming from the direction of New Dresden turned onto the township road. It passed beyond the intersection at the small hill and pulled up into Maynard's driveway.

"That has to be Kyle Fredrickson," said Byron.

"Rumors in New Dresden are that he's getting the listing," Tom said.

"Yeah, we've heard the same thing. Kyle's doing pretty well for himself. Competing with the Adam's franchise and all that."

"He's a quiet guy...haven't really met him, sure has a funny walk," Hastings added.

"Have you met the couple who bought the old farmstead located just west of your property line?" asked Byron.

"No, I haven't. Do you know anything about them?"

"Well, I bought that chunk of land about fifteen years ago, sold the farmstead the very next year. The people who bought from me turned around, sold it to those people."

"I stopped at their house one day. Names are Steve and Kim Wytorrak. They weren't very anxious to tell me where they were from—good job of sidestepping my question. Plenty of talk about the plans to improve the buildings and build a new house."

'Thanks for the coffee, Byron, I've got to go. Grass needs mowing."

"Thanks for coming by. I'll tell Eva you stopped."

# 12

THE ANSWERING MACHINE WAS BEEPING when Tom got home from New Dresden. The message was from Deputy Johnson, who announced the sheriff's department needed fingerprints from neighboring residents of Maynard Cushing. A temporary, convenient station was going to be set up in New Dresden.

Though the procedure was voluntary, anybody that refused to cooperate would be subject to a court order. Tom returned the call and waited a couple of minutes before the deputy came to the phone.

"Paul, some of my neighbors aren't going to go for this. Personally, I don't have a problem."

"Tom, the sheriff's department is setting up the session at the request of the BCA. Their reason is because numerous sets of fingerprints were lifted from the Cushing house. By matching them with the people in your neighborhood, they can use the process of elimination.

"For example, we expect to match the fingerprints of Maynard's house cleaner. We also expect your prints to show up. Others would include the gentleman from Rocky Point who regularly spent time playing checkers with Maynard."

"Yeah, that makes sense. I know Rollie Smith. He and Maynard played checkers almost every day. My neighbor Lisa Smilie's prints would be all over the place. She did regular house cleaning for Maynard."

"I think you've got the picture."

"When are you going to do this?"

"In a couple of days, Tom. You'll get a call."

"It sounds as if the BCA is still on the case. Are they still talking drugs as a motive?"

"Yup, they are still hung up on the drugs motive, something about a drug dealer possibility. But, darn it, all they have is the packets of methamphetamine found in a bedroom dresser drawer. There wasn't any drug paraphernalia."

Tom was taken aback when hearing the *meth* word. "Paul, I have a difficult time in believing anyone accusing Maynard Cushing of being a drug user."

"So, you don't think Maynard used drugs?"

"No, I don't, Paul."

"Personally, Tom, I tend to agree with you. The more I read of those memoirs, the more I think this Ranforth guy may be our man."

Two days later, the sheriff's department set up shop in a New Dresden City Hall meeting room. The large table was pushed to the end of the room and six of the eight chairs were lined up in a row, in front of a large window overlooking the street.

When Tom entered, he saw two people standing at the table. One of them had their right hand down on the table. Two uniformed technicians were administrating the fingerprinting task. He took a seat in one of the chairs and wondered who the two people were.

When they finished, one of the technicians waved and said, "You're next, sir."

Tom rose and approached the table.

"Would you sit down and write your name and address here please? Oh yes, your phone number too."

The procedure took about two minutes. One of the technicians stood up and said, "Thanks for coming in, Mr. Hastings. Would you like some coffee?"

Tom filled a Styrofoam cup and turned when hearing the door open. Rollie Smith and his wife Sarah entered. He had met Rollie previously at Maynard's house—the checkers playing buddy. Rollie and his wife spent their summers in a cottage on the extreme eastern tip of Rocky Point. Their permanent home was in Indianapolis.

The usually smiling Rollie was short and pudgy with no hair on top of a round face.

After they finished with the technicians, they turned and Rollie said, "Hello Tom. Have you ever met my wife?"

"No, I don't believe so."

"This is Sarah. She has joined me in retirement."

"Hi, Sarah. I'm Tom Hastings. I live on the north shore of the long bay."

She gripped his hand gently and said, "Hello."

Rollie went on, "Sarah enjoys the peace and quiet as well as the view. We don't even own a boat. One of our greatest enjoyments is sitting on the deck and watching the boats and birds go by. Just this morning we saw an osprey dive-bomb the water and come up with a fish."

Sarah continued, "Have you noticed the beautiful sailboat that comes out of your bay? I wonder why it doesn't sail."

Sarah was also a little pudgy and had beautiful, silvery hair.

"Sarah, the reason for no sails is because Sylvan is waiting for his order to arrive. He ordered the sails on the Internet and they were back-ordered. I talked to him yesterday."

Sarah poked Rollie and said, "We should get a computer, Rollie, the world is passing us by."

Tom couldn't pass up the opportunity and reached in his shirt pocket for a business card. Handing it to Sarah he said, "I can get you started."

She took the card and said, "Rollie and I will talk it over."

Pete and Lisa came through the door. Lisa gave Tom an affectionate hug after they walked over to where he and the Smiths were standing.

"Hey, looks like you two have the day off," said an energized Tom.

"Yup, very seldom both of us are home at the same time. How are you doing Tom? Are you doing any fishing?" asked Lisa.

"I'm plugging right along and would go out more, but I hear Pete has the lake all cleaned out."

Their home did not have direct lake access, so they used the public water access ramp to launch their boat. Tom would often see Pete and Lisa fishing the shoreline directly across the bay from his deck.

Lisa said, "I'm looking forward to seeing sails on that boat of Sylvan's."

Pete interrupted, "It should be soon because I noticed a UPS delivery truck head down the road to his house yesterday."

The road to Sylvan's lake home originated about halfway between Pete's place and Rocky Point.

Deputy Johnson came through the door and thanked all those present for coming and volunteering their prints. He said that no one in the neighborhood was under suspicion, but they needed the prints to narrow the search. He said that the person who killed Maynard may have worn gloves but they needed all the prints anyway.

The response by the people in Maynard's neighborhood to the fingerprinting session was mostly positive. The two technicians were kept busy most of the morning.

Tom Hastings was enjoying visiting with neighbors, some he had not met before. A strange couple came in and walked directly to the desk where the technicians were waiting. The man was reluctant to submit to the fingerprint process, but after some explaining on the part of Deputy Johnson, he finally agreed.

Thick, black stubble covered part of the guy's narrow face. He wore a baseball cap turned backwards. His mate had long, shoulder length blond hair which draped partially over the left side of the face. Her front teeth slightly protruded beyond the upper lip when she smiled.

"Those two are your neighbors," said Pete. "They bought the farmstead to the west of your big beaver pond."

"Yeah, I remember Byron talking about them earlier today."

Tom's nearest northern neighbors, a couple who lived on a small farm adjacent to the large beaver pond, came through the door. They shared the pond with the Hastings's property, readily viewed from the windows of their house. Glen and Lois Sterling's barn and house were plainly visible from Tom's most northern trail.

Tom recollected his last visit to their house. He was treated with a piece of fresh bread that was baked in their classic wood stove. Glen retired from farming about five years ago and currently rented his tillable acreage to the dairy farmers along the county highway.

Glen and Lois were currently pasturing four riding horses that were owned by Shady Acres Resort on the north shore of the main body of the lake. Shady Acres Resort was owned and operated by

Becky and Thor Anderson. Becky was an enthusiastic horse lady. She was often observed riding with her friends on the township road and occasionally rode down the Hastings's roadway.

Even though Lois and Glen were retired, they remained employed, part time. Glen worked as a carpenter for a firm in Big Lakes. Lois helped out in the kitchen of the hospital. They were a handsome looking couple, the tallest people in the room. Both had attractive graying hair and metal rimmed glasses.

After they were fingerprinted, Lois strolled over to the group and asked Tom, "When are you coming over for some coffee and cookies? I am baking tomorrow."

"It's a date," he answered.

Pete, Lisa, Glen and Lois departed and Tom was about to leave when Bill and Mary Jones from South Ridge Resort entered the room.

Bill walked a few steps into the room, looked at the technicians, and said to Tom, "This could be big trouble, agreeing to the fingerprinting will mean jail, for sure."

Tom laughed and said, "You won't be alone. I'll be there too."

Mary came over to Tom and said, "The coffee is always on."

"Hey super, I'll be by in a couple of days."

The couple walked across the room to the technician's table. They filled out the form and went through the process, while Tom continued to sip from his coffee cup.

After finishing, Bill said, "Our goose is cooked now."

Deputy Johnson overheard and laughed. After Bill and Mary left, no one came through the door for the next half-hour.

Deputy Johnson announced to the two technicians. "That about does it. Nice job, fellas. You did really well, only one person on our list didn't show up."

Tom overheard one of the technicians ask, "Isn't that the guy who owns Mary Ann's restaurant?"

"Yes, Harold Kraft," Deputy Johnson responded.

"Thanks for coming, Tom," said Deputy Johnson as Tom deposited the empty Styrofoam cup in a wastebasket.

Fred Hood and Sylvan Tullaby were engaged in conversation on the sidewalk next to the hardware store when Tom drove his pickup truck toward the railroad tracks.

"What's going on at the meeting room?" asked Fred.

"The cops are over there. They forced us to be fingerprinted."

"Fingerprinted? For heavens sake, why?"

"It all has to do with a ton of prints lifted from Maynard Cushing's house. We didn't have much choice. The thing was ordered by a judge."

"God, I don't know about that. Sounds like a big infringement on your rights, " said an angered Fred.

Sylvan was carrying a large coil of white rope and he tossed it onto the back seat of his van. "Talk to you later, Fred. Gotta go."

Fred Hood's sciatica flared up—the result of current frustration. The thought of the law forcing citizens to be fingerprinted irritated him. He experienced a low-grade, nagging pain while walking down the sidewalk toward the grocery store.

Business in this small town was a lot better than he had anticipated. Living alone had taken its toll on Fred, he needed to do something productive. During his initial visit to this part of Minnesota, he overheard some people talking, vacuum cleaners burned out often, because of the sand. The kids coming off the beaches wouldn't clean off the sand—it got in the carpet.

Fred tugged on the front brim of his beaten down golfing cap while turning the corner at the grocery store. This is the windiest intersection in the world, he thought.

# 13

TOM TURNED OFF THE COUNTY HIGHWAY onto a short gravel road leading to the cemetery. He watered two flower boxes resting on the base of his wife's gravestone. Looking around, he admired the wrought iron fence that enclosed the boundaries. Beyond the cemetery, westward, two geese were floating in a small pond that was surrounded by tall grasses.

Sitting on a masonry wall, he gazed out over the valley. A picturesque red farm building stood alone at the base of a high ridge. A sprinkling of tall trees adorned the ridge for its entire length. The wall rimmed the rear edge of an attractive monument. Five flagpoles projected from its base—the stars-and-stripes waving from the middle one.

From his position, the fresh dirt on Maynard Cushing's gravesite was plainly visible. The absence of a head stone diverted attention to his wife's site. Two names carved—one of them was his.

If his former wife could talk, he wondered what her comments would be regarding his recent lifestyle. Mainly, meeting and establishing a relationship with Julie. The deep thoughts of his former wife were interrupted by a speeding van headed toward New Dresden. It looked like Sylvan's, he thought. He said goodbye and headed for home. Julie was expected in about an hour.

Tom was working on his computer when the red convertible appeared in the driveway, close to 4:00 p.m. Anxiously, he hurried outside and experienced a long, warm hug.

"How are you, Tom?" asked a smiling Julie.

"Perfect. Especially right now."

"The weather's ideal for tennis. How about it?" asked Tom.

"I'll whip your butt," answered Julie.

After unpacking, Julie and Tom headed out to the court. The sun's rays penetrated the streaky clouds in the west on that windless Friday afternoon. He was surprised by Julie's ambitious agility, especially after a three-hour drive.

She extended the first set to ten games with a crisp forehand crosscourt winner. Tom needed a big serve to pull off a six to four win. The second set was all down hill for Julie as the tiring car drive took its toll. Julie plopped down on a courtside chair and Tom opened two beers.

"Hey, you played darn tough today," said Tom.

"I'll get you next time," she replied.

"Look at the eagle over there," pointed Julie.

The sun enhanced the white head and tail as the bird soared above the tree line. Shortly after playing tennis, they changed to hiking clothes. Equipped with cameras and binoculars, they began the hike on the north edge of the greenway just west of the tennis court. The greenway was originally created for his wife, to practice hitting golf balls. Tom experienced a moment of nostalgia while thinking about his wife and the hours she spent on the greenway.

He wondered what she would think seeing him holding hands with another lady. Suddenly embarrassed, he slipped his hand out of Julie's. She glanced at him without saying a word.

Walking the grounds and trails was a big part of his life during the past twenty-five years. Tom considered himself lucky to find a female person who enjoyed outdoor nature activity as much as he did. There they were again, Prancer's tracks. The deer had crossed the cultivated dirt area in the field of small trees.

"Look at the size of these tracks, Julie. Prancer was here."

"Who's Prancer?" she asked.

"Prancer is the king of deer. He rules the animals on this land."

After reaching the sunflower field, they turned left and followed the trail bordering the south edge of the sunflower field. Arriving at its termination, they walked slowly between the fence and trees looking for wildlife in a field of native grasses adjoining his property.

"Oh, look," said Julie.

She was referring to a marsh hawk flying low and fast, while hunting the length of the field. The hawk made three passes at field edge next to a large stand of old elm trees. On its fourth pass, it was intercepted and challenged by two crows. The crows harassed the hawk, forcing it to abandon its hunt.

After being convinced the hawk wouldn't return, they continued the hike into the woods. There wasn't any talk while stepping quietly along the main trail. A dead elm tree, long dead from Dutch elm disease, towered over a pool of water and a plank bridge.

Julie stopped and exclaimed, "What's that up there?"

Tom looked up at an old elm tree. Near the fractured top, a bushy tail protruded from a hole in the tree. "Looks like a raccoon," he said.

"Do you suppose it's alive?" asked Julie.

"Sure doesn't look like it. I bet it got stuck and died right there."

They continued to stare at the unfortunate raccoon for a minute before turning right to follow a cross trail leading to Tom's roadway.

Looking left, through a scattering of tall aspens and large oaks, they looked for wildlife in and at the edges of a large marsh. Clusters of bushes and small trees in the middle of the marsh marked the location of a small island. Some years ago, Tom built a narrow wooden walking bridge connecting the trail to the island. At the far end of the island, he added a sitting bench.

Stepping carefully, they crossed the bridge and sat down. Tom explained how he built the base for the bench from the remains of an old dock.

A shrill call of a pileated woodpecker violated the stillness of the marsh. The bird swooped down over the marshland and landed in a tree on the opposite side. After failing to spot the woodpecker with binoculars, they left the island and returned to the cross trail.

"Where does this lead?" asked Julie.

"Right out to my roadway. Let's go."

"Look at those cute little tracks," said Julie. She was pointing to a set of very small markings in the roadway.

"Looks like the fawns made those tracks within the last hour," said Tom.

The sound of their footsteps was barely discernible while walking the roadway back toward the house. They were hoping to catch sight of the fawns. Tom was not surprised when they didn't.

"Deer are ghosts of the forest, Julie, sometimes they appear out of nowhere, not infrequently they melt into the background."

Back at the house they snacked on appetizers. Tom pulled out the cork of a cold bottle of Chardonnay. Tom gave Julie a hug and said, "I'm so glad you're here. Thanks for being you."

"I'm very glad to be here," said Julie as she raised her head and pecked his cheek with her lips.

After Julie settled into the hot tub, Tom handed her a glass of wine. He set another on the rim and eased into the tub. The sky was beautiful. Large white popcorn clouds drifted by and created remarkable reflections in the still water of the bay. The echo of Minnesota loons danced playfully amidst a mild breeze. It was heaven on earth for the moment.

Julie's head lifted from her position in the corner and said, "That looks like a tent in that clearing, over there, across the bay."

Tom's eyeglasses were back in the house. His eyes strained while attempting to focus on the vague looking structure. Out of curiosity, he exited the hot tub and entered the house to fetch binoculars. After returning, he stood on the deck, in dripping wet trunks, and scanned the clearing.

"What's going on over there?" Julie asked.

"Nothing much, but you're right about the tent. Not only that, there's a man sitting on the grass."

A fishing boat trolled by the dock. "Look at that, Julie, all the people in the boat are standing. Geez, don't they know that standing in a small boat is dangerous? People drown every summer doing that. Why don't they sit down and stay safe?"

After the hot tub session, Tom and Julie barbecued pork loin. Darkness came as they were enjoying dinner in the dining room. They could see the flicker of a small fire in the vicinity of the tent.

# 14

**THE NEXT MORNING** Tom and Julie drove into New Dresden. There wasn't a single parking place available on Main Street. Neither was there a place available in Stillman's Super Market parking lot.

"Look at those license plates, Julie. Most of them are from out of state. Matt over at the hardware store and Mr. Stillman at the grocery love those out-of-state vehicles."

After circling the block twice, a parking place became available directly in front of the hardware store. Working the truck back-and-forth, Tom successfully squeezed the pickup into the space.

"Why does everyone insist at parking on Main Street?" Tom asked, knowing Julie was going to frown.

"Come on, Julie, let's get the mail."

"Darn, I have a package, but the business section of the post office is closed on Saturdays, except for a one-hour period earlier in the morning. It'll have to wait till Monday," Tom said.

"I think people are watching us," Julie said as they walked down Main Street toward Stillman's Super Market.

"Wouldn't surprise me one bit," laughed Tom. "Let's head over to the Borders Café."

A knife could have been used to cut the glares of onlookers as they entered. Julie was a new friend and she attracted more than the usual curiosity stares. Service at Borders Café was always top notch. People in the café were buzzing about an incident that happened in the community park next to the highway on Borders Lake.

Two grade school girls, while swimming at the beach, were approached by a stranger. According to their complaint, the man made suggestive, threatening remarks. The girls described the man as slim, wearing dirty, untidy clothing. One of the mothers reported the incident to the sheriff. The man disappeared before deputies arrived.

Julie was getting the look-over while the waitress was taking the order. When Tom glanced around the room after the waitress left, several heads turned away.

"Julie, the beach area they are all talking about is not very far away from the place where we saw the tent."

"Oh, maybe there's a connection."

"Have you heard about our local murder?"

"No, what murder?"

"My client and neighbor, Maynard Cushing, was killed about three weeks ago. He lived in the house you can see to your left when climbing the small hill on the township road. I'll show you on our way home."

"What's being done about it, anyhow? Has there been an arrest?"

"No, there hasn't, as far as I know. The sheriff's department paid me a visit the very next morning. The deputy had a lot of questions."

"Oh, how exciting," said Julie as she leaned forward and strained to hear.

Tom's words were subdued, his hand partially covering the face.

"What did you tell him?" asked Julie.

"He was mostly interested in a mysterious black car that I saw on the township road the day of the murder. He also was interested in the work I was doing for Maynard. The computer stuff and all that."

"Gosh, Tom, you're not a suspect, are you?"

"Well, I sure hope not. But then, I suppose, as far as the sheriff's department is concerned, me and all the neighbors could be on the suspect list."

"Hmm, you mean I'm going to have to start wearing dark glasses?" Julie joked.

"Most of Maynard's neighbors have been fingerprinted, me included. The deputy from the sheriff's department explained they needed the prints to eliminate unknowns found at the house.

"Maynard's checkers playing friend, Rollie Smith, must have left prints. So did I and Lisa Smilie."

"Who's Lisa Smilie?" Julie asked.

"She and her husband Pete are my closest neighbors. You probably noticed their roadway right next to the beginning of mine."

"Yes, the road into the woods."

"The BCA people from St. Paul were here. They even came to my house. They think drugs were the reason for the murder. The county sheriff people think Maynard was murdered because of something that happened during his CIA career."

"Was he shot, or what?"

"He was clubbed to death with a chunk of birch tree...a piece of firewood."

"Oh, how awful."

After eating breakfast at the Borders Café, they walked across Main Street and headed for Tom's pickup truck. There was an elderly gentleman standing on the sidewalk not far from the truck.

He greeted them and said, "I'm trying to remember why I came to town. I am not sure where I should go."

Julie and Tom were amused with the gentleman's humorous confusion. They had a good laugh on the way home. The incident initiated an up-spirited mood that lasted the rest of the day.

When evening came, Tom grilled steaks on the grill. After dining, they were sitting and relaxing on the deck when a small, single engine airplane flew low up the middle of the bay. The noise caused a family of loons to scurry for shelter in the weeds next to the shoreline.

"Oh look," said Julie, "the tent is gone."

Tom brought out his binoculars and focused on the clearing.

"You're right, Julie, the tent is gone. Nobody around either."

After Tom put down the binoculars, they heard the sound of another airplane.

They looked up and Julie said, "Looks like the same plane as before."

This plane was directly overhead and flying at a higher altitude. The wings dipped slightly as it crossed the bay. After it passed, two jet skis traveling at high speed emerged from the mouth of the bay. They roared past. The noise of their engines was louder than the airplane. The jet skis made a turn near the closed end of the bay and roared by a second time.

"Good riddance," said Tom as they disappeared from sight.

# 15

ALL GOOD WEEKENDS COME TO AN END. This was no exception as Julie was getting her things together early Monday morning. Tom helped carry her things to the car. Julie's job demanded she leave by six in the morning.

Tom watched her red convertible disappear around the curve of the driveway as it made its way up the roadway. From the feelings that were working through his body, he knew that Julie and he were going to become a serious relationship. Midmorning he drove to New Dresden, parked on Main Street, and headed for the post office.

Directly in front, on the sidewalk, he met Deputy Johnson. They chatted for a few minutes and Tom suggested coffee at the Borders Café.

"Wait right here, Paul, while I get my mail."

After returning from the post office, Tom and the deputy walked across the street and entered the restaurant. Tom's guest didn't gather as many onlookers as did Julie, a few heads did turn.

After finding an empty booth in the far corner and ordering two coffees, Tom said, "Paul, are you aware of an incident that occurred at the community park a few days ago?"

"Yes, I heard about the complaint filed by one of the mothers. We found the person who allegedly threatened the young ladies. He goes by the name of Leslie Richards and was living in a tent across the bay from your house. He's being held in the county jail, pending a hearing. Richards arrived in the neighborhood a few days ago. Would you believe he used an empty boxcar for transportation?"

"I suppose it's possible. Freight trains pass through New Dresden about four times daily, they often slow down or sometimes come to a complete stop. Waiting for a train to pass through town can take as long as twenty minutes," added Tom.

Deputy Johnson continued, "There isn't any current evidence that ties Richards to the Cushing murder. By the way, as expected, your fingerprints were among those lifted from the victims house."

"Well, I imagine besides mine you also found Lisa's and Rollie's."

"Yes, that's true. One print, not expected, belonged to Harold, owner of Mary Ann's restaurant."

"Didn't Harold refuse to be fingerprinted. Did you have to go to his home?"

"No, not at all. Mr. Kraft's fingerprints were already on file. He had some problems with the law a few years ago. I was surprised that the FBI had his prints."

"We also lifted prints from Leslie Richards, the man in the tent. His didn't match any in the Cushing house."

"How about the murder weapon?"

"The piece of birch log used as the murder weapon didn't have any prints. This isn't surprising. The killer may have wore gloves."

"Wow, Paul, I heard the skull was crushed severely. The murderer must have been someone with a lot of strength, a strong person."

"It would seem logical that the killer was a man," answered the deputy.

"So why were Harold's prints found in Maynard's house?"

Hastings could read that Deputy Johnson was not anxious to answer the question.

However the deputy did say, "Harold had visited Mr. Cushing a month before the murder. We don't really know why for sure, yet."

Tom didn't ask any more questions because he felt the deputy wasn't comfortable in discussing Harold's connection to Maynard Cushing. Tom picked up the lunch tab and they left the restaurant.

"Stay in touch," Deputy Johnson said as he returned to his car.

— —

SCISSORS CLATTERED TO THE FLOOR. Floyd Pella's fingers mixed in with the clusters of hair droppings to retrieve them. Eight years have passed since living in seclusion in this small dump of a town, he thought while watching an uniformed deputy and Tom Hastings cross the street.

"Sorry about that," he told his customer.

Opening and closing a drawer, he pretended to bring out a new pair. Floyd resembled Santa Claus, a full head of gray hair with accompanying beard. He lived in the back room, very seldom seen on the street, doing all his shopping in Cornwall. Occasionally, he was seen at Borders Café having lunch alone.

John Stillman, owner of the grocery store, was in the chair. "That Hastings guy and the deputy sure have been buddy-buddy lately. Johnson is his name, I think."

Floyd didn't comment. His hips were hurting, even stooping down for the scissors was difficult. Surgery was needed. He didn't have the money, nor the desire to get cut open. Rather a wheel chair then fear of going through surgery, he thought.

"Ah, what was that you said?" he asked his customer.

"Oh, I was just commenting on the sheriff across the street. He's been here a lot lately, the murder and all."

Floyd cringed when thinking about the sheriff. All these years gone by and he had gotten away with it, no one would ever know.

# 16

**R**OLLIE AND HIS WIFE SARAH WERE SIPPING WINE on the deck when he decided to go for a walk down the pathway that leads to the water's edge. After Rollie left, Sarah continued to sip wine and lost track of time. She was watching a sailboat slowly making its way past rocky point when two speedboats roared by between the point and the sailboat. She forgot about Rollie until almost dusk.

Sarah became alarmed and called out. When Rollie didn't answer, she chanced going down the pathway to look for him. Four steps from the bottom, she saw a body floating and bobbing against the rocks at the edge of the water.

She screamed, regained control, and hastened up the path and down the road to a neighbor's house. Steve Frederick and his wife Bonnie were watching television when they heard heavy, rapid knocking on their door. Bonnie opened it to discover a frantic, out-of-breath Sarah in the doorway.

"I need help...Rollie...he's floating in the water."

"Call 911," said Steve to his wife. "You stay here, Sarah, I'll get some help."

He ran down the road seeking help at Ken Smith's house. Ken was home and the two of them rushed back to Rollie's house and down the path to the rocky shoreline.

They lifted Rollie out of the water and laid him down on the shoreline. There was no breathing or pulse and it was obvious that any attempt at CPR would be futile. A rescue vehicle from New Dresden arrived in about half an hour. They verified Rollie was dead and called the sheriff's department.

— —

THE PHONE RANG A COUPLE OF TIMES at the Hastings's home during the evening hours. One of the calls was from Tom's son who lived in La Crosse, Wisconsin. Tom was pleased to hear Brad and his wife were planning on a weekend visit.

"Sure," Tom said, "Should be a great weekend."

Hastings's daughter, Kris, was single and lived in Dallas. He wasn't expecting her home until Thanksgiving. He had hopes for a get together during the holiday with both children. He reminded himself to invite Julie.

On Friday morning, after reviewing his grocery and beverage list, Tom headed for New Dresden. After picking up the mail, he visited the grocery store. Ellie, the grocery store clerk, was not smiling that morning, Tom asked her why.

She said, "Haven't you heard?"

"Heard what?" Tom asked.

"Rollie Smith is dead. He was found by his wife floating in the lake."

"Rollie, dead!" Tom exclaimed. "Not another one."

He just stood at the checkout counter staring at Ellie not really knowing what to do next. Tom picked up a paper and forgot about the items on his list. He crossed the street and was deep in thought about Rollie and the visits they had at Maynard's house.

Maynard and Rollie played checkers almost daily. Some of the time they wouldn't be finished with their game when Tom arrived to work on Maynard's computer. Often, Rollie would hang around after the game and watch. Tom remembered Rollie asking all kinds of questions while they were working on Maynard's memoirs.

During some of his Maynard visits, Tom would arrive just as Rollie was leaving. Rollie's wife usually came by with the car, picked him up because of his bad eyes. Rollie was legally blind and couldn't drive. His thick glasses worked well enough to see the checkerboard.

Tom was still in a partial daze when he entered the Borders Café. Henry was sitting at his usual table.

"Have you heard about Rollie Smith?" he asked Henry.

Tom liked Henry. Maybe it was his honesty—perhaps it was his soft, spoken mannerism—he loved to tell stories. Most of the stories were about events that happened within ten miles of New Dresden.

"I sure did, just now at the grocery store."

The waitress came by and Tom put in his order. Henry waited with his next comment until the waitress moved away from the table.

"I heard there were two packets of white stuff found in Rollie's pockets. Also, Rollie had a very large bruise and bump on his head. Someone said he fell and struck his head on a rock, got knocked out, and fell into the water."

"I don't know a thing, Henry. This is all news to me."

After Tom left the café and walked back to his vehicle, he wondered if Rollie's death was related to Maynard's murder. The two were friends and spent considerable time together. It was well known in the neighborhood that Rollie and Maynard would get together for checkers four or five times a week.

He remembered Deputy Johnson talking about Maynard and the fractured skull. Tom wondered how Rollie died. Was it from drowning or a blow to the head, similar to Maynard's?

While driving homeward from New Dresden, thoughts about Rollie and Maynard intensified. Just before turning onto the township road, he saw a black car stirring up dust. It was heading eastward on the township road. Tom slowed and watched. The car continued beyond Maynard's driveway. By the time he made the turn up the small hill toward home, the black car was no longer visible.

Increasing speed, Tom was hoping to get a better look at the car by intersecting it somewhere near Rocky Point. He was frustrated when the black car was nowhere to be seen as he approached the Rocky Point entry road.

Puzzled by its disappearance, he drove around the township road loop twice—no black car. Tom parked his truck and waited near the beginning of his roadway for a few minutes. Not a single vehicle came by.

After returning home, he walked out on the deck and looked across the bay. The tent was back.

# 17

TOM WAITED UNTIL THE NEXT MORNING to call the sheriff's office. Deputy Johnson was not available. The lady taking his call informed Tom the deputy was away on a personal holiday and would not return until Monday.

Tom's son Brad and wife of two years, Terry, arrived after the sun had set on Friday evening. Brad had light hair and blue eyes resembling Tom's side of the family. Terry was a neat, trim young lady with long dark hair. The dark eyes were radiant when she talked. Tom was pleased with Brad's selection.

Brad spent ten years in college and to his dad's relief, finally earned a degree in industrial engineering. Presently, he was employed by the city of La Crosse, Wisconsin. His dad was happy that his son was doing well financially, all that money spent on his son's education was paying off. Terry held a front office job at a major corporation, also in La Crosse.

They were both fascinated by his story of Maynard's murder and the death of Rollie.

"Small towns were usually dull and boring, but it looks like things in New Dresden have really picked up," Brad said.

Terry had it all figured out. "Rollie killed Maynard and then he committed suicide."

"Oh no," said Brad, "Maynard and Rollie were both killed by someone from out of town. Likely the Mafia."

Tom laughed and said, "I'm not sure why Rollie would kill Maynard. They were good friends. The Mafia is a little far fetched. Maynard's CIA connection may be behind the whole thing."

The next morning they drove into New Dresden. Brad and his dad had coffee at the Borders Café while Terry invaded the curio shops. Later that afternoon, Brad and Terry took the pontoon out on the lake while Tom tinkered around in the shop. Tom was sitting on the deck having a beer when the boat returned.

After they climbed the steps to the deck, Brad asked, “What should we do about dinner?”

“I’ll take you guys out to Mary Ann’s,” his dad said.

Terry sat down on a deck chair. Concerned, she said, “By the way, a red speedboat buzzed our pontoon boat about three times. Do you know anyone with a red boat?”

“No, I don’t. What did the driver look like?”

“Couldn’t tell you what he looked like, but I think he was wearing a flowered shirt and a green baseball cap.”

“Let’s go out and play some tennis,” Brad said to Terry.

“Okay, I’ll be ready in a jiff.”

After Brad and Terry returned from the tennis court, they bantered over who hit what, who missed what. Later, Tom drove them to Mary Ann’s. The restaurant was perched on a small bluff on the east shore of the lake. The lack of space in the parking lot hinted at a busy night.

“Hi, sweethearts, how’s your day going?” asked Mary Ann when they entered.

“Real good, Mary Ann, I would like you to meet my son, Brad, and his wife, Terry.”

“Where are you people from?” she asked.

“La Crosse,” said Brad.

“Great town. My first cousin, Alex, lives there. You people are lucky, I have just the booth.”

Mary Ann led the group to a booth by the window. She was a buxom lady with short, dark, straight hair. The stack of menus was wedged between her waist and left elbow. Her body leaned to the right, left fist supporting her chin.

“Nice place,” said Terry.

“See that guy sitting at the table by the flowers,” said Brad. “I think it looks like the man in the red boat, the one that buzzed us this afternoon.”

Tom’s eyes shifted, head turned slightly. He saw a small man with a thin face and black hair, combed straight back, a stranger. Tom glanced over at the table every few minutes. He didn't recognize the person across the table either. A cloud of cigarette smoke formed a halo over their table.

"So, Terry, how is work going?" Tom asked.

"Oh just fine, Tom. I'm so fortunate to be working with nice people—this is the best front office. Actually, I am hoping to get my first raise next month. The work is challenging and all is well."

"That's great, Terry. Keep up the good work."

After a delightful weekend, Brad and Terry left for home early Sunday afternoon.

The phone rang about eight Sunday evening—the caller was Pete.

"Tom, this Rollie thing has really shaken up Lisa. She is getting afraid to be alone at night when I travel."

"Look, Pete, when you're gone, I can keep an eye on your place. After all, you are doing a great job watching my roadway."

"Gee, thanks, Tom, Lisa will like that. She was especially concerned because her prints were found at Maynard's house. Lisa refuses to believe that Maynard was involved with drugs. She says Maynard had too much class."

"I imagine she got to know Rollie a little. He hung around Maynard's house a lot."

"Yeah, she sure did, but Lisa doesn't have any nice things to say about that man, even though he's gone. She said Rollie had an irritating mannerism, grin and wink. That's what he'd do when she caught him staring. Lisa didn't like that. Worse than that, if she came near him, sometimes he would touch her. She didn't like the whiskey smell either."

"I guess I didn't know Rollie very well. Sorry to hear about Lisa's experience."

"Lisa hasn't gotten paid for her last two cleaning visits and is concerned about getting her money."

"I think she should mail a note or statement to Maynard's son," Tom said. "Why don't you call Kyle's Realty office and get the son's number? His name is Norm."

"Yeah, thanks, I can do that."

"Hey, have you seen any small planes flying real close lately?" asked Pete.

"Yes I have. One came up the middle of the bay during the weekend. It flew back over our house a few minutes later."

"I was out fishing the other evening, trolling for walleyes in the sunken island area, when I noticed a small airplane flying real low, close to Rocky Point. You know where the sunken island is, don't you Tom?"

"Yeah, about quarter of a mile east of Rocky Point. Lots of boats hang out there, right?"

"Well anyhow, after watching it pass over the point, the plane dropped a white looking object. After the drop, it circled and flew off, toward your place."

"What did the plane look like? Was it silver-like with broad wings?"

"Yup, that's it. It must have been the same one you saw."

"Pete, did you see a red speedboat on the lake in the early afternoon?"

"No, I don't think so."

"Okay. Just remember, Pete, call me and let me know when Lisa is going to be alone. I can check on her once in awhile."

That evening, armed with camera and binoculars, Tom strolled up the greenway toward the sunflower field. As he followed the trail along the south edge of the field, slivers of water displayed between the tree trunks.

Tom used binoculars to scan the opposite shoreline. He saw a small column of smoke coming from the tent. Looks like Mr. Richards is home, he thought.

After reaching the property border, he followed a path leading down to the water. When closer, he saw two men sitting on the grass close to the tent—smoke coming from a small fire. Tom had never laid eyes on Leslie Richards before. He didn't recognize either of the two men.

Though a body of water separated his home from the tent, Tom felt threatened. A murder in the neighborhood, the mysterious tent across the bay. Hurrying back to his house, he quick stepped the stairs and entered the bedroom. His guns were stored in the closet.

Removing the rifle from its case, he worked the bolt making sure the action was free. His .32-automatic pistol was in a holster on the shelf. Neither had been fired for years. He went out to the garage brought back a box of shells for each gun. After filling the .32 clip with bullets, he placed the gun on the night table by the bed. He slipped five shells into the breach of the rifle and leaned it against a wall in the closet.

Tom went to bed and thought about Pete telling him about Lisa being afraid, alone at times. Tom was alone almost all the time. He became fearful for his safety—outside doors and windows were locked. The bedroom door was also locked. He reached over and touched the gun on the table. The feel of the hard steel dissipated some of his fears.

# 18

TOM SCHEDULED AN APPOINTMENT WITH A CLIENT for the Tuesday following his son's visit. After working four hours, he left the client's home and headed for New Dresden. Approaching the stop sign on Main Street, he was attracted to the sign at Hector's Bar. Yearning for a beer and pizza, he pulled into the parking lot.

Entering the building, he found a booth next to a window overlooking Main Street. Tom wasn't well known at Hector's, he didn't spend much time there. A semi-truck approached from the west, blocked his vision of Main Street for a few moments, and made a wide turn heading north.

Looking down the length of the room, he admired the classic mahogany bar lining almost the entire eastern wall. The wall behind the bar was decorated with shelves and large mirrors that were framed with ornate woodcarvings. Reflected in one of the mirrors was the back of a lady bartender. She wore a decorative, black western shirt and a black cowboy hat. After Tom sat down, he gave her his order for a mini-pizza and a Budweiser.

Each of the four television sets, placed in strategic positions, was showing a baseball game. On Sunday afternoons during the football season, they were all tuned to the Minnesota Vikings game. Remembering an afternoon last fall, the place was packed. There were yells and hoops when the Vikings were moving the ball. Mostly groans when the opposing quarterback was tearing apart the Viking's defensive-backs. The latter happened more often than the former.

The wooden booth that Tom occupied was replicated all along the west wall. Only three of them were occupied. A lady dressed in a plaid shirt and a white cowboy hat was tending a gambling counter in an area beyond the last booth.

Two large glass jars displaying colorful tickets took up most of the space on the counter. Leaning against the counter between the jars was a man, generously plump. His round shaped face was covered with a tangled, pepper-color beard. In the left fist, he clutched a wad of green bills. Peeling off a few, the lady handed him a stack of pull-tabs.

Beyond the bar and gambling counter, a large area in the back of the room housed two pool tables—not in use at the moment. In the space between the booths and the bar were several tables. It was just past eight o'clock and all the business establishments up and down Main Street were closed for the day. Hector's Bar was the only place in town that remained open in the evenings. Fridays were an exception when most businesses remained open until nine.

A party of five men and one woman were sitting around one of the tables. The center was heaped with green—the looks of an old-fashioned poker game. The lady wasn't playing and she didn't appear interested. She lit a cigarette and glanced around the room. The number of empty beer bottles stacked on the table explained the loudness of the voices.

Tom couldn't help but overhear two of the card players. They were having a heated discussion. The name *Rollie Smith* was mentioned. *Rocky Point* next.

"The two old fogies were doing a lot more than playing checkers," argued one of the men.

"You're talking about my uncle, and I don't like what you're saying," countered the other.

The discussion was rapidly developing into an intense argument.

Tom was looking out the window at the activity on Main Street when he heard a crashing sound. As he turned to look, one of the guys was getting up off the floor. The guy who knocked him down was standing over him and waving his finger.

"Don't you ever say that about my uncle," he angrily said. "Now get the heck out of here."

"I'll get you for this, you clown," said the guy getting up off the floor. He sneered at his attacker, staggered through the door and slammed it shut.

As Tom was finishing his pizza, the rest of the card players and the lady strolled out the front door.

"Good riddance," said the bartender. "They cause more trouble then they are worth."

The bartender's name was Peggy. She and her husband Norman owned the bar. They bought it two years ago and were working hard to make it pay. When Peggy came over to see how Tom was doing, he asked her if Rollie Smith ever came to their bar.

"Yes, Rollie did stop on occasion. Usually just before closing time. He always had a Beam on the rocks. I think there was something odd about that guy, the way he kept watching the door. It was if he was waiting for someone. One Beam and then he would leave."

Tom asked the bartender, "Did you ever notice Rollie meet someone in the bar?"

" I'm not sure about that but why are you asking me all these questions?"

"Rollie was my neighbor. I'm interested in knowing what really happened."

Peggy walked away from Tom and returned to her place behind the bar. A man sitting with a woman in one of the booths got up and walked over to the bar with his empty glass. His lady was sipping a tall reddish drink.

After Peggy prepared what appeared to be two Bloody Marys, he left some bills on the bar and carried off the two drinks.

On his way back to the booth, he stopped where Tom was sitting and asked, "Are you from around here?"

"Yes, how about you two?"

"We're from Illinois and vacationing at South Shores Resort. Did you know the two people who were murdered?"

"Yup, I sure did. However, I wasn't aware that the second death was a murder."

"Well, someone at the bar said that it was. Have a nice evening." The man rejoined his lady partner.

The couple from Illinois got up to leave just as Tom was finishing his second beer. He walked over to the bar to pay the bill. As Tom was walking out the door, he saw the Illinois couple get into a black sedan and drive off. When they were crossing the railroad tracks, Tom realized it was the same black car that he had been watching from the restaurant the other day—the car in the accident.

# 19

TOM HASTINGS WAS TREATED BY A BRILLIANT SUNRISE on Wednesday morning. While sipping coffee on the deck, he was deep in thought about Rollie and the black car. After hearing the bartender's story, he realized Rollie was a different person than the one he had known. Who were these Illinois people driving the black Buick? Tom remembered what Byron had said—the black car turned into South Ridge Resort.

Perhaps Bill and Mary would know more about the Illinois people who were staying there. Mary usually knows what's going on. Tom drove past the township road turn and pulled into the driveway at South Ridge.

After getting out of this truck, he noticed a group of people down by the beach. Both Bill and Mary were in the resort office when he entered.

"How are you doin', Tom?" Bill asked.

"Not too bad, Bill, but it's eerie around here with the Maynard thing and then Rollie."

"Yeah, I wonder what the heck is going on."

Mary interrupted and invited us into the kitchen, where she brought out three cups and filled them with coffee.

"The fishing is really good this year," said Bill. "Three of our renters filled with walleyes over the weekend."

"I met a couple from Illinois at Hector's yesterday. They mentioned staying at your resort."

"Oh, yeah, I know who you mean. They are staying in a cottage down by the water and are scheduled to leave on Saturday. The second visit this summer," reported Mary.

"They drive a black Regal, don't they?" asked Tom.

"A black something. Maybe it's a Regal. They stayed for an entire week about a month ago. Both of them were sure pleasant...not only that, they were so neat, their unit hardly needed cleaning after they left," Mary answered.

"There was this black car...the day of the murder. I wonder if it was them?" asked Tom.

"The lady said they were visiting relatives in the area. Both times they prepaid with cash. Hmm, is it possible?" an excited Mary questioned.

Bill interjected, "We don't know what's going on. The couple didn't hang around the resort much during daylight hours. When they were here, I never did see them down by the beach or ever use a boat either."

"Have you heard about the Leslie Richards guy?" asked Mary.

"Yes, I can see his tent from my deck. He must have a friend. There were two people sitting around the fire right next to the tent a couple of days ago," said Tom.

"I hear he's been released from jail. The sheriff's department didn't have enough on him. Talking to young girls isn't against the law, I guess," said a frowning Mary.

"Richards was hired by the big dairy farm along the county highway. They need the help and he needs the money," added Bill.

As Tom was leaving, Mary pointed out the cottage where the

Illinois couple was staying. The black sedan wasn't there.

"Thanks, Mary. Nice to see you two again."

Who were these mysterious people from Illinois? Did they have anything to do with Maynard's murder? These were the questions Tom had on his mind when he left the resort and headed for New Dresden.

The town was very quiet on Wednesday morning. There was no one to chat with at the post office. The same was true at the grocery store. Placing a small bag of groceries in the front seat, Tom headed for home. As he turned off the county highway onto the township road, he noticed a car parked in Maynard's driveway. Color was light brown. Three people were standing next to the car. Tom assumed it was the Realtor showing the property.

As his pickup climbed the small hill and continued down the township road, he slowed when seeing a gray-haired lady and a dog. She was restraining the dog's ambitions with a leash. Tom swung his truck close to the ditch to allow more than enough room. The lady smiled at Tom as he passed.

In his rear view mirror, he could see the lady had stopped and was watching him until he turned off onto the roadway. Tom heard his answering machine beeping when entering the house.

There was a short message from Deputy Johnson. He wanted to talk as soon as possible. Tom returned his call.

"Tom, I better come over. I have some information about Rollie Smith you need to know."

About a half an hour later the deputy's car appeared in the Hastings's driveway. Tom invited the deputy to join him for coffee on the deck. The deputy put both hands on the deck rail and stared out over the water. He was watching a shiny reflection in the water not far from the tent.

"Richards is still your neighbor, I see."

"Yeah, there were two guys over there a couple of days ago."

"Two guys?" the Deputy questioned, raising his voice.

"Yup, it looked like Richards had someone over for dinner."

The deputy sat at the table and accepted a cup of coffee.

"Tom, I have some news and it's important that you know."

"Uh, oh, is it about Rollie?"

"Yes, it is. Rollie Smith's death was no accident. He was murdered just like Maynard. It was not drowning, he was already dead when he fell into the water, likely pushed. There's a strong possibility that the two murders are related. Both men were clubbed to death."

"Wow, the rumors in New Dresden were right on."

Paul smiled and continued, "Maybe, that's why I hang around there so much, to get the latest news."

"I wonder how much buzzing went on as a result of the fingerprinting session? So, why do you think Rollie was murdered?" Tom asked.

"Our theory of motive for both murders has to do with one of the stories in Maynard's memoirs. Maynard was killed because he learned the identity of a missing, wanted CIA agent by the name of Robert Ranforth."

"Did Maynard ever talk to you about Ranforth?" asked the deputy.

"No he didn't, but I read about him in the memoirs."

"Well, the killer must have suspected that Maynard told Rollie, or Rollie may have been a witness to the murder. In either case, Ranforth was forced to get rid of him, also.

"Tom, the serious threat to your life, believed true earlier, has gotten bigger, we think. The missing business card is what I'm concerned about the most. It ties you to Maynard, especially working with the memoirs. The killer knows who you are and where you live."

"It's scary. Your warnings are being taken seriously. Your visits and information are appreciated. The more often your cars are seen in my area, the better for me. What about the drug theory the state people embrace?"

"According to state lab reports, traces of methamphetamine were found in the remains of Rollie Smith. Maynard had some of the stuff in his dresser drawer, but not in his remains.

"The Minnesota BCA has not budged from its position regarding motive...drugs in both cases.

"Our thinking is different...the drugs, we think, were planted in Maynard's house and had nothing to do with the murder. Rollie's case is more complicated because blood tests showed he was actually using the stuff."

"Paul, my two close neighbors, Pete and Lisa, are really worried about the Cushing murder. Pete is out of town a lot, leaving Lisa home alone. Is it possible you could stop to see them?"

"Okay, I'll give them a call. Even though Lisa was Maynard's house cleaner, she shouldn't be in any danger. You're the one that concerns us the most. Regarding any visitors in the future, you need to be extra cautious. Please call if you have any unusual conversations with anyone in the neighborhood, abnormal happenings as well."

"Well, that's not going to be easy. I'll certainly try," responded Hastings.

"If our thinking is correct, this Ranforth guy will stop at nothing to protect his identity. As I mentioned before, he knows who you are, a huge disadvantage to you."

After the deputy left, Tom sat in silence for a few minutes.

He went upstairs to the bedroom closet, removed the rifle and laid it on the bed. Getting down on his stomach, he reached under the bed and dragged out a dusty case containing a shotgun.

Carrying all three guns into the garage, he checked out the actions and placed a few drops of gun oil. After loading the shotgun, Tom carried all three weapons out onto the greenway. The pistol was first. After jacking a shell into the chamber, he pulled the trigger. Jerking slightly, it fired. The first shot from the deer rifle hurt his eardrums.

After firing two rounds from each weapon, he returned to the house and replaced the two shells in the rifle. Making sure there wasn't a shell in the barrel, he set the gun upright, leaning against an inner wall of the front door closet. The other two guns, shotgun and pistol, he carried upstairs to his bedroom.

Tom reloaded the shotgun and placed it upright in the bedroom closet. Next, he checked the clip of the .32, made sure it was full and placed it back in the holster and on his night table.

# 20

TOM PREPARED FOR HIS EVENING WALK. He found a belt to slip through the loop of the .32-automatic holster. Strapping the belt around the waist, he proceeded up the roadway. After walking half the distance, he heard the noise of a vehicle approaching. Clumsily, he removed the .32 from its holster. Grabbing the gun with the right hand, he stuck it into his jacket pocket.

His heart began racing when a pickup truck came into view. It was advancing steadily and he could see two men through the windshield. His right hand tightened on the gun when the vehicle pulled abreast and stopped.

Tom breathed a sigh of relief when seeing the power company emblem on the door, meter readers. After exchanging a few pleasantries they continued on to his house. Tom walked off the roadway onto a side trail and was hoping they didn't notice his hands were trembling.

When Tom returned to the house, he walked out on the deck and removed the hot tub cover. Before entering the tub, he brought out the automatic and laid it on the deck rail. Letting himself down into the water he felt good and delayed engaging the pumps. One of the best features of this hot tub was its location, an unobstructed view of the bay. His eyes wandered to the tent, no movements, no one hanging around.

His head jerked to the left towards the sound of a boat motor. Sylvan's sailboat moving slowly away from his dock. Tom watched as the main sail went up along with the rest of the rigging. Pete was right, UPS had delivered.

The sail caught the breeze and the boat moved eastward towards the mouth of the bay. Rays of the lowering sun generated an attractive spectacle for a few moments. Tom stepped out of the tub to fetch his camera. By the time he returned, the sailboat had moved farther away and the special effects had vanished.

Standing on the deck dressed in a robe, he had thoughts of vulnerability while in the hot tub. Anyone could drive up and he wouldn't hear a thing, especially when the water jets were active. Walking around the side of the house, an intruder could approach unnoticed.

The sun was approaching the horizon when Tom drove his pickup truck to Mary Ann's restaurant for dinner. There were a lot of empty spaces in the parking lot during weekdays.

— —

HAROLD KRAFT WAS SITTING IN HIS OFFICE tapping a pen on the desktop. The door was partially open and he could hear the background noise, people talking. He wished there were more people. Even though summer business was good, he could always use the money. The man on the other end of the phone just hung up, wasn't pleased. Sixty thousand dollars was the amount that Harold owed. If MaryAnn found out—he shuddered.

Thinking back to eight years ago, he talked his wife Mary Ann into purchasing this restaurant. Her ailing father put up most of the money. How could he face his father-in-law? His wife had soft-talked Ben into delaying any payments until after the summer season. Head between the hands, Harold wasn't anywhere close to coming up with that amount of money. If Ben died, his money problems would be solved, banish the thoughts, he loved Mary Ann.

The payments to the bank for remodeling and refurbishing the restaurant were two months behind. Harold gathered courage when he stood up. Ah, hell, it'll work out somehow. He was in good health, proud of being slim. The right hand stroked through his hair twice. Getting gray is one thing, but now it's thinning. He removed the wide, dark, thick glasses from his head and used a soft napkin to wipe away the smudges.

He left the office and walked into the bar area of the restaurant.

Tom Hastings was getting seated.

"Nice to see you, Tom. How are things with you?"

"Just fine, Harold. Thanks."

Harold glanced out the window and said, "There she goes again."

Tom looked out the window and saw the sailboat. A strong southwestern breeze was puffing the sails and the boat was moving along at a rather brisk pace.

Harold wished himself to be on that boat—away from all his problems.

"Hi, honey," said a smiling MaryAnn as Harold turned hearing the sound of her voice.

Harold gave her a kiss on the forehead and said, "Nice seeing you, Tom. The boss is here, I better get back to work."

Hastings laughed and said, "Hi, MaryAnn. What's good today?"

"Everything is good. You know that," she replied. "Here's Jane to take your order."

"What'll it be this evening?" asked the waitress.

She wrote down the order, a chicken fillet sandwich with a half-carafe of Chardonnay.

Jane made some comments about the murders and asked, "Aren't you scared living so close to where it all happened?"

Geez, even the waitresses at Mary Ann's know that Rollie's death was no accident, he thought.

"Pretty scary, isn't it?" Tom responded with a frown.

When the waitress raced off, Tom looked out the window and observed the large deck. An angled stairway led down to an elaborate dock at water level.

His table provided a favorable view of one of the television sets mounted on the wall. He was watching a baseball game when Jane arrived with the carafe.

She poured the first glass and said, "There you are, Mr. Tom. I'll be back with the rest soon."

"Thanks," said Tom as he brought the rim of the wineglass to his lips.

After dinner, Tom moved from the table to a barstool and continued watching the baseball game. The bartender served him a brandy and like most everyone else wanted to talk about the murders. Her name was Bette. Tight blue jeans didn't prevent the scramble needed behind the bar to meet waitress demands.

She stopped in front of Tom and placed a mat under his drink while saying, "I'll bet my bottom dollar the murders were committed by drug people. I hear they can get darn mean. Just the other day, four sinister looking men dressed in black and grays came in for dinner. They drove up in a snazzy, black Lincoln. Two of them were wearing dark glasses. They sure looked suspicious."

A waitress was standing at the bar station waiting for a drink order. Listening to their conversation, she commented,"Those four guys were a bunch of bozos. All they did was complain and give me a bad time."

Then she smiled and said, "Sure left a nice tip in spite of being a pain in the butt."

When returning home on his roadway, Tom became alarmed noticing a fresh set of tire tracks. The guns, all in the house, not good at all. Warnings from Deputy Johnson were real, better listen up. Future outings needed some protection, the .32-automatic would be easy. Tom pulled his foot back off the gas pedal as he neared the driveway. Feeling a sense of relief seeing no vehicle in the driveway, he parked the truck. Whoever made the track turned around and left.

He turned the key in the front door lock and pushed open the door. Nothing appeared to be disturbed. He checked the .32-automatic. Earlier in the day, he brought it down from the bedroom and placed it under a hat in the front door closet. After making sure the clip was full, he carried it with him upstairs.

Tom was having problems going to sleep. Windows open, noises were exaggerated. No less than four times he grabbed the gun from the bed stand and walked into the living room to check out the driveway. Daylight came, Tom was exhausted, deep sleep followed.

# 21

JULIE HOFFMAN WAS AT THE AIRPORT. Her job at Glacial Computers required attending a seminar in Dallas. She had been there since Monday. At last her luggage, the keys to the red convertible should be in her purse. Fingers digging couldn't come up with the keys. She dumped the contents on the hood of her car. With a look of relief, she grabbed the keys and replaced the contents of her purse.

Julie was exhausted after arriving at her apartment. She slept long and deep, arising mid-morning on Friday.

Dialing Tom Hastings's number, she said, "Hi, Tom, I'm back."

"How was the seminar?"

"Boring, but necessary. How about if I come out this afternoon...around four should work."

"I'll watch for you, Julie. Have a good trip."

The small red convertible made its appearance in Tom's driveway at four-thirty. He watched through the window as Julie swung out of the front seat and opened the trunk.

After transferring luggage from the car to the house, Tom was pleased to notice a pair of roller blades and a tennis racquet lying on the back seat.

"Remember the big deer, Prancer. It may have been him that leaped across the road while driving down your roadway. I had to hit the brakes."

"Did you see any antlers?"

"Yeah, I think they were in velvet."

"It's that time of year. Prancer is too smart to get hit by a car on the road," Tom said.

After she put her things away, they sat on the deck enjoying sips of a vintage chardonnay.

"Well, for heaven's sake, the tent is still there."

"Yes, Leslie Richards is certainly getting his share of attention. Does the grill appeal to you, or should we go out for dinner?"

"Oh, let's give Mary Ann's a try."

"That sounds great to me. Let's take the pontoon boat."

While Julie was readying for the drive to Mary Ann's, Tom removed his deer rifle from the closet and took it down to the pontoon boat. He placed it underneath the wide seat in the rear. An hour later, they were on our way to Mary Ann's.

Lack of wind contributed to a pleasant ride. The streaky clouds in the west turned into spectacular colors as the sun approached the horizon. Julie and Tom watched with wonderment. They cruised by several fishing boats that were trying their luck at the sunken island part way between Rocky Point and the restaurant.

Tom tied up to at the dock and escorted Julie up the long, angular stairway. At the first landing, parking lot level, they paused.

"Tom, look at that black car parked in the last row of the parking lot."

"I see it. Let's check it out."

Instead of continuing to the large deck above, they exited at the parking lot level. They stopped a short distance from the car. Tom noted the Illinois license plate, number *ATB100,* a Lincoln Continental Town. Not what he hoped for, a Buick Regal.

Because the car was black, he memorized the number. Entering the restaurant they were fortunate to find an empty booth in the bar area. Getting seated, Tom noticed the owner, Harold in the next booth. Two men wearing dark glasses and Harold were having a heated conversation.

Tom and Julie ordered wine and were studying the menu when they overheard Harold say, "Sorry, I just can't do it. Sorry boys."

Harold stood up, shook his head, and left the booth. Tom and Julie strained to listen, voices in the next booth were subdued.

Tom whispered to Julie, "Do you suppose the black Lincoln and the two men in the next booth came together?"

"I would bet on it," said Julie

Mary Ann came by and greeted Tom and Julie with a smile.

Julie asked Tom, "What's the latest on the murders?"

"Not much," Tom said softly, afraid of being overheard by the men in the next booth. Looking at Julie, his head slightly jerked, signaling a message to her.

Before Tom and Julie completed dinner, the two men in the next booth got up and left.

"I'll be right back," Tom said as he got up off the bench.

Restrooms were located next to the front door. He stepped outside for a moment.

After returning, Tom said to Julie, "Just as we suspected, the two guys in the booth, they came in the black Lincoln."

"Well they apparently came to see Harold. What do you suppose they were after?" asked a firm-faced Julie.

"Whatever it was, they got turned down," responded Tom.

"Maybe it's the drugs, you did mention the police finding some at Maynard's house," Julie said.

"Yeah, they did, but Maynard was not a user, not like Rollie Smith," Tom answered.

"Murder, drugs, mysterious tent, who said small towns were dull?" said a smiling Julie.

They finished dinner and left the dining room. Julie waited by the door as Tom took care of the charges at the checkout counter.

"How was your dinner?" asked Mary Ann.

"The dinner was great. Can you pass me a pen?" Tom signed the credit card slip and joined Julie at the door.

The sun had set and darkness was approaching as they cruised across the main body of the lake and entered the bay. Sylvan's sailboat was parked at his dock and all the fishing boats were gone. Returning to the house, Julie prepared two cups of coffee and they sat on the deck, waiting for the stars.

Tom sipped coffee, filled with satisfying thoughts. Julie's visit was going well. Julie was slumped in a deck chair facing east. She sat straight up and exclaimed, "Look, there's a fire."

Tom turned in his chair and saw a large area of flame light up the sky above the trees. The cloud of smoke above the flames was huge.

Within minutes, they heard sirens and saw the flashing lights of a fire truck as it made its way up the state highway, coming from New Dresden.

"Gee, the fire is right about where Mary Ann's is. I hope it's not the restaurant burning," Tom said.

As they sat and observed the fire, Julie said, "I hear more sirens."

"This is a big one, fire trucks coming from other towns," said Tom.

The glaring blaze continued to grow, smoke mass expanded and disappeared in the sky. Throughout the rest of the evening, Tom and Julie sat on the deck and watched the fire. In about two hours, the flame area reduced in size and the smoke was no longer visible. They watched the local ten o'clock news on television and there was no mention of a fire.

Tom awoke at 3:00 a.m. After a bathroom stop, he stepped out onto the deck. The flame was gone, but smoke was still visible against the background light of stars and moon.

The next morning Julie was anxious to drive to New Dresden and learn more about the fire. Their first stop was the grocery store and her wishes were fulfilled. The shoppers and clerks at Stillman's Super Market were buzzing about Harold and Mary Ann's house.

One of the ladies in the checkout line said, "I heard it burned to the ground."

The man with her said, "Mary Ann was unhurt. No one knows what happened to Harold."

Ellie, the checkout lady, added, "Our fire department saved the restaurant."

Tom said, "I'm sure glad to hear that the restaurant was spared. Hats off to the local fire department. They did a great job."

# 22

NEWS OF THE FIRE AT HAROLD AND MARY ANN'S WAS PUBLISHED in the *Star Tribune* the next morning. The article read,

*The house was totally destroyed but the restaurant, separated by just ten feet, was spared. Credit goes to the New Dresden Fire Department that arrived early and prevented the fire from spreading.*

*The fire was discovered by one of the owners, Mary Ann Kraft. She was locking the front door, after closing, and smelled smoke. Rushing down the sidewalk, she saw flames in the kitchen window. Mary Ann was unhurt but her partner and husband Harold has disappeared. The sheriff's department is searching for Mr. Kraft.*

*There were no bodies found in the remains. Mary Ann's restaurant and bar was not damaged and will reopen in a week. It is premature to ascertain whether arson was a possible cause. State fire marshals are being called in to investigate the fire.*

— —

SUNDAY AFTERNOON, THE DOORBELL RANG at the Hastings's residence while Julie and Tom were lounging on the deck. Tom opened the door and stood face to face with Kyle Fredrickson. Looking beyond him, he could see Kyle's light brown car parked in the driveway.

"I'm Kyle Fredrickson of Kyle's Realty. May I assume you are Tom Hastings?"

He talked with a slight lisp and Tom noticed his teeth were brown.

"Yes, I sure am. What can I do for you?"

"I've listed the Cushing property and thought it courteous to let you know."

"I appreciate that, Mr. Fredrickson. Do you have any buyers?"

"Not right now, but I know of at least two parties that are interested. If you ever hear of anyone that may be looking, please give me a call."

Kyle asked Tom what he thought of the two murders.

"Pretty scary," Tom answered. "What do you think?"

Kyle narrowed his penetrating cold, steel, gray eyes and said, "Tough on the neighborhood. Listings are good but I'd rather get them for normal reasons."

Kyle extended his hand. The thumb and forefinger were bruised, they shook and he left, sort of dragging one leg. Perhaps he's got an artificial leg, Tom thought.

"Who was that?" Julie asked when he returned to the deck.

"Have you ever noticed the Kyle's Realty sign on Main Street in New Dresden?"

"Oh yes, I remember seeing it."

"Well, that's who was at the door. His name is Kyle Fredrickson, the winner in the listing battle for the Maynard Cushing property. Only a courtesy call, but it's the first time since moving here, that I've had an opportunity to talk to Kyle Fredrickson."

"Well, it was nice of him to stop," said Julie.

"There goes the sailboat," said Tom.

Sylvan's sailboat had backed away from the dock and headed eastward, without sail, toward the mouth of the bay. There wasn't much wind—the sound of the engine reached their ears. An hour later the sailboat returned. It cruised by Tom's dock and made a big wide turn at the end of the bay. Julie and Tom watched as the boat made its way along the entire length of the opposite shore before settling in at Sylvan's dock.

On Monday morning it was time for Julie to return to the Cities, her apartment. Tom watched as the red convertible moved up the driveway and out of sight. Walking back to the house, he felt that sunken, lonely feeling experienced so many times in the past. His self-prescribed therapy for dealing with those feelings was to get busy with a project, soon as possible.

Tom got in his pickup truck and headed for New Dresden. He was anxious to learn more about the fire. The conversations he overheard at the post office, grocery and restaurant were all about the fire. Speculation about missing Harold was running wild. The visit to the hardware store was no different.

As Tom was browsing tools, he heard someone in the next aisle ask, "How did the fire start?"

"I think it was that Richards guy. He's the person who lives in that tent," answered a second voice.

A third person added, "Well, here's what I heard from Peggy, she was tending bar that day. The vagrant came into the bar a couple of days prior to the fire, he pulled out a wad of cash. After the fourth beer, Richards slouched down and laid his head on the bar. Richards was out of it, muttering to himself. He kept saying, *I didn't do it, I didn't do it, s*uddenly, the guy popped up off the stool and leaves."

Another voice Tom heard said, "Stookie saw Leslie Richards walking north across the railroad tracks after he came out of the bar...he said the guy was pretty wobbly."

# 23

TOM VISITED THE POST OFFICE BOXES ROOM two days later, talk about the fire resurfaced.

The lady, dressed in baggy shorts, told a guy in overalls, "Did you hear that Harold finally showed up?"

"Yeah, I heard he left the evening of the fire with two strangers. Betsy Olson said there was an argument. Harold was ticked off, but left with the men anyway. Betsy works there, you know, she's my granddaughter."

"Harold was in trouble with the Mafia," a lady was telling the postmaster at the business counter.

Jerry didn't respond and fetched Tom's package when he saw the yellow slip.

"I just knew it," the lady said as she moved over while Jerry handed Tom his package.

The fire stories continued at the grocery store.

Ellie was telling a customer, "Harold claims he needed to take care of some business in Chicago...meetings that needed his attention. Harold said he was shocked when hearing his house had burned to the ground....I wonder."

"I hear they bought a trailer house," said the lady who was writing out a check.

"They sure did, a long white one. That's the one Bert and Blanch had next to their house for about ten years."

"Oh, you mean up on the hill."

"Yeah, that's the one."

Tom entered the hardware store to buy tomato dust. After making a selection, he took his place in line at the checkout counter.

"The restaurant is reopening this coming Friday, I hear," said the tall guy with the hat.

The short man directly in front of Tom said, "I heard Harold was brought in by the sheriff for questioning."

"Yeah, I heard that too." replied the hat man. "Harold claims the fire started when he was gone. Chicago, that's where he went, I hear. Had some business with two men there the night before."

"Yeah, the sheriff released Harold, no charges, so it must be okay," the short man added.

Matt was telling one of his customers, "The state fire marshall is coming in to investigate the fire. It's going to take a long time before we hear the results."

The customer said, "There are some rumors floating around about gambling debts."

Matt firmly responded, "It takes more than rumors."

— —

MARY ANN KRAFT WAS STANDING in front of the window in the office. Harold was seated in the chair behind the desk.

Hands thrusting upward, Harold said, "I just don't have the money. Your parents will have to wait."

Mary Ann turned around—face red with anger, "Damn-it, Harold. How could you? It was my money too. I don't know if I can handle this."

"Well, what are you going to do, send me to jail?'

Harold met Mary Ann while he was stationed in San Diego during military service. They got married in California and moved to New Dresden after he was discharged from the service.

Mary Ann stormed out of the office. Harold got up from the chair. Oh well, what can they do to me? Pushing the desk chair aside, he walked into the restaurant lobby. Mary Ann was greeting customers.

Harold saw Tom Hastings enter.

Tom was thinking about the mass of twisted pipes and the charred remains outside the door. There were as many people touring the burn site as there were in the restaurant.

Inside it was business as usual. Harold was greeting customers, seemed upbeat and cheery.

When a customer asked him about the fire, he laughed and said, "Just a few days ago Mary Ann was talking about redecorating the house, now it won't be needed. I saved a ton of money."

Tom sat at a table near the bar, a good view of the main television. The bartender handed him the remote. Searching the channels, Tom settled on a baseball game. The couple sitting at a nearby table alleviated their boredom, all eyes went up to the television. They no longer needed an excuse not to talk.

Tom overheard Mary Ann telling a group. "Half-hour wait for the dining room."

People began stacking up at the hostess station. The crowd that was touring the destruction outside all came in at once. Harold was explaining to one of the customers about plans to rebuild the house.

The names *Harold* and *Mary Ann* were brought up at the next table.

Tom overheard one of the men, two tables down say, "Mary Ann is a good girl. Harold was lucky to find her. Darn good manager, too."

The couple occupying the far corner booth looked familiar. Tom remembered seeing them at the fingerprinting session. The couple that lived at the farmstead near the western border of his property, he thought. As Tom was about to leave the restaurant, curiosity got the best of him and he decided to find out who they were.

Walking over to booth, he said, "I'm Tom Hastings. I live just off Rocky Point Road. Aren't you two my neighbors?"

The guy stood up and said, "This is Kim and I am Steve. Yes, we are neighbors. Would you care to sit down?"

Tom sat next to Steve, who said, "Could I buy you a drink?"

"No thanks, Steve, I've had my share of wine with dinner."

"What did you think of the fingerprinting deal?" asked Tom.

"It ticked me off to tell you the truth. What right do the cops have to pull us in like that? If Kim hadn't talked me into it, they couldn't have dragged me over there."

Kim frowned and said, "Oh, come on, Steve, we have nothing to hide. There is no way either of our prints would have showed up at Maynard's house. Actually, I thought it was exciting to be fingerprinted."

"I can understand your frustration, Steve, but the sheriff's office simply wanted to narrow down the number of unidentified fingerprints. Nice meeting you two...it's time for me to get home. Besides, it looks like your dinner is here."

The waitress arrived with a tray full of food and Tom got up and left.

# 24

**K**YLE FREDRICKSON WAS PLEASED. Norm Cushing finally signed the papers. Time limit for the listing was a concern, only thirty days, but better than not at all. The Ebert's were hot to buy. He felt one more showing would produce an offer. The bathroom—darn the bathroom. It was too small and only one. Mrs. Ebert didn't like that. Everett was ready to sign—if I could get her to shut up, he thought.

Kyle pulled into the Cushing driveway. The Ebert's hadn't arrived yet. Kyle got out of his light brown sedan and unlocked the front door of the house. He walked inside and went over to the bathroom. It was indeed small—he needed to divert Mrs. Ebert's mind away from the bathroom.

Hearing a car door slam, he anxiously stepped onto the small porch. Kyle was taken aback, grabbing a railing for support, the car door opened and Linda Barr stepped out. She was wearing a yellow ribbon in her hair and her sunglasses were perched on top of her head.

She leaned on the door and said, "Hello Fredrickson. I see you're guarding the house. Are you afraid its going to get away?"

The urge to kill dissipated when a second car turned into the driveway—the Ebert's had arrived.

— —

TOM SAW THREE CARS IN MAYNARD'S DRIVEWAY as he made his way out to the county highway. Checking out groceries, he overheard two senior gentlemen discussing Maynard's house.

"Yeah, I hear that Kyle was close to selling Maynard's house," said one of them.

"I was at the hardware store and these Iowa people were excited, telling us about the deal," the other said. "They threw in an offer and I hear it was pretty low."

"Yeah, they were probably tired of paying rent in Big Lakes."

The very next day Kyle Fredrickson rang the Hastings's doorbell for the second time that summer.

"Hello again, Mr. Hastings. I have some good news. You are going to have new neighbors."

"Oh really, are they the Iowa couple I have been hearing about?"

"Yeah, their names are Everette and Ann Ebert. They originally are from Iowa City. Maynard's son Norm accepted their final offer and it looks like there's a deal."

"That sounds great, Kyle. What kind of people are they?"

"Everett is a retired equipment salesman and Ann a retired schoolteacher. They said they choose this area because of the great summers they spent in the lake area the past twenty years.

"The Everett's have grandchildren who love to fish, so you can expect some little people hanging around. They won't be here during the winter months...Arizona is where they go."

"Congratulations, Kyle, on your success."

"Mr. Hastings, I think your property could bring a tidy price. If you're ever thinking about selling, please give me a chance," Kyle said as he handed Tom a business card.

When the light brown sedan left, Tom was thinking about a story Henry passed on to him at the Borders Café. Kyle Fredrickson bought the realty business from Clark Belisle, a friend of Henry's. The business had been in the family thirty years—same little building. The name was changed to Kyle's Realty after the purchase, about six years ago.

"Kyle sure is a quiet fellow," Henry said. "He rarely comes in here for coffee or lunch."

"Does he live here in town?" asked Tom.

"Yes, in that apartment building down by the lake. By himself, I understand."

# 25

THE SOUND OF TENNIS BALLS PERMEATED THE STILLNESS of the evening. Tom Hastings looked up at the sky, clear except for thin blankets of bluish clouds in the west. The sun had slipped behind and was emitting reddish and purple streaks. The light western breeze cooled his perspiring forehead.

The tennis court was one of Tom's greatest joys. Planning the court was exciting—anticipations were high. The contractor came over in his pickup in middle of May—a deal was made. Tom signed the paper.

Excavation began in June. Topsoil was removed, tractor bucket at a time. It took a whole month. The trucks began arriving in late July. Scores of loads dumped fill into the excavation. Blades leveled the surface to prepare for the special asphalt. The smell of fresh blacktop filled the air during the middle of August. Engineers busied exacting the layout—Hastings built the fence. In early September, the painters came. The job was done. A UPS panel truck delivered a tennis ball machine a week later.

That day's workout began well over an hour ago, Tom was tired. Picking up the balls, he dumped them into the hopper, snuggled the cover over the top, and rolled it to the back fence.

Two drops fell on his chin—leaked from the first swallow of a beer. Tom lit up a cigar and scanned the western sky. A small flock of fast moving ducks flew over the greenway. They circled and landed in a small pond at the edge of the woods.

The air was still, not a sound. Tom was still watching the area where the ducks landed. He saw a deer. Prancer was standing on a trail watching him from about one hundred and fifty yards away. What an awesome rack, Tom thought. Remaining still, he continued to watch. Prancer's slim right leg raised off the ground, the knee was bent, the warning. Moments later, as Tom expected, the deer bounded away into the woods.

Carefree, Tom closed the gate on the court and walked the asphalt pathway toward his house. Rounding the corner of the garage, his stomach tightened. A black auto was parked in the driveway. Not moving, he stared at two strangers standing on the porch by the front door. A man and woman. The man was pressing the doorbell. Tom experienced panic thoughts about the warning from Deputy Johnson. His guns were ready, but they were in the house.

Taking advantage of the landscape, he hurried around the West Side of the smaller garage, out of sight from the visitors. Tom turned the knob of his lower level door. It was locked. Double-stepping up to the deck, he tried the deck door, it opened. Tom was able to enter without being seen.

Dashing up to his bedroom, he hurried back down with the .32-automatic. Tom jacked a shell into the chamber and held it in his right hand while approaching the front door. He peaked out a window overlooking the driveway and saw that the two people had walked back to their automobile. Tom opened the front door, as the two visitors turned.

"Can I help you?" Tom asked.

They moved forward a couple of steps. The man said, "We're from the FBI and would like to talk to you."

Tom's right hand was gripping the .32-automatic, tucked in behind the wall, out of sight from his visitors. They began advancing slowly down the sidewalk. Their hands were out front, displaying badges.

Recognizing the face of the male, Tom remembered him from Hector's Bar, the couple from Illinois. Approaching within a few feet of the door, Tom held up his left hand, they stopped.

"I need to look at your IDs," Tom said nervously.

The lady handed him hers. Tom grabbed it with his left hand and raised it to eye level. The gun was still in his right hand, tucked in behind the wall.

Susan Crenshaw was the name beneath the picture. It looked like her, he thought. He handed it back.

The man was next, handing Tom his ID in the same manner. Bill Brown was the name. Again, the picture matched the face. Since Tom had never seen an official ID before, he assumed they were okay.

Handing the ID back to the man, he asked, "How can I help you two?"

"I'm Agent Brown," the man said. He pointed at the lady and added, "This is my partner, Agent Crenshaw. We're investigating the murder of your neighbor Maynard Cushing, and need to talk to you."

Tom began to relax and set the gun down on the computer desk.

"Just one second," Tom told his visitors.

Returning back inside, he placed the .32-automatic under a newspaper on the dining room table. Tom returned to the door, asked the agents in, and had them sit on a love seat next to a bay window. Tom sat on a chair at the table within reach of the newspaper. The large oak table separated him from his visitors.

Agent Brown began, "This is a little complicated. We, the FBI, are investigating the Cushing murder at the request of the CIA. As you may already know, Maynard Cushing was a former CIA agent. Your local sheriff's department is doing their job, working with us, to find Cushing's murderer. Deputy Johnson has made it clear that you can be trusted."

"Treating you guys the way I did, not trusting, the IDs, I'm sorry," said a contrite Tom Hastings.

"Oh, don't feel that way. We understand what you are going through. Not a problem, I respect what you did, asking us for identification. Having a clear understanding is the first step to success, Mr. Hastings. Thanks for your comments." answered Agent Brown.

Tom Hastings felt the strenuous load leave his shoulders, the black car, two of his neighbors dead. The only people he trusted, until now, were Deputy Johnson and Pete Smilie.

"You guys can laugh if you want to, but I have a loaded gun on the table, beneath the newspapers. Talk about mistrust"

Agent Crenshaw looked out the window, she was grasping for the right words, "Mr. Hastings, its not your fault. You're doing what you feel is right, to protect yourself."

She continued, "Now down to business. We believe Deputy Johnson who insists your life is in danger. It's time to level the playing field. Some of this you may already know. A set of fingerprints found at the scene of the Cushing murder matched a former CIA agent, who is wanted by the FBI. His name is Robert Ranforth. We know for certain that the former Agent Ranforth is living somewhere in your community, under an assumed name, of course."

Tom eyed the two agents, confidence growing.

Agent Brown added, "We need your word not to discuss this visit or anything about us with your neighbors or anyone else. The people at the county sheriff's office are an exception."

"I promised Deputy Johnson to keep our discussions confidential and will do the same for you," said a serious-faced Tom Hastings.

Agent Brown continued, "Fifteen years have passed since Ranforth disappeared. If you read the Cushing memoirs, you know Ranforth was arrested for selling classified information to a foreign government. Maynard Cushing was the key witness.

"There's more to the story," said a smiling Crenshaw.

"The FBI had been looking for Mr. Ranforth ever since his disappearance. Your neighbor, Mr. Cushing, called us about a week before the murder. He was sure Ranforth lived in the community, he asked for help. We responded by posing as tourists and taking up residency at a local resort.

"Much to our disappointment, Mr. Cushing was killed before we succeeded finding the missing agent. Your county sheriff's department was not initially aware of our presence. The Cushing murder changed everything."

Agent Brown continued with the explanation, "As you are aware, computer disks containing copies of Mr. Cushing's memoirs are missing, a sure thing they were taken by the killer. If Ranforth is responsible, and we think he is, he also has your business card."

Tom experienced a numbing feeling—he was thinking about that word "target" again.

Tom responded, "I can sure use the help. Deputy Johnson has been more than generous with information and protection. His warning is why I was so cautious with you two."

Agent Brown smiled and said, "Hey, nice job checking us out."

Agent Crenshaw continued, "Agent Brown and I have orders to remain in your community, to assist in any way we can with the investigation into Maynard Cushing's death."

Crenshaw added, "Our stay at the resort has ended. Some of the locals didn't like the color of our car. They became nervous having us around. We've moved to a motel in Big Lakes."

She chuckled and said, "We were reported to the sheriff's department by the owners."

"Well, some of that was my fault. After Deputy Johnson questioned me about the black car, I visited the resort, other places too, inquiring about the black car," Hastings confessed to his visitors.

Agent Brown said, "Mr. Hastings, we have a favor to ask you. Our work will be done here soon. A third agent is going to replace us in a few days. After discussing the case with your sheriff, we are asking you to provide housing for our replacement. By doing this, the agent will be able to continue assisting in the investigation and also provide you with a certain amount of protection. Deputy Johnson really liked the idea."

"That's quite the strategy. I like the idea, too, but let me think on that for a day," Tom answered.

"If you agree to this, the agent will be here soon, in a matter of days," said Brown.

Crenshaw added, "You give it some thought and we'll get back to you soon."

# 26

**A**FTER THE TWO AGENTS LEFT, Tom retrieved the .32-automatic from underneath the newspapers. He stood next to the table and held the gun in both hands. Warnings were now coming from two sources, first it was Deputy Johnson, now the FBI.

Tom set the gun back down on the table and retrieved the holster from the closet. The gun went into the holster, he threaded a belt through the loop. After buckling the belt, Tom experienced feelings of power in spite of the threats.

The windows in the dining room and den gave him a view of the bay and the landscape on both sides of the house. From the living room windows he could see the entire driveway plus some of the path leading to the tennis court. How much time, each day, could he devote to sentinel work? Danger could rear its ugly head at any time, he thought.

Hot tub sessions, though occurring for less than an hour, definitely left him vulnerable. On the other hand, he couldn't foresee holing up in a closet. In spite of the potential dangers, Tom felt a level of excitement realizing that he was part of a CIA and FBI investigation.

Ranforth was for real, a threatening, faceless enemy. Tom thought about the men he knew in the community of New Dresden—which one of them is Ranforth? Is it Steve Wytorrek? No, too young, he thought. Living in a secluded farmstead would have advantages. His neighbor, Sylvan, moved here just a few years ago. So did Kyle Fredrickson. Fred Hood, also a recent resident, appears to have a mysterious past. It could be any of them. The barber, Floyd Pella, he moved here about six years ago. Perhaps Ranforth does not live in the New Dresden community, Big Lakes and Cornwall are not that far away.

Poor Rollie must have stumbled upon the truth, to end up floating in the lake. The more Tom thought about the complications of protecting himself, the more he liked the idea of an FBI agent staying at his house. Agents have guns, too. Better yet, they know how to use them.

Tom needed to drive into New Dresden for the mail. Before backing the pickup truck out of the garage, he placed the holster and gun in the glove compartment.

The experience of being armed while driving up the township road was a new feeling. Thoughts of carrying a gun wherever he went every day was not very appealing. The scare he got yesterday, when the black Buick showed up unannounced, was enough to force a change in lifestyle. Getting caught away from the house without a weapon shouldn't happen again.

After parking on Main Street, he walked across to the post office to fetch the mail and then proceeded to Stillman's and bought a *Star Tribune*. Once again, there weren't any articles regarding the Maynard or Rollie murders. The fact there were two murders in the same community didn't seem to attract the big city media's attention as much as one would hope.

While Tom was browsing through the newspaper at the grocery store, Ellie asked, "Is there anything new in your neighborhood about the murders? I hear the FBI has moved in. That's exciting."

"Yes, Ellie, the FBI is here. That fact should make us all feel safe, shouldn't it?"

Tom didn't know if she was referring to Brown and Crenshaw or the new agent taking their place. Tom chose to honor the confidentiality promise he made to agents Brown and Crenshaw. The local residents were probably going to figure things out, regardless of well-meaning strategy.

Harold Kraft came through the door.

Ellie asked him, 'How are your new house plans coming?"

"Ah, the builder was at our place last night. He had some good ideas. If it wasn't for that darn insurance thing, the contractor could start digging next week."

Harold picked up a basket and proceeded to walk towards the far aisle.

Ellie told Tom, "I heard that someone started that fire, no accident."

"Wow, arson, I sure hope not. That could delay an insurance settlement for a long time."

Ellie and Tom ended their conversation about the fire when a customer approached the checkout counter with a cart full of groceries.

Tom picked up the small bag. Before pushing open the exit door, he made sure no one was in the way.

As Tom was placing the grocery bag onto the passenger side of his pickup truck, he noticed a man standing on the curb at the far end of the block. Tom felt that he was being watched. He gazed back for a moment and then proceeded to walk around the truck. After opening the door, he paused and took another look. The man was gone.

Tom got in the pickup and drove around the block hoping to get a better look. After failing, he drove around the block a second time. Main Street sidewalks were empty. Heading homeward on his final pass up Main Street, he saw someone behind the picture window at Adam's Realty, it wasn't Linda Barr.

My fears are out of control, he thought while crossing the railroad tracks—need to get hold of myself. The threatening feelings generated by listening to FBI and sheriff warnings were playing tricks on my mind.

# 27

ALLAN BURNSIDE WAS SITTING ACROSS THE DESK from a supervisor, in a FBI office in St. Paul, Minnesota.

"Well, what do you think? Does an expedition up north into the lake country interest you?"

Allan cleared his throat and got up from the chair. He walked over to the window that overlooked the skyline in St. Paul.

Turning around he said, "I miss my family. Melissa isn't going to like this. She'll have to tell the kids. I was hoping to get home and see them by next week."

"Tell you what, Allan, I'll see what I can do about getting a summer lake vacation lined up for your family. Perhaps they can come out and visit."

Allan took a step forward, smiled and said, "Really, do you think that's possible?"

"I'll do the best I can."

Deputy Johnson dialed the Hastings's number. Tom answered on the fourth ring.

"Tom, do you remember the FBI agents asking you about housing an agent? "

"Yeah, I remember."

"Have you given it some thought? The agent has arrived. He's here right now."

"I've decided to go along with the plan. Living alone and all that, besides, the company will be appreciated right now," said Tom Hastings.

"Well, since you have agreed, and the agent is here in the next room, how would you feel about meeting him today?"

"Sure, that would be fine."

"Good, we'll be over in about an hour."

Tom was working at the computer desk when the deputy's car arrived in his driveway. He watched as Deputy Johnson opened his door and walked around to the front of the car. Putting one hand on the hood, he pointed toward the basketball hoop. Tall and slender, Agent Allan Burnside was dressed in a suit. He smiled and pretended a jump shot. The deputy gestured in the direction of the front door and they came down the walk.

Tom opened the door and Deputy Johnson said, "Tom, I want you to meet Allan Burnside. He's the FBI agent I've been telling you about."

Tom was surprised by the youthful appearance. The handshake was firm and warm.

"Hi, Allan, I'm Tom Hastings. Welcome to my home."

"I love the looks of this place. Thanks for taking me in."

"So, where are you from, Mr. Burnside?"

"Monroe, Michigan."

"Oh, really. Isn't that where, General Custer was from?"

"Why yes, there is the statue in the park."

" I've read all about the controversial statue. Is that the one of the general astride a horse, saber lifted, simulating an upcoming charge?"

"Yes, you have it right."

"There's an interesting story about the statue."

"Well let's hear it."

"The statue itself was no problem, its location and position in the city-square was. The first thing people saw when walking down the steps of a local church was the horses butt.

"The pastor of the church didn't like that one bit. He successfully lobbied the city council to move it."

Deputy Johnson and Allan Burnside laughed.

"Well, Mr. Hastings, you have one over on me. This is the first time I've heard that one."

Agent Burnside added, "I would like to move into your house within a week. I need some time to get my things together and rent a car."

"A week would be fine. Sooner the better as far as I am concerned."

"Well, good. That'll work out just fine," said Deputy Johnson.

Tom looked at the deputy and asked, "Is there anything new on Ranforth?"

Deputy Johnson said, "Not really, but by having Agent Burnside working on the case full time we're hoping for an early solution to the murders. The other two agents that visited you have returned to St. Paul."

He added, "Would you mind if I showed Allan around?"

"No, not at all. I'll help."

Tom gave Deputy Johnson and the agent a tour of his house, including the bedroom where Agent Burnside was going to sleep.

They proceeded outdoors where he led them on a tour of his property.

When they got out to the tennis court, Agent Burnside said, "Oh, I'm going to like this."

"Are you a tennis player?" Tom asked.

"Yup, I hit the ball around in high school and college a little," Allan answered. "Your place looks ideal for setting up shop, it's nice and private. I hope my electronic stuff doesn't interfere with your computer network or satellite television system. If it creates any problems, just let me know and I'll get someone over here to fix it."

They reviewed door locks and Tom provided the agent with a key for the front door.

"Thanks, Tom," he said.

"After I move in, a plan will be needed to monitor my departures and arrivals. We can work on that later. I'll call you in a couple of days when I am ready to move in."

Deputy Johnson said, "It's time for us to leave."

"Nice meeting you...talk to you in a couple of days."

Tom and Allan shook hands and the two officers returned to the deputy's car. Tom Hastings watched as it turned around, and drove up the roadway. A whole new ballgame, he thought.

# 28

AGENT BURNSIDE PARKED HIS RENTAL IN THE MOTEL PARKING LOT. He wasn't too fond of Chrysler cars but this one was going to have to do. His interviews that afternoon were productive. The field of Ranforth suspects was narrowed to four. His evening plan was for dinner and a good nights sleep. Tomorrow, he would move to the Hastings's residence.

He changed into jeans and began a walk that took him along the north shore of Big Lake. He stopped at a monument along the way and sat on the masonry bench. The fishing boat trolling down below reminded him of his son. Spending more time with him was a priority. If his supervisor came through as promised, he would see his son soon. Thoughts of his two children and wife coming to visit this piece of heaven were exhilarating.

The LongBoat Bar and Grill served Allan's purpose well. Service was top-notch. He was seated in a shadowed corner, quite independent of the main traffic.

"What'll it be, sir?"

"I'll have the walleye and chips. Ah, also, would you bring me a Bud?"

Allan was finished with dinner and about to leave when he observed two men, one with a strained, weird walk and the other who looked like an actor in Casablanca. *Rick, do something. You've got to save me.*

He had seen that walk before. Yes, it was in New Dresden—on Main Street.

Burnside was pleased. He exited the restaurant without being seen by the suspect across the room. He was looking forward to the call to his family.

Melissa Burnside anxiously answered the phone, "Hello."

"Hi, honey, how are you? How are Robby and Debbie doing?"

"We're just fine."

They talked for about ten minutes and Melissa said, "Would you like to talk to Robby and Debbie?"

Allan Burnside slept well. Talking to his kids and wife was the ticket he needed to face tomorrow.

— —

TOM HAD RETURNED FROM NEW DRESDEN. Agent Burnside left a message on his answering machine announcing that he would be arriving in a medium green Chrysler Intrepid about 3:00 that afternoon.

Tom did some scrambling to clean up the house. There was a pile of magazines and papers stacked on the dining room table. By the time Allan arrived, he had vacuumed the floors and rearranged the items in the refrigerator to create extra space. The Intrepid had Minnesota plates and looked like any other car in Minnesota.

Burnside had dark, thick hair and was tall and lean. He had a very peaceful, soothing voice and smiled when he talked. Tom helped him move his things into the spare bedroom. Allan carried in two bags of groceries and placed them into the refrigerator. Allan volunteered to take care of his own needs, and Tom could pretend that he was not even here. Allan's words were comforting and Tom was beginning to appreciate his presence.

Tom left Allan to the unpacking. The grass needed mowing, recent rains and all the activity at his house—he was behind with daily chores. Tom worked outdoors for a couple of hours and went back into the house to check on his new guest. Allan was sitting on the loveseat in the dining room, conversing on his cell phone.

After Allan finished, Tom asked, "Are you settled in okay?"

"Sure am. Thanks for all your help. Tom, Since I'm going to be coming and going a great deal, as mentioned before, you and I need to have a plan. It'll save you a lot of worry, knowing exactly when I leave, and the time of an expected arrival."

"That's a good idea. What do you suggest?"

"If you aren't home when I am leaving, I'll leave a note on your computer desk, time of departure and expected time of return. If this changes, I'll call and leave a message."

"That sounds fine."

"Also, I think it best if I call twice before returning. Once when leaving and again from the township road. So, before I get to your home, you will get two calls. Arrival should happen within a couple of minutes after the second call."

"I like your idea, but during the daylight hours I'm outdoors most of the time. You better take my cell phone number. I'll try to remember to clamp it on my belt when spending time outdoors. Perhaps you should call the cell phone first, prior to my regular number.

"Okay, if the time of day is between nine in the morning and nine in the evening, I'll ring your cell phone first. We'll have an opportunity to test our strategy today, because I'm leaving right now. Return should come in about two hours. Would you give me your cell phone number?"

After Allan wrote it down, he dropped the slip in his pocket and said, "Hey, how about checking out the rest of your grounds, before I leave?"

"Sure, let's take a walk."

They walked around the house and down to the dock. After that, they followed the pathway out to the greenway and the tennis court.

"Holy smokes, this is real nice," Allan said. "What's beyond the greenway?"

"Some fields and trails through the woods."

"I'll explore them later, Tom. If you would loan me a tennis racquet, perhaps we can hit some balls tomorrow."

"I have plenty of racquets, no problem," Tom answered.

Tom and Allan talked about tennis while walking back to the driveway. Allan got behind the wheel of the Intrepid and put on his sunglasses. In moments he was gone. Tom went for a walk that evening. A cell phone was clipped to his belt on the left side, the .32-automatic in a holster on the right waist.

Tom was in the hot tub when he got the first call. Quick as possible, he scurried out of the tub and answered the cell phone. Allan announced his pending arrival from five miles away. The second call came in about five minutes. Two minutes later, Tom saw his car emerge from the roadway and onto the driveway.

After he came into the house, Allan said, "Well, how did the system work?"

"Just fine Allan, It's not going to be perfect, but it's sure going to help."

They sat in the den for the balance of the evening watching a baseball game. Allan was a Detroit Tigers fan, not surprising since his home was in Michigan.

The next morning when Tom got up and made his way down to the kitchen, Allan was up and making some breakfast.

"Good Morning, Tom. After breakfast I'd like to explore the rest of your property including the trails through the woods. Would you like some eggs?"

"No thanks, Allan. I'm a late morning person and will make myself a bagel later."

After he finished breakfast, Allan excused himself and walked down the pathway toward the tennis court. While Allan was gone, Tom sat on the deck with a coffee.

A bald eagle was hunting the opposite shoreline of the bay. After swooping down close to the water, it pumped the wings and soared to a position above the tree line. No mistake, it was an eagle, white body markings caught the rays of the sun.

After Allan returned, he said, "Tom, I need your help. My boss planted information about me in the community. I'm a nephew of yours from out west, visiting Uncle Tom Hastings. Could you help keep my identity as much of a non-event as possible."

The thought of an armed agent living in his house appealed to Tom, especially if his potential enemy, Ranforth was aware.

"You can call me Uncle," said a grinning Tom Hastings.

Allan left midmorning. He planned to spend most of the day at the sheriff's office going over records. Tom continued his outdoors work, spending very little time in New Dresden that morning.

Allan's coming home call came at close to 5:00 p.m. Twenty minutes later he called again from the township road. In just two minutes, the Intrepid pulled into Tom's driveway.

"Well, this is a second testing of our system. It's working for me, how about you?" Allan asked.

"Just fine, Allan. I really appreciate your keeping me informed. How did your session at the sheriff's office go?"

"I spent most of the day studying the investigative reports about the Cushing and Smith murders. I also browsed the Maynard Cushing memoirs. The most interesting part was about this Robert Ranforth person."

"Did you come to any conclusions? Do you think Ranforth is the killer?"

"No conclusions, but many suspicions."

"How about some tennis?" Tom asked.

"Sure, be ready in a couple of minutes."

Allan was a little rusty, but hitting for half an hour his shots improved. Tom and Allan hit the ball around for another hour.

"That's enough for me," Allan announced.

Later in the evening Tom chose Bayside Restaurant in Big Lakes for dinner. It was located on Big Lake about fifteen miles west of New Dresden. Tom was well acquainted with the owners, Howard and Jane Iverson. They owned and operated Bayside for the last twelve years. The two men drove to Big Lakes in Allan's green Chrysler. The parking lot was full, but Allan found a curbside parking spot in the street. Howard and Jane were greeting customers when they entered.

"Hey, Howard, I want you to meet my nephew Allan from California."

Howard and Allan shook hands.

"This is Howard's wife Jane," added Tom.

Allan shook her hand.

"What part of California?" asked Jane.

"The northern part, near San Francisco," answered Allan.

"Were all full up right now, but you're on the list and I'll let you know soon as a table is available."

"Thanks, Jane, we'll head over to the bar."

Tom took possession of a couple of empty stools. He introduced Allan to bartender Sam. They ordered a couple of beers. Sam eyed Tom's guest with curiosity. The bartender was known for his fishing prowess. He was telling them his latest fishing story when the sound of a glass tapping on the other end of the bar drew him away.

The bar was crowded. Every stool was occupied. The Minnesota Twins were playing the Detroit Tigers on television. The game attracted Allan's attention while waiting for a table. He clapped when one of the Tigers drove a baseball into the left field seats. Two more innings went by before the hostess came looking for them.

"Your table is ready, Tom, please follow me."

She led them to a table next to a window and said, "How's this?"

"It's great. Jeepers, what a nice view," said Allan.

Tom and Allan were studying the menu when a waitress strutted up to the table. They each ordered a glass of wine and continued to study.

After the waitress returned with the wine, she said, "Are you gentlemen ready?"

"Yes," said Allan. "I'll have a half-rack of ribs, a baker and the house salad."

"And you, sir?"

"I'll have the halibut, also a baked potato and salad with honey mustard dressing. Bring me another glass of wine. How about you, Allan?"

"No, I'm fine."

Looking around the dining room, Tom didn't notice anyone he knew until spotting his neighbors, Byron and Eva Schultz. They were dining with another couple in the far corner.

"See that couple in the far corner, the two facing us?" Tom asked Allan.

"Yeah, anybody interesting?"

"They're my neighbors. The farmhouse overlooking the township road."

"Strategic location, camera behind their picture window would be perfect. All the vehicles coming and going on the township road on film," Allan said and smiled.

Jane came by carrying four menus. She seated a foursome at the next table.

"How are you two doing?" she asked.

Jane appeared to be very interested where Allan lived and what he did for a living. Then she asked Tom about setting up an appointment to help here with their inventory program. Howard and Jane were not only Tom's good friends, but also clients.

Tom had worked hard updating their accounting system and integrating it with an inventory program.

"I can come over next Tuesday, right after lunch, Jane. How will that work?"

"Sounds good to me."

They were partially into their dinner when Allan said, "I have a favor to ask you Tom. I haven't seen my family for about a month, and I would really like to bring them out to your home this coming weekend. My wife's name is Melissa. I have a ten-year- old son, Robby and a seven-year-old daughter, Debbie."

"That sounds like a great idea. I'll look forward to their visit."

Allan's mood became very upbeat after he got the okay from Tom for his family's visit.

"I'll get on the phone after getting home and arrange for a flight for my family this coming Friday."

"You probably know this Allan, but the closest commercial airport is at Brownstown, sixty miles to the west."

After a delightful dinner, they moved back into the bar area. The baseball game was in the ninth inning with the Twins ahead by a run. The Tigers had two runners on with only one out. Allan uttered a sigh when the next batter struck out. The third out came on a groundout. The Twins survived a Tiger rally in the ninth to the delight of most of the people sitting at the bar. Allan, of course, was not too amused. They got up to leave after the game was over. On their way out, Howard and Jane were at the door chatting with a group of other customers.

"Nice meeting you," Howard said to Allan.

"You've got a great place here. I really enjoyed the view and the food."

"Thanks, Allan, come back and see us again."

The day was still partially light as Allan and Tom drove back to the Hastings's residence. Tom called Julie later that evening and told her about the potential company for the weekend. She was delighted.

— —

BILL JONES WAS TRIMMING THE SHRUBS fronting Unit 4. Mary was inside cleaning. She was upset—the renters had left a mess. Pieces of food stuck to the kitchen sink—noodles on the floor in the corner—dirty dishes.

"Damn-it, Bill, we've had a pack of animals in here. Just come and look at this."

Bill set down the shears and went inside. He chuckled and said, "It takes all kinds, doesn't it?"

"You can laugh Bill, but I don't think we should rent to these people next year. I'm going to tell them we're full up."

"You need a break. Come on out and let's sit a bit."

Bill went back out and lit a cigarette. He sat down on the small deck. In a minute, a disheveled and frustrated Mary joined him.

"You've got to learn how to relax," Bill told his wife.

"Relax-smax," she replied.

"The green Intrepid is going by again. Yesterday, I think I saw it about four times," said Bill.

They watched the car reduce speed as it approached the speed zone.

"That car has been up and down that township road about four times a day. Must be someone visiting the Point," added Mary.

Bill took another drag and he looked at the cloud of dust on the township road.

He said, "There goes Tom's pickup headed for town."

"I wonder how he's doin'. I can still see that funeral procession going by," Mary sadly said.

"Woah, he's not going to town. He's coming in here," Bill said as he stomped out the cigarette on the ground.

— —

AFTER ALLAN LEFT FOR BROWNSTOWN to pick up his family, Tom headed for New Dresden in the pickup truck. When he was approaching the stop sign at the county highway, he turned right instead to pull into the drive at South Shores Resort. He knew they would be noticing Allan's car. So would Byron and Eva.

There wasn't anyone in the office when he entered, however there was a note. *We're in cottage 4.*

Tom walked down the slope toward a group of cottages.

Bill spotted him from the bench and yelled out, "Hi Tom, come on over."

Tom stopped on the grass below and placed his elbows on the top rail.

"Hello, Tom, how are you? Is it time for some coffee?" asked Mary.

"Yeah, Mary, I think you two need a break. I'm just fine, thank you."

Bill lit another cigarette and said, "What's up, Tom?"

"Just came over to chat, Bill."

They walked up the slope to the house, up three wooden steps to a deck and into the office. The door back of the counter led to the kitchen.

"Have a chair," said Mary.

Bill and Tom sat at the kitchen table while Mary readied a pot of coffee.

"What's new?" asked Bill as he snuffed out his cigarette in an ashtray.

"Well, I have a new visitor. My nephew Allan has arrived from North California. He is going to stay with me for a few weeks. You may have noticed a green Intrepid coming and going along the township road."

"I was wondering who belongs to that green car," said Mary.

"Yeah, I noticed it, too," said Bill. "Since the two murders, Mary and I pay a lot more attention to the vehicles driving up and down that road. A lot of them are probably sightseers, curious about the murders."

Mary said, "The couple from Illinois who drive the black Regal haven't returned. I'm really concerned they may have something to do with the murders. We're darned worried. What if people stop coming? There have already been a couple of cancellations, one just yesterday. I'm afraid there could be more."

"It's time for me to run to town," Tom said. "Besides, you two need to get back to work. Thanks for the coffee, Mary. Talk to you later."

After leaving the resort, Tom stopped at the Schultz farm. Byron and Eva were both home. He was offered coffee for the second time. They sat at the kitchen table.

"I saw you guys at the Bayside the other day. Did you have a good dinner?" Tom asked.

"Sure did. I saw you sitting by the window," replied Eva. "Who was that young man with you?"

"That was my nephew Allan, visiting from California. You may have seen his green Intrepid driving up and down the township road."

Byron gestured with his arm towards the window and stated, "Yeah I noticed the green car. Is he staying with you?"

"Yes, Allan is going to be around about a month. I'm glad to have someone around, especially after the two murders."

Eva added, "Isn't that awful about Rollie? I'm glad we know who belongs to the green car. It circled the loop about three times the other day, got me suspicious."

Just like Bill and Mary, Byron and Eva were also watching the traffic on the township road, Tom realized. After leaving the farm, he drove to New Dresden.

The string of red lights on the arms of the railroad crossing began to flash just after Tom crossed the tracks and entered Main Street. The blast of the horn penetrated his ears as he emerged from the pickup truck. He stood by the truck for a moment and watched the train lumber through town. Saved about ten minutes, he thought.

Pete emerged from the hardware store as Tom was walking back to his truck from the post office. He waved and Tom retraced his steps back to the sidewalk.

"I hear your nephew is visiting," Pete said.

Wow, word really gets around, Tom thought.

"Yes, his name is Allan. Perhaps you and Lisa will get a chance to meet him."

"Yeah, bring him over sometime. I'll check with Lisa. Perhaps she would be interested in having you and your nephew over for dinner. She's a darn good cook, you know. Lately, Lisa is a little less concerned about the murders. We don't feel involved and other than a short visit by the sheriff's department and the state people, we have been left alone."

Tom saw Fred Hood approaching from the direction of the grocery store. Fred looked up and nodded before entering the hardware. Pete's eyes followed him into the store.

"Now there is one quiet, keep-to-himself man. We took our vacuum in the other day and he hardly said a word."

"Gotta go Pete. See you later."

# 29

JULIE HAD ROLLED HER SUITCASE DOWN THE CORRIDOR and out into the parking lot. After hoisting it into the trunk, she brushed off the car dust from her slacks. Being hungry was not going to delay her departure. I'll eat along the way, she thought.

The little red convertible dodged in and out of traffic lanes attempting to avoid heavy truck traffic on I-94. Most of the cars competing for space on the highway were headed for the lake areas of central and northern Minnesota.

She swung off the Interstate onto Federal Hwy-10. The less traveled highway wound through rolling hills and small towns. Lakes and small ponds frequented the landscape. Julie pulled into the parking lot of a sub-sandwich restaurant after an hour of driving.

Julie held her breath passing through one of the smaller towns. She saw a local police car parked at an intersection—the speedometer showed ten miles over the speed limit. Julie experienced relief when the officer didn't pull her over.

— —

TOM WAS FINISHED WITH YARD WORK for the week. He was looking forward to Julie's visit. Allan would be returning with his family. Julie will have ideas for dinner, he thought. Tom looked at his watch—almost 3:30. He was standing in the garage door opening when the red convertible drove up.

Tom was careful not to injure her ribs while giving her a big hug. "Hey, its Friday. How was the drive?"

"Enjoyable. I just love this drive. When is your company coming?"

Julie was delighted that Allan was bringing his family to visit.

She liked people, especially kids. Shortly after her arrival, Julie and Tom were out on the tennis court. There was very little wind and the conditions for tennis were ideal. Julie's forehand was exceptionally strong that afternoon, and she combined the power with a natural drop shot to pick up more than the usual number of points. Tom had his hands full.

When they returned to the house, the phone rang. Allan was calling from Big Lakes.

"I have my family aboard and should be there in about twenty minutes."

"Okay, Allan, I'll wait for your next call."

When the second call came, Julie and Tom moved outside to greet their new guests.

Melissa, Allan's wife, was tall and slim with attractive, short black hair. Robby, his son, was also tall but had a head of bushy blond hair. Little Debbie had long, dark hair and looked like her mother. She was all smiles and very bubbly. The next hour, the Hastings's visitors experienced a celebration, new friendships and a joyous homecoming.

Robby and Debbie were anxious to explore. Their dad gave them a tour of the tennis court and the surrounding greenway and trails. Julie and Tom were visiting with Melissa in the house when Debbie came running in all excited.

"Guess what, we saw two fawns. Out by the tennis court."

Julie asked her, "How is Robby doing?"

"He's playing tennis with dad."

Julie, Melissa and Tom were relaxing on the deck when Sylvan's sailboat backed away from his dock. When the boat reached the middle of the bay, the sails were untied and raised to the top of the mast. They captured the southwest breeze that propelled the boat eastward toward the mouth of the bay.

Julie looked across the bay and said, "The tent is gone."

"Yeah, I noticed it missing a few days ago. Maybe Leslie Richards is in jail again, or better yet, he left the country. I'll ask Deputy Johnson next time we get together."

Robby and Debbie came in from the tennis court and joined the group on the deck.

"Oh look," said Debbie. "What's that huge bird down by the dock?"

"That's Old Blue," Tom said. "He's part of the family. The dock is in his territory. Every single day during the summer, Old Blue hunts the shoreline."

Robby asked, "How's fishing in this lake?"

"It's quite good. You should talk your dad into getting a license. The hardware store in New Dresden sells three-day fishing licenses and there is a bait shop right next to the store. My fishing boat is available."

Robby was excited. When his dad came out to the deck, he said, "Dad, Mr. Hastings said it's okay to use his boat for fishing. Can we go?"

"Yeah, that sounds like fun. How about early tomorrow morning?"

Melissa said, "While you boys are fishing, Debbie and I will drive into New Dresden and do some shopping. I hear there are several interesting small shops and curios on Main Street."

Julie filled four glasses with wine and set them on a deck table.

"Time to think about what's available in the fridge for dinner," she said.

Tom announced, "There are a couple of packages of chicken breasts in the freezer. Help yourself."

The two ladies moved into the kitchen and began searching for fixings to prepare for dinner. The mood at the dinner table was high-spirited. Thoughts of danger and murders were put aside. Tom was delighted to see the Burnsides spending time together.

When dinner was completed, Allan and Tom sauntered out to the deck. They sipped on coffee and Tom puffed on a panatela cigar.

"So, how's your investigation going so far, Allan?"

He said, "Tom, I'm following some leads, Ranforth isn't too far away. I'd rather not mention any names right now, need to be sure."

Allan's statement excited Tom.

"Is this going to be someone I know?" he asked.

"Yes, likely you do," Allan answered.

Tom noticed Allan's withdrawn expression and wished he had not brought up the subject. They began talking about baseball.

A gray sky and light drizzle greeted the Hastings's household the next morning. Allan and Robby had gotten up early and made enough noise to be heard. They were headed for the bait shop. Since they were expected back in about half an hour, there was no need for Allan to call on his cell before returning.

Tom was making coffee when he heard the car return. Allan and Robby headed down to the dock with the bait and fishing gear. Tom was checking the Internet weather as Melissa and Julie came down in their robes. They settled down with some coffee at the dining room table.

"Going to be sunny this afternoon," Tom said to Julie.

"Oh great, how about some tennis later?"

"Sure sounds okay to me."

The ladies learned they both had college degrees in political science. Tom was preparing a batch of bagels while the girls discussed the world of international politics. Melissa walked out on the deck and spotted Allan and Robby in the boat across the bay.

She said, "There are a couple of happy guys."

While Tom was buttering the bagels, the phone rang. The caller was Deputy Johnson. Feelings of excitement quivered through Tom's body. The call sounded urgent. The deputy requested coming over to talk with him and Agent Burnside.

"Sure, how about right after lunch?" replied Tom.

"That's fine. I'll see you then."

Debbie made her first appearance of the day. She was rubbing her eyes and trying to hide a smile. She snuggled to her mother and avoided good morning greetings.

The fishing guys returned to the dock just before noon. Robby stepped out of the boat onto the dock, got on his knees and reached down. He retrieved a stringer that everyone could see: resounding cheers from the occupants on the deck.

Debbie ran down to the dock to get a closer look. Robby came up to fetch a fillet knife for his dad. Later, Allan packed the fillets in a plastic container and stored them in the refrigerator.

"Looks like a fish dinner coming up soon," Julie said.

"When do we eat?" asked a hungry Robby.

"Well how about making you a sandwich?" Julie asked.

"Boy, I'm really hungry," he replied.

Julie and Melissa got busy making lunch. When they were finished, everyone gathered around the dining room table. During lunch, Julie spotted a break in the clouds.

"Hey, looks like some tennis this afternoon."

Tom added, "How about a doubles game?"

The tennis match discussion was interrupted by the sound of a vehicle coming up the driveway.

"It's a police car," said an excited Robby.

— —

DEPUTIES PAUL JOHNSON AND ARLIN LARSON turned left off the county highway, onto the state highway.

"It's about three miles down the road, Arlin."

The two deputies drove in silence.

"It's the next left, a farm field road," said Deputy Johnson pointing.

Arlin Larson was driving and he eased the car over a tractor road of rocky bumps and gopher mounds.

"Let's park over there," said Paul.

After stopping the car, the two men got out and checked their pistols. They both put them back in the holsters but didn't button the strap.

"It's over this way," said Paul.

The two deputies followed a grassy trail through a stand of trees. Johnson stopped and put his right hand up.

"There it is. Let's go."

They walked over to the tent and Deputy Johnson called out, "Anybody in there? This is the sheriff."

Hands went down to their guns when a rustling sound was heard from the tent. They held their breath when a shaggy looking man emerged. They gave him a chance to stand and adjust to the daylight.

"Are you Leslie Richards?" asked Johnson.

"Yeah, who wants to know?"

"I have a paper right here that says you are under arrest for suspicion of arson."

"Now, what the hell is all that? I haven't done nothin."

"Read him his rights, Arlin."

— —

DEPUTY JOHNSON STARTED DOWN THE SIDEWALK but turned around and returned to his car. He jotted down the license plate number of Allan's rental. After reaching through the window, he laid the notepad on the front seat. Walking down the sidewalk, he rang the doorbell.

Tom answered the door and invited Deputy Johnson into the house.

After introductions, Tom said, "The deputy needs some time with Allan and I.

"Let's go out on the deck."

Shortly Debbie knocked on the screen door and entered with three glasses of ice tea.

"Thanks, Debbie."

After she left, Deputy Johnson said, "I have news. Leslie Richards has been arrested for burning down the Kraft house."

"Is that why the tent is gone?"

"It sure is and he isn't coming back. His tent has been searched, several articles hidden under a stack of blankets belonged to the Kraft's."

Allan asked, "How about any connection with the murders?"

"Nothing so far, Allan. His prints don't match any of those lifted from the Cushing house. There are no ties to former Agent Ranforth. On the surface it looks like Richard's motive was robbery, but deeper down we're guessing he torched the house for other reasons. He needed more money than he got from the farm job to pay for his drug habit."

Tom sat in silence as the deputy continued.

"The main reason for coming here is because of a crank phone call received at the office yesterday. It came from an apparent male. Whoever it was claimed to know who committed the murders. He didn't tell us whom, but he did say *two down and one to go.*

"The caller hung up before we could trace the call. Crank calls do happen now and then, but this one scared me. I think it was real."

"I appreciate the warning, Paul," Tom said with a quivering voice.

The discussion ended and they moved into the dining area where the ladies, Robby and Debbie were working on a fifteen-hundred-piece picture puzzle. The deputy said his shift was done for the day and he was heading home for a nice quiet weekend.

Julie suggested, "Why don't you join us for dinner? We have plans for a sausage cookout on the grill, over by the tennis court. Do you have a family?"

"Yes, I do. My wife's name is Toni and we have two daughters, age nine and seven."

Julie expanded the invitation to include his family.

He smiled and said, "I'll check with her and give you a call. Thanks for the invite. It's time for me to go."

Julie and Tom drove into New Dresden to pick up the mail and a newspaper. While shopping at Stillman's Super Market they picked up two packages of brats and two dozen buns. They also purchased some soft drinks and salad ingredients.

Walking from the grocery store to the pickup parked on Main Street, Julie noticed Kyle Fredrickson standing in his shop doorway.

"Tom, I think that man is watching us."

Tom looked across the street. Kyle remained standing by the doorway, watching.

A couple of hours later, Julie had a reason to celebrate. She defeated Tom in a set of tennis. It was her first victory since they began playing a few months ago. Following their singles match, an ecstatic Julie challenged the Burnsides to a doubles match.

Tom and Julie found out the hard way that Melissa was a former high school tennis champion. The first set was reasonably close at six-three, however they got burned in the second set, six-one.

"Melissa, you are some kind of mean tennis player. I've now lost three sets in a row and on my home court."

"Hey, Tom, if you hadn't blown so many shots, we may have had a chance," joked a grinning Julie.

The Johnson family arrived later that afternoon. Deputy Johnson introduced himself as Paul. He put his arm around his wife and said, "This is Toni and over here are our daughters, Becky and Cherith."

The two Johnson girls warmed up to Debbie and soon the three girls were off on their own exploring the grounds. After tennis matches were all done, they gathered around the outdoor grill next to the court. Soon the aroma of sausages cooking over charcoals permeated the air. Dinner on the picnic table on that beautiful evening was a treat for everyone. Robby had just wolfed down his third brat.

"How about another one?" asked Julie.

"No thanks, I'm stuffed," he answered.

"It doesn't get much better than this," said Melissa to Toni. "How old are your girls?"

"Becky is twelve and Cherith is ten."

As darkness was approaching, the Johnson family began its preparation for leaving. There were some heartwarming good-byes and those remaining watched the taillights of the Johnson car as it moved down the driveway and out onto the roadway.

The remaining group slowly made their way back to the house. The Burnsides appeared exhausted. A very pleasant day had come to an end.

There were more good-byes the next day as Melissa, Robby and Debbie prepared to depart in the green Intrepid. Julie and Tom helped carry the luggage to their car. Allan packed the suitcases into the trunk and the car made its way down the driveway slope and out onto the roadway.

They were gone. Allan would soon deliver them to the airport in Brownstown where they would board a plane for the return trip to Monroe, Michigan.

Tom put his arm around Julie and gave her a hug. He knew she felt bad that the company was leaving.

"Did you have a good time?" Tom asked.

"It was wonderful—what a couple of great families. I sure hope to get to see them again. Tom, I need to get packed and hit the road. Tough day coming up tomorrow."

Julie left before Allan returned from Brownstown. After Allan returned, he and Tom spent the rest of the evening watching the

Braves-Mets game on television. Neither one was very sympathetic for the Mets when the Braves scored ten runs in the eighth inning.

# 30

ALLAN WAS UP EARLY ON MONDAY MORNING. Tom could hear him rummaging around in the kitchen. Next, he heard the front door open and close—Allan's car had left the driveway. Tom was satisfied and confident seeing a note lying on the computer desk.

Allan didn't return until late that evening. This routine went on for the rest of the week. Every morning Tom expected a note from Allan explaining departure time and expected arrival time.

The agent was reluctant to discuss details of his investigation. He did mention following some leads regarding the mysterious phone call received by the sheriff's department. It appeared that he was working closely with Deputy Johnson and the rest of the department.

On Thursday morning, after parking on Main Street in New Dresden, Tom noticed a green Chrysler Intrepid car parked next to the post office. He walked up close to the car and was quite certain it was Allan's. The car was still there after he returned from the grocery store.

Tom hesitated in front of the hardware store for a few minutes attempting to satisfy his curiosity—was it Allan's car?

Beetles were eating up his potatoes. Tom entered the hardware store.

Matt Nelson was proud of the hardware store. Several years ago, he and his wife made the decision to move. He always wanted to run a country hardware store—big change from living in Chicago. Matt, his wife and family have never looked back. The store was doing well financially even though sales slowed in Minnesota during the winter months. Customers were steady even then, a lot of regulars. The place was a madhouse in the summer months.

Matt had been working in the office for an hour. He came down the steps, yawned, and meandered over to the counter. The only customer in the store was browsing garden tools. Matt had seen him before, the guy who bought the farmstead north of Borders Lake. Wytorrek, yes, that was his name.

"Hello sir, finding what you're looking for?" asked Matt.

"Just shopping," answered the customer.

Matt approached the counter. Susan, the head clerk said, "Matt, did you see that creepy guy that was in here a few minutes ago?"

"No, what did he buy?"

"A knife...the switch."

"Why did you think he was creepy?"

"He reminded me of Casablanca, the movie. Remember *the letters of transit*...the creepy guy who stole them?"

"Yeah, Rick's...the piano. Rick hid the letters in the piano."

Matt heard the front door open. He watched as Tom Hastings came up the center aisle.

"Hi, Tom, what can we do for you today?"

"Beetle dust...my potatoes are in trouble."

"Over there in the garden aisle."

While Tom was browsing through the chemicals, he noticed Steve Wytorrek fiddling with yard and garden tools. Steve wasn't too happy during the fingerprinting session, but sure was friendly during dinner at Mary Ann's, Tom remembered. Tom's neighbor had a menacing looking two-handed grip on a spade.

"Hi, Steve," Tom said.

"I'm looking for a good inexpensive spade, a handle that doesn't break."

"How are you coming with your plans for the new log house?" Tom asked.

"Our plans are on hold until we raise more money," his face saddened.

After picking out a bag of potato dust, Tom made his way to the checkout counter.

While waiting his turn to pay, Tom admired the impressive and elaborate computer system that Matt had recently installed. The bag of dust was scanned, a receipt printed noiselessly—high technology for a small town.

"Would you add a tube of popcorn to the bill?" Tom asked the clerk.

While waiting for the popcorn, Tom shelled a few peanuts from a wooden barrel next to the counter. The floor got messy, acceptable practice, fitting the personality of the hardware store.

After the clerk handed Tom the popcorn, he was about to leave when Matt said, "Hey, Tom, do you ever have any problems with networking?"

"What's the problem?" Tom asked.

"Sometimes my number-two terminal loses its connection to the server."

"Likely it's the cabling."

"Yeah, maybe I should get some new cables."

When Tom left the hardware store, the green Intrepid was gone.

— —

EVA SCHULTZ WAS WATERING PLANTS on the side of the house when Byron arrived from town. He was carrying a bag of groceries and paused before entering the house.

"Hope I didn't forget anything," he said.

Eva stood up, reached her hand behind her back and stretched.

"Ooo, that hurts," she cried. I'm getting too old for this, Byron."

"Looks like we have some company," said Byron.

"That looks like Tom's pickup," Eva added.

The pickup truck kicked up a small whirl of dust when it stopped in the driveway. Tom hopped out and waved. He walked over to the house and shook Byron's hand.

"Hi, guys," he said.

"Well, hello, Tom. How did you know I baked cookies today?" Eva said.

"I could smell them from the highway," Tom chuckled as he answered.

"Come on in, Tom."

They entered the house. Byron and Tom sat at the kitchen table overlooking the highway.

"How's the traffic on the township road?" asked Tom.

"It's picked up lately. There sure has been a lot of activity in Maynard's driveway. I saw three different vehicles there at separate times just yesterday."

"Say, Byron, when you raised cattle, how did you dispose of dead calves? When I passed by the dairy farm yesterday, I noticed someone was dragging a dead calf behind an ATV. An ugly scene at best, the tight noose around the small stretched out neck."

Byron laughed and said, "Losing calves was a problem. I used to dig a hole with the tractor bucket and bury them, sooner the better."

Eva set down a plate full of cookies on the table. "Have some...just baked them this morning."

"It's a deal," Tom happily responded.

Byron's fingers weren't far behind as Tom reached for the plate.

While they were sipping coffee and munching cookies, a light brown car turned off the county highway onto the township road. They watched as it went straight down the north branch and continued on beyond Maynard's house.

"That looks like Kyle Fredrickson's car," Eva said.

"We have been seeing a lot of that car the last couple of months," Byron added, "I hear the Iowa couple got a good deal on Maynard's house."

A pickup truck slowed and made the turn onto the township road. "There goes Pete Smilie," Tom said.

"What does Pete do for a living?" Eva asked. "He sure is up and down the road a lot with his pickup."

"Ah, I believe he works for a construction company. Have you noticed any strange vehicles on the township road since I was here last?"

Byron responded, "Not really. Usually it's the same ones day after day. Ah, I forget, there's this little red convertible once in awhile—but then, you may have an explanation for that." He chuckled as the last piece of cookie went into his mouth.

Tom laughed and said, "Yup, I guess everyone around here knows who belongs to that car. Well guys, I have work to do. See you later and thanks for the coffee and cookies."

"You are most welcome, Tom," said Eva.

Tom slowed the pickup just before entering his roadway. He glanced left and saw Kyle Fredrickson's car coming from the direction of Rocky Point.

After reaching his home, Tom parked the truck in the garage. He spent the afternoon mowing grass with the riding mower. Forgetting to carry the cell phone, Tom returned to the house to check for phone messages. He listened to Allan's voice announce an arrival at about six o'clock. Tom smiled when Allan suggested dinner out.

"I'm buying," Allan said before hanging up.

Tom clipped on the cell phone and it rang two minutes after six.

The Intrepid entered the driveway a couple of minutes later.

"Hi Allan. I saw a green Intrepid in New Dresden this morning, parked in front of the post office. Was that your car?"

"Yeah it was. I was checking into some people up and down Main Street. There sure is a lot of local talk about you and the murders."

"What kind of talk?"

"Well, everyone knows you worked for Maynard Cushing, on his computer. Rollie gets brought into the conversations, since he visited there almost every day."

"Geez, am I a suspect?"

Allan laughed and said, "Not in my mind, you're not."

Tom selected Mary Ann's as the choice of restaurant for dinner that evening. They drove in Allan's car and arrived shortly before 8:00 p.m. The sun was responsible for an amazing array of colors and effects in the sky and water. Before entering, they stood in the parking lot for a few minutes absorbing the beauty.

Mary Ann's wide smile greeted Tom and Allan when they entered. Tom introduced Allan to Mary Ann as his nephew and she took one of his hands into both of hers, a warm welcome indeed.

She led her two guests into the dining room. Tom was pleased when Mary Ann placed two menus down on a table next to a window, overlooking the lake. As a result, they were able to continue to view the colorful sky. The sun was just beginning to slip behind the tree line at Rocky Point when a waitress came by to take their order.

Allan's scotch and water and Tom's gin and tonic arrived in a couple of minutes. The waitress explained the specials and they put in their dinner order. Tom looked up and saw Sylvan and his wife enter. Mary Ann escorted the Tullabys to a table at the other end of the dining room. Sylvan smiled and nodded as they walked by.

Tom explained to Allan, "Sylvan lives in the house just down the shoreline from mine."

"Is he the guy with the sailboat?" Allan asked.

"Yup, and you have probably noticed his roadway entrance about half the distance from my roadway to Rocky Point."

"Oh yeah, I noticed that road. Just down from Pete's, right?"

The sun was totally down when their dinners arrived.

After they finished, Allan and Tom sauntered over to the bar area. They selected the only high, round table available, even though it hadn't been cleared. Two empty beer cans and three one-dollar bills.

The bartender lady came over, snatched up the money and the beer cans, wiped the table and asked, "What can I get for you two gentlemen?"

"Bette, this is Allan. He's a long-lost nephew from northern California. He's going to be around for a few days. I'm only going to have a cup of coffee. How about you, Allan?"

"A coffee is just fine."

"Nice to meet you. Two coffees it is."

When Bette returned, she asked Tom, "Have you heard the news?"

"What news?" he asked her.

"Harold and Mary Ann are selling the restaurant."

"First I've heard about that," Tom said. "When is this going to happen?"

"Not sure, but the rumors say the end of the month."

Tom felt badly, he would miss Mary Ann. She filled some of his voids, living alone and all that. Julie is going to be disappointed, he thought. Here he was, sitting at dinner with an FBI agent, worrying about a mini-change in his life.

The television above the bar was showing the Atlanta Braves-New York Mets game. Piazza, the catcher, just hammered a fastball into the left field seats. Rocker, who was on the mound for the Braves, didn't appear pleased. When the pitcher hit the next batter in the back with a blazing fast ball, both benches cleared. There was a lot of pushing and shoving before order was restored.

"Wow," Tom said to Allan. "Imagine getting hit in the head by one of those rockets, look at that mess."

Allan laughed and asked Tom, "Would it be all right if I brought my family to your home again this coming weekend?"

Without hesitating, Tom answered, "Yes, Allan, Julie will be coming again. She really enjoyed your family during their first visit."

The parking lot was dark when they left the restaurant. There were only seven or eight vehicles remaining. A car, alone and parked at the far end of the lot, attracted Allan's attention because the parking lights were on.

After getting behind the wheel of the Intrepid, Allan said, "Let's check this out,"

The Intrepid made a wide swing, headlights exposing a light-colored car. The person in the driver's seat was shielding his face with a hand, from the headlights. Barely visible was the shadow of another person in the front passenger seat. The Intrepid left the lot and headed out to the state highway. Allan drove in silence, made no mention of why he was interested in the car, Tom didn't ask.

While on Tom's roadway, Allan said, "I'm hoping to bring the investigation to a close soon. Hopefully, I can tell you more before long."

# 31

FRED HOOD WAS IN THE BACK ROOM. He knew the ding bell was going to ring. Mrs. Paulson had called earlier in the day. She was bringing in the Electrovac, twenty years old it was. That damn thing was never going to work for more than one day at a time.

Fred was worried. He was out in Big Lakes the other evening and saw that new FBI agent. There was no way he would have known, his guest pointed him out. The ding bell sounded.

"Hello, Mrs. Paulson, still having a problem?"

"Yes, I am. It worked fine for only half an hour and then it quit. Surely, I won't have to pay for it again."

"Just leave it here and I'll try to get it fixed."

"Well, you better. When will it be ready?"

"I have your phone number. I'll call."

Good riddance, Fred was thinking when the door closed. Fred walked over to the door and locked it. He had enough for one day. His car was parked in the rear of the building. Instead of using Main Street, he drove through an alley and headed north across the railroad tracks.

— —

MELISSA, ROBBY AND DEBBIE ARRIVED at the Hastings's residence the following Thursday. The happy family was reunited once again, and it was quite obvious the two children were glad to see their dad. Julie was not scheduled to visit until Saturday, so Tom decided to spend a couple of days in Brownstown. His guests needed some privacy. Tom had tickets for baseball games on Thursday afternoon and Friday night. He left Allan in charge of his home and headed for town.

The Thursday afternoon game was interrupted by rain showers twice. That evening after the game, Tom met some friends and they gathered at a bar where the ball players hang out. The team had won the game and the players were in a rather festive mood.

On Friday during the daylight hours, he did some personal shopping and called on two of his clients. In the evening the weather cooperated and the game was played without interruption. His team won again. Afterwards Tom was satisfied to return to his motel room and hit the sack.

Tom returned home mid-morning on Saturday, about two hours before Julie was to arrive. His guests were obviously having a delightful time. Fishing was slow, Robby reported, but they took advantage of the walking trails and the tennis court. Debbie just had to show Tom her new pet frog that she captured down by the dock. She thanked Tom for the use of his piano. Debbie was in the midst of taking lessons and took advantage of the opportunity to practice.

Julie arrived just before noon. She exchanged hugs with Robby and Debbie. Her initial attentions were demanded by Debbie, who narrated descriptions of exciting adventures experienced the last two days. Debbie and Julie were developing a strong buddy relationship.

That evening at dinner, Melissa invited Julie and Tom for a visit to their home in Monroe. Julie appeared to be very receptive to the idea, as was Tom. Wow, I could actually see the General Custer statue in person, thought Tom.

After dinner ended, everyone went for a walk in the woods. They were following the main trail and came to a fork. It led downward to a beaver pond—a large deer flashed across.

"It's Prancer," Tom said.

"Who's Prancer?" Robby asked.

"He's the king deer in this territory," Tom answered just as the deer bounded away.

"What's his territory?" Robby asked.

"I don't really know. That's a tough question, but I am sure it includes at least all of my fields and trails. Did you see the antlers?"

"They were big," Robby answered

At the beaver pond, Robby was fascinated with the tree cuttings and the small pile of wood chips surrounding the remaining stumps.

"Who dug out all that mud?" Robby asked as he observed the mud-banked water channels created by the beavers through the dense and tall grasses.

"The beavers did that to create waterways for floating logs and branches to their dens."

There was much sadness the next day when Melissa, Robby and Debbie prepared for their departure. Tom helped them load their luggage into the trunk of the Intrepid while Allan was busy engaging in conversation on the phone. It was a beautiful sunny morning. Allan continued on his phone while the rest of the group walked out to the tennis court. They observed a large bird, clumsily swooping up the middle of the greenway.

"That's a pileated woodpecker," Tom said.

The bird turned and flew north into the wooded area. When the group returned to the parking lot, Allan was standing next to the car.

He said, "Thanks for loading the luggage. I'm all done on the phone. Let's go."

Tom noticed that Allan appeared nervous while finalizing preparations for his family departure. Julie's eyes turned to tears as she and Tom watched the Burnside car disappear up the roadway.

Tom and Julie went for an extensive walk after their company left. Wonders of nature helped lift their spirits, especially when Julie spotted a strange looking bird in a tree near the beaver pond. Sitting on a stump, she researched the bird book.

"That was a cedar waxwing, Tom."

Tom admired Julie's curiosity of nature's creatures, especially her skill in identifying birds. When they emerged from the woods, Julie held up her hand.

"Look, Tom, its Prancer," she whispered.

Sliding fingers slowly across the chest to the bag hanging from his left shoulder, he fetched the camera. Tom was surprised the deer hadn't bolted by the time it became visible in the viewfinder. Distance is not a factor—hundred feet at the most, he thought.

Tom pressed the exposure button five times. He lowered the camera and Prancer remained. The front legs of the deer were planted firmly in the grass. The neck was extended and the ears were cocked, at attention. There wasn't a sound as two people and a deer stared at each other.

Finally, Prancer turned his head, showed off his antlers, and trotted off into the woods along the lake.

"That was amazing," said Julie.

"I have the feeling he was trying to tell me something. I've seen this before," Tom told Julie. "I think the big deer is upset because of the two moose that show up once in awhile."

"Moose, when was that?"

"Couple of weeks ago. I haven't seen them lately."

After their walk, they played two sets of tennis and spent the rest of the evening on the deck. They had wine in the hot tub and Tom grilled steaks.

The bay was quiet that evening. From the deck, they viewed the tall mast of Sylvan's sailboat. It remained dockside all evening. There was only one fishing boat in the water, directly across near the opposite shoreline.

The sun had just set and Julie said, "I sure like the smell of that cigar."

Tom continued to puff on the cigar and did not respond.

"Allan hasn't returned," added Julie.

Tom removed the cigar from between his lips and said, "Allan comes and goes as he needs. Returning at odd hours is common."

The next morning, as Julie was preparing for departure, Tom peaked out in the driveway. Feelings of alarm were generated when failing to see the green Intrepid. He checked out Allan's bedroom and noticed the bed hadn't been touched last night. Regardless of his serious concern, there was no mention of Allan missing to Julie. He didn't want her to worry.

Until now, Allan always called regarding any changes in plans. Tom was struggling with his thoughts, *something is wrong*. He hoped that Julie wouldn't notice that the green Intrepid was not in the driveway.

Tom and Julie had a light breakfast and some coffee before she departed in the sporty red convertible. Julie didn't mention the missing Allan, but Tom felt she was silently aware of his concern. He appreciated her not asking.

After Julie left, Tom hurried to the phone and called the sheriff's office. The lady dispatcher understood the urgency of Tom's call.

She said, "Hold on for a moment, Mr. Hastings, he'll be right with you."

"Paul, Allan didn't return last night. He drove his family to the airport in Brownstown and didn't come back to my house."

"What time was that about? Leaving from your home, I mean."

"Shortly before noon. I think the flight was scheduled for 2:30."

"Thanks for calling. I'll look into it. Hopefully, he got busy with something and forgot to call you."

# 32

SYLVAN TULLABY SAT ON THE DECK SMOKING A CIGARETTE. Casper was lying in a corner. He could hear the clatter of plates from Missy filling the dishwasher. She had prepared a great meal. He shuddered at the thought of ever losing her. Sylvan was waiting for the right time to tell her about getting fired. That snake of a Val Peterson stuck it to him for missing too many days. Missy's parents will just have to wait until he gets another job.

Sylvan was wondering why there wasn't as much fuss over Rollie Smith dying compared to Maynard Cushing—after all, they were both murders. That Hastings's place is like a police department, sheriff cars coming and going. The green car belongs to the FBI. Perhaps his girlfriend, the red convertible, is also an agent. Maybe Tom Hastings is an agent.

Missy walked out onto the deck and asked, "Did you like the dinner, honey?"

"Yeah, it was great. Save any bones for Casper?"

"They're in a plastic bag in the fridge."

"Okay. Say Missy, there's something I need to tell you. Here, have a chair."

"What, Sylvan, what?"

"I've quit my job."

"Oh Lord, when did this happen?"

"Last week."

"Why in the heavens did you do that? You know the money is needed. My parents...they have been asking."

"Yeah, I know. I've been talking to a manufacturing business in Cornwall. It looks promising."

"Sylvan, I wish you would have discussed it with me before you quit," Melissa said angrily as she closed the deck door.

He lit another cigarette, lifted the binoculars to his eyes, and focused on Tom Hastings's deck.

— —

AN ENTIRE DAY HAD PASSED and there wasn't a phone call or any other sign of Allan. It was already Wednesday morning. Allan disappeared on Monday. Deputy Johnson had stopped at the Hastings's home the previous day to discuss Allan's disappearance. Allan's family had arrived safely in Monroe, the deputy had talked to Melissa. She indicated Allan's intention was to return to the Hastings's home after leaving the airport.

With Allan missing, Tom sensed a feeling of vulnerability and began carrying his gun. On the way to New Dresden that morning, he stopped at the Smilie home. Pete was busy working on his tractor. Both hands were stained with grease and he looked a mess. Tom felt it was time to level with Pete.

"Hi, Pete. Need any help?"

"Yeah," he said. "A new tractor."

"Say, Pete, have you heard anything about my nephew who was staying with me?"

"Yeah, some people were talking about that in the hardware store a couple of days ago. I wasn't paying much attention, but I heard your name mentioned and a green car and a nephew from California."

In spite of agreeing to Allan's request for anonymity, because he was missing Tom decided to confide in Pete.

"Well, Pete, the guy was not my nephew. He was an FBI agent looking into the Maynard-Rollie thing."

"Geez, that's exciting."

"There's a new problem. Allan has been missing for a couple of days. His family stayed at my house the past weekend. After driving them to the airport, Allan didn't return. No one knows what's happened to him. The sheriff's department is out looking for him and so far not much luck."

Pete was excited. "Wait here," he said, "I'll be right back." He returned carrying his deer rifle.

"Geez, Pete, what do you plan on doing with that?"

"I'm going to keep the rifle handy just in case. Now that your friend is missing, the murders and all the other stuff going on...Lisa and I need some protection."

Pete and Tom walked out to his deer stand at the edge of the woods a short distance from the house. A lot of time and money was used for its construction. The stand overlooked a small field, a popular passageway and feeding area for deer. The stand was built to last, supported by four large posts, towering about eight feet above the ground.

"You know, Pete, your idea about being on your guard doesn't include just yourself. This morning I started carrying my automatic. We should both be extra alert until this whole mess gets cleared up. Strange vehicles on my roadway scare me. I would appreciate letting me know if you see any.

"You know what I drive. Julie, the red convertible, sometimes there's a sheriff's car, the meter people, Allan's green Intrepid...anything else could be a threat."

"Do you think the green car will return?" asked Pete.

"Pete, I'm afraid to even think about it."

"I'm working part time the next four weeks. During my free time I'll keep an eye on the roadway whenever possible," said a serious-faced Pete.

Tom followed Pete up the ladder. He was amazed with the expansive view of the field and the surrounding landscape, including a section of his roadway. Pete remained in the deer stand after Tom left. Tom's truck generated a massive dust cloud on the gravel road as he drove up the township road, lack of rain was obvious.

Tom noticed the dairy farm was almost as quiet as the cemetery on the way to New Dresden. As he approached the town, railway warning lights began blinking and the long arms came down as a long freight train rumbled slowly through town.

Ten minutes passed before the last boxcar jiggled through the intersection. The arms went up and he crossed the tracks followed by a long caravan of vehicles. Tom found a parking spot directly across from the grocery store.

He was hoping to see a green Intrepid amongst the vehicles parked on Main Street. Tom had a nagging, negative feeling about Allan's disappearance while paying for the *Star Tribune* at the grocery store.

Ellie asked him, "How is your nephew doing?"

"He went away for a few days."

Jerry the postmaster sported his usual smile when Tom entered the business room. Tom laid a package-too-large slip on the counter and Jerry began shuffling through a stack of packages lying on the floor.

"Here it is," he said.

"Thanks, sure a nice day out."

"I hear the FBI is investigating the murders," Jerry said.

"Yes, I guess they are. Hopefully, they will help get this whole thing solved soon. Have a nice day Jerry."

# 33

**K**YLE FREDRICKSON WAS STANDING IN THE DOORWAY of his office. The couple from Brownstown should have been here half an hour ago. He was watching for a Ford SUV—black. He didn't know how it happened, the Cushing house sale fell through. Linda Barr, I bet that witch has something to do with it, he thought.

Small problem, the FBI hanging around was his real worry. A guy came into his office last week. Even though the man showed a genuine interest in buying some property, Kyle suspected there was an ulterior motive. Typical FBI, he thought. Kyle was watching when the guy got into a green Chrysler parked around the corner from the grocery store.

That visit occurred last week, at the moment he was frustrated because the clients from Brownstown were not showing up. He saw Tom Hastings exit the post office. That's another problem, he thought. That Hastings guy is in bed with the sheriff's department, worse than that, the FBI. That green car spent a lot of time driving around that Cushing area. Recently, Kyle had learned the man in the Chrysler was staying at the Hastings's house.

— —

WEDNESDAY NIGHT, Tom got out of bed four times to look out the windows overlooking the driveway. There was no sign of the green Intrepid. After returning to the bed, each time he put his hand on the automatic lying on the small bed table.

The next morning, Tom slept late. He was exhausted by the lack of sleep and didn't awaken until after nine. On his way down the stairs, headed for the coffeepot, he paused to peer out the windows, still no sign of the green car.

Tom remembered to strap on the .32-automatic after getting dressed. Before heading for New Dresden, he unbuckled the gun belt and placed it into the glove compartment. The early sun had disappeared as low, dark clouds had moved into the area. Tom drove the pickup truck slowly up the roadway and onto the township road.

He was pleased when thinking about the threat of rain, particularly when looking into the side view mirror and seeing the huge cloud of dust.

Approaching New Dresden on the county highway, he noticed flashing lights in the vicinity of the public park. Tom reduced speed when nearing a cluster of vehicles parked on both sides of the road.

On the crowded highway ahead, he could see a highway patrolman directing traffic. A tow truck was blocking most of the northbound lane. Tom decided to pull in behind the last vehicle parked on his side of the road.

Tom sat in the truck for a couple of minutes attempting to gain understanding, what's going on here? He noticed a long cable attached to the rear of the tow truck, extended into the water. People were gathering into small clusters as near to the tow truck as they dared. By this time, traffic was moving very slow.

Joining one of the clusters, Tom asked, "What's happening?"

A guy wearing a baseball cap said, "There's a car in the lake."

A man standing nearby added, "A couple of guys out fishing this morning spotted a car down there."

Tom felt a weight drop into the pit of his stomach. Allan was missing, there was a car in the lake. At that moment, a diver bobbed to the surface. He was attempting to hook a cable to the vehicle in the water. The diver paused for a couple of minutes and submerged. A minute later, two divers came to the surface, one of them signaled the tow truck operator.

The cable reel on the tow truck began to move. As it slowly rotated, the cable tightened. Tom heard a gasp from someone standing close to him as a vehicle began to emerge from the lake.

"There it is," the person said.

As the water began to gush off the vehicle, Tom's stomach dropped to the pavement. The vehicle was a green colored car.

One of the people standing close to the water shouted, "There's someone in there."

It took a few minutes for the tow truck to drag the car up the steep slope. Tom wandered closer to the car and saw the Chrysler Intrepid emblem. That was enough for him and he walked back onto the highway.

A second state highway officer had arrived to assist with traffic. The lanes were blocked in both directions. Tom walked a few steps toward his pickup and stopped. He was trapped.

After the green car settled onto the highway, two sheriff's deputies approached the driver side door. One of them jerked on the handle but it didn't open. Noticing their failure, the tow truck operator reached into the box area just back of the cab and brought out a long metal bar. He joined the two deputies and began prying on the door.

There was a hush amongst the viewers gathered along the shoreline when the door sprung open and a rush of water escaped. One of the deputies began examining the body while the other put a cell phone to his ear. They made no attempt to remove the body from the car. Of all the officers and people witnessing this ordeal, likely only Tom Hastings knew who was in that car.

Ten minutes later, they succeeded in opening all the other doors. There was a pause in activity and the sound of a siren could be heard in the distance. In minutes, an ambulance was being escorted to the site by a sheriff's car. As the two vehicles slowed, Tom recognized the driver of the lead car, Deputy Johnson.

The ambulance parked in the middle of the road next to the green Intrepid. Two attendants in white uniforms jumped out and hurried to the place where the two deputies were standing, near the front seat of the Intrepid. One of them ducked in the car and began to probe the body. In moments, he stood and shook his head. A third member of the crew opened the back door of the ambulance and drew out a gurney. He was joined by one of the white clad attendants.

They snapped the wheel legs into position and rolled it to the green Intrepid. Carefully, they removed the body from the vehicle and placed it onto the gurney. One of the crewmates covered the body with a sheet. Tom was standing a few feet away from the ambulance when they slid the loaded gurney through the open rear doors.

The Patrolmen created a path for the ambulance driver, allowing it to turn around and head north. Tom was liberated from his trance when the siren was activated. He had been infused with fear and remorse while the gurney was being loaded into the ambulance.

The ambulance made its way up the county highway through a corridor established by the highway patrol. Deputy Johnson walked over to where Tom was standing.

His only words were, "I'll stop by."

After the ambulance was gone, the lanes were reopened and Tom continued on into New Dresden. His mind was in a daze while getting mail and buying a newspaper. As he was leaving the grocery store, the cash register lady called out.

"Mr. Hastings, you forgot to pay for the paper."

On the way back home, he slowed while passing the accident site, noticing that officers from the sheriff's department and the highway patrol were still present. Two of them were marking and measuring, another was making notations on a clipboard. Tom passed by the scene and proceeded homeward.

He was passing by the cemetery and his thoughts were with Melissa, Robby and Debbie. After arriving home he tried watching the market news on television but couldn't concentrate.

Half an hour later a sheriff's vehicle entered his driveway. Tom looked out and saw Deputy Johnson open the car door and step onto the driveway. The deputy's head was tilted down as he walked down the sidewalk, toward the front door. While watching the deputy, Tom knew for certain that Allan was the victim. Hastings and Deputy Johnson experienced an emotional moment while clasping hands after the deputy came through the door. Tom led the way onto the deck where they both sat down.

"Paul, it was Allan, wasn't it?" Tom said, holding his breath.

"Yes, it was. I'm in shock."

"Do you think it could have been an accident?"

"Hell no," said the deputy. "There's no way a trained person like Allan would accidentally drive into a lake."

Deputy Johnson looked up at Tom and added, "It's a little early to be jumping to conclusions, but I think we both know what happened. You can bet your bottom dollar that Ranforth guy had something to do with it. I'm going to get that bastard."

Once again Tom thought of Melissa, Robby and Debbie. "Who is going to notify his family?"

Paul said, "We have already notified the FBI headquarters in St. Paul, and they will take care of that distasteful chore."

The two men sat in silence for a few minutes and then Deputy Johnson said, "Tom, you will have to watch out for yourself more than ever. The sheriff's department doesn't have enough staff to give you and your neighbors perpetual protection. Patrolling your neighborhood daily is a possibility, I'll talk to my boss."

"Paul, how do you think the FBI office in St. Paul is going to react to losing Allan?"

"They are going to investigate and you can bet there will be some new people in your neighborhood. The FBI is likely going to expand its investigation to include the Smith murder. They'll send out the A-squad this trip, you can count on it.

"This man Ranforth will stop at nothing to protect his identity. Be very careful, Tom, and please give us a call if you notice any unusual activity in your neighborhood. Oh, I almost forgot, Allan's bedroom needs to be sealed."

The deputy returned to his car and brought back a roll of yellow tape. Tom led him to Allan's bedroom. Johnson glanced inside the room, locked the door, and placed three strips of tape over the door.

"Tom, please keep this door locked until you hear from either our technicians or the FBI. I'm positive they will be contacting you."

After Deputy Johnson left, Tom called Julie. There was a deafening silence at the other end of the phone. He could hear her sobbing.

"What about Melissa and the kids?" she cried. "Who is this monster?"

# 34

THE NEXT DAY TOM HASTINGS RECEIVED A SPECIAL PHONE CALL.

"Hello, are you Tom Hastings?"

"Yes, I am."

"I'm Brenda Mitchell from FBI headquarters in St. Paul. I've been in touch with the Big Lakes Sheriff Department. They tell me you're the person who owns the house where Agent Burnside was residing."

"Yes, that's true. What can I do for you?"

"Our office is sending two special agents to check out Agent Burnside's room. They will arrive in a gray Chevy Celebrity at approximately 4:00 p.m., today. Do you have any problem with that?"

"No, I don't. I will look forward to their visit."

"Fine. If you have any questions, feel free to call this number, 888-825-1000."

"There aren't any questions at the moment. I'll expect their visit at four."

"Thank you very much, Mr. Hastings."

Time seemed to crawl for Tom Hastings on that day. Feelings of tension and sorrow were overwhelming. He sat in the living room with his deer rifle leaning against the wall. At 3:45 that afternoon, the car described by the lady from the FBI pulled up in front of his house. Two men got out of the car and looked around for a couple of minutes before walking down the Hastings's front sidewalk. Tom heard the doorbell ring and with feelings of apprehension, turned the knob and opened the door.

The person nearest said, "I am Agent Anderson of the FBI. He turned towards the second man and said, "This is Agent Mikish. Are you Tom Hastings?"

"Yes, I am."

"Did someone from our office notify you that we were coming?"

"Yes, I was expecting you, Thanks for informing me in advance about the gray car."

"We're here to investigate the death of one of our agents, as you know, Allan Burnside. According to our information, he was residing at your home. Is that correct?"

"Yes, it is."

"Fine," said Agent Anderson. "We need your permission to enter your house and access Agent Burnside's room."

"I will be happy to give you that permission if you both show me identification."

Both agents reached inside their jacket pockets and brought out leather folders. Agent Anderson displayed first, flap open and badge exposed.

"Thank you Agent Anderson. How about you, sir?" Agent Mikish did the same.

"Okay. I'll show you to Allan's room."

Tom led them up the stairs and into his living room. He gestured toward the door, sealed with the police tape. They seemed pleased noticing the tape while advancing toward the bedroom door.

Carefully, they pealed the tape and placed it aside. Agent Mikish used a pointed instrument to release the lock. He opened the door and they entered the room. Tom remained standing outside the door.

In a few minutes Agent Mikish came out and said, "Nice place you have here."

He walked by Tom and headed out to the car. Through the window, Tom could see the agent reach into the back seat and remove a briefcase.

After Agent Mikish returned, he re-entered Allan's room. The two agents remained in the room for at least an hour, later they locked the door and replaced Deputy Johnson's tape.

Agent Anderson said, "We are finished for now, but you can expect a team of technicians tomorrow. After they are done, you can have your room back. Meanwhile, make certain no one, including yourself, enters the room."

They left a card with names and a phone number where they could be reached at any time.

After the agents left, Tom drove his pickup truck to Pete's house.

"Who belongs to the gray Celebrity?" Pete asked. "I was in the deer stand when it went by. The car scared me, so I grabbed my rifle and sneaked over to your place. I figured they were cops, but hung around for about half an hour, making sure."

"Thanks for checking it out, Pete. I wish there was some way I could signal you when things are okay. In this case, they were FBI agents checking out Allan's room. Tomorrow, you can expect to see the gray Celebrity again, plus there will be another vehicle."

"I'll be watching your roadway as usual. You can count on that."

"When expecting a strange vehicle, if possible, I'll let you know in advance."

Later that evening, Tom drove to Mary Ann's feeling the need for dinner and hopefully, some conversation. As he drove up the roadway, he noticed that Pete was in the deer stand. Tom waved and saw Pete raise the rifle over his head. What a great neighbor, Tom thought.

When Tom entered Mary Ann's, he could feel stares, all eyes in the room were watching him. He took a booth by the window and sat down. He began reading a business magazine. After completing page three, he couldn't remember a single thing he read. Tom glanced up and noticed at least three sets of eyes turn away.

Mary Ann came by and sat down opposite him. "Mercy, you are living an exciting life. Isn't it scary?"

"Yes, it's very scary."

Tom had a quiet dinner and hastened to get home before daylight ended.

Pete was no longer in his deer stand when Tom drove down his roadway. Sitting on the deck, he watched the blue water and blue sky turn into darkness. His thoughts were about Allan and his family, the loss of two neighbors and a friend. The home he loved so well was being threatened. Blue darkness was closing in around him.

# 35

ADJUSTING TO ALLAN BEING GONE WAS DIFFICULT for Tom, even though his guest had lived there for less than a month. He realized his feelings were miniscule compared to what Allan's family was going through. Tom missed not only Allan's companionship, but also the security from his presence. Sleep for Tom that night was sporadic at best.

Late next morning the phone rang.

"Good Morning, Mr. Hastings, this is Agent Mikish, How are you doing today?"

"Well, I didn't sleep too good. What's up?"

"Not surprising about your feelings...you've gone through a lot. The technicians we mentioned yesterday are arriving here today. Our objective is to get them over to your house by about 11:00. Hope that's okay."

"That's fine, Mr. Mikish, I'll be home."

Tom had just completed his session on the Internet when a white van pulled into his driveway. The van was followed by a gray Chevy that belonged to agents Anderson and Mikish. Tom opened the front door before they had a chance to ring the doorbell. Agent Anderson introduced the man and woman that arrived in the van. Tom escorted them to Allan's room.

Tom watched as they took down the tape, unlocked the door and entered. Each of them was carrying a large case. Tom decided to do his errands in town since the technicians work was going to take two or three hours. Agent Anderson was sitting in the living room and nodded when Tom announced his intentions.

While in New Dresden, Tom chose to avoid specific places where he would surely be questioned about Allan. As he unlocked his post office box, he heard a lady's voice.

"So you have the place where all the strange things are going on. I feel sorry for you. What is this world coming to, anyway?"

Tom guided the contents of the post office box into his hands and turned to see who had spoken.

He did not recognize the lady and responded by smiling and saying, "Have a nice day."

Tom looked through the grocery store window to make sure there wasn't a line at the checkout counter before he entered to pick up a newspaper. Ellie was kind enough not to make mention of the loss of his nephew.

When Tom returned home, the two FBI vehicles had not moved from his driveway. Agent Mikish was standing outside by the corner of Tom's house smoking a cigarette.

After parking his truck and approaching the house, the agent said, "They're almost finished."

Tom stood outside and visited with Mikish until the two technicians emerged a few minutes later. They had their arms laden with carrying cases and bags. Agent Anderson was carrying Allan's suitcase and a plastic bag. They loaded all the items into the van.

Just as they were ready to leave, Agent Anderson walked to where Tom was standing and said, "We're all finished with Allan's room. Thanks a lot for your cooperation. It makes our job a lot easier. Hopefully, you understand the reason we spent so much time in your house. Our goal is to find Agent Allan's killer. We will be working closely with your sheriff's department until the case is solved. Just remember, if you come up with any new useful information, please contact your Deputy Johnson."

Tom's feelings warmed toward the FBI agents. He responded, "I sure will. Nice meeting you."

The two vehicles turned around and drove up the roadway. Tom remained standing in the driveway and listened to the fading sound of tires on gravel. The incredulous stillness was interrupted by the shrill call of a blue jay.

Tom turned and slowly walked toward his house. Gone, he thought, they were all gone, Maynard and his computer, Rollie and his checkers, Allan and his family. Tom wandered the grounds for a few minutes. The tennis court was empty and quiet. Feelings of remorse occurred when he entered what had been Allan's bedroom.

The next day he received a surprise phone call from the director of the FBI branch office in St. Paul. As an expression of gratitude for his cooperation with their agents, the caller offered Julie and Tom accommodations to attend Allan's funeral in Monroe, Michigan.

He wasn't sure if this was normal FBI courtesy or perhaps there was another motive. Nevertheless, he called Julie, and after some discussion they decided to accept the offer. Tom was reluctant to leave his home unattended for two days but concern was alleviated by a call from Deputy Johnson.

"My boss has approved patrolling your roadway during your absence."

Two days later Julie and Tom flew out of Minneapolis/St. Paul Airport on their way to Monroe, Michigan. After they landed, Melissa and her sister Jane were there to meet them. The composure of Melissa during the hugs and greetings was impressive. Her loss had reached a level of acceptance. Melissa proudly explained that Robby and Debbie were dealing with the loss of their father rather well, thanks to the kindness of church counselors.

After Tom and Julie retrieved luggage, Melissa dropped them off at the hotel. They spent most of the evening relaxing in their room. The funeral service was scheduled for 10:00 the next morning.

Tom reserved a cab for the drive to the church. As most funerals, the atmosphere at the church was solemn and reserved. They noticed a number of men and women milling about the lawn, next to the steps leading up to the main part of the church.

"Must be FBI people," Julie said.

They entered the church and were seated just behind the reserved area. Tom could hear Julie sobbing softly and quietly as the procession made its way down the middle aisle.

The family led by Melissa, Robby and Debbie followed the coffin to the front part of the church. Tom was impressed with their courage and composure. As the coffin passed, a long line of FBI agents stood at attention, right hands at salute. They were all dressed in dark blue jackets and blue neckties. Tom and Julie were experiencing a very touching moment.

A former high school classmate of Allan's delivered the eulogy. It was a simple story about a quality young man that did everything right. The story ended with a simple statement, "My friend and classmate Allan died while in the line of duty."

After the service a long, slow-moving parade of limousines and cars made its way to the cemetery. Final respects were spoken at the gravesite by the local pastor, *dust to dust*. Tom experienced difficulty in saying goodbye to his new friend. Only one month, but Tom felt he had known Allan for a long period of time.

The most emotional moment came when the sound of a bugle penetrated the air. Tom was holding Julie's hand and he could feel her short, irregular jerks. He knew what she was doing. Tom kept his head down during the bugle taps. Tom's eyes were misty and he didn't dare look up. After the last note, they remained standing and Tom continued to look at the ground. Julie snuggled close and tight. He could feel her heart beating.

Tom and Julie joined many of the people who attended the funeral at the church hall, for a post-funeral lunch. An hour later their cab arrived and they took one last look at the church as the cab moved away from the curb.

On their way to the airport, Tom requested the cab driver to detour if needed and drive by the statue of the famous General Custer.

"No problem, just a few blocks out of the way."

"There it is," the driver said as he slowed the cab to allow them a good look.

Over one hundred years had passed since this brilliant young cavalry officer lost his life at the Little Bighorn in Montana.

Later that day Tom and Julie arrived at the airport in the Twin Cities. He spent the night in the Cities and returned home the next day. Tom called Pete when he got home.

Pete said, "The only vehicle that drove down your roadway was a sheriff's car. My plan was to walk the roadway down to your house, the sheriff's deputies may have given me a bad time, especially when carrying a rifle."

"Thanks a lot, Pete. I think the deputies will stop round-the- clock surveillance of my house now that I'm back home."

After unpacking, Tom checked the status and location of his weapons. The shotgun was in the bedroom closet. The rifle was in the closet by the front door. The holstered .32-automatic was in the drawer of the small table by the bed.

Tom called Deputy Johnson to announce his return from Monroe.

"Glad to hear you're back. The guys didn't see anything worth mentioning while patrolling your roadway and the house while you were gone. Well, not exactly. One of the deputies said he saw a guy out by the deer stand carrying a rifle. Fortunately, they were informed about your neighbor, beforehand."

"Leave it to Pete," Tom said. "He's out there watching."

"I talked to the two FBI agents who visited your house and cleaned out Allan's bedroom. They agreed that Allan's murder is related to the deaths of Maynard Cushing and Rollie Smith—also the missing Robert Ranforth".

"Ah, yes, Anderson and Mikish."

"I am disappointed Allan didn't have a chance to pass on his findings before going into the lake. It's important to keep in mind that Robert Ranforth was a professional CIA agent and therefore is trained in the skills of physical assault, just as are agents of the FBI."

Tom found it difficult to adjust to daily routines after returning from Monroe. However, later that morning he drove his pickup truck to New Dresden for mail and the newspaper. On the way, he noticed a rather chubby lady mowing a very large area of grass along the county highway. She was doing the ditch with a push mower. That should take off some pounds and I should consider that too, he thought.

Because Tom was gone for a couple of days, his post office box produced an armful of mail. He discarded most of it into the wastebasket, no end to junk mail, he thought. Leaving the post office, he heard the blast of a horn announcing the arrival of a freight train. He placed the mail in the truck and was walking down the sidewalk toward Stillman's Super Market when the train began rumbling through town.

A line of vehicles had formed on Main Street. Tom noticed that Sylvan's blue van was the last in line. He saw a man with a wide brimmed hat sitting in the passenger seat. The window was open and the man had his hand out, gesturing towards the tracks. His hat was pulled down low over his forehead so Tom couldn't see his face.

Tom stood and watched until the final railroad car passed. Continuing to lean against the hood of the truck, he waited, allowing the long line of vehicles to pass before leaving for home.

# 36

FRED HOOD SAW the ambulance leaving. He pulled over to the side of the road while it was being cleared of spectators. The wrecker truck towing the car was allowed to leave first. He watched Tom Hastings walk across the road and get into a pickup truck.

Fred was on his way to a meeting in Big Lakes. Though late, he didn't care. His mind was made up, a decision he hoped would never be necessary. Moving and starting over in a new location was mandatory, after what happened.

Driving north, he caught up with the wrecker even up with the cemetery. Too hilly here, couldn't pass. Glancing at his watch, he was now over half an hour late. He would wait, Fred thought—money talks. The terrain flattened out and he passed the wrecker—at last, clear road ahead. He glanced to his right, noticing the Maynard Cushing house before increasing speed.

— —

THE FUNERAL HAD EASED TOM HASTINGS'S TENSION. He was sitting on the deck enjoying a panatela cigar. The fishing boat cruising by his dock didn't get more than a glance. His eyes were watching two large birds swooping and circling over the tree line, opposite shoreline. Bald eagles, he thought, but they could be golden eagles or perhaps large ospreys.

Binoculars were inside—they were needed. There's one—a baldy. After glassing the bird for about a minute, he put the glasses down, manually searching for the second bird.

Just as it came into view, Tom was startled by an explosive sound, accompanied by a zing and pieces of glass falling to the floor behind him. Dropping down on all fours, he scurried behind the hot tub. His mind was racing and confused—that was a gunshot!

There was no further sound, as he lay on the deck for a few moments, except for the clang of a latent piece of glass falling to the floor. The sound of a boat motor running at full throttle broke the silence. Tom elevated to a crouched position from behind the hot tub, and peaked over the top. He saw the rear end of a boat retreating towards the mouth of the bay. After it rounded the bend, he turned to look at the window. Only jagged edges of glass remained.

Reentering the house, he saw glass scattered all over the floor. Looking through the shattered window, he saw the pontoon boat bobbing. Only about a minute had passed since the shot.

Hurrying to the front closet, he brought out the deer rifle. Checking the breach, he made sure there were shells in the gun. Before going back on the deck, he jacked a shell into the barrel and secured the safety. Tom became watchman over the bay for a few minutes, rifle cradled in his arms.

Convinced no further threat remained, he returned inside and dialed the sheriff's office. Deputy Johnson was not available.

His backup said, "Okay, don't mess with anything and I'll get someone out to your house right away."

In about half an hour, Tom heard the sound of a vehicle enter the driveway. Looking out the window, he was relieved to see a sheriff's car. Two uniformed deputies emerged from the car and came down the sidewalk.

"Hello. You're Tom Hastings, I assume. You called about a shooting. Are you all right?"

"Yes, I am, thanks for coming over so quick."

"I'm Deputy Larson and this is Deputy Weismann. What happened out here?"

"I was lounging on the deck watching a couple of eagles when this fishing boat came by. I heard this noise and the window behind me shattered. It had to be a rifle shot."

"Do you think it came from the boat?" asked Larson.

"I don't know for sure, but assume it did. The boat left at high speed right after the shot. No one else was around."

"Which direction did it go?" asked Weismann.

"Towards the open part of the bay."

Deputy Larson began searching the far wall near the computer for a bullet hole.

"I think I found it," he said.

He unsnapped a small case attached to his belt, brought out a small pointed instrument and began prying in the oak window frame.

"Ahah, here it is."

The deputy held up a small piece of lead between his fingers. His physical similarity to a sitcom character was uncanny, Tom thought. The sitcom was about a sheriff and his bungling deputy, in a small town—name was *Barney*. The bullet had missed the computer screen by only a few inches.

"Looks like a .30-06," said Larson.

He handed the bullet to Weismann who held it up to the light.

"Yup, I think you're right, a deer rifle."

The sound of another vehicle pulling up in the driveway drew Tom's attention. Deputy Johnson got out and hurried down the sidewalk. Larson opened the door and the deputy came to a stop when spotting the broken glass.

"Anybody hurt? Are you okay, Tom?" he asked.

"Yeah, I'm fine. Scared as hell though."

"What happened?"

"Someone took a shot at him from a boat, went through the window and hit the wall over there," answered Deputy Larson.

"Where were you, Tom?"

"I was standing on the deck watching a pair of bald eagles."

Deputy Larson said, "Here's the bullet, Paul, looks like a .30-06."

Deputy Johnson examined the bullet and said, "I think you're right, Arlin. Where did you find it?"

"Right over there next to the computer, in the window frame."

"This is lucky. Not only did it miss Tom, but also the computer by inches. Let's get some pictures first...then help Tom with the window."

He followed Tom out into the garage. They brought back a metal garbage can, big pieces of cardboard and a roll of duct tape. After Deputy Weismann finished the photography, the deputies assisted Tom Hastings in picking up the broken glass and securing the cardboard over the window.

"We've got to get going," Larson said.

After Larson and Weismann left, Deputy Johnson remained. He and Tom sat down at the dining room table.

"Let's go over this thing again," the deputy said.

"Okay. I was on the deck viewing a couple of eagles with my binoculars when I heard this noise...sounded like a gunshot...then broken glass. I wasn't sure what was happening but ducked behind the hot tub. I heard a boat motor. When I peaked up over the tub, I could see the back end of a boat leaving the bay...going wide open. The shot must have come from the boat."

Deputy Johnson spent a few minutes writing Tom's explanation on a notepad. He snapped the small folder shut and placed it into a breast pocket.

"I wonder if there's any chance the shot could have come from the opposite shoreline?"

The deputy walked out on the deck, leaned on the rail, and gazed out over the bay.

"I think you have it right...the opposite shoreline is a little too far away. Since the boat left right after the shot, it must have come from there. How many places are there on this lake where you can launch a boat?"

"Just two that I know of. The public boat access, just off the township road, and a small private one across the bay, not far from here."

"We'll check out the two landings and talk to the neighbors. Someone may have been around and seen something. I'm just glad the shot missed. You're lucky. I've never fired a gun from a boat...wouldn't be too steady."

The deputy gazed eastward and said, "Tom, would you be up to calling the office twice a day? If so, I have a plan."

"Yeah, what's that?"

"I want you to call my phone number each day at ten in the morning and at four in the afternoon...leave a message. If we don't hear from you, I'll send someone over."

Tom thought for a moment, "Yes, I can do that."

"You'll be allowed a half-hour leeway on those calls."

The deputy and Tom walked out to the driveway. Tom was carrying the empty window frame.

"I'm glad it was the window and not the French door," he told the deputy. "I'd like to thank you and the other deputies for coming out."

"That's our job, Tom."

Deputy Johnson got in his car, turned it around, and left. Tom followed in his pickup truck. The deputy's car turned right on the county highway and Tom headed for New Dresden.

— —

"WHAT YA' GOT THERE?" asked Matt.

"Broken window, can you fix it soon?"

"Hmm, special dual-pane glass. Shouldn't be a problem. Tomorrow be okay?"

"Sure, thanks, I'll be in late morning."

Arriving back home, Tom spent the rest of the day patrolling, automatic strapped to the waist. He was carrying the deer rifle. Possibilities of being attacked again were high. Paranoia had the lead. He stayed away from cleared areas—opting to remain close to a tree or the corner of a building.

When darkness came, he kept the house lights off and remained on nervous alert.

Next day, Deputy Johnson phoned at ten in the morning.

"I've got some news, Tom. Larson and Weismann found an abandoned fishing boat pulled up on shore at the private landing.

The one you mentioned. There wasn't anyone at home in the house next to the landing...no witnesses."

"The people who own the house live in California, I heard," added Tom.

"The boat is registered to a man who lives about half a mile down the shoreline. Both him and his wife were at work when the boat was taken from their dock," the deputy continued.

"Did Larson and your other guy, ah, Weismann, talk to the neighbors?"

"Yes, no one saw the boat being taken. The people who own the empty house have been contacted. They're still in California and have not been here since spring. You'll be seeing them sometime later this summer."

"So, I'm the only one who saw the shooter and I wasn't paying any attention when the boat cruised by."

"The boat and motor are being checked out in the county garage. Maybe the shooter dropped something."

"Whoever fired the shot must have had a good idea of the comings and goings of the residents along this shoreline," Tom added.

"Yes, that makes sense."

"I'll call about 4:00," said Tom.

"Okay."

The phone rang again after Tom hung up.

Pete called and said, "I heard about the shot."

"Would you come over, Pete?"

"Okay. I'll be right there."

After Pete arrived, they went out on the deck and Tom pointed toward an area in the bay."

"Over there, about a hundred yards from the dock."

"Good thing the guy was a lousy shot," Pete remarked "You're lucky it wasn't me doing the shooting."

"Pete, surely you jest. I'm at war. Someone is out to get me or, at the least, scare the hell out of me."

"Yeah, I was just kidding," answered Pete.

"Would you like to see my deer rifle?" asked Tom.

"Sure, let's have a look."

Pete remained on the deck while Tom fetched his deer rifle from the front closet. After returning, he held the rifle up, in both hands, for Pete to see.

"That's a real classic."

"It hasn't been fired for about ten years, but it's in great shape. No rust anywhere. Look," Tom said, working the bolt and action.

"That's real smooth," said Pete.

Nostalgic memories passed through Tom's mind about his deer hunting days. He purchased the Model 270 Winchester after graduating from college, a rifle that was a veteran of many deer hunting seasons.

He rubbed his fingers along one side of the stalk that had burn marks. They happened during a tent fire in Canada many years ago, while hunting with his older brother. Tom could visualize the flames when the blankets ignited. He was attempting to light a propane heater—some of the fuel spilled. The rifle was lying on the blankets.

They got the fire out in time to save the tent and gear. As years went by, the charred rifle stalk served as a reminder of the good times he had with his brother. His brother died of cancer eighteen years ago.

# 37

**PETE WAS FASCINATED WITH TOM'S STORY.** He showed Tom his rifle—a bolt action .30-06.

"Do you need a ride home?" asked Tom.

"No, I'll walk."

"Thanks for coming over."

"Anytime."

Pete left Tom's home and walked home. When Tom drove up his roadway headed for town, the deer stand was empty. After picking up the mail and buying a newspaper at Stillman's Super Market, he walked across the street to the Borders Café. Tom was glad to see Henry sitting alone at a corner table. Henry looked up when Tom approached. He motioned for him to have a seat.

The conversation began with the local weather but eventually drifted to Maynard.

"Have you ever met Maynard's son Norm?" asked Henry.

"No, I haven't."

"Norm said his dad listed the house for sale about a month before he died."

"Boy, that's sure news to me. Maynard had never mentioned putting his house up for sale when I was there."

Henry continued, "At one time, Maynard owned the property across the road. He sold it to his son, who in turn sold it to a group of investors. They had it platted into about twenty lots. I heard Norm held onto a share. You've probably noticed the old house that still stands on the lot nearest the public access. Norm lived in the house for a few years until he moved to an apartment in Big Lakes."

"Yeah, I've noticed the house. It sure looks abandoned, but someone is keeping the grass mowed and tilling the big garden."

Henry was born and raised in the New Dresden community. He was accepted as an authority on local history. Henry wrote a weekly article in the local newspaper.

"Did you hear you are going to have full-time neighbors?" asked Henry.

"No, I didn't. What's that all about?"

"The California people who own the house across from you are both retiring and they plan on moving this fall. I went to school with the lady. Well, it's time to get back to work."

Henry scooped up his slip and headed for the checkout counter. After paying his bill, he returned to the table and dropped off some change.

"See you later," he said.

As Henry was ambling to the door, Kyle Fredrickson entered and took a booth across the room in the smoking section. When Tom got up from the table and approached the checkout counter, he glanced and noticed that Kyle Fredrickson was watching him.

As Tom turned to leave, he noticed Fred Hood was sitting by himself in the adjoining booth—head lowered. He didn't look up.

Two booths down, head buried in a newspaper, sat Sylvan, Tom's neighbor.

One of the waitresses entered the kitchen. "The special for Santa Claus," she told the cook.

Outside, Tom walked to his pickup truck. Before easing out of his parking spot, he checked the glove compartment to make sure the .32-automatic was in place.

— —

HE SNUBBED OUT ANOTHER CIGARETTE and took a sip of coffee. Without turning his head, he could see Henry and Tom Hastings sitting at the corner table. Thoughts of anger—how could Vince miss a target like that? He had it all set, scouted the bay for weeks, then the fool misses.

Vince was a thorn. What choice did he have? The slime knew everything. Once the job was done, his debt would be paid. Vince would disappear. Out of the corner of his eye, he was watching the two in the corner. Henry rose from the chair, reached in his jacket pocket and dropped some change on the table, a quarter escaped and rolled to a stop near the edge. Hastings remained, reading a newspaper. Henry was out the door. Hastings followed a few minutes later. They're both gone. I can relax, he thought.

# 38

TOM HASTINGS WAS CROSSING THE RAILROAD TRACKS in his pickup. His thoughts focused on the private boat landing, the site where the sheriff's deputies found the abandoned fishing boat. There weren't any doubts about the boat, its use during the shooting.

After driving past the lake, he stayed on the state highway instead of turning left toward home.

The road leading down to the landing exited three miles beyond the county-state intersection. An abundance of tall grass between the two dirt tracks hinted that the road was used very little. The tracks ended near the edge of the water on a hard-based, sandy point.

Short of the landing, the tall grass showed evidence that vehicles had parked there.

Before walking down to the water, Tom strapped on the gun belt. In the wet sand, he could see the markings where the fishing boat had been pulled out of the water.

Looking across the bay, he saw Sylvan's house and dock. His house couldn't be seen from this location because of a bend in the bay. Sylvan's dock was long, its six sections projecting into the water. The sailboat was tied to the side of the dock, nearest Tom's place. Large white bumper guards protected the rails of the boat from getting bruised. Impressive was the mast that loomed high over the cabin. The horizontal piece near the top reminded Tom of a Christian cross. A fishing boat was tied to the other side of the dock.

Sylvan's house was two-story with a large wooden deck extending from the upper level. An outdoor stairway led down from the deck to the lower level and the dock. His lakeside landscape was very similar to the Hastings's, except for a greater number of trees on the slope between the house and dock.

The slope of the opposite shore, where Tom was standing, was not as extreme. As per Sylvan's landscape, a large number of trees reduced the view from the lake.

Walking back to his pickup truck, Tom wandered into the grassy parking area. Looking down into the trampled grass, he spotted the remains of a cigarette. As Tom stooped to pick it up, he wondered if either of the deputies smoked.

He picked up the butt and held it up close to his eyes. There were no markings. The butt was fresh white, burned down almost to the filter. Tom placed it into his shirt pocket. Further searching in the tall grass uncovered a second one, identical to the original, he thought. Tom was getting excited. If neither of the sheriff's deputies smoked, the cigarette discoveries could be important.

He looked back to the place where he found the first one—about thirty feet distance. Tom visualized a man pacing around and smoking, waiting, enough time for two cigarettes. Was he waiting for an accomplice? Tom didn't smoke cigarettes but he estimated the time needed to smoke two. Was Ranforth standing right here when the shot was fired? Feelings of fear, Tom reached down with his right hand and clasped the holster.

Beyond the grassy parking area was a dense, brushy area separating the landing from a green lawn. The lawn belonged to the empty house owned by the people from California. Henry talked about them at the Borders Café. Cautiously, Tom worked his way through the brush until reaching the edge of the recently-mowed grass. Looking through a stand of trees, across the bay he could see his own dock and part of the house. The lack of trees on his slope allowed anyone on the lake to plainly see his deck.

Working his way back through the brush to the grassy parking lot, he spotted a third discarded cigarette. It was lying at the base of a thorny bush. Careful not to get scratched, he successfully retrieved the butt. Comparing it to the first two, they all looked alike.

Tom remembered Henry talking about the private landing property. A couple from Big Lakes owned it and intended to build a retirement home on the site. Very few boaters were using the private landing because the DNR had greatly improved the public boat access on the main part of the lake.

He looked to the east. Around the bend were several homes. His attacker could have parked in the grass, walked over there and taken a boat. After the shot, he could have come ashore here and driven off. The sheriff's department needs to know about the cigarette butts.

# 39

TOM PLACED THE BELT AND HOLSTER into the glove compartment. He turned around the pickup and headed back out to the state highway. Turning right at the fork, he drove up the county highway. He was forced to slow, a tractor and wagon were chugging along, blocking the road.

Vehicles accumulated behind him as the tractor continued up the northbound lane of the county highway. The driver of the tractor didn't seem to pay any attention to the long line of vehicles. Tom heard a horn honk—the red sports car right behind was getting impatient. Too risky to pass, Tom thought.

To his amazement, the red sports car crossed the yellow line and scooted by the pickup and tractor. Tom held his breath, hoping no one was approaching from the other side of the hill. Soon as the red sports car dipped in ahead of the tractor, a milk truck appeared at the crest of the hill, close call.

The tractor turned off at the farmyard just beyond the peak of the hill. The red sports car was no longer visible when Tom picked up speed and continued up the highway.

Tom slowed as he approached the turnoff onto the township road. He saw Bill from South Shore Resort perched on his tractor, mowing the roadside. Tom pulled the pickup truck over onto a farm field approach. He parked and walked down into the ditch.

Bill waved and pushed in the clutch on the tractor mower as Tom approached on foot. He lit a cigarette after getting off.

"Craps," Bill said. "I hear someone took a shot at you from a boat."

"Bill, I hope it wasn't you or Mary getting ready for hunting season," Tom joked.

Bill laughed and said, "No, it wasn't, but you might be interested in this. On the same day as your shooting, a stranger stopped by and asked about renting a boat. He was a small, skinny guy and driving a light blue car."

"Wow, Bill, would you recognize him if you saw him again?"

"Yeah, I think so. The voice, I would remember it."

"I don't suppose you noticed the license plates, the state?"

"No, darn, I was busy at the time and told him we don't rent boats. I didn't even notice which way he went after I talked to him. You know the hassle...adjusting the deck height on a small riding mower...frustrating."

"Bill, I think the sheriff would be interested in your story. Do you mind if I mention it? I'm going over there today."

"No, that would be fine. Tell them to stop by if they want to hear it from me."

"Thanks, Bill, I will."

" I suppose you've heard about the fire at Mary Ann's?" asked Bill.

"Yeah, The flames could be seen from my deck."

"Well, you may also have heard that the restaurant is for sale."

"Yeah, I heard something about that, too."

"This may sound crazy, but Mary and I are thinking about buying Mary Ann's. Business has been good here this summer. A restaurant might be less work than this. Of course, we would have to sell this place first."

"I bet you could get a darn good price for your resort."

"I sure think so. The selling price for Mary Ann's is reasonable, according to Kyle at the realty office. First this would have to sell."

"Knowing you and Mary, you'd run a good place. Besides, you both like challenges."

"Well, I don't know about that, but if we pull it off, it would mean building a new house. Mary would kill for a new one. Kyle told us that he has showed Mary Ann's to only one other buyer, so far. No offers yet—a little more time and a lower number, perhaps.

"Kyle has offered arranging temporary financing until the resort sold. Mary didn't like the idea of having two places, even for a short period of time."

"Good luck with whatever you decide. I suppose you know by now about the couple and the black car that stayed at your place. They were with the FBI."

Bill laughed and said, "Ever since that deal, record keeping in the office has improved—Mary and I are more alert. Only last week we rented a cabin to an Ohio couple. They weren't using the beach or dock facilities. Just like the other couple, they either spent their time in the cabin or on the road. Looked okay to me, but Mary thought they were CIA agents. At least they didn't drive a black car."

"Did you see a red sports car go by just before I came?"

"Yes, I sure did. Some crazy guy going about hundred miles- an-hour, he almost rear-ended one of our renters after they turned onto the highway. I wish I could have gotten the license number."

"He passed me and a tractor just in front of the big hill. I held my breath on that one."

"Mary and I really get ticked at vehicles going by our driveway like rocket ships. The forty-mile-per-hour speed zone sign doesn't seem to help. Some day one of those lunatics is going to kill someone."

"Well, Tom, I need to get back to work."

Bill started up the tractor mower and Tom returned to his pickup truck.

Tom was in a detective mode. He had already recovered three clues from the shooting site. Just now he learned a stranger asked to rent a boat at South Shores the day he was shot at. After leaving Bill, he drove by Maynard's house.

After passing by the house and following the long curve, he noticed two cars parked by the side of the road, both unoccupied. Tom slowed to get a good look. One was a gray Grand Am Pontiac, the other a light brown Toyota Camry. He stopped in the middle of the road and noticed both vehicles had Minnesota plates.

Tom removed the automatic from the glove compartment and placed it into his jacket pocket. He got out of the pickup, looked in all directions seeing no one. Returning to the pickup, he retrieved a pen. On the back of his vehicle registration card, he wrote the license plate numbers.

The brown Toyota looked like the car driven by Kyle Fredrickson of Kyle's Realty, he thought after getting back in the truck and continuing up the road.

After reaching the south branch of the township road at Rocky Point, he turned right. The pickup slowed when passing by Sylvan's roadway, half way between the point and Pete's.

The deer stand was empty as he drove down his roadway. Tom was expecting Julie the upcoming weekend. He wondered whether to tell her about the shot.

Perhaps not, at least at this time—news of the shooting might frighten her. On the other hand, Julie was the type of person who thrived on adventure and danger.

After entering his house, he dialed Deputy Johnson's number. The deputy wasn't in. Tom left a message with the deputy's voice mail. He mentioned finding the cigarette butts and Bill's story about the man looking for a boat.

Checking in on the Internet did not help his mood. The markets were all down. He wasn't happy with the declining prices of his equity holdings. After signing off the Internet, he noticed two boats directly across the bay. Using binoculars, three people were observed in one of the boats and two in the other. They all appeared to be fishing.

A noisy jet ski violated the peaceful serenity of the bay. It came into view and roared by his dock. A blue heron hurriedly took to wings, two loons escaped by diving. It made a sharp turn as it approached the closed end of the bay and roared back, not far from the two fishing boats. Tom could see the displeasure by a couple of the people fishing.

Peace and quiet returned to the bay after the jet ski left the area. Tom remembered reading about the laws passed to control jet ski usage. He was proud of the high majority of jet ski drivers that respect the laws and regulations. He didn't have much respect for the aggressive few that violated them. Enforcement of personal watercraft laws was difficult because the sheriff's department and the Department of Natural Resources didn't have enough people.

Tom put the binoculars down on the table and checked the markets again—numbers were worse. A rally was needed.

At dusk, the sound of a barking dog drew him out to the deck. He noticed lights in the vacant house across the bay, hoping the owners had arrived for their summer visit. Tom remembered they arrived about the same time last year.

The lights are a welcome sight. Their presence added to my security—the longer they stayed the better, he thought. Tom remembered Henry mentioning these people during their conversations at the Borders Café.

Henry explained the lady was a former high school classmate. Tom promised himself to meet his new neighbors. Within an hour, dense fog reduced visibility across the bay. In a matter of minutes, he could no longer see beyond fifty feet into the bay. The dog had stopped barking.

After double-checking the door locks, he watched television while lying in darkness on the sectional in the den. The .32- automatic lay on the table next to where his head was propped on a pillow.

# 40

THE WEATHER REMAINED CLOUDY AND FOGGY for the remainder of the week, including daybreak on Friday. Mid-morning, after leaving his 10:00 a.m. message with Deputy Johnson's voice mail, Tom drove his truck into New Dresden. As he drove by the dairy farm, two ATV were being used to direct a Holstein cow through a grassy field and toward the farmyard. The cow disappeared as it entered the underpass beneath the county highway. It reappeared on the other side but was soon lost in the fog as it galloped towards the barn area.

Arriving in New Dresden and parking on Main Street, he got the mail and walked to Stillman's.

Tom was thinking about Julie's visit later that afternoon. She was planning on spending the weekend—groceries were needed.

Ellie punched his grocery items into the cash register and handed him a pen to use for writing a check.

"Was the highway foggy? I hear it's going to clear off later today."

"I'm glad to hear that. A friend from the Cities is driving up this afternoon."

"You've had an accident at your house, people are saying. Is it true your window was broken by a rifle shot?"

"Yeah, it's true. What have you heard?"

"Oh, not much. Just someone, a few people, mentioned it this morning."

Tom finished writing a check and left the grocery. Not surprising, the shooting news was all over town, the broken window at the hardware store—everybody knows.

He carried the grocery bags up the sidewalk of Main Street and deposited them in the rear of his truck topper. After closing the flip-up door, he walked across the street to the Borders Café.

After pulling the door open, Tom saw Henry sitting at his usual table. His back was to the door and a newspaper was lying folded next to his plate. Tom walked to the table, Henry looked up and gestured for him to sit. The start to the conversation was about Tom's neighbors across the bay.

Henry said, "I hear they moved in yesterday. As I probably told you before, Betsy, the lady of the house, and I went to school together. She retired from nursing a couple of years ago. Archie, her husband, is an engineer and will be retired by this time next year. You'll be seeing remodeling activity in the future. We expect to do some extensive work there next spring."

"What's new in the paper?" Tom asked.

"Oh, not much, the usual stuff."

After a few minutes of small talk, Henry left some change and left.

Tom finished lunch, paid his bill, added to the change and returned to his pickup truck. The slip on the seat contained one item—filter bags. He started the truck, drove around the corner and parked next to Fred's Vacuum Cleaner Shop.

Fred Hood started the business a few years ago, taking advantage of the availability of an abandoned fire hall. The display room was dotted with all sorts of new and used vacuum cleaners. Interesting and practical accessories filled the shoulder-high display cabinets in the center.

The service room in the rear wasn't as neat but it was the core of his business. Fred had a reputation for repairing any brand. He was behind the counter when Tom Hastings entered. Looking up, Fred waited for his customer to speak.

"Hi, Fred, I need some vacuum filter bags."

"What model vacuum do you have?"

Tom reached in his breast pocket and handed Fred a slip of paper. Fred didn't say a word as he grabbed the slip and passed through the door into the back room. He emerged moments later with a packet of filters.

"These will work."

Fred used a ballpoint to fill out a purchase slip. He handed it to Tom who had his checkbook ready.

"How's business, Fred?"

"Can't complain. I have all the business I need. Sometimes I wonder if it's worth the effort. People just keep calling. One would think vacuum cleaners are manufactured for the purpose of failing."

"Lots of carpets out there, Fred."

He was a quiet person and didn't spend much time visiting with customers. After leaving Fred's Vacuum Cleaner Shop, Tom was careful in manipulating his truck out of a tight parking slot. He noticed Sylvan and his wife emerge from Hector's bar down at the end of Main Street. Both were smoking cigarettes—Tom wondered what brand they smoked. Focusing back on the road, Tom drove the pickup toward home to prepare for Julie's arrival.

The answering machine was beeping when Tom entered the house. The message was from Deputy Johnson. Something about new information on Allan's murder and the sniper shot.

Tom returned his call immediately.

"I'm only a few miles down the road and should get to your house in about fifteen minutes," said the deputy.

Tom was working at his computer when Deputy Johnson's car appeared in the driveway.

He met the deputy at the front door. They sat at the dining room table.

"Well, it's conclusive," the deputy said. "Allan's death was not an accident. It was murder."

Tom wasn't really surprised or shocked by what the deputy said about Allan—his mind was on *Melissa, the children, Allan, the great visits*.

Deputy Johnson continued, "The autopsy showed Allan was unconscious when the car left the road and plunged into the lake. There were bruises and marks on his head consistent with wounds caused by the impact of a hard object."

"Did you guys find the weapon?"

"No, we didn't. Likely it was a metal pipe or some type of club."

"Was the gear lever in neutral?"

"No, it was in drive and there weren't any skid marks. The seat belt wasn't fastened. It looks like a clear case of being pushed into the lake. Drowning was the cause of death on the autopsy report."

"You know, Paul, I would rather not hear any more about what happened to Allan."

"Sorry, I'll stop on that subject. Would you like to hear what I have on the shooting?"

"Sure, go ahead."

"A group of school kids were picking up litter along the state highway, six miles east of the landing. They found a deer rifle in the ditch. It's been checked out. Without any doubt, it was the rifle used to fire the .30-06 caliber bullet pried from your window frame."

"Were there any fingerprints on the rifle?"

"No, but get this, we traced the serial number and it belongs to Harold Kraft. Yes, the same person who owns Mary Ann's."

"I imagine you checked that out."

"Yes, sure did. Mr. Kraft said the rifle was missing since the night of the fire."

"Leslie Richards, the tent vagrant, has also been questioned about the rifle. He's the one in jail awaiting trial for arson. I questioned him myself. He denied knowing anything, no memory of a rifle...almost believable," said the deputy as he chuckled.

"So, the boat is in our hands, so is the rifle. Next, we need to catch the culprit who goes around shooting at people."

"Did you find anything in the boat?"

"Yes, we sure did, some odds and ends. There was a short piece of rope, two beer bottle caps, two yellow twisters and some denim threads.

"The owner of the boat wasn't sure if the items were there when he last used the boat. The denim threads were caught in a small splinter on the rear bench, right about where the motor operator would be sitting. The denim was analyzed and it was conventional material sold at most discount clothing stores. Not much to go on there."

"Paul, I'm not sure if you are going to like this. I found three fresh cigarette butts at the private landing yesterday. They all seem to be alike. Do the deputies that found the boat smoke?"

"Let's see, that would be Larson and Weismann. I don't believe either smokes, but don't know for certain. I'll find out."

Tom opened a cabinet drawer and removed a sealed plastic bag containing the cigarette butts.

"Here, you better take these."

"Hey, nice job, Tom. I'll check this out with Larson and Weismann. These could be very important. Meanwhile, I better get going."

"Thanks for coming, Paul, and sharing all the information. Since it's getting close to four o'clock, I'll not call your office until ten tomorrow morning."

Deputy Johnson carried the plastic bag to his car. He waved after he turned his car around and drove down the driveway. If neither of the deputies smoked, they might be embarrassed for not finding the cigarette butts.

Tom continued to be concerned about the fog. Even though it had cleared some, visibility was still limited. He assumed Julie was on her way. Much to his relief, Julie called from her cell phone an hour after the deputy left.

"Hi, Tom, I'm only about ten minutes away. The fog isn't too bad out this way."

After arriving, she parked the red convertible in Tom's garage. He helped her with luggage. She was having a tough time coping with the death of Allan and the effect it must be having on Melissa and the kids.

Playing tennis helped get the tragedy off her mind. Julie's tennis game was getting stronger each visit. In the second set, she rallied to make it close—lost only four-six. After tennis, they spent time relaxing in the hot tub. Tom kept glancing at the bay and watching for boats. To his relief, there weren't any in the bay that evening. Julie didn't notice the rifle covered by a towel next to the tub.

"I'd like to take you to Mary Ann's for dinner," Tom said.

"Sounds great," she responded.

Tom was concerned that Julie, even though courageous and an adventure seeker, would have a problem with him carrying a gun. He got cleaned up and dressed hurriedly, sooner than Julie, to return the rifle to the closet. Also to place the automatic in the glove compartment.

Hiding the automatic when Julie was present would be difficult, especially when going for walks and working in the gardens.

Pete was in the deer stand and waved as they passed. Tom wondered if he was watching when Julie's red convertible came down the roadway a couple of hours ago. Now that Allan was gone, it was a comfort for Tom to have Pete so alert and so near. He parked the car and they entered Mary Ann's.

"How are you two?" asked the hostess as she scribbled something in her book. "Looks like about a fifteen-minute wait."

They sat at one of the tables in the bar area. Glancing around, Tom spotted Henry and his wife sitting in a booth under one of the windows overlooking the lake. Henry looked their way and waved. Tom had the feeling he and Julie were the subject of most the conversations in the room.

Bette was tending bar that evening and she brought Tom and Julie each a glass of wine.

"How are you folks this evening?" she asked.

"Just fine," answered Julie. "I like the wine."

In about twenty minutes, the hostess stopped at their table and announced a place was ready for them in the dining room. Following her, they passed the front door, Kyle Fredrickson and a lady had just entered. Kyle nodded a greeting as Tom and Julie followed the hostess. They were offered a window booth and gladly accepted.

"Hey, look, the fog has lifted," said Julie.

Tom looked out the window and was fascinated with the dancing, silver-like glitters caused by the rays of the setting sun. They were grouped like a pyramid, the point, not far from the dock, the base far out into the water.

Down on the lake surface, two speedboats towing skiers were racing back and forth. Water sprays, created by the leaning skiers, were absorbed into the glitter as they moved across the rays of the sun.

Beyond the skiers, close to Rocky Point, Tom spotted a sailboat.

"See that sailboat, Julie...must be Sylvan's."

Tom and Julie watched the sailboat for a few moments and Tom added, "His sailing skills have sure improved since the season begin."

Harold made an appearance in the dining room. He sauntered in a few steps and Tom watched his eyes wander across the room. After nodding, Harold headed for a table in the far corner. He paused to greet customers on the way, finally sitting down at Kyle Fredrickson's table. A cocktail waitress with a tray full of glasses stepped over to their table. She carefully set down three drinks and moved on to the next.

Tom and Julie's waitress arrived with a bottle of Chardonnay. She uncorked the bottle and poured a tad into Julie's glass for tasting. Julie smiled, nodded and the waitress filled both glasses. Julie ordered a walleye dinner after asking a number of questions concerning the preparation of the fish. Tom ordered a small rack of ribs. In spite of the restaurant being very busy, their entrees arrived in about fifteen minutes.

"Julie, I haven't seen Mary Ann yet. She makes this place tick. The efficient and well-trained staff is her doing."

As they were enjoying dinner, the sun was just beginning to disappear over the tree line at the point

"I'm all done, how about you?" Tom asked Julie.

She nodded and said, "My dinner was great."

"Let's make a stop at the bar for an after-dinner drink."

When they got up from the table, Tom noticed Harold was still sitting with Kyle Fredrickson and the lady. Tom held Julie's hand and led her into the bar area. Henry and his wife were still at their booth when they entered.

Henry's head turned their way and he waved. Tom led Julie toward their booth.

"Henry and Jan, this is my friend Julie."

"Have a seat," said Henry.

"Thanks," Tom said and guided Julie into the booth next to Jan.

He sat next to Henry. A cocktail waitress stopped over and Julie and Tom ordered an after-dinner drink.

"What's that I hear about your house having a window shot out?"

asked Jan.

"It's true, the bullet went through my dining room window."

"Who do you think fired the gun?"

"The sheriff's department is investigating. The shot came from a fishing boat, at least that's what they think and I agree."

"We have lived on this lake for over thirty years. First, two murders and now someone shooting at our houses. That is frightening," said Jan.

Tom looked at Julie and was afraid of what she was thinking. I hadn't told her about the shooting—big mistake, he thought.

"I guess I should have told you about that, Julie."

She handled the startling revelation well. It must have been because of her adventurous, spirited background.

Tom was taken a little aback when she said, "How exciting."

"You are joking, of course," Tom said.

Julie laughed and said, "Of course I am."

After the after-dinner drinks, Tom and Julie said goodbye to Henry and Jan and walked out into the parking lot. When they arrived at Tom's home, he carefully removed the .32-automatic from the glove compartment and carried it into the house. Julie wasn't in the room and he placed it under a pair of gloves in the front closet.

Tom joined her on the deck.

She looked up at him and said, "Tom, what the heck is this about a shot fired at you? I'm getting a little concerned here."

"Julie, there isn't much more I can do. You've met Deputy Johnson. He and his staff monitor my place twice a day. They patrol the neighborhood daily."

"Well, that helps," replied Julie, somewhat satisfied.

"I suppose I could run away, but you know I'll never do that. Maybe Pete and I will become heroes and catch this Ranforth guy."

Julie turned away, looked across the bay and said, "I hope and pray this whole thing will get settled soon."

The rest of the weekend passed without incident. Julie left for her home in the red convertible on Sunday afternoon. At four, Tom called the sheriff's office and left his check-in message for Deputy Johnson.

# 41

MONDAY MORNING AND A CLEAR SKY greeted Tom Hastings while looking out the lakeside bedroom window. The weekend fog had dissipated. Rays from the sun were radiating through the dining room windows when entering the kitchen to start the coffeepot. Tom poured a cup and carried it onto the deck along with a pair of binoculars.

His rifle was only a few feet away in the front closet. The automatic was lying on the night table in the bedroom. He glassed all around the bay and saw no one. Catching his eye was a section of dock projecting from the shoreline of the house across the bay. A small fishing boat was tied to its side.

Scanning east of Sylvan's to the mouth of the bay, he could see only a single boat in the water. It wasn't moving and was hardly a threat from that distance.

Tom's calls to the sheriff's office at ten in the morning and again at four were made as agreed. That evening he worked out on the tennis court using the ball machine. His rifle was leaning against the near fence. Returning to the house, he walked out on the deck and saw a boat parked next to a weed bed only 50 feet from his dock. There was a man sitting on the rear bench next to the motor. Calmly, he returned into the house and brought out his deer rifle and binoculars.

The man was leaning forward and holding a fishing pole in both hands. As Tom continued to watch, he didn't observe any casting activity. Tom's nerves were beginning to unravel. Was this man actually fishing? There was no sign of a bobber. He continued to watch the man, hoping to see some movement.

Tom tried seeing the face with binoculars. The dark colored baseball cap was pulled down low, covered most of it. The collar of a camouflage jacket was pulled high up on the neck. There wasn't a tackle box on the bench in front of him. Was that a rifle lying there?

Tom rotated the focus mechanism in an attempt to define the object lying on the bench. He wasn't sure—it could be a rifle. As Tom continued to observe, the man finally began reeling in the line. There was a bobber attached to the stringer at the end. Perhaps just a guy relaxing and enjoying a peaceful day of fishing, he hoped.

Tom wasn't taking any chances. Before going back into the house to refill his coffee cup, Tom left the deer rifle lying on a small table close to the deck rail. Picking up his camera, he returned to the deck and proceeded to take a series of digital photographs.

The man in the boat wasn't paying any attention to Tom Hastings the photographer. He just continued to lean forward and hold onto the pole. After a third cup of coffee, Tom went indoors to do computer work. Frequently he left his chair and walked onto the deck to check on the status of the mysterious fisherman. There wasn't any change to boat, man or line. The suspicious looking object remained on the bench seat.

Tom went online to check e-mail and the weather forecast. After finishing, he made another trip to the coffeepot and peeked out the kitchen window. There still wasn't any change in the position of the fisherman and boat. Tom looked up at the clock. The guy had been down there all this time with almost no movement. Tom concluded the man was not a serious threat. Retrieving the rifle from the table, he returned it to the closet and headed for town. After lunch, he had a date with a client.

— —

SNIPPING SOUNDS PERMEATED THE AIR. Floyd Pella grimaced from the pain in his right hip. Maybe I should have the surgery, he thought, it couldn't be much worse than this.

Bill Jones was patiently waiting, sitting on a chair by the window. Mary had been on his case, his hair was too long, she insisted. Floyd glanced at Bill and saw Tom Hastings's pickup truck maneuvering into a spot across the street. His right hand, holding the clippers, lowered to waist level. Walking to the customer's front, he removed the apron.

"All done,"

"Thanks," said the customer as he removed a billfold from a hind pocket and slipped out a ten. "Will this do it?"

"Sure will," said Floyd as he accepted the bill and commenced to prepare for the next customer.

"Okay, Bill, your next."

Bill eased into the barber chair and sighed, "Well, Floyd, are you staying out of trouble?"

Floyd didn't answer immediately. He smiled and thought *if the fools only knew.*

The pain, there it was again, felt Floyd as he positioned on the other side of the chair.

"Speaking of trouble, there it is over there, across the street."

Bill looked out the window and saw Tom Hastings get into his pickup and drive off.

— —

AFTER RETURNING FROM THE CLIENT SESSION, late afternoon, Tom looked out the window. The troublesome boat and man were gone. Two other boats had arrived and were positioned next to a weed bed across the bay. There were two people in each boat and Tom concluded they were fishing.

Tom opened a bottle of beer and took the cover off the hot tub. The soothing feelings from the bubbling warm water overcame some of his fearful thoughts about threatening people in boats.

He continued to watch the activity in the bay while resting in the hot tub. Half an hour later he dried, dressed and noticed the two boats across the bay hadn't moved. The occupants continued to cast and retrieve. Tom felt safe. He spent the rest of the evening watching a baseball game on television.

Shortly after 9:00 the phone rang. His neighbor Pete was on the line.

He reported, "Other than Julie's red convertible, your vehicles and the sheriff's vehicles, I hadn't seen any other vehicles on your road since last talking to you. Everything okay over there?"

"Yes it is, Pete, and I appreciate your call. Some of the boats out front scare me a little, but no problem since the earlier sniper."

"I was wondering if you heard any shots from my direction. Lisa has been doing some target shooting from the deer stand."

"No, Pete, I haven't heard the shots. Maybe I wasn't home when Lisa was shooting. I really appreciate you two watching my roadway. So Lisa's becoming a pretty good shot, huh?"

"Hey, you better believe it."

"Great, Pete. If anything changes over here, I'll let you know."

"No problem, Tom. I appreciate you letting me know what's going on."

"I'll sure try."

"Oh, by the way, there's been a lot of activity on Sylvan's roadway, more than on your road. From the stand, we can see over there real good, even though it's a little farther away. So far, mostly people walkin and jogin. It's not always Sylvan or his wife either."

"Thanks for calling, Pete, I have some work to do."

— —

JUST BEFORE DAWN BROKE on the next day, it rained buckets. There was considerable lightning and thunder. The lights blinked off and on several times. The computers were equipped with battery backups, therefore not affected. Most of the clocks needed resetting. As expected, there weren't any boats out on the lake. A strong eastern wind churned up the water and was pushing Tom's pontoon boat against the dock.

Rainy days were made for running errands. First stop was for the mail in New Dresden, before heading for Big Lakes. After dropping off some of his shirts at the dry cleaners, he parked in a municipal lot.

Using an umbrella to keep from getting soaked, Tom sloshed his way to the local bookstore. He knew the owners, Joe and Susan—they were old friends. Their store was packed with new and used quality books and a generous assortment of magazines and newspapers. The bookstore was busy this morning, a number of customers browsing the racks of paperbacks and magazines.

"Hi, Tom," said Susan from behind the counter. "How are you doing?"

"I'm still alive," he answered.

She came out front and gave Tom a big hug.

One of the customers browsing the magazine section looked up and appeared interested as they talked.

"How is Joe?" Tom asked.

"Oh, just fine. He's in the back room taking a nap. Is there anything new about the murders?"

Tom guessed she hadn't heard about the sniper so he might as well tell her. She was going to find out anyway.

"Susan, have you heard about the sniper?"

"No, Tom, what happened?"

"Some jerk took a pot shot at me from a boat while I was relaxing on the deck."

"Gosh, that's awful. Did they catch him?"

"No. Whoever it was got clean away."

"Do you suppose it was the same person who did the murders?"

"I can only guess, Susan, but I would bet my last dollar there's a connection between the murders and the sniper."

Tom bought a couple of newspapers and said, "Say hello to Joe."

He walked out the door, back into the rain.

On his way home, down the roadway, he stopped the truck abreast of Pete's deer stand. After making sure the deer stand was empty, he took the .32-automatic out of the glove compartment and strapped it around the waist. Leaving the truck parked, he walked down the road toward his house. At approximately a hundred yards from the truck, he spotted shoe tracks on the edge of the road. The tracks were made by one person, likely a man. They were headed in the same direction as he was.

Origination of the tracks was a small wooded area just beyond the field visible from the deer stand. Tom looked in all directions and could not see anyone. The size of the tracks appeared to be about his size. They weren't Pete's for sure. His boots were a heck of a lot bigger.

Tom followed the tracks for a short distance until they led back into a cleared section of the wooded area. Again he stopped and looked around. Being satisfied no one was about, he crossed a broken-down barbed-wire fence and stepped into the grass. He noticed there were spots where the grass was trampled. Somebody had walked here recently.

Tom followed the grassy trail cautiously, stopping often and looking in all directions. He was well into the clearing. Peering into the deep grass, he spotted another discarded white cigarette butt. Stooping down, he gently picked it up with his fingers. The butt looked much the same as those found at the private landing.

Continuing to follow the grassy trail, he paused at the edge of a narrow stand of trees. After working through the branches and coming out the other side, he paused again. Directly in front was a field of corn. Across the field, he could see a pickup truck parked on Sylvan's roadway.

*Darn! I don't have the binoculars.*

Tom scolded himself while snuggling close to the trunk of a large oak tree. He watched the truck for about ten minutes. Seeing no one, he returned to his roadway and walked toward the truck.

Driving home, he was careful not to disturb the fresh shoe tracks. Tom parked in the driveway and went into the house to make the morning call and check out his answering machine. There were no messages. He turned the pickup truck around and headed back to New Dresden.

There was a parking spot directly across from the hardware store. After parking, he crossed the street and entered the store.

"Can I help you?" asked a clerk.

"Yes, do you have plaster of Paris?"

"Sure do, follow me."

Tom selected a bag and said, "How about some silicone lubricant?"

She led him to an aisle near the front door where there were several spray cans of silicone. He picked out a product and hoped it would work as a separator between plaster of Paris and road gravel.

Returning back home, he parked the truck in front of the house. Inside, he found a plastic container and mixed a batch of plaster.

Rushing up the road to the shoe tracks, he selected one of the deepest and sprayed it with the silicone product. After waiting a few minutes for the silicone to set, he filled the imprint with a fresh mix of plaster of Paris. Removing a peace of plastic from behind the pickup seat, he covered the fresh plaster. To prevent the plastic from blowing away, he rounded up a few medium-sized rocks. According to the directions, the plaster would take a few hours to cure. Tom returned home and parked the pickup in the garage.

Tom didn't mention the tracks when making the four o'clock call to the sheriff's office. Just before dark, he strapped on the holster containing the .32-automatic and walked up the roadway to check out his project. Every few steps he stopped and looked around. The plastic cover looked undisturbed. He probed a finger underneath the plaster. It had begun to harden—too early to attempt a recovery.

The .32-automatic remained at his side all evening. Tom watched a movie on the television, lying on the couch in the dark. That evening, shortly after 10:00 p.m., he called Pete.

"Did you walk any part of my roadway today?" Tom asked.

"No, I didn't, not today. Why?"

"I found some shoe tracks on the road next to the wooded area."

"It wasn't me and I didn't see anyone from the deer stand. I was up there for a couple of hours right after lunch."

"Thanks for your help in watching the roadway, Pete."

"No problem," he responded.

"Have a good night, Pete," Tom said and hung up.

All the lights were out in the house. The outdoor lights were on. His doors were locked. The .32-automatic lay on his bedside stand.

# 42

ANOTHER MORNING DAWNED FOR TOM HASTINGS. His routine of carrying the automatic from window to window, scanning the outdoors, was completed. No cars in the driveway and no people moving relaxed his fears. Setting the gun on the dining room table, he carried his deer rifle onto the deck. There weren't any boats on the bay.

After getting dressed and checking out the news on the Internet, he fetched a plastic bag and picked up the deer rifle from the dining room table. With the plastic bag in his back pocket and the rifle over his shoulder, he walked up the roadway, frequently glancing into the wooded area and clearing where he followed the grassy trail yesterday.

The small rocks did a good job of holding the plastic down. Tom pried the plaster cast from the shoe track. He was delighted that it didn't fracture. After placing the cast in the plastic bag, he began the walk back to the house. Every few steps, he paused and looked in all directions. No one was in sight. Arriving back at the house, he set the bag with the plaster model on the table. Fetching a cardboard box from a storage area, he placed the plaster model and a small plastic bag containing the cigarette butt into the box.

Palms resting on the table, Tom debated whether to call in his recent discoveries to the sheriff's office. Thinking of possibilities, he considered the person who made the track and dropping the cigarette being simply out for a walk.

Walking out onto the deck with a cup of coffee, he became alarmed when seeing the same fishing boat parked in the same place as yesterday. It was the same guy, wearing the baseball cap and camouflage jacket.

Tom had intended to drive into New Dresden for the mail after finishing with coffee, but he didn't dare to leave while the man and boat remained. Retrieving the rifle from the closet, he placed it on the deck table just as he had done yesterday. Tom sat on a deck chair, absorbed more caffeine and watched. He was flabbergasted that the man moved so little.

Bringing out the camera, he took another series of photographs. Anxiously, he copied today's photos to his computer hard drive. Comparing these with yesterday's left no doubt, it was the same man.

Two red shouldered hawks were circling over the trees at the edge of the shoreline, near the man and boat.

*Keeya, keeya, keeya*, the birds cried as they swooped and soared.

The hawk's noisy banter didn't appear to disturb the man in the boat.

When Tom returned into the house, he called Deputy Johnson.

"Anything happening?" the deputy asked.

"Paul, there is a lone man, he may or may not be fishing, real close to my dock for the second straight day. It's really bothersome."

"Tell you what I'll do," he said. "I'll see if I can get hold of one of our boat patrol units. I'll try talking them into patrolling your lake today. If the guy is still around, they can check it out. Do you have a description?"

"Yup, I sure do, several photographs."

"Great. Can you bring them into New Dresden this morning? I'll meet you for lunch."

"Super idea."

After Tom hung up the phone, he printed the two best photographs.

# 43

JUST BEFORE THE NOON HOUR, Tom Hastings was sitting at a corner table in Borders Café. The restaurant was almost filled and he was lucky to find a place to sit. A manila envelope was lying on the table. He had run usual errands earlier.

Tom was reading an article about the U.S. missile defense system when the deputy came through the door. Many heads turned as he worked his way between the other tables and sat down with Hastings.

"What's new in the paper?" the deputy asked.

"Our hundred-million dollar missile interceptor failed to hit the target yesterday. There were some red faces at the Pentagon. The Minnesota Twins lost again and are in danger of losing their best player to free agency. The salary of their weakest player is probably higher than the entire staff at the sheriff's department."

Deputy Johnson chuckled and added, "Hopefully, our won and lost record is a lot better."

"Paul, I'm anxious to hear if there is any news?"

"Well, for starters, the FBI has turned over the entire Cushing and Burnside murder investigations over to Big Lake County."

Tom nodded and remained silent.

The deputy continued, "We're staying with our earlier theory regarding the motives. All three murders were directly a result of the victims learning Ranforth's identity. However, there's some new thinking about why Ranforth is after you."

"What?" asked Tom, anxiously.

"This Ranforth guy may be playing games with you. Surely, he must realize that if you knew his identity, we would have that information some time ago. You may be a victim of a twisted mind, the kind that needs to win, at all costs, part of an ego trip. He may consider you a threat to his expertise."

"You know, Paul, I cannot imagine what this Ranforth guy has against me, ego or no ego. As you say, he has to know that I don't know his identity. Why doesn't he simply leave me alone?"

"He may be obsessed with terrorizing you."

"Yesterday, I found some shoe tracks on my roadway that were made by someone else...they weren't my neighbor's either. I have the feeling Ranforth or whoever took the shot at me was here. The reason is because I found another one of those discarded cigarette butts. It looks the same as the others."

"Tom, your findings could be important. Do you have the cigarette butt?"

"Better yet, Paul, I have a plaster model of one of the shoe tracks."

"Tom, you are really getting into this case. Perhaps that's why Ranforth considers you such a threat. Did you bring the photographs you took of the guy in the boat?"

Tom pushed the manila envelope toward the deputy and glanced around the room, He noticed at least six sets of eyes turn away. Deputy Johnson and Tom took advantage of the noisy atmosphere during the noon hour. They could talk normally without fear of being overheard.

"Thanks, I'll pass these photographs to the guys who are doing your lake this afternoon."

"What's the latest on the Harold fire?" asked Tom.

The case is out of our hands right now. The county prosecutor has taken over. The only arson charges filed so far have been against Leslie Richards. A jury is going to decide. For certain, some of our staff will be called as witnesses. Another matter, Harold is suing the insurance company. It may take him a long time to get the money," added the deputy.

"Anything new on Allan's murder? It's surprising to me that Allan could have let his guard down. He appeared so cautious, so sure of himself," said Tom.

"I'm disappointed that Allan didn't report more often to us or his headquarters in St. Paul. They didn't get any of his reports, must have been in his car and the killer took them. The tape recorder Allan used is also missing.

"It's looking more and more like Ranforth used an accomplice. Together, they may have set a trap for Allan. One could have been used in the shooting at your house.

"It makes sense. Ranforth could have dropped the accomplice off to steal the boat. Then, he waited at the private landing, smoking cigarettes. After the shot, the accomplice landed the boat and they escaped unseen. That would also explain the three cigarette butts you found."

"Do you think the accomplice was used in Rollie's murder?" Tom asked.

"We really don't have the answer to that question. The killer likely took advantage of knowing that Rollie often walked down to the water's edge in the evenings. It wouldn't have been that difficult to come ashore with a small boat. Rollie's widow told us there were three or four boats not far from the point that evening.

"She also mentioned seeing a sailboat in the area on the evening of the murder. We found out it belonged to your neighbor, Sylvan, just down the shoreline. We visited Sylvan at his home and neither he nor his wife noticed anything unusual the evening Rollie died. They admitted sailing in the vicinity of the point that evening."

Deputy Johnson continued, "It's apparent Ranforth has solid knowledge of the lay of the land surrounding your lake...along with perhaps, the personal habits and routines of your neighbors."

A lady approached their table and addressed Deputy Johnson. "Hey, I want to complain about a herd of cows that have trampled my garden. Could you talk to the owner of the cows and stop them from getting out of the fence?"

"Why don't you stop by at the office and file a complaint? If you do that, we will talk to the owner of the cows."

"Those darn cows did it to my garden about three times already this year, and this time I am going to do something about it. Thank you, Mr. Deputy."

She left our table and stormed out the door.

They both laughed after the irate lady left the restaurant.

Tom remembered a couple of times in the past when cows strayed onto his property. Some years ago, a large Black Angus bull decided to lay down and nap on one of his trails. All his attempts to scare off the bull ended in failure. Other then the bull, he has been invaded by a herd of cattle, two horses and three peacocks. The three peacocks were the worst. They did a great job of messing up his deck.

Deputy Johnson said, "Call me at home the next time Julie comes down, my wife and I'll take you two out for dinner."

They got up from the table and approached the checkout counter to pay.

"I'll get this today," Tom told the deputy.

"Thanks for the treat, my turn next time."

After Tom wrote a check, they shifted around the busy tables and through the door. Kyle Fredrickson saw them come out onto the sidewalk. From the grocery store window, Fred Cook watched them shaking hands. Floyd's barber chair was empty. He was sitting on one of the chairs by the window and watching when the deputy and Tom Hastings parted.

As Tom approached his pickup truck, the feeling of being watched caused him to pause and scan Main Street. He saw about a dozen people meandering up and down the sidewalks. None of them appeared to be paying him any attention. After opening the door to the truck, he looked up and saw a man standing in front of Hector's bar. That's the one, he thought. The distance from his truck to Hector's was too far to recognize anyone.

Tom slipped into the pickup truck and opened the glove compartment. Before leaving the parking place, he took the .32-automatic out of the holster and laid it down on the seat. He eased the truck out and anxiously drove towards Hector's bar. The person who had been standing there was gone. Could be my imagination, he thought.

# 44

MEETING WITH DEPUTY JOHNSON WAS ENCOURAGING. When Tom arrived back at his house he headed right out to the deck. The man and boat hanging around earlier were not there, a relief. Staring at the empty bay, he thought about the man in the boat—by now the sheriff deputies had checked him out. Tom was curious about the boats seen near Rocky Point when Rollie died. He telephoned Rollie's widow and asked her if she was up for a visit.

Tom was pleased to hear. "Yes, do come over."

"I'll be over in a couple of minutes," he told the widow.

Driving the pickup truck toward Rocky Point, he noticed a car coming his way. When the vehicles came astride, he got a look at the driver. It was a man wearing dark glasses and a wide brim hat—a short man. The car was strange to Tom, light blue in color. He continued to observe the vehicle in the rear view mirror while continuing toward Rocky Point. Tom was glad to see it turn right instead of down his roadway.

Tom continued on into the Point and parked in Sarah Smith's driveway. She answered the doorbell immediately.

Her smile appeared strained, but she extended a warm hand and said, "I am Sarah and you must be Tom."

"Yes, Sarah, we met in town earlier this year. Do you remember the fingerprinting session?"

"Oh yes, we talked about computers. Would you like some coffee?"

Tom accepted her coffee offer, and followed her through her house, a sliding door opened onto a deck.

"Have a chair." she said before excusing herself to return to the kitchen for the coffee.

Tom walked to the front railing and looked down. He could see the beginning of a path below that led down to the lake. The shoreline directly below was not visible because of a cluster of bushes and trees; however the deck's elevation allowed a great view of the lake. Two fishing boats were floating about in the area of the sunken island. Well beyond the boats, perched on a prominence of the opposite shoreline, he could make out Mary Ann's restaurant.

Glancing back into the main part of the house, Tom could partially see through an open door into a room just off the living room. There was a desk in the room, atop sat a computer monitor. He remembered the conversation at the fingerprinting session. Sarah was chiding Rollie about getting a computer.

Sarah entered the deck carrying a tray containing two cups of coffee and a plate of cookies.

"Help yourself," she said.

"The view is spectacular, Sarah. You must really enjoy this deck."

"Yes, I spend hours out here each day. Rollie used to sit in that corner lounger for hours. He lived for those binoculars."

"You must miss him a lot, don't you?"

"It gets very lonely without someone around, but I will have to get used to it, I guess."

After seating herself, she elaborated on the history of Rocky Point.

"Rollie's dad purchased the property some seventy years ago. It seems just like yesterday when Rollie and I built this place. Gosh, that was over forty years ago."

She placed a hand over her face and added, "We spent our honeymoon here at this cottage."

Sarah didn't accept the murder theory, "He slipped when he reached the bottom of the path and hit his head on a rock. Poor Rollie fell into the water and drowned. I don't care what the paper says. Rollie was not murdered."

Tom's feelings warmed for the lady. Murder was a bad word.

Sarah continued, "Rollie had three or four drinks before he walked down the pathway to the water's edge. He may have been a little tipsy before slipping and hitting his head."

"What are your plans for the future?" Tom asked.

"I'm not sure what my plans are. It's difficult to think about leaving this place. There are so many memories. This is where I am going to die. My two daughters in Kansas City are encouraging me to sell the cottage and move there. They tell me their children were sickened by the loss of their grandfather."

Sarah smiled and added, "Both of my families are coming for a visit in two weeks. I am so looking forward to seeing them again. They haven't been back since the funeral."

After the second cup of coffee, Tom asked, "Would you mind if I walked down the pathway to the lake?"

"No, please do, but be careful. Recent rains have made the steeper sections slippery."

Tom walked down the rough, wooden stairway to a small landing and then followed a path to the lakeshore. After reaching the bottom, he could visualize someone slipping and losing balance. Especially if they had been drinking beforehand. He reached the flat, clear area where the path ended.

The shoreline was lined with large rocks, at the point, they extended out into the water. He remembered fishing the edge of the rocks years ago, snagging the line.

Looking out over the lake, he saw a cluster of fishing boats in the area of the sunken island. A short distance to his right, along the shoreline, a space between rocks. Someone could have landed a boat there and waited for Rollie. Tom visualized Rollie slipping and hitting his head.

He remembered what Deputy Johnson said *the nature of the wound wasn't consistent with falling on rocks.*

Tom made his way back up the pathway and onto the deck. Sarah was standing, leaning on the deck rail as he approached.

"Yes, I could understand how someone could slip and fall into the water. Thank you much for the coffee and the visit."

It was obvious to Tom that Sarah was a very lonely person with Rollie gone. He thought she enjoyed his company.

"Good luck with your family," Tom stated as she grasped both of his hands.

"Sarah, does anyone here at the point drive a light blue car?"

"No, I don't think so, but then I can't be sure. Why don't you ask Nick? He would know."

She waved as Tom backed out of the driveway. He watched as she stood in front of her door with hands on hips. Real lonely, he thought.

Sylvan's roadway was empty. Because his roadway terrain was flat, Tom could see almost all the way down to the house. Pete's roadway was also flat, but it curved, preventing the house from being visible. Driving down his own roadway, he passed by Pete's deer stand. It was vacant.

Approaching his house, he glanced at the grass in the greenway and noticed it needed mowing. Some of Tom's maintenance had been put on the back burner since the shooting incident. The .32-automatic was strapped to his side for the entire two hours needed for mowing the greenway. After finishing, he made his 4:00 p.m. call to the sheriff's office.

# 45

THE LIGHT BLUE CAR turned down Sylvan Tullaby's roadway. Short of the house and out of sight, it turned onto a field approach and stopped. Vince remained in the vehicle for a few minutes. Convinced of being alone, he opened the door and walked around to the other side. Reaching into the glove compartment, he withdrew a paper bag, an Ace Hardware emblem stamped on the side.

He reached in the bag and grasped the switchblade. Placing it into his pocket, he threw the bag into the tall grass and closed the car door. Smiling when seeing no one, he advanced into the cornfield. The corn stalks brushed against his hips while approaching a wooded area.

He had agreed to this deal. Time was running out. If he was lucky and could finish, right now, today, he could be headed back to Chicago by this evening.

After reaching the wooded area, he glanced back at his car. This must be his lucky day, he thought. There wasn't anyone around. Working across the corn rows northward, he spotted the deer stand. No problem with that, he thought. The deer season didn't open till fall.

As he turned the corner of the wooded area, he stopped when hearing the sound of a chainsaw.

— —

TOM WAS EXAMINING HIS BUILDINGS for damage. A severe thunderstorm wakened him at three in the morning. The wind had been ferocious. While walking around the house, he was pleased the shingles had not been damaged. Between the house and garages, oodles of small branches were scattered throughout the driveway.

Moving toward the beginning of the driveway, his hand swirled upward to repel pesky black flies. They were buzzing around his head in droves—their peak season.

He walked a short distance up the roadway and could see a large tree lying across the road. Tom was relieved it had not damaged the power lines. His right hand dropped to the waist. Careless of me, he thought. He turned and quickly walked back toward the house. After fastening the holster around his waist, he went out to the garage and readied a chainsaw.

Placing the saw into the tractor bucket, he drove the tractor to the site of the fallen tree. The chainsaw started on the third pull. In a few minutes, he had the fallen tree cut into several two-foot chunks. Cutting firewood was a favorite task of Tom Hastings. He liked the winters in Minnesota—wood fires were cozy.

Loading the wood into the tractor bucket, he looked up and saw a person standing in the cornfield. Tom stared, concern grew, a male, he thought. Whoever it was, the corn stalks, a few rows in from the wooded area, were well above the knees. A small man, something about this scene looked grossly wrong, binoculars were back at the house.

After throwing another chunk into the tractor bucket, Tom unsnapped the holster and put his hand over the automatic. The two men stood and stared at each other. The metal feeling of the .32-automatic usually made Tom feel confident, his hand was shaking.

After a couple of minutes, Tom resumed loading chunks of wood into the tractor bucket. Pick up a chunk—look at the man—dump the chunk—look again. The statue-like person wasn't moving.

In his haste, he dropped a heavy wood chunk on his toe. Accepting the pain, he continued loading and finally tossed the last piece into the bucket. He got into the tractor cab and laid the automatic on the dash. Proceeding down the roadway toward his house, the statue passed from view. Frequent glances through the rear window up the roadway, through the side window into the wooded area revealed nothing.

After arriving in the driveway, he parked the tractor and rushed into the house—binoculars were on the table. Tom paused when passing through the front door. He reached in the closet and brought out the deer rifle.

He opened the pickup door and laid the binoculars on the seat. Jacking a shell into the barrel of the rifle, he flipped on the safety and placed it barrel down on the passenger seat. Tom removed the automatic from the holster and laid it next to the binoculars.

After backing out of the garage, he slowly drove up the roadway and stopped the truck at the point where the tree had fallen across the road. The man was gone. He sat there for a few minutes and saw no one. Satisfied no one was about, he continued up the roadway and drove into Pete's yard. Pete came out of the house when he heard the vehicle.

"Pete, did you see anyone standing in the cornfield the last few minutes?" Tom asked while remaining in the truck.

"No, I just got back from town. What did you see out there?"

"I saw a man wearing a hat standing in the edge of the cornfield, just next to the wooded area. Let's walk over and check for tracks."

Tom placed the automatic back into the holster, grabbed the binoculars and opened the pickup door. He stepped out, walked around to the passenger side and retrieved the rifle.

"I'll be right back," said Pete.

While Pete was gone, Tom buckled the gun belt around his waist. He was not surprised when Pete returned carrying his deer rifle. They made their way across the narrow field to the approximate spot where Tom had seen the man.

Carefully, Tom sifted through the short corn stalks until spotting shoe tracks in the soft soil.

"Over here, Pete, I found some tracks."

They followed the tracks toward Tom's roadway. A few steps later, they came to the spot where the man was standing. On the ground next to one of the tracks were two discarded cigarette butts.

"Look at this, Pete, the guy was a smoker."

Tom picked up the two butts, showed them to Pete, and put them in his pocket.

"Are you collecting cigarette butts?" a grinning Pete, asked.

"Well, not exactly, but I've been finding a lot of these lately. Let's follow the tracks to see where they came from."

Step by step, Pete and Tom retraced the shoe tracks towards Sylvan's road. The tracks continued through the cornfield and disappeared right next to Sylvan's roadway.

"Whoever it was came from here," Tom said.

"Darn, I wish I had been in the deer stand," said Pete.

They walked back to Pete's place.

"Thanks for the help, Pete. I don't like the looks of this. It could have been another sniper."

"I better not tell Lisa about this. She's scared enough the way it is. Are you going to tell the sheriff about this?"

"You darn right I am. Hey, Pete, I appreciate you keeping an eye on things. Thanks so much. I need to go. I know you are going to stay alert."

After driving out of Pete's driveway and onto the township road, he turned right toward Rocky Point. After pulling even with Sylvan's roadway, he stopped the truck. There wasn't anyone or any vehicle in sight. He thought about the foot tracks—those duplicated in plaster. Were the foot tracks on the roadway made by the statue man?

How did he get there? Where did he park a vehicle?

Tom remembered Deputy Johnson talking about ego. *Ranforth is playing a game with you. He needs to win—his ego, you know.*

Continuing on the township road towards Rocky Point, Tom turned left onto the north branch when he met a car. There was a man behind the wheel and a lady in the passenger seat. Probably heading to Rocky Point, he thought. While approaching Maynard's driveway, a mother raccoon and three baby coons scurried across the road.

A light brown car was parked in Maynard's driveway. It looked like the Realtor's car, Kyle Fredrickson. Continuing on beyond Maynard's driveway, he turned onto the county highway and headed for New Dresden.

After picking up the mail, Tom was anxious to visit with Henry at the Borders Café. Much to his disappointment Henry wasn't there. Tom sat at their usual table and opened the newspaper. When the waitress came by for his order, Tom asked about Henry.

"Normally, I could set my clock by when Henry enters. He's missing. What's going on?" Tom asked.

"Henry and his wife are visiting relatives in the Cities," she said.

"Well that explains it. I'll have the special," Tom said as she poured the coffee.

"Have you heard that the sale of the Maynard Cushing house has fallen through?"

"No," Tom responded. "I haven't heard."

"Oh well, Kyle will find another buyer," she said.

Tom continued reading the newspaper and eating. After finishing, he headed for home.

The answering machine was beeping when Tom arrived back in the house. There was a message from Deputy Johnson asking Tom to call back. Tom dialed the deputy's number and got an immediate reply.

"Hey, Tom, how's it going today?"

"Well, I'm still alive, if that means anything. I was about to call your office anyhow. I think I'm being stalked."

"Now, what's that all about?"

"I saw a man in the cornfield. Just standing there. About a hundred yards from my roadway."

"Did you recognize him?"

"No, but he was a short guy, wore a Panama hat. Didn't have my binoculars."

Tom explained how he and Pete found the tracks and the cigarette butts.

Deputy Johnson said, "Oh man, that doesn't sound good at all. Maybe it fits."

"Fits what?"

"Yesterday, one of our patrol cars ticketed a speeder on the county highway in your area.

"The driver wore dark glasses and sported a Panama hat. The car had Illinois plates and was registered to a Vince Cameron of Chicago. As far as model and make of the car, it was a light blue late model Bonneville Pontiac. Everything appeared to be in order, regarding the ownership of the vehicle, so the driver was simply ticketed for speeding."

"The hat! I've seen it around before," said Tom excitedly. "I saw a guy with dark glasses and wearing a Panama hat in the passenger seat of Sylvan's van a few weeks ago. They were waiting for the train to go by. Also, I met a light blue car on the township road just the other day. The driver had a wide brim hat."

"I'll check this out with Sylvan. Oh, by the way, your photographs produced some results. A couple of the guys patrolled your lake yesterday afternoon and found the boat you described. It is registered to a Ned Ruzinsky from Brownstown. His cottage and dock are located on the east shore of your lake."

"Did your patrol guys talk to the guy?"

"No, there wasn't anyone home but that man doesn't appear to be a threat...by what was learned, the man does a lot of fishing. Oh, by the way, neither Deputy Weismann or Deputy Larson smoke."

After Tom got off the phone, he spent the rest of the day mowing grass and working on the grounds. He did take a break to make the four o'clock call. The gun and binoculars were strapped to his waist all day long. Julie called that night and, in spite of the threatening circumstances, she insisted on driving out for the weekend.

# 46

JULIE'S RED CONVERTIBLE was a welcome sight to Tom as it entered his driveway mid-Friday afternoon. After unpacking her stuff, they moved out on the deck with two bottles of mineral water. Tom wasn't convinced to share the cornfield, stalking story with her.

"Tom, something awful has happened at work. One of my co-workers has been charged with embezzlement. Cindy has been accused of stealing more then eighty thousand dollars."

"Geez, Julie, how can things like that ever happen? Someone must be asleep at the switch somewhere."

"Everyone at the office was just shocked when the news broke.

Cindy is a trustee in the church. Her husband is successful financially. They have three children, all school age. I can't imagine what possessed her...and so much money. I keep hoping the entire thing is a dream and will be gone in the morning.

"I need to forget about the problem for now. What should we do for dinner?" Julie asked.

"How about Mary Ann's?" Tom responded.

"Sure, sounds great."

At 4:00 p.m., when Tom made his call to the sheriff's office, he informed Deputy Johnson that Julie was here and they were heading to Mary Ann's for dinner.

"Have a good time," the deputy said. "We can't join you today, but will another day."

An hour later they were on the way to Mary Ann's in Tom's truck. Pete waved from his deer stand as they passed. The parking lot at Mary Ann's restaurant was almost full. After circling the lot twice, Tom found a spot at the far end. He left the gun in the glove compartment and locked the car. While they were walking towards the restaurant, he noticed a light blue Bonneville Pontiac with Illinois plates. Tom stopped for a moment and considered returning to the car to retrieve his gun.

"Tom, what are you looking at?"

"Oh, nothing really, Julie. I was just trying to remember where I saw that car before."

"Which car are you talking about?"

"The Pontiac," he said.

They walked into the restaurant after they stood and looked at the car for a minute, Mary Ann greeted them in the vestibule. She appeared to be in a festive mood.

"There's going to be a short wait, but I'll see what I can do about getting you two a window booth."

"Thanks," said Julie.

The bar area was busy and they were lucky to find an open table. Tom gazed around the bar area. Other than staff, he didn't recognize anyone. Jeannie, the cocktail waitress, brought Julie a wine and Tom a gin tonic.

"How are you people?" Jeannie asked. "It is sure nice to see you two again. Have you heard that Mary Ann's has been sold?"

"No I haven't, that's a surprise," Tom responded.

"Yes, the deal is final and the new owners are going to take over in two weeks."

"Gee, what are Harold and Mary Ann going to do?" he asked.

Jeannie said, "I heard that they are moving to Florida."

About half way through Toms' gin-tonic, Mary Ann came by and happily announced she had found them a booth. They followed her into the dining room. Tom was about to ask her about the Florida move, but she hurriedly scurried away.

"What a great view," said Julie. "Look at all that glitter on the water."

Tom watched a pontoon boat, crowded with people, cruise by northward, through billions of sparkles caused by the sun. The waitress came and they ordered dinner. The glitter on the water continued to draw their interest. It shifted and changed in size as the sun lowered.

Sunset was just beginning when their dinners arrived. By the time they finished, the dining room had several unoccupied tables.

Across the room in a darkened corner, Tom noticed two men sitting at a table. They sat across from each other and were smoking cigarettes. One of the men was big and he was busy gesturing with his hands. He couldn't see the face because his body was partially turned. The other man was much smaller. He could see his thin face and slicked-back, black hair.

The smaller man was slightly hunched over the table and was listening to the bigger man who was waving his hands as he talked.

"What are you looking at, Tom?" Julie asked.

"Oh, I was watching those two guys in the corner, over there. I was wondering who they were—they look familiar."

Tom was thinking about the deputy's story, about the speeder. The man he saw in the cornfield, was this the one? Then, he remembered the light blue Bonneville out in the parking lot.

"Let's go," he said to Julie.

As they were leaving the dining room, Tom glanced at the two men, and he suspected the smaller one was watching them. As Tom and Julie passed by their table, his eyes and the smaller man's locked together briefly.

After Tom paid the bill, they walked directly out into the parking lot. As he expected, the light blue Pontiac with the Illinois plates was still there. When they got in his pickup, he wrote down the license number, *TBJ452*.

"How about a dip in the hot tub after getting back to the house?" he asked Julie.

"Sure, that would be great. Say, Tom, did you notice one of the men in the far corner staring at us during dinner?"

"Was it one of the guys sitting at the table by the wall smoking a cigarette?"

"Yes, it was the small guy...he sure had an evil-looking stare."

Saturday dawned bright and clear. Julie looked out the window and was looking forward to a delightful day. She looked at the thermometer. The temperature was in the seventies and the sky was mostly blue with a small number of scattered clouds.

"How about an early morning walk?" she asked.

Tom readily agreed to the walk and they began preparing. Each packed a camera, binoculars and insect repellent. He did not forget to buckle on the holster containing the .32-automatic. They walked by the tennis court and followed the edge of the greenway toward the sunflower field in the west.

When they reached the field, they walked northward toward the origination of the main trail. They moved slow and quiet.

They were into the main trail for a few minutes when Julie said, "Oh look, Tom, fawn tracks."

"Yeah, they're really small."

Tom wasn't looking at the deer tracks. He was looking at a human shoe track that he didn't make. The most recent rainfall was only two days ago. The track was fresh and pointed in the opposite direction. Tom wasn't positive but he thought the size resembled the plaster cast. He did not mention the track to Julie.

As they continued the walk up the main trail, he kept watching for more shoe tracks—there weren't any.

They walked the entire length of the main trail that diagonals through the woods and ends at the beginning of his roadway. After arriving there, they walked onto the township road and Tom eyed the surroundings.

"Let's walk the roadway back home," he said.

They spotted all kinds of animal tracks on the way back, mostly deer and raccoon. No one was in Pete's deer stand as they passed. When they reached the area where the tree was downed and removed yesterday, Tom stopped.

"What do you see?" asked Julie.

"Oh nothing...just looking over the cornfield." He wasn't ready to tell her about the statue-like man in the cornfield.

"Look at the big deer," Julie said excitingly as the greenway came into view.

Prancer was standing stiff legged along the north edge of the woods.

"That's Prancer," Tom said.

"How do you know?"

"I can tell by his size and the big rack. You know something, Julie, that deer may be trying to tell me something. Normally, he'd have bolted by now."

"Oh, how weird."

They both took several pictures of Prancer as he remained in a fixed position.

"Let's go and leave him alone. I know he's sending me a message. I think it's about the moose that showed up near my woods, close to a month ago."

"Yeah, I remember you telling me about them. Have you seen them lately, the moose I mean?" Julie asked.

"No, not for at least a couple of weeks."

"Were the moose very big?"

"Lot bigger than Prancer."

"So, how do you know Prancer didn't like the moose?"

"He told me."

"Oh come on, Tom, now you're talking to the animals."

"Well not exactly, but this deer is different, a lot different."

After their walk, they were having coffee on the deck when a small airplane, flying just a few feet above the water, roared up the middle of the bay. The plane looked similar to the one Tom had seen fly over his house a few weeks ago.

"Julie, would you believe there are rumors this plane was seen dropping something into the water near Rocky Point. As a coincidence, Rollie Smith was a user of drugs and there were some drug packets found in Maynard's house."

"Wow, that really sounds mysterious."

"Deputy Johnson told me some time ago his department checked out the plane. A former World War II pilot owns it and flies out of a small private airstrip about five miles from here. He said they didn't find any connection between the drugs and the plane."

After Tom made the ten o'clock morning call, he and Julie got busy in the gardens. He had followed Julie's direction during the planting season. She was responsible for the finest garden his home had ever produced.

"Well, Julie, the dinner at Mary Ann's last night was great. How would you feel about doing some cooking this evening?"

"Fine, do you have any ideas?"

"Sure, why not steaks? I'll do them on the grill. I've got this new sauce...mushrooms and all that."

"Yum, it's a deal."

"After making my four o'clock call, let's break out a bottle of wine and get the cocktail hour underway."

A pontoon boat cruised by heading westward not far from Tom's dock. Julie waved and some of the occupants waved back. She began working on the salad, and Tom got busy preparing the steak sauce. Preparing dinner was an enjoyable experience, especially while sipping wine. For a couple of hours, Tom forgot about shoe tracks and bullets.

After dinner, Julie filled two coffee cups, placed them on a tray, and carried them out to a table on the deck. Tom lit a cigar and they sat, sipped coffee, and watched the action in the bay.

A speedboat cruised by slowly. There were several people in the boat, and some of them looked up and waved as they passed. Tom and Julie remained on the deck and watched darkness overtake daylight. They watched the stars and the occasional satellite making its way across the sky.

On Sunday morning, while Julie prepared breakfast, Tom drove into New Dresden and stopped at a gas station. Paying for the newspaper, he became aware of his carelessness. Julie was at his house—alone.

He jumped into the truck and drove home as fast as he dared. Entering the house, he was relieved to see Julie setting the table. After eating, they lounged around the dining room table, sipped coffee and read the newspaper.

"Time to pack," said Julie. "Have to get going a little earlier today, one of those special meetings at work tomorrow morning."

Tom watched the small red convertible bump slightly as it hit the gravel on the roadway. He continued to watch until the last streak of red disappeared. After Julie was gone, his thoughts returned to the shoe track on the main trail. He prepared a backpack, filling it with camera, binoculars and a tape measure.

After strapping on the .32-automatic and slinging the bag over his shoulders, he headed up the main trail and into the woods. The shoe track that he spotted on the trail yesterday had not been disturbed. It measured four inches wide by nine and one-half inches long. Tom took two photographs of the shoe track.

He continued walking the trail towards the roadway, continually scanning the ground for new tracks. Except for Julie's and his, he didn't see any others, until reaching the roadway. There were more new shoe tracks along the edge of the roadway just off the township road. He measured a couple of them and they were identical in size to the track on the trail. Tom took several photographs.

After walking the entire length of the roadway back to his house, he transferred the photo images from camera to hard drive. He studied the photographs and they seemed to match the plaster cast from a few days ago. Thinking about the man standing in the cornfield, the tracks on my trails, the cigarette butts and the shot from the boat—are they all related?

At close to 10:30, Tom called the sheriff's office. He called again at four but because it was a Sunday, he didn't mention the new shoe tracks. Tomorrow morning will be soon enough, he thought.

# 47

THE MAN IN THE CORNFIELD and the shoe tracks on the trail produced uneasy thoughts for Tom Hastings on Monday morning. He didn't wait until 10:00 to call the sheriff's office. A few minutes after eight, Tom dialed Deputy Johnson's number.

"Good morning, Paul, hope it's not too early for you on a Monday morning?"

"I'm still half asleep, but what's up?"

"Remember that talk you and I had the other day? You mentioned that Ranforth's inflated ego might be the reason for getting rid of me. Well, I think he has his plan in high gear."

"What do you mean? What happened?"

"During the weekend, I found some strange shoe tracks on my roadway and in the woods. They appear to be the same. That's not all, I think the guy standing in the cornfield was at Mary Ann's for dinner on Saturday evening."

"Tom, those shoe tracks need checking out. I'll get someone over there later today."

"How about the two cigarette butts my neighbor Pete and I found out in the cornfield?"

"Would you save them for us? I'll have the guys call you before they come over."

"Okay, Paul. I'm heading into New Dresden right now and should be back in an hour. I'll be around for the rest of the day."

Tom made his morning trip into New Dresden. Henry was at his usual table at the Borders Café.

"Have a chair," he said.

After ordering the special and a cup of coffee, Henry said, "I heard Harold was forced to sell the restaurant because of gambling. Rumors are that he owes some people out east a lot of money. To make things worse, there were complications with the insurance."

Henry continued, "I hear Mary Ann isn't too happy."

"Have you heard who bought the restaurant?"

"Someone from Wisconsin, people around here are saying. Have you heard the latest on the Maynard Cushing house?"

"No, I haven't. What's that all about?" asked Tom.

"The sale has fallen through because the Ebert guy had a heart attack. Maynard's son was at the store the other day and didn't seem too concerned. Kyle Fredrickson has assured him there were other people interested in the house."

Tom opened the newspaper and they discussed some of the news articles on the front page.

Just before Henry got up to leave, he said, "Your new neighbors are staying the rest of the summer."

"Do you mean the people from California?"

"Yes, both of them are now officially retired. You will likely see some lights across the bay until winter comes. They have a place in Arizona, you know."

"That explains all the lights over there recently."

Henry dropped a few coins on the table and proceeded to the checkout counter. Tom folded up the newspaper and followed.

"Have a nice day," Henry said as he began crossing the street.

— —

MATT NELSON CROSSED THE STREET and looked in the barbershop window. Only Floyd sitting there, he noticed. Chimes clattered when he opened the door.

"Got time for me now, Floyd?" Matt asked.

"It's all yours, have a seat."

"Did that adapter work, under the sink, I mean?" asked Matt.

"Yes, just fine, thanks."

Floyd watched Henry crossing the street. Another ally of Tom Hastings, he speculated. The two of them compare information a lot, too much. Last week, Floyd was attempting to eavesdrop, it didn't work, Hastings keeps his left hand, palm open, next to the cheek all the time. Henry had his back turned.

"How do you like it around the ears?" the barber asked.

"Just touching is okay."

Floyd finished the left side and turned his body slightly to get at the right. He saw Tom Hastings walking toward the grocery store. Matt jerked a little as Floyd nicked his ear.

"Sorry, Matt, my fault."

"That's okay. I've got two of em."

Haircut finished, Matt opened his wallet and dropped a ten on the counter next to the sink.

"Thank you, sir," said the barber.

Matt was holding his hand up to his right ear when crossing the street. Tom Hastings was coming up the sidewalk toward his pickup.

"Hello there, Tom, what's new today?" asked Matt.

"Tough question to answer, Matt, gotta get home."

Floyd Pella clutched a pair of scissors tight while watching Tom Hastings and Matt Nelson talking.

— —

ON TOM'S RETURN TRIP HOME, his thoughts were on the shoe tracks. Part of his main trail in the north part of the woods was visible from a farmhouse next to his property line.

His friends Glen and Lois Sterling have lived on that farmstead all their married life. They were aware of Tom's trails. Lois called him a couple of years ago and asked for a favor during the holiday seasons. Her daughter and family were visiting and they needed a place to ski. Tom was delighted to have her family use the ski trails.

When Tom drove into their driveway, a large white dog greeted him as he opened the pickup door. The dog seemed friendly enough so he proceeded to their front door. Lois answered his knock and when the door opened, Tom could smell the aroma of fresh-baked bread.

"Well, gosh sakes, come on in, Tom. Glen is working today."

"Hello, Lois. So does Glen have a new job?"

"Yes, he's doing welding over at Norkins Manufacturing in Big

Lakes. He likes to stay busy."

Lois's gray hair complemented her above average height. She wore thick glasses that hung down low on her nose. When they shook hands, Tom could feel the hard calluses. Lois and Glen never backed off from doing hard, physical work. The large garden next to the house demonstrated the beautiful fruits of her labor.

"You sit right there, Tom, and I'll bring out some goodies."

Lois brought out a plate of cookies and set them on the table. He noticed the classic, cast iron, wood-burning cook stove snuggled against the far wall. Tom couldn't remember seeing one of those since being a kid. The stove oven door was partially open and from it radiated the aroma of baking bread.

"The cookies are just great, Lois, what a treat."

She smiled.

"Lois, you have a pretty good view of my woods. Have you or Glen ever seen anyone besides me on the trail?"

"No, I can't remember that I have. But wait a minute, I remember Glen had mentioned seeing a person on the trail near the pond a couple of days ago. You'll have to talk to Glen. He was standing by the picture window over there and mumbling something about a hat."

"Will Glen be home tomorrow?"

"Yes, he will, drop by if you wish."

"Thanks for the coffee and cookies, Lois. Company is coming today and I must be on my way."

Just after the noon hour, Deputy Johnson called and said he was bringing out a technician to check out the shoe tracks. An hour later, a sheriff's car appeared in the driveway. Deputy Johnson emerged from the driver's side. His companion was Deputy Larson. Tom recognized him from the sniping incident. He and Weismann were the deputies who found the boat at the private landing.

"Tom, do you remember this guy?"

"I sure do. Deputy Larson, right?" He was easy for Tom to remember because of his resemblance to *Barney*, the television sitcom character.

He led the two deputies up the main trail to the location of the shoe track. Deputy Larson opened the black case he was carrying and brought out a camera. Adjusting the lens, he took a series of photographs of the shoe track. After he put his camera away, he sprayed the track with a lubricant and filled the hollow with a greenish material. It set in a matter of minutes, and the deputy pried it from the depression and displayed what appeared to be a quality duplication of the track.

Tom led the deputies along the trail to the roadway where he showed them additional tracks. Deputy Larson selected one and repeated the process of foot track duplication. After he finished, they walked back down the roadway to Tom's house.

"Come on in, guys. I would like to show you what I did yesterday."

The two deputies followed him into the house. Tom showed them the photographs of the tracks.

"Boy," said Larson, "they sure look alike."

Tom also brought out the plaster cast he had retrieved from his roadway. They compared it to the two casts Larson had just made.

"They all look identical," Larson said.

The freezer bag containing the cigarette butts Tom and Pete found in the cornfield was lying on the table.

"Nice job, Tom. Those must be the cigarettes you told me about. Okay if we take those too?" Deputy Johnson asked.

"Sure can. I'll do anything possible to help catch whoever is behind all this...it's not any fun to get shot at...or get stalked. What do you guys think?"

"Well, you could be getting stalked...not for sure though. People do strange things all the time. You'll probably like this, our patrols on the township road have increased. So far, no one has reported anything unusual. You are providing most of the clues."

In a few minutes the two deputies were gone.

# 48

THE CAR CAME TO A STOP ON THE GRAVEL ROAD. "You get out right here. I'll pick you up in exactly one hour, check your watch.

"Now remember, Vince, this is your last chance. Do you have the tool?"

Vince was standing outside by the driver's door of the car. The window was open. He reached into his pocket and raised the switchblade so the driver could see. The man in the car nodded and drove off.

Vince plodded down the ditch and emerged in the thick corn on the other side. Taller today, he thought. The higher corn curls flopped against his shoulders as he made his way toward the wooded area. He moved steadily and quickly in a crowded, narrow space lined by two rows of plants. Reaching a fence, he followed it northward expecting to round the corner and come out on the roadway where he saw Hastings with the chainsaw.

Arriving at the corner, he was perturbed to see someone perched in the deer stand. Instinctively, he retreated behind a tree. Looking at his watch, five minutes so far, *damn-it anyhow*. Retracing his original route along the fence line, he crossed the fence and worked toward the roadway, through the wooded area, not his original choice.

At last he stepped onto the roadway. He stopped to listen and heard a strange popping sound. Sneaking along the edge of a greenway, he saw a high fence towering over a row of spruce—a tennis court. Perfect, he thought. Hastings is busy and hopefully not armed. Returning to the roadway, the popping sound was still audible. Feeling secure, Vince Cameron grinned widely while walking up the driveway and entering the house. This should be easy, he thought.

— —

AFTER TOM MADE HIS SCHEDULED CALL to the sheriff's office promptly at four, he headed out to the tennis court. The ball machine was positioned and set to spit out balls to the backhand court. He scolded himself for being careless and leaving the gun in the house. Oh well, he thought, the deputies were just here, he should be safe. The weather was perfect and Tom was really enjoying the workout. After returning from the court and opening the front door, his heart skipped a beat. Flocks of butterflies invaded his stomach.

There was a man standing next to the dining room table. An ugly grin, the same person Tom saw at Mary Ann's last Friday in the evening.

His stature resembled the man in the cornfield. For a brief moment, the intruder stoically stood there—right hand elevated. Tom heard a click and saw the glint of a knife blade.

"This is for you," the man sneered, advancing toward Tom, blade gripped in the right hand.

Lucky for Tom, one of the intruder's shoes stubbed on the edge of a small carpet extending beyond the computer chair. The man stumbled, allowing Tom a fraction of a second to dodge. Tom felt the sting of the knife blade as it penetrated the left side of his waist.

The forward momentum of the intruder's body forced both of Tom's arms high and to the left. Tom Hastings continued to hold the tennis racquet handle with both hands. In desperation, using his elbows, he shoved and pushed the attacker backward. With all the power Tom could muster, using his backhand, he swung the racquet at the intruder's head.

He saw the edge of the racquet hit the bridge of the nose. The shorter man cursed and pulled back his right arm, knife still in hand, preparing for a second strike. Tom felt terrorized by the intruder's watery eyes. Another lucky break, blurring vision caused a momentary delay. By the time the intruder's right arm began moving forward, Tom swung the racquet again, this time with more force, aided by the advantage of a strong forehand.

The small man's mouth was partially open when the racquet made contact with his face. Tom heard a cracking sound and saw the gap in the mouth widen. He heard the intruder utter a groan. Tom's racquet had scored a direct hit on the mouth. He could see fragments of teeth floating in the bloody foam accumulating between the lips. Tom heard a rattling sound when the knife fell to the wooden floor.

Both of the intruder's hands went to his face. Tom wasn't finished with that bastard yet. In spite of the wound in his side, he generated considerable force, using his entire body, and swung the racquet for a third time. The racquet caught the smaller man just in front of his right ear and he dropped to the floor like a rock.

Tom stepped over the body and ran upstairs to his bedroom to retrieve his automatic. Climbing the stairs, he thought of the rifle in the closet just a few feet from where the intruder lay. Tom was confused at the moment—not knowing for certain where his guns were located.

To his relief, the gun was lying on a night table next to the bed. He picked it up and jacked a shell into the barrel. Hesitating to catch his breath, he headed back downstairs. Passing through the kitchen into the dining room Tom was shocked to see the intruder standing. The small man had picked up the knife and was attempting to steady it in his right hand. In spite of the awful-looking, glossy, reddish eyes, he advanced a step in Tom's direction.

Tom Hastings's right hand jerked upward as he heard the deafening roar of his .32-automatic. Even though the bullet appeared to strike his chest, the intruder's right hand continued to grasp the knife. The fingers of the left hand spread out across his chest. Slightly staggering, the intruder took another step forward. Tom steadied the gun by grasping his right wrist with the left hand. He pulled the trigger a second time. To his amazement, the man continued to smile and advance.

The intruder was close enough to touch when Tom fired a third time. Missing at this distance was impossible, Tom reasoned. After the third shot, the smile disappeared and the knife clattered to the floor. The man staggered for a moment and fell into a heap. Tom remained standing, finger still on the trigger, left shoulder leaning against a cabinet, watching anxiously as the body began to convulse.

Quivers became intermittent. Soon the intruder's movements ceased and the room got deadly still. All Tom could hear was his own heavy breathing. The knife lay on the floor next to the body.

Tom stepped around the body and dashed over to his computer chair in the opposite corner of the room. He put the gun down on a mouse pad and clumsily removed the wall phone from its cradle. Hands were trembling—he had difficulty punching the right phone numbers. Instead of the sheriff's office, he reached a wrong number, very frustrating, impossible to apologize.

Tom sat for a moment, set the phone down on the desk and placed his head between his knees. After the shaky fingers regained composure, he made another attempt to call the sheriff's office. Listening to the phone ring at the other end, he glanced at the far end of the room and was relieved to see the intruder still lying on the floor. A large of pool of blood had gathered around the body. Tom was positive the man was dead.

After the second ring, a lady dispatcher at the sheriff's office answered. She had difficulty understanding Tom's explanation.

"Who, what, a shooting?"

He regained composure, "This is Tom Hastings, I've just killed an intruder."

The lady said, "Just a minute, hold on."

There was a short pause. Moments later, Tom heard Deputy Johnson's voice, "Stay on the phone, Tom. Someone will be over there as soon as possible."

The dispatcher returned and continued talking to Tom. She insisted he stay on the line until Deputy Johnson arrived. Glancing at the body on the floor, Tom noticed the pool of blood surrounding the upper part of the intruder's body was turning dark red—it had ceased to spread.

"Are you still there, Mr. Hastings?" the lady asked.

He was holding the phone in his left hand, the fingers of the right hand were compressing the wound—they were feeling sticky.

"Yes, I am, but I need to fetch a towel. Please hold on."

Tom got a towel from the kitchen and pressed it tight against the wound.

"I'm back, are you still there?" asked Tom.

"Yes I am, please tell me when Deputy Johnson arrives and I can let you go."

A few minutes later, Tom told the dispatcher, "I can hear a siren. Hopefully, it's Deputy Johnson."

"It should be," replied the lady.

Within minutes a sheriff's car pulled into Tom Hastings's driveway. Looking out the window, Tom could see Paul Johnson and another deputy rush out of the car. With guns drawn, they approached the front door.

"I'm hanging up now, they're here."

"Okay, Mr. Hastings, and good luck."

He heard Deputy Johnson yell, "Are you okay, Tom?"

Before Tom could respond, the two men came charging through the door. Deputy Johnson lowered his gun when seeing Tom.

"I think I'm okay except for the cut in my side."

"Wow, what a scene," said Deputy Johnson's partner.

Johnson hurried over to Tom and examined the wound. The other deputy went over to examine the body of the attacker.

"Nothing here, Paul, he's gone."

Deputy Johnson helped Tom get his shirt off. Tom cringed when he saw the nasty cut in the left side of his waist for the first time.

"Where do I find a clean towel and some antiseptic?"

"In the bathroom just around the corner."

"I'll get them, Paul," Tom heard the other deputy say.

Deputy Johnson's partner dashed off and returned moments later.

Together, using the ointment and towel, they wrapped the wound.

"Arlin, would you get on the phone and call the office? We're going to need technicians and the coroner. I'm taking Tom to the hospital in Big Lakes. Would you stay here and wait for them?"

Paul put the back of the passenger seat down and helped Tom into the car. The deputy drove the car slowly up the gravel roadway, respecting Tom Hastings's wound.

When they were nearing the township road, Deputy Johnson said, "God, that's a big deer."

"Does he have antlers?" Tom asked.

"Yup, he sure does."

Tom knew it was Prancer.

"How are you doin' over there?" asked the deputy.

"I'm a little woozy, should get better when you get on the blacktop."

After turning onto the county highway, Paul pushed a lever until the siren reached intensity above wail. It didn't take very long to reach the emergency room in Big Lakes. Two medics placed Hastings on a gurney and carried him into an examining room.

A doctor was waiting, and after examining the wound said, "You're lucky the knife didn't damage any major blood vessels. There's tissue damage, I think it best surgery be done immediately...no point in delaying."

This wasn't exactly what Tom had in mind, but he succumbed to the doctor's advice. When he awoke the next day, Julie was sitting on a chair by his bed.

When Julie noticed Tom had awakened, she came over and gently grasped his right hand and said, "Oh, it's so good to see you wake up. How do you feel?"

"Lousy, but lucky to be alive. Thank heavens for that small carpet."

"What carpet?"

"The blue one on the floor under the computer chair. It saved my life. The guy with the knife caught his toe and tripped, giving me just enough time...time to let him have it with the tennis racquet."

"It's all over. You have eliminated Ranforth and he will not bother you or anyone else again."

"Prancer knows," he said.

"What are you talking about, Tom?" asked Julie slyly.

"Prancer was standing by the road to see me off yesterday."

Julie didn't respond. Tom's thoughts drifted to the evenings of fear, sitting out on the deck watching daylight turn to darkness. He felt elated that the days of blue darkness were over.

Two days later, Tom was very happy to be leaving the hospital. His doctor came into the room mid-morning and examined the wound.

"Congratulations, Mr. Hastings, you're healing real well. I think I'll let you go home today."

"I like your place of business, but going home really appeals to me...thanks," replied a smiling Tom.

"I'll sign your release, but you have to promise to return in a few days and have the wound checked. If you notice any bleeding or have any pain, let me know. The nurse will give you some pain killers just in case."

"Thanks, Doc. I appreciate all the attention."

Julie and one of the nurses wheeled Tom into the rear parking lot.

"Boy, it's sure nice to be outdoors again," he said.

Julie helped Tom into her car and in minutes they were on their way to Tom's home. The soreness in the wounded area was surprisingly mild during the drive. They were both ecstatic.

"Just think, Julie...no more worrying about Ranforth and what was going to happen next. I can sleep normally for a change."

When Julie drove her car into the Hastings's driveway, she was careful to avoid two parked sheriff vehicles. Deputy Johnson greeted them as they walked down the sidewalk. He was sporting a big smile and held the door open as they entered.

Tom's eyes glanced at the place where the body of his intruder lay after the attack. The floor had been cleaned. Chairs were tucked into their correct places under the table. Julie and Tom sat on the love seat.

"How's the wound feeling, Tom?"

"Not too bad."

Besides Deputy Johnson, there were two other deputies in the room. One of them poured Tom and Julie a cup of coffee. Tom was ecstatic at seeing the bay again. Looking out over the dock area, he saw a column of baby ducklings hurriedly scooting beyond the dock, catching up to their mother. They formed a single line, just like people at grocery checkout counters.

Glancing out the window to the east, plainly visible was the crosspiece high up on the mast of Sylvan's sailboat.

Deputy Johnson said, "I've got some news."

The tone of his voice sobered the faces of Tom and Julie. They both looked up to the deputy, anxiously waiting for a statement.

They sat in silence as he explained, "Your stalker and intruder was not Robert Ranforth, but a man known by the name of Vince Cameron.

Julie cupped her hands around her face. Tom anxiously leaned forward, his back straightened, the game wasn't over.

"Tom, your attacker was the guy caught speeding on your county highway about a week ago, remember? Cameron is known by a multiple of aliases. The FBI informed us Cameron was an established hit man, operating out of Chicago. He has been on the FBI's most wanted list for the past ten years."

Deputy Johnson smiled when he brought up the extent of the wounds the intruder suffered.

"Tom, you really did a number on that guy. A broken nose, sixteen broken teeth, a fractured skull and three bullet holes in the chest. The FBI owes you one...for putting an end to him."

After the chuckles and reactions by the room's occupants subsided, Julie asked the inevitable question, "If that wasn't Ranforth, who is Ranforth and is he still in the area?"

Deputy Johnson slowly shook his head and said, "I'm real sorry but I just don't know. As a matter of fact, we don't know if Ranforth is responsible for any of the murders. The only connection we have between him and the murders are the prints found at the Cushing house...the memoirs, too. Cameron could have committed all the murders. If he did, there shouldn't be any more. You took care of that, Tom." He added, "Now that Ranforth is on the run, we should be able to track him down."

"So do you think I need to remain armed like before? Also, how about the two check-in calls every day?"

"That's a tough call, Tom. Until Ranforth is caught and put away, you need to take all the precautions possible. That means checking in with us twice a day, as before. I'd sure continue to be armed, if I were you."

Tom's head tilted downward, Julie place a hand on his arm. He looked up and said, "Yeah, okay, I can handle that."

"Another thing you may consider is to have your cell phone with you at all times. Be sure to program in our number."

"Yeah, I programmed your number in some time ago. The cell

will be with me at all times."

"Good. Meanwhile we are going to continue to patrol the roads in your neighborhood. Also, you can expect to see one of our cars on your roadway at least once a day."

The other two deputies took their leave. Deputy Johnson remained behind for a few minutes. Before heading out the door, he handed Tom a paper bag.

"This is just between you and me, until you get the .32-automatic back, you may need this."

Tom looked in the bag, It contained a .38-special revolver and a box of shells.

"I think you should fire a couple of rounds and get used to the change...this gun has quite a bit more punch than your .32-automatic. You can use it until the technicians are finished with your gun," added the deputy.

Tom set the bag on the table.

"Oh, by the way, the cigarette butts from the cornfield were different than the three butts you found at the private landing. Good luck, be careful—talk to you soon."

Deputy Johnson walked out the door to his car. The flashers on the roof reflected the sun while turning around in the driveway.

# 49

TOM WATCHED THE SHERIFF'S CAR LEAVE. He turned to Julie and said, "Maybe I should give up and move, damn far away."

"Tom, you're so close to winning. Don't give up now."

"Yeah, you're right, running may not work anyhow. If Ranforth thinks his secret is in my hands, he'd come after me no matter where I'm living. Besides, the thought of that creep intimidating me makes me angry. Deputy Johnson loaned me a gun and I need some practice."

"Okay, you go out and practice, and I will see what I can do about dinner."

As the deputy mentioned, the .38-special was heavier than the automatic. Tom rummaged a piece of plywood from the garage and, with a hammer and a couple of nails, walked out onto the greenway. Locating a bare tree trunk, he pushed through a small patch of Northern prickly ash, received a couple of scratches, and nailed up the plywood.

Backing off approximately fifty feet, he fired a round at the plywood target. Tom was pleasantly surprised that all six shots hit the plywood. The .38-special had noticeably greater recoil than his .32-automatic. Since it was also heavier, he was expecting it to be more accurate. The noise stirred up a covey of crows, they responded noisily and flew off to a group of trees at the end of the greenway.

Julie's chicken dinner that evening was delicious. Along with the food, the Chardonnay went down especially well on this first evening home from the hospital.

The temptation to forget about the tragedies of the last couple of months was overwhelming. Regardless, their conversation eventually drifted to the mysterious, tantalizing Ranforth.

"Do you think that Ranforth was behind the earlier shooting and also the intruder?" Julie asked.

"Yes, I do, but it's unlikely he will make another attempt. His risk of being exposed is higher than ever. Regardless, I plan on remaining alert. I need to get Pete more involved. He needs to know about the recent attack. I liked the idea of Pete wandering up and down the road with his deer rifle."

The temptation of the warm water in the hot tub was just too great and Tom succumbed. The water was delightfully soothing that evening, especially in the area of the knife wound. Tom suspected that his doctor would have frowned on soaking the bandages.

Next morning while Tom was making coffee, Julie was packing. She had taken extra time off from work because of the intruder incident and needed to return home. He got the usual sinking feeling watching the red convertible disappear around the corner at the end of the driveway.

On the way to New Dresden later that morning, he turned down Pete's roadway and pulled up in his driveway. Pete was sipping coffee on the front deck.

"Cripes, you sure did a number on that hit guy. The word around town is that you shot him full of holes after beating him up with a tennis racquet."

"Well, you have it partly right. It was a frightening experience, never one to wish onto anybody."

"No doubt, you are the top gun in this territory. *Don't mess with that guy*, that's what I hear around town."

In spite of the seriousness of the intruder incident, Pete and Tom had a good laugh.

"Pete, the man who I killed was likely hired by the person who killed Maynard, Rollie and Allan. Until the person who hired him is put away, we need to be on our guard more than ever."

"You can count on me," said Pete as he padded the stalk of his deer rifle. "I was in the deer stand for part of the day when you were attacked. I did see a car parked on Sylvan's road about half the distance to his house. I couldn't make out the exact color, but it did seem to be light.

"No one entered or left the car while I was in the deer stand. Perhaps no big deal, but the car may have been used as a drop-off for your attacker," added Pete.

"Gee, I don't remember the sheriff's people talking about how the intruder got to my house. There was no mention of finding an abandoned car, specifically a light blue Pontiac. Pete, do you remember those foot tracks in the cornfield? I think the person who made those tracks was the guy who attacked me."

His stop at the grocery store in New Dresden was greeted with a *do not mess with that guy* statement by someone in the checkout line. While he was picking up the newspaper, Tom overheard someone else say, a *gunfight at OK Corral.*

Things did not change much when he visited the post office. Jerry, the local postmaster had some questions and comments. "What does it feel like to have a guy with a knife come at you?

"Have you ever shot a criminal before? You're famous, the hero of New Dresden."

Tom wasn't interested in having lunch at the Borders Café that morning—far too much attention. He got in the truck and turned the key only to hear an irritating clicking sound. The darn battery he was supposed to replace about three weeks ago was dead—no more delays in getting it replaced. Tom walked to the corner gas station and asked for a booster start.

"Sure," the guy said, "I'll be over in a few minutes."

As Tom walked back to the truck, he could sense the guys at the station staring at him. When he glanced back, one of them was gesturing in his direction.

Ten minutes went by before a vehicle from the service station came by and pulled up next to Tom's truck. The guy opened the hood and connected the cables. The pickup engine started immediately after he turned the ignition key. The service attendant came over to the open side window and got paid ten bucks. Swinging the truck around the block, Tom headed north. His luck wasn't improving, the railroad warning signals began flashing and the long white arm came down as he approached the tracks. Ten minutes went by while his truck and other vehicles waited for the freight train to rumble through town.

Tom was the first vehicle in line and made sure the engine ran at fast idle. When the last boxcar finally passed, a caravan consisting of about twelve vehicles were lined up behind his truck. He led them up the county highway.

Tom was thinking about the discussion with Pete and the lack of a get-away car. If Byron and Eva were watching the township road as he hoped, they may have seen something. He turned off the county highway, onto their roadway. After stopping the engine in front of the house, he tested the starter. A turn of the ignition key was positive—it started.

Eva answered the door. "Byron isn't feeling too well, but why don't you come in for a few minutes," she said.

Byron was sitting in a lounger, a blanket in his lap when Tom entered.

He lifted a hand and said, "Have a seat."

The lounger was facing the window, the county highway and township road below. He had a perfect view.

Eva was all smiles as she directed Tom to a chair in their living room close to where Byron was sitting.

"Don't bother with any coffee, Eva. I won't be staying long," Tom said.

Byron forced a smile. Obviously his feelings were not up to par. He made mention of hearing about the incident that happened at Tom's house.

"I always thought this was a safe neighborhood. Things have changed with all these killings and shootings." His right arm motioned towards a rifle hanging over a closet door. "I keep it loaded."

Regardless of Tom's no coffee request, Eva brought in a tray with three cups of coffee and a small plate heaped with cookies. She tempted Tom with the cookie plate, he smiled and grabbed one. Byron was offered the plate next, in spite of the flu, he removed a cookie from the stack.

"Oh have another," a smiling Eva said after Tom finished off the first one.

"I sure will."

"See anything unusual on the township road lately?" Tom asked.

"No, but there sure has been a lot of traffic, more this summer that ever before. Maynard's house being for sale must be part of the reason. I see Kyle Fredrickson's car coming and going a lot."

"Do you remember ever seeing a light blue Pontiac?" Tom asked.

Eva was in the kitchen, and she peeked around the doorway and said, "Hey, I remember seeing a light blue car the other day. I couldn't tell what brand it was, though. The car looked a little older, like something from the early eighties."

"Do you remember what day that was?" Tom asked again.

"Well, not for certain, but I think it was the day I went in to have my hair done. That would have been last Monday."

The day before I was attacked, Tom thought.

"Hey, Eva, thanks for the coffee and the cookies. Lots of work to do at home today."

"See you later, Tom," said Byron.

"Now you get well fast," Tom responded as he left their house.

His truck battery cooperated and the engine started when he turned the key. Pete was in the deer stand, he waved when the pickup truck passed by. Farther down the road, he saw two fawns and a doe grazing the roadside. They looked up as he approached and quickly dashed into the woods. Go find Prancer, he thought.

# 50

THE LONG WAIT FOR THE FREIGHT TRAIN to pass through New Dresden along with the visit at Byron and Eva's home delayed Tom's return home He was anxious to check for phone messages. After parking the truck, Tom cautiously walked down the sidewalk to the front door. Before entering, he jacked a shell into the .38. Pushing the door open, he was relieved no one was there. Stepping into the kitchen, he could hear the phone answering machine beeping. Tom pressed the play button and waited for the message.

Expectations were for a message from Deputy Johnson. The strange, garbled voice was not the deputy's. He replayed the message, Words that Tom could understand, *Better watch your step* generated a numbing feeling in the pit of his stomach.

After regaining composure, Tom called Deputy Johnson.

"Could be a crank. I'll come by and check it out," said the deputy.

Before moving outdoors to mow grass, Tom buckled on the gun belt. He grimaced as the belt tightened on the tender spot in his waist. The sun was partially peaking through the clouds and it was a bit cool with a slight breeze coming from the northwest. He returned to the house to put on a jacket. Two eagles with huge wingspans were soaring and circling over the fields just west of Tom's property line as he mowed the greenway. Were they golden or bald, he wondered?

Mowing completed, he drove the tractor mower into the garage. A sheriff's car was parked in the driveway, the tall deputy was standing and admiring the yellow day lily flowers in full bloom, flower bed next to the house.

"Hi, Tom. Let's have a listen to that message. How's the wound feeling?"

"It's a little tender but I can't complain. The work's getting done. Come on in and I'll play it for you."

They listened to the playback, five times.

Paul said, "Boy, it sure doesn't tell us much, does it? Would you play it again?"

After three more, the deputy said, "That's enough, I guess. Not much to go on there. We receive several hundred complaints every year about crank phone messages. The country is full of whackos who are enjoying making life miserable for everyone."

Tom, with hands in pockets firmly said, "I almost wish this Ranforth guy would simply show up and the two of us could have it out. He has a huge advantage knowing who I am and where I live."

The deputy said, "I wonder what he's thinking now after what you did to Cameron. But then, all he has to do is hang around New Dresden to find out what's going on. Do you remember the pictures Larson took of the shoe tracks on your trail and roadway?"

"Yeah, I sure do. I would guess they belonged to Cameron."

"Well, yes and no. The shoe tracks on your trail and the cast you made on your roadway were the same, likely Cameron's.

"The prints near the township road at the beginning of your trail were different."

"Hmm, maybe Ranforth himself," Tom remarked.

"By the way, Tom, the county has set a hearing date to rule on Cameron's death. You are the primary witness and will be mandated to attend. The investigator is going to ask you a lot of questions. All you have to do is tell the story as it happened."

"When is this going to happen?" Tom asked.

"In about a week."

"That is going to be a dreadful experience for me. Getting it over with, dropping the incident into the past will be the consolation."

"Well, Tom, I have to go. Be careful...keep making those calls, we'll be watching."

That evening, long after the deputy left, Tom began a cautious walk up the roadway. Pete's deer stand was empty, there were two deer browsing in the cornfield just beneath the stand. Lucky for them it wasn't deer hunting season.

As Tom walked out onto the township road at the end of his roadway, he didn't move for about fifteen minutes. He was thinking about answering a barrage of questions, facing an investigative panel. God, they have to believe me.

No vehicles came by, a jogger with a dog was coming his way from Rocky Point. Tom did not wait, he moved onto the main trail, walking softly. Well into the woods, crossing a small bridge, he spotted a cloth-like object in the adjacent tall grass. Kneeling on the planks, he reached down, a glove.

Not his for certain, it wasn't a work glove. Material appeared to be leather, the kind country club people wear in the winter. Thoughts of how it got there, Tom felt a chill in his spine, Ranforth walking his trails. He didn't recollect Cameron wearing gloves during the attack. Tom carried the glove back to the house and carefully placed it in a plastic freezer bag, another clue for his collection.

Smell of pizza penetrated the air in the deck area that evening. Tom was waiting for the oven to buzz. Looking across the bay, he noticed the trees lighting up from the rays of the lowering sun. The western sky was speckled with red-and-blue-tinted clouds. He was mesmerized by the color changes in the sky and tree line. The sun had not set and his oven timer began beeping. Ah, the pizza was ready.

Lounging on the deck eating the pizza, he watched the water turn dark blue after the sun went down. His deer rifle was leaning against the rail, within reach. The .38-revolver was strapped to his waist. Blue darkness, another night, wondering when Ranforth was going to launch an attack. As customary, he double-checked the locks on all the doors, the.38-special revolver lay on the bedside table. His thoughts were about Ranforth—was his enemy in bed, thinking about him?

The next morning Tom awoke to the shrill squawking sound of crows. The noises sounded like a battlefield, Custer and the Little Bighorn. After rising, he strolled through the house, utilizing the windows to search the surroundings. Justifiable paranoia, he thought.

Instead of an enemy with a gun or knife, he saw two bald eagles perched in a birch tree near the west side of the house. The next few minutes were spent photographing the beautiful birds. Flashes of white were visible as the morning rays of sun filtered through the trees.

After the eagles flew off, Tom returned to the kitchen, grabbed a cup, and took up a sentry position on the deck, rifle leaning against the rail. A lone fishing boat across the bay didn't appear threatening. Using binoculars, he could see a single occupant casting into the weed bed,

After re-entering the house, Tom returned with a second cup of coffee. Moments later, he heard the sound of a boat motor, coming fast. He set the cup down and picked up the rifle. The boat, occupied by two people, thundered by. After passing the dock, it veered south and made a stop about a hundred yards west of the other boat.

Setting the rifle down, he sipped coffee, watching the wake splash against his pontoon boat. An hour later, the pot of coffee was empty. One of the boats left the bay, the other moved to a position farther east, toward the mouth of the bay. Tom became convinced the remaining boat didn't pose a threat.

Grocery list was tucked into his shirt pocket—wallet in his jacket. Grabbing the gun belt from the table, he headed for New Dresden. Tom looked for Prancer while driving up the roadway. The deer had the morning off—it didn't make an appearance.

As Tom approached town, he passed by the lake and thought about Allan, his wife and children. The only consolation was that Allan's family was not there to witness the dreadful scene, the green car getting pulled from the lake.

Main street parking spots were all taken on both sides, and there were two sets of double-parked vehicles, including an UPS truck. Tom found a parking spot on the side street just beyond Stillman's Super Market. First stop was the post office. The lobby was empty when he entered. Unlocking the box, he heard the door swish open, a voice.

Sylvan Tullaby said, "I hear you've had some excitement at your house."

Tom felt a chill, turned and said, "Hello, Sylvan, yes. You've probably heard. A man attacked me with a knife. I'm lucky to be standing here."

"I've sure seen a lot of sheriff cars around the past month, especially going into your place," added Sylvan.

"Yeah, they're working on the murders, trying to catch the person who committed them. I hope they do it soon. They've been over to see you too, haven't they?"

"Yeah, they've been at my house. They gave me a bad time about my cousin Jeff. Only because of the hat he was wearing. God, you would think it was against the law to wear a straw hat around here."

Tom had finished discarding junk mail, Sylvan was sorting through his.

"Look at all that junk stuff," said Sylvan as he tossed several pieces of mail into the wastebasket. "See you around," he added and exited through the lobby door.

Tom bundled up his remaining mail pieces, including a yellow slip indicating a package. He took the slip into the business room.

Jerry came in from the back room and said, "How's it goin'?" He began rummaging through the packages on the floor.

"Oh, not too bad. It's been at least a week since I have been shot at or attacked with a knife. What do you hear from the people that come in here?"

"You're our number one guy. I've heard all kinds of stories. One person said you are a special agent, working undercover for the CIA. A lady yesterday said you take your orders from the Mafia in Chicago. So take your choice, Tom."

"Interesting. I'll just keep them guessing."

Jerry found the package and laid it on the counter.

"Thanks, Jerry, have a nice day."

Tom walked down the sidewalk in the direction of the grocery store. Stillman's wasn't busy and he didn't take much time to make selections.

Ellie asked, "How are things out your way?"

"Very quiet and I like it that way." After writing a check, he picked up two bags and left the grocery.

— —

HAL FILLED A BUCKET WITH WATER and dumped in two dozen minnows.

"Thanks," he said and deposited the cash in the drawer. "Hey, Martha, would you watch the store? I'm headed over to the barbershop."

"Sure," his wife answered.

His timing was right on. Floyd wasn't busy.

When the apron was being tightened around his neck, he looked outside and said, "Uh, oh, looks like Kyle and Linda are going at it. Look at that, Floyd, was that a shove?"

"Those two have been at it ever since she moved here, nothing would surprise me."

"It was a shove, she pushed his chest, see that?"

Floyd didn't answer, he was watching Tom Hastings walk up the sidewalk.

— —

AS TOM DROVE DOWN THE TOWNSHIP ROAD, he saw a large flock of crows, about two hundred, feeding in a field. An early sign of fall, he thought. The deer stand was empty. Frightened from its perch by the approaching pickup truck, a pileated woodpecker flew ahead of the truck. The big, swooping bird had difficulty maintaining safe distance ahead of the truck, it veered off the roadway.

Tom parked the truck in the garage and carried the mail and groceries into the house. After putting the groceries away, he walked onto the deck. The fishing boat at the mouth of the bay earlier was gone. A mother duck trailed by a few ducklings scurried by the dock. The little ones were growing and they swam faster. There weren't as many. Tom smiled. Did an eagle or owl have some ducks for dinner?

# 51

SYLVAN'S SAILBOAT CRUISED UP THE MIDDLE OF THE BAY. Late evening, chill in the air, Tom was relaxing on the deck with a glass of wine. Almost relaxing—his deer rifle lay on the table. The unusual number of passengers aboard attracted his attention, sound of loud voices, Sylvan was having a party. Even though the southwesterly breeze appeared adequate for sailing, the mast wasn't rigged. The purring sound of the boat motor could be heard in spite of laughter and din.

Tom heard the phone ring. Julie was on the line. After the customary, how-are-you exchanges, she said, "I'd sure like to come out today. How about some fishing?"

"Sure, it will be great having you here. If you get out this afternoon, there'll be time to buy a fishing license, a couple of hours of fishing before dinner."

"That sounds like fun. I'll see about getting off early. Shouldn't be a problem."

"Okay. I'll be looking forward to your visit, the bait will be taken care of when I go in for the mail tomorrow morning."

Tom went to bed that night a little less fearful and more upbeat. He didn't feel as threatened and Julie was coming.

The next morning Tom was driving up the roadway, he had forgotten to bring the revolver. *Heck with it today,* he thought. The truck came to a stop, *don't be stupid.* Tom turned it around and headed back to the house. The .38-special was in the glove compartment when the pickup drove up the roadway a second time.

Pete was in his deer stand. Probably took his morning coffee out there, Tom thought. He parked in the hardware store parking lot and headed for the post office.

Two young boys, riding bicycles on the sidewalk, brushed up against a gray-haired lady as Tom approached.

"Hey, watch it, guys," he yelled.

To no avail, the boys increased their speed and continued down the sidewalk.

"Are you okay, ma'am?" asked Tom.

"Yes, thank you. I'm glad there's someone looking out for us."

"Hi, Jerry," Tom said as he entered the room. "I need a roll of stamps."

"I've got a registered letter for you," Jerry said as he laid a form on the counter.

Tom stared at the heading, *Big Lakes County Attorney.*

He knew what it meant.

"Sign right here, please."

Tom signed the form and brought out his checkbook.

As Tom was writing the check for the stamps, Jerry asked, "Have you ever heard of a man named Ranforth?"

Tom was staring at the envelope, he was thinking about sitting on the hot seat for a couple of hours, mentioning of the name *Ranforth* was not expected.

"I have. Why do you ask?"

"I have a letter addressed to a Mr. Robert Ranforth with just an address of New Dresden, Minnesota. He doesn't have a box here."

"Jerry, aren't you aware that a man with that name is the leading suspect of all three murders. I think you should contact the sheriff's department. This is serious...they need to know."

"Do you think so?" asked the postmaster.

"By all means, that letter could be critical."

"Okay. I'll give them a call."

To his dismay, the grocery store was out of newspapers for the second straight day.

Ellie apologized about the newspapers and said, "You'll have to get up earlier this time of year. They sell out fast."

Tom tightened his lips, narrowed his eyes, smiled and said, "This is early, Ellie."

Before leaving for home, he visited the hardware store to buy a fishing license. Pete was in the store browsing fishing tackle.

"Wow, are you quick or what? I just saw you in the deer stand a few minutes ago," said Tom.

"Yeah, I saw you go by. Guess what I caught yesterday, two nice size walleye. Fishing is picking up."

"Ah, and Julie is coming later today. We're going to give it a try."

"Lisa's got a touch of flu and didn't go to work today, but I'm hoping she will be up for some fishing later this afternoon. We'll see you out there."

"How's the public access working out for you?" Tom asked.

"Big improvement over the first year I had the boat. I got my pickup stuck over there, not fun. The new slab is just great."

Tom left the hardware store by the rear door where his pickup truck was parked and proceeded to Hal's bait shop a half block away.

"What can I do for you?" Hal asked.

"Two dozen large leeches should be enough."

Hal opened a refrigerator and brought out a plastic container.

Lying it on the counter, he said, "That'll be three-fifty."

Back in the pickup truck, Tom opened the registered letter. The death hearing was scheduled for a week from tomorrow. He wasn't looking forward to that. On the way home he was thinking about the letter Jerry showed him. Could the sheriff's department legally open it? If so, this whole thing would be cleared up shortly and his life could get back to normal. The glove, Tom had forgotten, the sheriff needs to know.

After arriving home, he readied the fishing boat for usage and placed the container of leeches under the seat. He was looking forward to fishing. Julie will like that.

Tom was sitting at the computer—it was just after 3:00 p.m. when Julie's red convertible emerged from the roadway and onto the driveway.

While he was assisting Julie with the luggage, she said, "Pete was standing at the edge of the field, next to your roadway, when I went by. He was holding a rifle."

"Pete's doing his job. Let's head into town and get you a fishing license. Pete said the walleyes are biting."

As they drove up the roadway, Pete was nowhere in sight. How could I expect him to be watching the roadway all the time, not practical, Tom thought.

At the hardware store, Julie filled out a fishing application as Tom stood near. He felt the stares as she handed the clerk the completed form. After Julie paid for the license, they left the store and headed for home.

Arriving home, Tom carried the tackle box and the fish poles down to the dock and placed them in the boat. He went back up and strapped on the .38. Julie helped carry a cooler of water and beer.

The engine started on the second pull. Before leaving the dock, Tom looked at Julie. She was perched on the forward bench, an extraordinarily wide smile. Life can be wonderful, Tom thought as he backed the boat away from the dock.

He directed the boat along the north shoreline toward Sylvan's place. After they passed Sylvan's dock and the beautiful sailboat, Tom set the engine to neutral and worked on baiting their lines.

Julie watched with interest and insisted she would bait her own hook the very next time. Tom rotated the handle of the motor, the forward gear engaged, and they dropped the lines in the water.

They were out only about four minutes when Julie exclaimed. "I got something."

Her pole almost vanished as the tip disappeared in the water. She tensed and held on with both hands.

"Looks like you've caught a real big one. Do you need any help?"

"No, I can bring it in," she said.

Julie worked the fish like an expert and brought it along side. Tom was in the process of getting the net under the fish when it jerked free and was swallowed up by the deep water.

"Darn it," she said.

"Sorry I was so slow with the net," Tom said.

Ten minutes and a beer later, she hooked another one. This time she succeeded in bringing it close, Tom scooped it up with the net. They had caught their first walleye of the day. Continuing to work the shoreline, they brought in two more walleye, pound-and-a-halfers, Tom guessed. The small pikes they caught were released.

A pontoon boat cruised by and the people aboard waved as they passed. A few minutes later, a large boat traveling at high speed went by. It left them bobbing up and down for a couple of minutes. When the wakes passed, Tom made for the dock. After docking, he filleted the walleyes and carried them up and placed them in the refrigerator.

Tom was aware of Julie's culinary skills, especially in the preparation of fish. He opened a bottle of wine and Julie began dinner.

"How about dinner on the deck?" asked Julie.

"That sounds like a great idea."

Tom ambitiously laid the plates and silverware on the table. Before returning for the cups, he gazed out over the water.

"Look at the trees across the bay," he said to Julie.

Spectacular colors in the leaves due to concentration of light from the sun. Reflections of the trees in the blue water were picture perfect. As Tom passed through the French door leading back into the dining room, he glanced at the table. The wineglasses glittered as narrow rays of sun slipped through the heavy wall of trees. The trauma of the last couple of months was lost for the moment.

# 52

"ALL WEATHER'S GOOD, REALLY," Tom said. The sky was gray and threatening rain. Julie looked at him and chuckled, a sly-like glance as they sipped coffee in the dining room.

"Well, if it insists on raining, let's go into town and buy a paper and have some breakfast," Tom said to Julie.

"Before we go, the carpet in the den needs vacuuming," Julie announced.

"Okay, sounds productive to me."

A couple of minutes later Tom heard the vacuum cleaner start. It stopped and started—once again.

"Darn this thing," said Julie. "I think it needs fixing."

Tom messed with the power cord for a few minutes, no avail.

"Forget the carpet for now, let's take this thing in. We've got a vacuum shop in town."

After backing the pickup truck out of the garage, Tom went back in the house, retrieved the vacuum cleaner and laid it in the box.

Julie braced for the jar at the railroad track crossing, as Tom didn't slow the pickup. He did slow down for Main Street. Julie said, "I wonder what's going on over there?"

There were several people milling about, near the front entry to the post office.

"Uh-oh, that's a sheriff's car parked next to the building," Tom said.

He drove past the post office and found a parking spot around the corner on the side street. Tom and Julie walked hand in hand past the grocery store, and up the Main Street sidewalk Tom knew something was wrong, the body language of the people gathered on the sidewalk looked similar to what he observed when the car was in the lake.

Matt Nelson was standing at the periphery of a cluster of onlookers.

"What's going on, Matt?" Tom asked.

"Hello folks, there's been an accident."

"What happened?" an anxious Tom asked.

"Jerry's been hurt."

Oh no, not another one, Tom thought—the Ranforth letter.

"Is he hurt bad?" Tom asked.

"Don't know."

"Do you think I can get my mail?"

"Oh yeah, the side room is opened."

As Tom and Julie entered the postal box room, they heard a siren.

As he was readying a key to open the postal box, Julie said, "Oh, look, there's an ambulance."

Tom looked up and saw it slow before making a left turn into an alley that led to the rear of the post office. The door to the business part of the post office was closed and the lights were out. They could hear voices from behind the wall.

"Here they are," exclaimed someone.

"Let's go, Julie," Tom said.

They stood outside for a few minutes and the chatter hushed when the siren re-started and the ambulance darted onto Main Street and headed northward toward the county highway. They were still standing on the sidewalk when two sheriff officers emerged. One of them was Deputy Johnson. He saw Tom and nodded his head and gestured with his right hand toward his vehicle.

"I think he wants to talk to me," Tom whispered to Julie.

They began walking slowly toward the sheriff's vehicle. Deputy Johnson had gotten behind the wheel and slammed the door shut. He lowered the window when they approached.

Keeping his voice low, he said, "We need to talk. I'll be by in a couple of hours."

The deputy's car followed the ambulance out of town.

"So what do you suppose happened to Jerry?" asked Julie.

"Darned if I know but it sure has the feel of...of a Ranforth."

While walking down the sidewalk returning to the pickup store, Tom said, "Julie, yesterday Jerry showed me a letter in the post office, it had Ranforth's name on it.

"I advised him to call the sheriff, bet he never did. I'll find out more when Deputy Johnson comes over."

Tom's thoughts were about Jerry when they entered the grocery store. Hurriedly, they picked up the newspaper and some miscellaneous grocery items and made their way back to the truck.

Tom and Julie originally planned to have breakfast at the Borders Café.

"I think we should skip breakfast in town this morning," Tom told Julie.

"Just as well, I wonder what the chatter at the Borders Café will be about this morning?" Julie said.

"I can about imagine," Tom answered.

As they headed out of town and passed the post office, the cluster of onlookers on Main Street had dissipated.

They were beyond the railroad tracks when Julie exclaimed, "The vacuum, Tom, we forgot to drop it off."

"Oh shoot, I almost forgot."

He turned the truck around and returned to Main Street. Driving around the block, he parked in front of Fred's Vacuum Cleaner Shop.

Julie accompanied Tom as he carried the vacuum across the curb.

"Look, the door's partly open," said Julie.

Tom pulled it wide and he followed Julie into the shop. There wasn't anyone in the room. Fred was not in his usual spot behind the counter.

After waiting for a few minutes, Tom asked, "I wonder what's happened to Fred?"

A pen and pad were lying on the counter. Writing down his name, number and a short note, he placed the vacuum on the floor.

They drove home in silence, both glancing at Pete's deer stand when passing. It was empty. After arriving back at the house, they shared the task of putting away the groceries.

"That takes care of that, Julie. Why don't you take the newspaper on the deck? I'll bring out the coffee."

"Oki-doke," she said. "When is the deputy coming?"

"He said he would be over in a couple of hours."

They began reading the newspaper and sipping coffee. They were still on the deck when Tom heard the sound of tires on the driveway.

"Probably the deputy," he said.

He walked into the house and peered out. Tom was relieved that it was a sheriff's car. He hustled to the front door and saw Deputy Johnson and another deputy coming down the sidewalk. Julie entered the room.

He opened the door and Deputy Johnson said, "Do you remember Deputy Larson?"

"Yes, I do, but I don't think Julie has met him."

Tom introduced Julie to Deputy Larson and the two deputies sat down at the dining room table. Tom went into the kitchen, filled four cups and set them down on the table.

"Thank you," said Deputy Larson.

"Hey, you guys make great coffee," added Deputy Johnson.

Julie brought out some napkins. Tom and Julie sat on the love seat.

"So what happened to Jerry and how is he?" Tom anxiously asked.

Deputy Johnson grimaced and spoke slowly, "I didn't think Ranforth would make a move this soon, it was the letter. Jerry was still unconscious as of about fifteen minutes ago."

"Oh no," Julie responded with a strained voice.

"Was he shot or what?" Tom asked.

"Jerry was hit on the back of the head with a club of some kind."

"Oh, my God, here we go again. Do you know what the prognosis is?"

"I talked to the doctor at the hospital and he didn't sound too optimistic," said Deputy Johnson.

"The letter, Jerry showed me the letter yesterday. I told him he should call you right away."

Deputy Larson said, "Jerry called us earlier this morning...it was about the letter. The problem was, we needed a judge's order to open it. Bad news is, the judge was in session and the approval didn't come until later...too late."

Tom's hope of exposing Ranforth via the letter had vanished. His lips tightened and he asked, "I think I already know the answer. Is the letter missing?"

Deputy Johnson took a deep breath and answered, "Yes, as you suspect, Tom, it's gone."

"I wonder who else Jerry showed the letter to, other than me. Probably Ranforth himself."

"That possibility looms high. Ranforth has to be someone living right there, in New Dresden. I would like to stay here the rest of the day...impossible to do. Let's go Arlin. Thanks for the coffee, nice seeing you, Julie."

"Before you go, I've come up with another clue." Tom brought out the plastic bag containing the glove.

"What do you have there?" Larson asked.

"I found this a couple of days ago along the main trail not too far from my roadway."

Deputy Larson took the plastic bag, held it up to the light and handed it to his partner.

"Hey, nice job. Our lab guys are going to check this out," he said.

Deputy Johnson added, "You found it along the trail, you say. You're sure it's not yours?"

"Not mine...that's for sure."

"I don't imagine you need another warning to be careful. You've already been through so much."

"Thanks for coming," Tom said.

The deputies returned to their car. Julie and Tom stood in the driveway and watched as the car disappeared up the roadway.

"Julie, this latest event has reduced my enthusiasm for fishing. But, what the heck, let's go anyhow."

They went fishing again late that afternoon. This time they crossed over to the other side of the bay and began trolling the edge of the popular weed beds. They were trolling only a few minutes when Julie hooked a walleye. She demonstrated considerable skill in working the fish close to the side, allowing Tom to retrieve it with the net.

As he dropped the stringer with the walleye into the water, Tom noticed a large boat coming up the middle of the bay. Julie was busy baiting her line and didn't notice him unsnapping the holster strap and placing the revolver in his lap.

The operator glanced at them as the boat sped by and continued on deeper into the bay. Tom brought out the binoculars and watched the boat make a wide turn and began the return. As the boat drew near, he grasped the revolver in the right hand and pulled back the hammer.

He watched with anxiety as the boat operator pushed the throttle forward and the boat sped by. The fishing boat began bobbing up and down and Tom put down the binoculars.

"Who was that?" asked Julie.

"I'm not really sure but it sort of looked like Kyle from the realty office. The driver was wearing a baseball cap, similar to what Kyle wears."

After the boat passed from view, Tom placed the revolver back into the holster and snapped the strap. They fished for about another hour before returning to the dock.

After the boat was secured, Julie said, "I'll go up and get a container while you fillet the fish."

When Julie returned, Tom was tossing the fish remains back into the water and said. "The turtles love what I am doing."

After washing the fillets in the lake water, he placed them into

Julie's container and they walked hand in hand up the hillside to the house.

Sunday afternoon Julie packed her things and Tom helped load her stuff into the car.

"See you soon," she said, and the red convertible was gone.

Only a few minutes passed after she left when Tom's phone rang. It was Julie calling from her cell phone. "I saw a strange man standing at the edge of the township road right next to the entry to your roadway."

"It wasn't Pete, was it?"

"No, I'm sure it wasn't Pete. I didn't see any vehicles around either."

"Do you remember what he was wearing?"

"Oh yes he had a baseball cap on his head. I believe it had some white but mostly green. His shirt and trousers were brownish. Glasses, he was wearing glasses. The man was staring at me as I drove by."

"Thanks, Julie, I'll check it out."

"Be careful Tom," she said. "Talk later."

"Have a safe trip."

Strapping on the gun and grabbing the rifle from the closet, he quickly made his way to the garage. After backing out the pickup truck, he jacked a shell into the rifle and propped it against the passenger seat. Placing the revolver on the seat, he opened both windows and slowly drove up the roadway. Pete's deer stand was empty.

As he approached the end of the roadway, he steered with the left hand and grasped the revolver with his right. He stopped and looked left when drawing abreast of the beginning to the main trail. Prancer was standing only about forty yards away. The deer's front legs were stiff and planted on the turf.

Tom's anxiety lessened. Whoever Julie saw had to be gone, otherwise Prancer wouldn't be there, he thought.

Tom got out of the pickup and watched Prancer retreat into the woods. Carefully, he pulled out the rifle and walked to the end of the roadway. Looking in all directions, he saw no one. At the edge of the gravel road, in the smooth area created by the township road grader, he saw fresh shoe tracks. They were shallow, but definite.

After turning the pickup around on the township road, he drove back to the house. Returning to the intersection a few minutes later, he traced the tracks onto a sheet of computer paper. Looks pretty darn good, he thought. Tom did a second tracing of another track.

After getting back to the house, he thought about calling Deputy Johnson. Tom had a nagging fear that the front office people were getting tired of all his tracks and clues, he didn't make the call.

As evening approached, Tom's fear changed to a burst of inspiration. Adrenaline surged through his body. He had been stalked, attacked and victimized. His trails and roadway had become a private battleground. This was his turf, nobody was going to drive him out. Tom confidently spun the cylinder of the .38, placed it back into the holster.

He grabbed the deer rifle from the front closet and walked out to the greenway. Slinging the rifle over his shoulder, he began walking the main trail through the woods. Moving along with confidence, the fingers of his right hand were resting on the revolver.

Reaching the end of the trail and stepping onto his roadway, he tucked in behind a tree and remained for close to an hour. The strategy of laying in wait, to catch Ranforth, was losing momentum. Not a single vehicle came by. Not a single person seen. He stepped onto the township road. Not even Prancer made a showing.

The only sound came from a barking dog, from the direction of Sylvan's house. After hanging around the township road for another hour, he began the walk back to the house.

Passing Pete's empty deerstand, a penetrating screeching sound alarmed Tom, scared the pants off him. He crouched and jerked out the revolver. The gun slipped from his hand and landed in the gravel. With embarrassing relief, he watched a red shoulder hawk flying down the roadway. The hawk will never know the fear it generated in Tom Hastings that late summer evening.

# 53

CROWS AWAKENED TOM HASTINGS on Monday morning. Sometimes the crackling screeches crows make are warnings, hopefully local confrontations with hawks. To be certain, he scanned the landscape using the strategic location of his windows.

All is well, he thought. After starting a pot of coffee, he sat at the computer and accessed the Internet. There was news of a plane crash in the San Francisco bay area and of forest fires sweeping across western Montana. The sun was rising by the time he heard the sound of coffee perking.

E-mail was completed, the Internet session ended. He placed the two paper tracings in an envelope and headed out to the garage. Driving up the roadway, he stopped just short of the township road. No one was around and he took the gun belt out of the glove compartment and fastened it around his waist. He was startled to see that a tire track had obliterated some of the shoe tracks that he traced the previous day.

Leaving the pickup truck parked in the middle of the roadway, he followed the tire tracks toward his house. Just short of the site where the large tree had fallen, the tracks disappeared. He imagined Ranforth turning the vehicle right around, right there. Mixed feelings of satisfaction and apprehension went through his mind as he rapidly walked back to the pickup truck.

He planned to visit the sheriff's office in Big Lakes after New Dresden errands. A lady postal worker was behind the counter serving a customer when Tom walked through the door to pick up a package. She and the man were discussing Jerry's condition. Tom listened while waiting for his package. His stomach sickened when hearing the postmaster's condition was not improving. He picked up the package off the counter and headed for Big Lakes.

"Hi, Mr. Hastings," said the receptionist at the sheriff's office. "What can I do for you today?"

Tom interpreted the lady's expression to mean that she was tired of him coming around with clues.

"I need to see Deputy Johnson," he said firmly.

"Okay, let me see if I can find him." She spent a few minutes on the phone. After hanging up she said, "He'll be with you soon."

A minute later Deputy Johnson emerged and gestured Tom to enter his office.

"What do you have there?" he asked.

"I found some more prints yesterday and produced these two tracings. Paul, Julie saw a man standing on my roadway near the township road when she drove out on Sunday. I went out there and found these boot tracks."

"Nice job with the tracings, Tom. Let's see how they compare with the other stuff that's in our file."

He brought out a folder from his file cabinet and removed an artist tracing of the shoe tracks found on the trail in the woods a couple of weeks earlier.

"Boy, that's real close," Tom said.

"Yes, it sure is," the deputy agreed.

"How about the plaster casts?" Tom asked.

The deputy left the room and returned with two boxes.

"The casts gotten from your trail and roadway, not from Vince Cameron, closely match your paper tracings. This could mean Ranforth. Oh, by the way, regarding the leather glove you brought in the other day, a new set of fingerprints. They matched one from Maynard Cushing's house."

Usual feelings of insecurity after leaving the sheriff's office were not dictating to Tom that day. He walked out brimming with confidence. After leaving Big Lakes, he drove to New Dresden. Tom stopped at the Borders Café for an early lunch. Henry was sitting at a table reading the newspaper.

"Have a chair," the senior gentleman said.

Tom accepted, sat down across from him and asked, "What's new in the paper?"

The waitress interrupted and said, "Are you ready?"

"Yes, I'll have the special."

Henry asked Tom, "Have you heard any news on how Jerry is doing?"

"No, I haven't. What about you?"

"Yes, I've heard Jerry was coming out of the coma."

Tom wondered why Deputy Johnson had not mentioned Jerry earlier, he may have forgotten. If what Henry told him was true, surely the sheriff's department would know. Perhaps news traveled faster to New Dresden than to the sheriff's office. Regardless, the news about Jerry was encouraging.

"Henry, if Jerry recovers he will talk, and our lives, especially mine, will become a lot easier."

Driving home, Tom decided to visit Byron and Eva, yet another visit. The location of their house, overlooking the township road, was strategic. Their vehicle report could be important.

Byron answered the door and Tom was glad to see that he was feeling better.

"Come on in, Tom."

"Byron, you look a lot better today...goodbye to the virus, huh?"

"Yeah, I'm even taking daily walks on the township road."

"Do you see many people during your walks?"

"Yes, I usually meet other walkers, most of them from the resort. I made it all the way around the loop the other day."

"Have you ever seen anyone near my roadway recently?" Tom asked.

"No, I don't think so."

Eva came in from the kitchen and said, "Yesterday when biking around the loop, I saw someone, a man. It was at the entrance to your roadway. I thought it might be you."

"What time was that about?" asked Tom?

She added, "About 5:00. The man moved out of sight just before I got to your roadway. I couldn't see who it was. By the way, Tom, how do you just happen to show up on the days I bake cookies?"

"I can smell them all the way from the highway."

"Oh yeah, so that's your excuse for stopping."

"Yup, I make sure my window is down every time I drive by your house."

Tom's confidence remained high the balance of the day. That evening, he decided to dine at Mary Ann's. Driving up his roadway, he noticed Pete in the deer stand. The parking lot at the restaurant was nearly empty. The sign was different, *Sally's*. Tom stood by the truck and stared at the sign, end of an era, he thought.

Two yellow tractor-loaders were parked next to the burn site. The debris was gone. Construction of the new house was underway. According to Henry, the new owners were going to build a log home.

As Tom walked across the parking lot, two couples were leaving.

One of the ladies paused, looked at Tom, and said, "The food's real good."

"Glad to hear that," Tom responded.

He had the feeling the lady intended to say something else, she knew who he was. Tom didn't know any of the four.

The hostess was new and introduced herself, "Hi, I'm Sally. Richard, my husband, and I are the new owners."

"I'm Tom Hastings. My home is on the other side of the lake."

"Welcome aboard. Can I help you get a table or booth?"

"Yes, you sure can."

Tom decided to take a seat in a booth next to the window in the bar area.

Sally's voice was soft, lightly singing her words. She was tall and well proportioned. Her hair was blonde and she had a lot of dark stuff around her eyes. A country western musical program was on the television.

"Sally, would you mind if I changed the channel to a baseball game?"

"Not at all. I'll ask Richard to help you."

Moments later, a man came by with the remote control. He said, "Hi, I'm Richard, and you are?"

"I'm Tom Hastings from the other side of the lake. I really appreciate you bringing over the remote."

Richard's voice crackled slightly when he talked—perhaps a

smoker, Tom thought. The new owner's large, dark brown eyes were busy glancing around the room. The brown, bushy mustache matched his dark hair that was fighting a receding hairline.

After a few clicks with the remote, Tom found the Twins game. They were playing the division-leading White Sox.

A waitress appeared. "Anything to drink?" she asked.

"Yup, I'll have a bottle of Bud."

She returned with the beer.

"I think I would like some cordon bleu this evening," said Tom.

"Anything else?" she asked.

"Yes, would you bring over a glass of Chardonnay when the dinner arrives?"

"Sure thing."

Tom raised his elbows and watched as the waitress filled his glass and laid the plate down. He felt the first sip of the Chardonnay sooth the walls of his stomach while re-focusing on the Twins game. Their new first baseman was rounding third, touching them all, two-run lead. Watercraft activity on the lake was sparse, only two fishing boats, they were a distance away, close to Rocky Point.

As Tom was finishing dinner, Sylvan and his wife appeared, coming from the direction of the main dining room. They sauntered over to the bar and sat down at one of the small high tables. Sylvan glanced in Tom's direction and waved. Tom returned the wave.

Sally came over and asked, "Was everything all right?"

Tom smiled and responded, "It sure was."

Sally sat down across from Tom and asked, "Have you been coming here a lot in the past?"

"About once a week," he told her.

"How was the service?" she asked.

"I've never had a problem. But then, I'm not very fussy. Mary Ann and her staff took care of me pretty darn good."

Sally said, "I hope you visit us often. Thanks for coming."

After dinner was completed, Tom left the booth and approached the cash register at the bar. He wrote a check and stopped to visit with Sylvan and his wife.

"Have you met my wife, Missy?" Sylvan asked.

"Yes, I think I have...right here at the restaurant some time ago."

Missy asked, "Do you know how our postmaster is doing?"

"I've heard two stories today, and am hoping the one about him coming out of the coma is true."

"I cannot imagine why anyone would want to harm Jerry."

Sylvan remained silent during the discussion about Jerry. Darkness was setting in when Tom left the restaurant. The name change *Sally's* is going to require a mental adjustment, he thought.

# 54

MAYNARD CUSHING DESCRIBED RANFORTH as a youthful and intelligent young man. Tom Hastings was re-reading section four of Maynard's memoirs. Looking upward over the computer display, he saw a group of finches fighting for position at one of the bird feeders. Deep in thought about the memoirs, he wondered, did youthful mean a real early age, perhaps in the twenties? If so that would place Ranforth's present age at late forties or early fifties.

Reading on, it became apparent that Maynard did not trust Ranforth during the time they worked together. He mentioned the number of times Ranforth's automobile would be the last vehicle remaining in their underground garage at the end of the day. After Maynard Cushing reported his suspicions to a superior, a lookout operation caught Ranforth red-handed, loading a satchel full of classified documents into the car trunk.

In the final paragraph, Maynard described Ranforth's cold, steel, gray eyes, as he was being led away in handcuffs. Do I know anyone with gray eyes, wondered Tom? But then gray could mean hazel or bluish. He dwelled on the last two pages of the Ranforth section for a few minutes.

Tom set down the document and walked out on the deck. There weren't any boats near his dock. The only boat he could see was well east of Sylvan's dock, silhouetted in a haze, no threat, he thought. A small break in the eastern sky, sun peaking through, was attempting to disperse the haze. In moments a bright orange circle appeared, dispensing reddish-colored streaks above and along the shoreline trees.

Heading for New Dresden, Tom drove beyond his roadway entering the township road, creating a large dust cloud behind the pickup truck. He slowed when spotting a person walking. It was Byron taking his daily stroll. Tom stopped and opened the window.

"Real quiet around here this morning except for the dust. We could sure use some rain," Byron said.

"No use getting a car wash today. Have a good walk."

Tom closed the window and generated another large dust cloud. The lack of wind and dry air enhanced the aroma from the dairy farm as he passed.

Tom parked the truck and entered the grocery store, Listening to the conversations, he knew there was good news. The employees were in an unusually cheery mood.

"Haven't you heard?" said Ellie, the till clerk.

"Heard what?"

"Jerry came out of his coma last night," She said.

"That's great news...the best I've heard in a long time."

The news of Jerry's recovery was great news for New Dresden. They missed their postmaster.

Ellie added, "Jerry drifted in and out of sleep a few times and finally woke up for good."

"Did he say who hit him over the head?" Tom asked.

"I hadn't heard about that. I only know he is going to be okay."

When Tom returned home, he dialed Deputy Johnson's phone number.

"It's true, Tom. Jerry has recovered from the coma but the doctors won't permit him to be questioned right now...perhaps tomorrow. We have someone at the hospital around the clock waiting for permission."

Tom Hastings was in good spirits driving home. He wondered how long it was going to be necessary to carry a gun. The noose was tightening around Ranforth's neck.

Arriving home, he checked the .38-special revolver. There were five bullets in the magazine, empty chamber in front of the hammer. The magazine clicked as it closed and Tom pushed the gun down into the holster.

After snapping the strap, he filled the tractor mower with fuel and began trimming the greenway. While heading in an eastern direction and making a turn, he glanced at the roadway and glimpsed some motion.

Tom made the turn and headed the opposite direction, glancing back over his shoulder frequently. Perhaps it was a deer, he thought. Continuing to mow, he began to have doubts. Could the motion be for real—Ranforth?

Tom felt reasonably secure with the gun strapped to his side. Looking over the greenway, he estimated another half-hour mowing remaining. Reaching down with his right hand, he unsnapped the strap. Curiosity and fear won him over. Stopping the tractor, he got off and removed the revolver from the holster.

Creeping up the side of the greenway toward the roadway, he paused periodically and snuggled next to a tree. After reaching the point where the roadway was visible, he could see no one. His left hand gently rubbed the healing wound in his left side. The house—was it safe?

Sneaking by the side of the garage, he advanced toward the west side of the house. Moving quickly, he entered via the lower-level furnace room door. Stopping to listen, he couldn't hear anything except an occasional crow. Tom opened the door that led to a bedroom and spiral staircase. Again, he stopped to listen.

Hearing nothing, he tiptoed up the spiral stairway. Before raising his head to floor level, he held the revolver in both hands and held it above his head. The next step could seal his fate, or Ranforth's, he thought.

He pulled back the hammer and heard the cylinder advance. Up he stepped, ready to fire—a sigh of relief. The dining room was empty. Tom checked out the rest of the house, the revolver ready.

Satisfied the house was secure, he looked for deer tracks or human shoe tracks on the roadway, but found none. It could have been a large bird. Perhaps a pileated woodpecker or a hawk, he thought.

As he continued walking up the roadway, his thoughts were with Jerry and how his innocence and service to others had almost cost him his life. Tom considered himself to be either lucky or Ranforth's intentions were simply to frighten. Perhaps the frequent visits by sheriff deputies discouraged Ranforth from chancing another attempt.

At dinnertime Tom called Pete to ask him if he was aware that Jerry was recovering.

"Yeah, I was in town earlier this morning and heard the great news. It would have never been the same at the post office without Jerry. Lisa and I are hoping he will be back to work soon."

"Have you seen any vehicles on my road lately, other than the expected, of course?"

"A couple of days ago I saw a car coming up your roadway from your house. It was light in color and at first I thought it was a deputy's car, but after another look, I knew it wasn't."

"The car you saw may be the one that turned around on my roadway yesterday. Thanks, Pete."

Tom spent most of the evening sitting in the den watching a baseball game on television. Between innings he visited the deck and scanned the surroundings. The bay was quiet that evening. He saw only one fishing boat, it was directly across the bay. That boat remained in the same area all evening. Just before dark he heard the motor startup. Glancing out the window, Tom saw the boat speed out of the bay.

# 55

JULIE CALLED THE NEXT MORNING. "Good morning, Tom, how are things with you so far today?"

"No problems yet. Nice to hear from you, Julie."

"The *Star Tribune* has a story about your postmaster this morning. I was elated to read about the news of his recovery. Very soon you should know who Ranforth is and he will be arrested."

"Yup, I heard the good news too. Hopefully this whole thing will be over before long. How about coming out on Thursday?"

"It's hot and humid here and I'm looking forward to another visit soon. I'm looking forward to playing tennis. Thursday should work."

On his way into town later that morning, he stopped the pickup truck just short of the end of his roadway. Before getting out of the truck, he looked around in all directions and saw no one. Slowly, he pushed the door open and got out onto the roadway. Carefully walking the edge of the roadway, he didn't see any new shoe tracks.

Satisfied there wasn't anyone about, he walked back to the truck and drove onto the township road. Approaching the turn at the bottom of the small hill, he glanced over towards Maynard's house. The driveway was empty. A car coming from the public access road cut right out in front of him. Tom reached the intersection first, but needed to apply brakes to prevent a collision.

When the car halted at the county highway stop sign, the dust settled enough so Tom could see the license number. It was a Minnesota car with a number *AWY462*. The first three letters were the same as his truck, a local vehicle. Tom waited behind the car while a milk truck and two pickup trucks passed heading northward. When the car turned left towards New Dresden, in spite of all the dust, Tom could make out a light brown color. The huge dust cloud hid the driver.

The car ahead of him accelerated after it passed by the dairy farm. A small pickup truck jumped onto the road, forcing Tom to slow down. He passed the red pickup and tried to catch the car. All he got was a glimpse when it crossed the railroad tracks. The car turned left after it reached the end of Main Street. By this time, Tom wasn't sure whether it was the same one.

There was a parking slot directly across from the post office. Tom began walking across the street. A delivery truck slowed to allow him to cross. After retrieving the mail, he stopped at the counter to buy stamps. Jerry's replacement was all smiles as she completed his transaction.

Leaving the post office, Tom saw Kyle standing in front of the realty doorway conversing with someone in a car, next to the curb. Tom crossed the street and walked past Kyle on his way to the bank.

The tellers were all busy. Tom stood in line waiting a turn. The lady in front of him was finished with business, she was using up the teller's time with a story about her granddaughter. Tom almost flipped when the lady brought out a picture. He was experiencing bank teller rage. She finally packed up her stuff, gave Tom a dirty look, and stormed out.

"Sorry, Tom, not much I could do, nice pictures," said the teller. "I hear that Jerry will be coming back soon. That's what Henry has been saying."

Tom laughed and said, "It takes all kinds. Yeah, I like what I hear about Jerry. He sure has gone through a lot. It will be good to have him back."

After leaving the bank, Tom walked across the street to the grocery store. The people in the grocery were upbeat about Jerry.

"We're going to get our postmaster back," a man dressed in overalls said.

Tom picked up the grocery bag and headed up the sidewalk toward his pickup truck. He noticed Kyle Fredrickson was still standing by his door. He was smoking a cigarette and appeared to be watching.

When Tom got back in the truck, he remembered the vacuum cleaner. Parking in front of Fred's Vacuum Cleaner Shop, he entered and saw Fred sitting behind the counter. He was on the phone and gestured Tom to wait.

In a couple of minutes, he hung up and said, "Loose wire. I have it ready."

Fred went into the back room and brought out the vacuum and set it on the floor.

"How much is the bill?" Tom asked.

"Eight-fifty," Fred replied.

Tom wrote out the check and said, "Thanks, Fred, nice job."

When Tom was getting in his truck, he noticed Fred watching from the window. He drove around the block and glanced through the back window as he headed toward the railroad tracks. The Realtor continued standing in front of his office door.

Tom met a sheriff's car when passing the cemetery. The driver wasn't Deputy Johnson, probably a routine patrol, he thought. Tom saw a jogger on the township road as he approached the entry to his roadway. The male jogger was a stranger.

Parking the pickup truck in the garage, he removed the gun belt from the glove compartment and fastened it around his waist.

After carrying the bag into the house, he walked out on the deck. There wasn't anyone on the lake except for two loons drifting and diving a few yards away from the end of his dock.

He watched the loons while eating lunch and reading the newspaper. A third loon had joined the original pair. After lunch he walked outside and took mental note of clusters of weeds invading his flower gardens. The small tiller was noisy. Tom worked it through the weedy areas and felt satisfied when the job was completed.

— —

FRED HOOD WAS SEETHING after Tom Hastings left the store. His world was coming apart. Vince Cameron had failed him. The thought of his hire being dead was pleasing, except that Cameron didn't get the job done. Twice Fred sent him to the Hastings's home. Twice Vince had failed.

Fred opened the counter drawer and removed an envelope. He grasped the ticket to Mexico and held it up to the light. Smiling, he reviewed his travel itinerary. The flight was leaving from Brownstown this evening and he would be on the plane, leaving behind a room of used vacuum cleaners. Mrs. Paulson's vacuum was in the room. It wasn't fixed, she wasn't going to stick him with another freebee.

Fred locked the front door, grabbed the envelope off the counter and headed out the back door. He drove to his apartment and walked up the long narrow stairway for the last time. His belongings were all packed, stuffed in the trunk. Under the cover of darkness, he took care of that last night.

It's time, thought Fred. I'll show that Tom Hastings.

— —

BYRON SAID, "Hey, Eva, isn't that the vacuum cleaner guy's car?"

"Look at that dust...how can you tell whose car it is, anyhow?"

"I saw it before it left the pavement."

Pete was almost dozing. He had been in the stand for close to an hour and heard the sound of wheels on the gravel. Looking toward Tom's roadway, he saw a light colored car go by. Wonder who belongs to that?

— —

LATER THAT AFTERNOON, Tom placed the .38-special in the tennis bag and headed out to the court. There was little wind and the temperature was perfect. After working out for a solid hour, he picked up the balls and put away the machine.

Sauntering back to the house, he came to an abrupt stop—there was a car in the driveway. It was light brown in color and parked on a slope short of the sidewalk. Tom ducked back behind the corner of the garage and set the tennis bag down. He stooped and retrieved the revolver from the holster.

Peeking around the edge of the garage and looking in all directions, he saw no one. The house wasn't locked, he was certain.

Tom walked around the back of the garage, to the other side, giving him a better look at the car. Similar to the one that cut him off this morning, he thought. Tom was hesitant to walk out into the open area of the driveway, or approach the house. His right hand was feeling numb from the tight grasp on the revolver.

Walking back to his original position on the west side of the garage, he tucked in behind the large corner bush. A few minutes passed and there wasn't a sound except for the purr of a boat motor somewhere on the bay.

Tom shifted the revolver to the left hand and stretched the numbing fingers. The voice he heard from behind shocked him beyond belief.

Words heard on television so many times, "Drop the gun."

He searched his mind to remember where he had heard that voice before, a male voice. The initial fear he felt was gradually dissipating. Adrenaline surged through his body as racehorses out of a gate. Tom was pleased with himself for remaining cool.

"I said, drop the gun," the man repeated.

The voice—Tom knew where he had heard it last, the vacuum cleaner shop. Reluctantly, he dropped the revolver on the grass near the corner of the garage.

"Now turn around," the man said.

Tom slowly turned and was not surprised that the voice was that of Fred Hood—Tom's suspicion was right. Fred's cold, steel gray eyes were glowing with excitement. He held a small pistol in the right hand. For what seemed like an eternity to Tom, the two men stared at each other. Tom was preparing for the worst when he noticed movement, near the tennis court.

Pete Smilie was bracing against a large oak tree and drawing a bead on Fred with his deer rifle.

"Come on shoot...shoot damn-it, Pete," Tom whispered. "Shoot!"

Fred was watching Tom's eyes. When seeing them shift toward the tennis court, he turned. Tom was amazed how quickly Fred got off a shot, toward Pete. Within a split second of Fred's shot, Tom heard the thundering sound of Pete's deer rifle.

Taking advantage of the spectacular distraction, he dropped to the grass, picked up the revolver, and dove behind the corner of the garage. Lying on his stomach and out of sight, he pulled back the hammer of the revolver and heard it click. Keeping the gun pointed out in front and placing his finger on the trigger, Tom was ready to shoot. He was expecting Fred to appear at any moment. The feel of his heart, becoming more and more evident, beating at about two-hundred-times-a-minute.

The moments passed. No one came into view and Tom's curiosity was soaring. Silence was deafening. He didn't dare call out to expose his position. His stomach was super bubbling while continuing to keep a finger snug on the trigger. More time passed. Just how much time, Tom will never know. Unable to maintain the strained position, he got up on his knees and began to creep away from the corner of the garage. Eventually, he reached the other end.

Staying between bushes and the outside wall as much as possible, he made his way to the northeast corner. Cautiously, he chanced a peak. To his immense relief, Pete was standing where Fred had been earlier.

"Hey, Pete, what's happening? Are you okay?" Tom yelled.

Pete looked at Tom and waved. Tom kept the revolver in his right hand while walking to where Pete was standing.

"Oh, there you are," Pete said. "Blood."

Tom looked down at the grass and saw the red splotches. He felt his voice quiver, "Thanks so much, Pete, You've saved my life."

"I know I hit him," Pete said. "After I shot, he ran for the woods right over there." He pointed towards the trees.

"I'm going to call the sheriff's office," said Tom.

"Okay," replied Pete.

Tom ran to the house with gun in hand. Pushing the front door open, he crouched and swept his arm from side to side. Much to his relief, there wasn't anyone in the room. He dialed Deputy Johnson's phone number. The deputy answered and listened to Tom's confusing explanation of what was happening.

"Don't take any chances," he said, "we're on our way."

Tom returned outdoors to join Pete, who had followed the blood drops to the edge of the woods.

"The bleeding has increased. Let's follow the trail."

"I don't think they want us to do that, Pete, the sheriff people are on their way. Let's leave it to them."

Pete looked at Tom and seemed disappointed, anxious to follow the blood trail. He pointed his rifle toward the woods where Fred's trail led and said, "I think we can take this guy."

"Finally, Ranforth's identify is known. Oh God, Pete, he may attempt to get back to his car. Stay right here, I'm going to check and see if the keys are in there."

Tom loped over to the light brown car, opened the front door, and looked at the ignition. The keys were missing. At that moment, he heard a car coming down the roadway. Two speeding sheriff vehicles, bouncing because of the wavy roadway, were approaching the driveway. Tom put the revolver back in the holster when the vehicles stopped. Four uniformed deputies, including Johnson, emerged from the two cars. Three of them had their guns out.

"What's happening?" asked Deputy Johnson.

"It's Fred Hood, the vacuum cleaner guy. He pulled a gun on me over by the garage. Pete wounded him with his deer rifle. Fred shot at Pete first."

Tom led the deputies to the edge of the woods where Pete was standing, still holding his deer rifle.

"He went right in there," said an anxious Pete.

"Where was Fred when you shot?" asked one of the deputies.

Pete showed them the spot. The deputies examined the bloodstains and followed them to the edge of the woods.

"Doesn't look like he will get far," said one of the deputies.

One of them questioned Tom as to the layout of the woods and land west of the house. Deputy Johnson trotted back to his car. Returning, he was carrying a pair of walkie-talkies. Handing a unit to one of the other deputies, he directed two of them to follow the blood trail.

"Arlin and I will flank you to the right along the woods. Tom, I want you and Pete to go into the house and remain there until we return."

After the deputies disappeared into the woods, Tom led Pete into the house. Pete laid his deer rifle on the love seat and they stood near the table. Pete was watching through the window where the cars were parked. Tom was looking out beyond the deck toward the dock. The deputies were gone for about ten minutes when Tom spotted motion down by the dock.

"Stay low, Pete, let's check this out."

They crouched and entered the deck through the French door. Tom peaked over the rail and saw Fred attempting to start the motor of the fishing boat. Pete went back into the dining room and came out with his rifle. He jacked a shell into the barrel and Tom watched in disbelief as he lifted the rifle over the rail and fired. The noise was jarring. Fred looked up, dropped to the bottom of the boat. Only a hand holding the pistol was visible.

Pete yelled down at Fred. "Throw that gun on the dock or I'll blow your head off."

To Tom's relief, Fred obeyed. He tossed the gun onto the dock.

Then he stood up, hands at his side. Two of the deputies came running out of the woods. They raced onto the lawn above the dock.

One of them looked up and said, "You can put that rifle down, up there."

The other deputy yelled at Fred, "Step out onto the dock and put your hands on your head, NOW!"

Fred obeyed and the officers trotted down to the dock. One of them spun Fred around, the clicking sound of the cuffs was audible up on the deck. The other officer picked up the gun lying on the dock. While Pete and Tom watched, Fred, head down, was escorted by the two deputies up the front slope and around the side of the house.

Pete and Tom walked back through the house, out the front door in time to see Fred pushed into the back seat of one of the sheriff cars. Deputy Johnson and the other deputy came running from the direction of the greenway.

"We got him, Paul, thanks to those two over there." He gestured toward where Pete and I were standing on the sidewalk.

# 56

JULIE AND THE RED CONVERTIBLE arrived the next day. She was sorry about missing all the action. They celebrated that evening by taking Pete and Lisa to dinner at Sally's. Several people dropped by, many comments and questions regarding the dramatic capture.

"I heard you caught him single-handed," one of them said to Tom.

"Not really, it wasn't I who did the capture. It was Pete. Without him I wouldn't be here today."

Pete showed off a big smile as he raised his glass.

"Here is to you and your deer rifle," Tom toasted.

Sally came over and said, "The bottle of wine is on Richard and I. Have a nice dinner...have a nice life."

Julie looked up at Sally, smiled and said, "We will."

After dinner, Tom dropped off Pete and Lisa at their home. As Tom and Julie drove down the roadway, Julie exclaimed, "Look, there's Prancer."

The big deer was standing by the edge of the woods. They saw him raise the right front leg slightly and take two huge leaps and disappear into the woods.

"The moose are gone, Prancer is king of the woods, once again," Tom said while glancing at Julie.

She looked off into the distance and said, "You are so right, the moose are gone, and so is Ranforth."

Later Julie and Tom sat on the deck watching daylight diminish. No revolver or rifle needed, thought Tom Hastings. He leaned over and kissed Julie.

The days of blue darkness were over.

# EPILOGUE

TWO YEARS LATER, JULIE AND TOM WERE SITTING on the balcony of his 20th floor apartment in Minneapolis. They were visiting with guests, Paul and Toni Johnson. Tom sold his country place in central Minnesota, and moved to the Twin Cities over a year ago. Paul Johnson, former deputy, joined the state highway patrol and moved his family to the Cities about the same time.

Paul called two weeks ago, they agreed to meet at Tom's apartment. Paul and Toni were all smiles when Tom greeted them at the door.

"Greetings, Tom and Julie, what a nice location," said Paul.

After hug exchanges, Tom led them onto the balcony. They spent the next two hours munching on goodies and talking. The balcony was getting chilly and Julie suggested they move inside.

Gathering around the dining room table, Tom took a sip of wine and asked, "Paul, do you ever think about the Ranforth killings?"

"Yes, I do, almost every day. That case was unique considering all the events took place in a rural, small-town community. Ranforth is in prison but it wasn't until recently that he talked. Would you like to know what he said?"

Julie excitingly said, "Oh, let's hear it."

Paul smiled and said, "Well, here goes. As most of us suspected early in the case and learned for certain later, Ranforth killed Maynard Cushing. What started it all was Maynard's vacuum cleaner. When he took it in for repair, Fred recognized the signature on the check.

"Many of the documents Ranforth had stolen from the CIA office contained Maynard Cushing's signature. Even though Fred wasn't positive he was recognized, his mind was tortured with the possibility. Fred drove to the Cushing home and in a moment of panic hit Maynard over the head with a piece of birch.

"One thing we'll never know is whether Maynard suspected or knew Fred was the missing CIA agent. Remember now, he called the FBI about Ranforth a week earlier. That's when the black car entered the scene. Maynard Cushing tipped them off and they were secretly searching for Ranforth.

"As Fred was driving away from the Cushing house, Rollie was walking in from the township road where his wife had dropped him. After Rollie discovered the body, instead of reporting the killing to authorities, he phoned Fred and demanded money.

"Fred agreed to pay Rollie fifty-thousand dollars to keep quiet. Because Rollie was aware of Maynard's memoirs, he took the diskettes and deleted the files from the hard drive. He also took one of your business cards. What you didn't know was that Rollie was an ex-computer programmer.

"Rollie agreed to meet Fred at water's edge in front of his house. As part of the deal, Rollie agreed to turn over the diskettes. Rollie gave Fred the diskettes and Fred hit Rollie over the head with a club.

"Because of your business card, Fred worried you had a copy of the memoirs. He read about himself in the memoirs and assumed you must have done the same. By simply hanging around the grocery store and post office, he learned the FBI was getting involved. He also learned, they, along with the sheriff's deputies, were hanging around your house. His paranoia grew. He concluded you, Tom, would learn his secret.

"Fred didn't buy the nephew thing when Allan Burnside was assigned to your house. He actually overheard someone say at the post office that a FBI agent was staying with you."

Paul laughed and added, "That's where the sheriff gets most of his information, Main Street New Dresden."

Paul continued, "Besides being blackmailed by Rollie, Fred was also blackmailed by a man named Cameron. The Chicago-based hoodlum moved into a motel in Big Lakes for the purpose of either getting a lot of money from Fred or exposing him. Cameron was originally involved in the scheme when Ranforth was selling information as a CIA agent. Fred made a deal with Cameron to help dispose of two men for a hundred thousand dollars.

"The Sunday evening after delivering his family to the airport in Brownstown, Allan stopped at a gas station in New Dresden. He laid his billfold on the counter while fishing out a credit card. Fred was next in line and spotted Allan's ID. His paranoia caused him to panic again. He knew Allan was staying at your house.

"When the two of them returned to their vehicles, Fred started a conversation with Allan and eventually lured him to his apartment. After Fred hit Allan over the head with a pipe, he called Cameron. The two of them placed the unconscious Allan into the Intrepid and pushed it into the lake.

"Fred made a deal with Cameron, to scare you at first. That changed after you visited Fred at his Vacuum Cleaner Shop. He was convinced you, too, knew his secret. Cameron took the shot at you from the boat while Fred waited at the landing. Failing with that, together they stalked you at your home. Fred talked Cameron into coming after you with a knife.

"The news about you killing Cameron spread around New Dresden like wild fire. When Fred heard the news, he was furious. He couldn't understand how an amateur, such as you, could upset his future.

"A few days later when Jerry showed him the Ranforth letter, as he did you, Fred went around back of the post office, picked up a pipe, sneaked in and hit Jerry over the back of the head.

"When Fred learned, at the grocery store, that Jerry was recovering, he became desperate and knew he had to get out of town real soon. Before leaving, his ego demanded a settlement with you. You were a constant thorn in his side since he murdered Maynard Cushing. You were fortunate that Pete was watching your road that day. He saw the strange car go by and hustled right over to your place."

"Thanks for sharing your story, Paul. I take comfort in knowing what really happened. I miss the country, especially the deer. I wonder how Prancer is doing without me. It's darn quiet for him, I bet," said Tom Hastings.

Paul's eyes widened and said, "Speaking of deer, it was amazing how many times I saw a big deer hanging around your road. I saw him so many times...it's almost as if he was trying to tell us something."

"Prancer was concerned about the moose, Paul," Tom said, yearning for his country home.

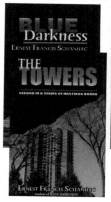

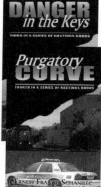

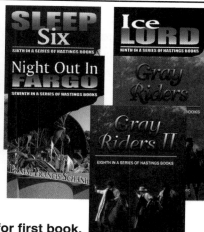